THE REALMGATE WARS
LORD OF UNDEATH

AGE OF SIGMAR™

The Gates of Azyr
Chris Wraight

Legends of the Age of Sigmar

Fyreslayers
*David Annandale, David Guymer
and Guy Haley*

Skaven Pestilens
Josh Reynolds

Black Rift
Josh Reynolds

Sylvaneth
*Robbie MacNiven, Josh Reynolds,
Rob Sanders and Gav Thorpe*

The Realmgate Wars

War Storm
Nick Kyme, Guy Haley and Josh Reynolds

Ghal Maraz
Guy Haley and Josh Reynolds

Hammers of Sigmar
Darius Hinks and C L Werner

Call of Archaon
*David Annandale, David Guymer,
Guy Haley and Rob Sanders*

Wardens of the Everqueen
C L Werner

Warbeast
Gav Thorpe

Fury of Gork
Josh Reynolds

Bladestorm
Matt Westbrook

Mortarch of Night
Josh Reynolds and David Guymer

Lord of Undeath
C L Werner

The Prisoner of the Black Sun
An audio drama by Josh Reynolds

Sands of Blood
An audio drama by Josh Reynolds

The Lords of Helstone
An audio drama by Josh Reynolds

The Bridge of Seven Sorrows
An audio drama by Josh Reynolds

The Beasts of Cartha
An audio drama by David Guymer

Fist of Mork, Fist of Gork
An audio drama by David Guymer

Great Red
An audio drama by David Guymer

Only the Faithful
An audio drama by David Guymer

THE REALMGATE WARS

LORD OF UNDEATH

C L WERNER

BLACK LIBRARY

For Chelsey and her adoration of vampires.

A BLACK LIBRARY PUBLICATION

Lord of Undeath first published in 2016.
This edition published in Great Britain in 2017 by
Black Library,
Games Workshop Ltd.,
Willow Road,
Nottingham,
NG7 2WS, UK.

10 9 8 7 6 5 4 3 2 1

Produced by Games Workshop in Nottingham.
Cover illustrations by Mac Smith and Julia Zolotareva.

A CIP record for this book is available from the British Library.

ISBN 13: 978 1 78496 566 2

See Black Library on the internet at

blacklibrary.com

Find out more about Games Workshop
and the world of Warhammer at

games-workshop.com

Printed and bound by CPI Group (UK) Ltd, Croydon, CR0 4YY

From the maelstrom of a sundered world, the
Eight Realms were born. The formless and the divine
exploded into life.

Strange, new worlds appeared in the firmament, each one
gilded with spirits, gods and men. Noblest of the gods was
Sigmar. For years beyond reckoning he illuminated the realms,
wreathed in light and majesty as he carved out his reign. His
strength was the power of thunder. His wisdom was infinite.
Mortal and immortal alike kneeled before his lofty throne.
Great empires rose and, for a while, treachery was banished.
Sigmar claimed the land and sky as his own and ruled over a
glorious age of myth.

But cruelty is tenacious. As had been foreseen, the great
alliance of gods and men tore itself apart. Myth and legend
crumbled into Chaos. Darkness flooded the realms. Torture,
slavery and fear replaced the glory that came before. Sigmar
turned his back on the mortal kingdoms, disgusted by their
fate. He fixed his gaze instead on the remains of the world he
had lost long ago, brooding over its charred core, searching
endlessly for a sign of hope. And then, in the dark heat of
his rage, he caught a glimpse of something magnificent. He
pictured a weapon born of the heavens. A beacon powerful
enough to pierce the endless night. An army hewn from
everything he had lost.

Sigmar set his artisans to work and for long ages they toiled,
striving to harness the power of the stars. As Sigmar's great
work neared completion, he turned back to the realms and saw
that the dominion of Chaos was almost complete. The hour
for vengeance had come. Finally, with lightning blazing across
his brow, he stepped forth to unleash his creations.

The Age of Sigmar had begun.

CHAPTER ONE

Darkness filled the great hall, a blackness more sinister than that of night and shadow. Great braziers of gilded bone blazed from their pillared stands, tongues of flame dancing up towards the vaulted ceiling dozens of feet above. Crystal lanterns carved into the shapes of skulls hung from marble columns, their translucent surfaces aglow with the sapphire, emerald and ruby lights of the soulfires imprisoned within them. From the ceiling, a colossal chandelier of volcanic glass and fossilised skeletons glimmered with the light of a thousand corpse-candles, each flicker fed by the fat of a slaughtered killer. Through the vastness, darting around pillar and column, weaving through the bony arms of the chandelier, ethereal wisps of ghostly luminescence flew about the hall.

The chamber was a riot of lights, but still there wasn't enough to fend off the darkness. A darkness that went beyond a diminishing of vision. A darkness that struck at the soul with terror and oppression. A darkness that lounged languidly upon a divan fashioned from a mammoth chunk of drakstone and upholstered with silks stained in the heart-blood of unblemished maidens. A darkness that raised a goblet of sanguine wine to velvet lips and took the most delicate sip of the morbid liquor.

To those mortals assembled in the hall, the sight of their sovereign drinking the blood-brew was a forceful reminder of their place in the scheme of things. They were servants, subjects and, if they provided offence, cattle. Some among them wondered who it was who had been bled for their monarch's grim repast. Older and wiser men no longer entertained such questions, well aware there was no good to come from curiosity.

The immortals among the court were no less struck by the exhibition. They could smell the blood in the goblet, could almost taste it flowing across their tongues, the fiery bite of the mournweed used to spice the wine as it burned down their throats. A terrible longing rushed through them, pulsing in their blackened hearts. Had their sovereign taken some mortal, ripped his throat out and drained him dry, they would have known only a sense of envy. Seeing this display of control and restraint, these dainty sips in the face of their lust, struck them at a level not so different from that of the mortals. Without a word being said, they were being told how great was the gulf between their own status and that of the one they served.

Stretched across her divan, her bare flesh cool and pale where it wasn't obscured by the sable veils of a web-like gown, the vampire queen regarded her subjects with regal detachment. There was no hint in either motion or expression of the agitation within her, of the anxiety that had been steadily mounting since the first reports had been brought to her throne. It was the first rule of power, the first lesson any ruler, no matter how experienced – never show weakness. As her eyes drifted to the armoured figure of Lord Harkdron, the slightest hint of a smile pulled at her crimson lips and exposed the gleam of a fang.

There were, of course, exceptions to every rule. Times when a show of weakness made it easier to exploit the aspirations of others. In all the numberless centuries of her unnatural existence, Neferata had made use of many would-be paramours. There was no loyalty so easy to abuse, no slavery so complete, as that which hoped for love. Even for a Mortarch, a mistress of death and the infinities beyond death, there was a delicious savour to preying upon the dreams and ambitions of lesser beings. The loftier the height they wanted to ascend, the more satisfying their inevitable fall.

Once the foolish swain had served his purpose, of course.

Neferata turned her attention from Harkdron to regard the rest of her court. She could see the fear that pulsed through the veins of her mortal subjects, a fear that, for once, was not provoked by the dread queen who ruled over them. Among the vampires and liches who swore allegiance to her, she could likewise sense unease. It was less visceral than the fright of mortals, but there nonetheless. Their anxiety vexed her, for it was a sign of faltering belief in her power. Her subjects were losing confidence in her ability to protect them.

She took another sip of her wine, but the taste was soured by the turn her thoughts had taken. It had taken many centuries to build her great city of Nulahmia. Every street and building had been translated from the dreams of memory into constructions of limestone and marble, into basalt walls and obsidian pillars. A thousand times had the colonnade leading to the Palace of Seven Vultures been built and razed, its workers impaled upon spikes of copper and gold, before the vision in her mind was perfected. Four hundred slaves had been entombed alive beneath the foundations of the Jackal Gate before the proper aura of death and despair lurked beneath its brooding archway. Ten generations of men had laboured to excavate the cavern of Nehb-kotz below the necropolis of Themsis, their bodies plastered into the cavern walls to entice the corpse-moths to nest within the empty skulls.

In all the Realm of Death, Nulahmia was hers alone. Every contour of the landscape, every brick in the walls and tile upon the roofs, every curl in a maid's coiffure, every thread in a farmer's tunic, all of them had been nurtured by her dark dreams of primordial memory. When the hordes of Chaos poured through the realmgates to conquer the lands of Shyish, it was to Nulahmia that Neferata had withdrawn. It was for Nulahmia that she directed her forces and powers. To keep and hold the kingdom she had built in accordance with her own vision, she had devoted spells of such magnitude that a mortal sorcerer would be reduced to ash merely trying to sound the letters of the first incantation.

Long had Nulahmia been hidden, veiled from the marauders of Chaos by a web of illusion and terror. Impenetrable shrouds of gravefog cloaked every approach. Spectral mires of liferot waited to drain the vitality of any invader. Ghostly echoes distorted the perceptions of any who drew too close to Neferata's dominion, and phantom whispers excited their fears. While the rest of the realm had been despoiled and defiled, while the devotees of Chaos ravaged and pillaged at will, her city had remained inviolate.

Now that sanctuary was threatened. After years of seclusion, the enemy had finally pierced the skein of terror and illusion to strike at the city secreted within. It was a possibility that had haunted Neferata often when Shyish had first been overrun, but time had dulled her worries until she had come to share the belief she had nurtured amongst her subjects – that the defences of Nulahmia were inviolate.

Slowly, Neferata lowered her goblet and motioned one of her handmaidens to remove it. Then her gaze roved across the anxious visages of her court. There was a predatory quality in her eyes now. Among her subjects, the fear of Chaos was eclipsing fear of their queen. This was a situation she couldn't abide. She needed a victim to remind them all what it meant to fail a Mortarch.

'Repeat for me again what was revealed in your seance,' Neferata commanded, pointing a pale finger towards one of her mortal retainers. He was a spindly, almost fleshless man, his skin afflicted with a leprous cast. The dark robe he wore was an imitation of those worn by the priests of immemorial ages, eldritch hieroglyphs embroidered into the fabric with purple threads. Ahkmet-bey, chief of Nulahmia's necromancers, bowed his shaved head when his queen addressed him. Though magic had enabled him to extend his life beyond the usual mortal span, the mystic had never lost his terror of Neferata. It was one of the reasons he had been suffered to live so long, the other being that spirits were more readily drawn to a living conjurer than one who had already been given the blood kiss.

'My dread queen.' Ahkmet-bey abased himself at the foot of the dais. 'The spirits have shown me many dire things. The enemy has penetrated the spells that have protected your kingdom for so very long. An army marching under the banner of the Serpent descends upon us to lay siege to the city.'

Neferata glowered at the necromancer, her pointing finger

lengthening into a blackened claw. 'Have the phantoms bound to my dominion not plagued these invaders? Have they not filled their minds with doubt and fear? How much of this horde has already deserted their snake flags? How many of them are lost in the gravefog?'

A tremor of fear shook Ahkmet-bey's voice as he answered. 'Highness, the enemy has lost few to the mists and fewer still to the phantasms. Their leader pushes them unerringly across the boneyards and mouldmires.' The necromancer shook his head. 'It is as though he is being drawn to us by some infernal enchantment.'

'You speak nonsense, mortal,' Lord Harkdron sneered. 'Since the first realmgates were breached by the Everchosen, neither sorcerer nor daemon has been able to find Nulahmia.' The vampire's fangs glistened as he smiled at Ahkmet-bey. 'Do you dare cast aspersions upon our queen's powers?'

'I report only what I am commanded to reveal,' Ahkmet-bey declared. 'The spirits have shown me the invaders marching into the kingdom. They have found a way...'

Neferata dropped down from her divan, descending the steps of the raised dais with a panther-like menace. She hesitated an instant beside Harkdron, letting her claw slide down his cheek in a languid caress. She could feel the vampire's excitement at the display of affection. 'Ahkmet-bey wouldn't risk the life he's used so much magic to sustain simply to spread disquieting rumours in my court. What the spirits have shown him must be true. The enemy has found a way to reach Nulahmia and threaten my domain.'

Harkdron brought both of his fists crashing against his breastplate in martial salute. 'Allow me to command your armies, my queen. I will bring them against these invaders and give them cause to repent whatever doom allowed them to slip through your spells. They will be exterminated before they can even lay eyes upon your city.'

'No, my eager champion,' Neferata told Harkdron. 'You will not sally forth to confront the enemy out in the open where the horde's numbers can be brought to bear. You will stay here and hold the walls.'

'It will be my honour,' Harkdron vowed. 'The Chaos vermin will smother the wormfields with their dead, and after the battle, I shall build an ossuary taller than the Throne Mount from their bones. The tribute of a general to his queen.'

Neferata smiled at Harkdron's enthusiasm, enjoying how fully his devotion had trapped him. 'Bring me victory first. Allow no harm to befall my city and it will be Lord Harkdron who is paid tribute.'

'If your armies can hold the walls,' Ahkmet-bey said, 'then we might light the spirit-beacons and summon aid from the other Mor–'

The suggestion died on the necromancer's tongue. Fast as a striking tomb-scorpion, Neferata spun about and raked her claw across Ahkmet-bey's throat. Bright arterial blood sprayed from the man as he crumpled to the floor, his extended life extinguished in a heartbeat. The vampires of Neferata's court gazed hungrily at the gory puddle that surrounded the twitching corpse, but none made a move to indulge their thirst.

'Nulahmia has stood on its own strength this long,' Neferata told her courtiers as she turned to face them. 'We will not light the spirit-beacons. We will not be so weak as to beg for help from those who abandoned us long ago. When the enemy comes against us, we will hurl him back with our own magic and our own armies. It will be the might of Nulahmia alone that brings them to destruction. No others will share in our victory!'

Neferata climbed back onto her divan, letting the cries of

devotion and praise rising from her subjects fill her ears. There was always a quality of fear in the voices of her courtiers, a quality she usually found pleasing. Now it had turned sour. The fear she detected wasn't provoked by her, but by the advancing hordes of Chaos. Even after her callous slaughter of Ahkmet-bey before their very eyes, her court was more frightened of the invaders.

A wave of her hand dismissed her court. She watched Harkdron march away with the captains of her armies, listened for a moment to their mutterings about strategy in the coming battle. None of them dared so much as whisper about seeking aid, not when their queen's sharp ears might hear them, but she knew the thought was on their minds.

She would not countenance the humiliation of begging the other Mortarchs for help. It would be a show of weakness they would be quick to exploit for their own ends. Neferata had worked too long to protect what she had built to share it with one of her rivals. Certainly she was anxious about the horde now moving against her kingdom. Any army that could breach her spells might likewise breach her walls.

Still, she wouldn't order the spirit-beacons lit. To do so would undermine her dominion over her subjects. They would look to the outside for deliverance rather than to their queen. If that help never came...

Neferata stared down at Ahkmet-bey's corpse. Almost absently, she waved her hand and allowed her entourage to feed. As she watched them lap up the necromancer's blood, she pondered the futility of the man's suggestion.

After so much time, with so much of Shyish overrun by Chaos, was there even anyone left to see the spirit-beacons? Was she the last of the Mortarchs?

* * *

Lascilion closed his eyes and leaned back in his saddle. Pursing his lips, he flicked out his forked tongue. The slimy organ quivered a moment, each prong licking the misty air and feeding observations to his brain. Much like a true snake, the Chaos warlord smelt with his tongue. Unlike a serpent, the smells Lascilion tasted were not scents or odours, but residues of emotion. They were spiritual stains imprinted upon their environment, fierce passions and terrible frights that had blazed up like bonfires for an instant and left their essence seared into their surroundings.

Yes, it was still there, borne upon aetheric waves of anguish and agony, the taint that had guided him through the grave-fog and mouldmire. A delicious flavour of cruelty and sadism that sent a thrill of envy pounding through his veins. Lascilion had long been in the service of the Prince of Chaos, the sensuous god Slaanesh. Pleasure and pain had become his food and drink, each new experience feeding off those that had come before, creating within his soul a tapestry of excess and depravity. He had presided over numberless atrocities and outrages, glutted himself upon suffering until his senses had become jaded and dulled. Sometimes, for a rare moment, a single tear might evoke his old passion, a scream might once again echo through the corridors of his spirit, but such moments had become increasingly rare. All felt empty to him now.

There were those who said the god Slaanesh had been destroyed, consumed by his own sensual gluttony. Lascilion, in his darkest moments, wondered if such myths were true, if the god he had given himself to was indeed vanquished. If the Serpent no longer waited to reward him for his devotions, then what was the purpose of any of it? Mere indulgence of flesh? A wanton abandonment to shallow hedonism? Such simplicity might be enough for the half-witted marauders and bestial gors who marched under his banner, but for him, there had to be more than that. Something of value. Something of meaning.

As his tongue flickered in the air, Lascilion felt old urges stir deep within him – half-remembered lusts, half-forgotten desires. The suffering he sensed was beyond any he had tasted before. He had drunk often from the well of torment, but never had he encountered something of such terrible purity. It was like a fine vintage, set down long ago and carefully tended so that it might reach a perfection of cruelty. The air of horror that drew him on had been cultivated not over the lifetime of a single murderous tyrant, but was steeped in the malignity of centuries. A pall of nigh-incomparable agony clung to Nulahmia, and it was calling out to him as though drawing back to itself one of its own.

That was why, where so many others had failed, Lascilion would succeed. The disciples of Nurgle, the warlords of Khorne, the acolytes of Tzeentch, even the verminous spawn of the Rat God had all tried to discover the secret city to which Queen Neferata had retreated. Man, daemon or monster – all had failed. Lascilion wouldn't fail. His devotions to Slaanesh would see him through. Bloodking Thagmok, overlord of the armies of Chaos in Shyish, would learn that, broken or lost, the power of the Serpent lived on in his servants.

The monstrous steed upon which Lascilion rode lurched beneath him, its sinuous body undulating with ripples of agitation. It was a gift from the Realm of Chaos, a daemon sustained by his own depraved spirit. In the Mortal Realms, daemons demanded certain conditions to exist – mighty relics, lavish sacrifices, mantles of flesh to possess or, most propitious of all, a landscape in harmony with their own dark essence. In all his wanderings, Lascilion had never sensed a place more in tune with the power of Slaanesh than Nulahmia. The warlord opened his eyes and gave his daemon steed a reassuring pat on its fluted proboscis. Only when the thing had quieted somewhat did he turn his attention to the being that had upset his mount.

Amala crouched in the mouldy filth of the ground across which the army marched, gossamer wings folded against her back. She stretched forth a ropey tendril and offered to Lascilion a curled portion of skin. The warlord noted the blood that dripped from the scroll as he plucked it from the chitinous tentacle. The insect-like mutant was a capable scout, but her lack of a mouth made it necessary for her to render her reports in writing. She was often too impatient to wait for stylus and clay, so made do with the horde's stragglers.

Lascilion dismissed the mutant with a flick of his hand. There was only so long his steed could abide the sight of the luminous organs that oozed up from beneath Amala's skin. When the winged scout withdrew to the branches of a gnarled tree some distance away, it was as though his mind surged up from beneath black waters.

Tokresh-khan, chieftain of the Sorroweaters, marched towards Lascilion when he had seen Amala fly away. The barbarian was a huge man, nearly as tall on foot as the warlord was in his saddle. Tokresh wore only a few ornaments and talismans, preferring to display his scarred and tattooed body and prove his devotion to Slaanesh by exposing himself to the slashing blades and raking claws of his enemies. The masses of grey scars etched across his sallow skin had transcended ugliness to become beautiful in their own right, weaving and flowing into one another like the coils of the Serpent himself.

Lascilion, by contrast, took great care to protect the magnificent body and handsome visage with which Slaanesh had gifted him. Once, he had been as ugly as one of Tokresh's lizard-skin boots, but his devotions had transformed him into an entirely different being. His body was strong and fine, wondrous as a marble god and powerful as a daemon. His skin was as smooth as eiderdown, and the great mane of hair that cascaded down from his head and tumbled across his shoulders was like spun gold. His face transcended the limitations of human beauty, blending the nobility of a lion with the wisdom and determination of a king.

To guard these gifts, Lascilion wore plate armour cast from great slivers of pearl plundered from the noxious depths of the Obsidian Lagoon. Each segment of his shimmering armour had been etched with esoteric sigils and the secret names of his god, soaked in wyrd-dust until every piece was saturated in powerful magics. At his side, he wore twin swords crafted by the crazed swordsmith Nakadai, the vicious blade named Pain and its smaller brother Torment. Each new victim fed the blades, swelling their power with the anguish of those they cut down.

Lascilion let one hand slip down to Pain's ivory grip, feeling the hungry hum of the aroused blade pulse through him. He fixed a stern gaze upon Tokresh. It had been an arduous ordeal, bringing his army through the arcane veils that guarded these lands. Many times he had been challenged, confronted by despairing chieftains and sorcerers who wanted to turn back. Their path through the grave-fog was littered with the bodies of those who had tried to oppose his command.

Tokresh halted when he saw Pain inching from its sheath. The barbarian looked from the blade to the face of the man who held it. 'You have sent the moth-eater ahead of us?' he asked, nodding towards Amala. There was a woeful lack of deference in the chieftain's tone. Lascilion would remember that.

'I have her words,' Lascilion declared, waving the fleshy scroll in his other hand. He looked across the bleak landscape through which his army marched, a jumbled terrain of barren mountains and winding ravines, dead trees and yellowed weeds. 'We will soon be quit of these lands.'

'It cannot be soon enough,' Tokresh cursed. He slapped a calloused hand against his tattooed breast. 'This place chills my heart and would unman me. Every step I take, I can feel my courage falter. There is witchery here, the stink of the necromancers and their ilk.' He waved at the marching Sorroweaters as the marauders were approaching one of the withered stands of trees that spotted the edges of the trail the army followed. 'My warriors sense it too. I can see it in their eyes, watch it crawling across their faces. We have heard much of Neferata and her might. There are some who worry you lead us not to glory but disgrace.'

Lascilion gazed across the ranks of the Sorroweaters. They were a formidable force, hundreds strong, each man built along the same hulking lines as their chieftain. Standards crafted from the still-moaning bodies of their victims rose above the heads of the marching marauders. Their shamans knew spells of such horrific potency that they could remind even the undead what it was to suffer. For their living victims, even more unspeakable tortures were their reward. Normally, the Sorroweaters drew strength from the misery of their living totems. Now, Lascilion could see that their ardour was dimmed. They glanced at their surroundings with furtive, worried looks.

Among the rest of his horde, he could see similar traces of trepidation. The brays and bleats of the Vorkoth war-herd had fallen to almost nothing, the horned beastmen moved to silence by the oppressive atmosphere. The fratricidal Hellcast had drawn close to one another, something the gold-armoured knights usually did only when they charged into battle, all too aware of the Khornate curse that hovered over their heads and spurred them to strike one another when no other foes presented themselves. Even the Scalp-finders, the most savage and brutal of the tribes who followed Lascilion, had a subdued air about them, clutching their axes and flails as though they were talismans rather than weapons.

Mendeziron, the gigantic Keeper of Secrets, was less circumspect in his agitation, plucking gors and marauders from the midst of their tribes as though they were choice morsels in a box of sweetmeats. The more the army surrendered to their fear, the more they excited the appetites of the daemon. The four-armed monster needed such victims to invigorate him. The obscene reliquary Lascilion had stolen from the Crying Tower was enough to sustain Mendeziron in the Mortal Realms, but not enough to lend the daemon any measure of strength. That required more substantial offerings. Early in the march, there had been many among his army who considered giving themselves to Mendeziron a sacred honour. Now they fought or fled when the daemon came for them.

Lascilion scowled at the unquestionable lack of valour and determination on display. It was small wonder the followers of the other Ruinous Powers had come to hold those who served Slaanesh in such disregard. Was this the best that could be expected of them? Were they merely decadent hedonists, grown soft in their vices, no longer capable of the intensity of desire that drove them to ever more profound revelations of experience?

'Can you truly be afraid?' Lascilion sneered at Tokresh. 'Can you not delight in the chill that curdles your blood? Is it not something new? Is it not something you haven't felt before?' He could see that his questions made no impact upon the barbarian. Creatures like Tokresh were too simple to understand the extent of experience the true disciple of Slaanesh must be willing to embrace as an offering to his god. 'We have fought the coffin-worms before. The whole of Shyish was once their domain. But with sword and spell, we have brought them to ruin. The Lords of Chaos have conquered the Masters of Death. All that is left of them are lingering echoes, remnants hiding in the night. Can you not imagine the delights that await us? The wonders of pillage and conquest that stand before us?'

'Their magic is strong,' Tokresh protested.

'The very magnitude of their spells should whet your desires,' Lascilion told him. 'The greater the effort to protect, the more magnificent the reward that waits for those with the determination to press on.' He tapped the fleshy scroll against his breastplate. 'Amala has seen the walls of a city just beyond the mountains. A day, less than a day, and we shall stand before those walls.' A cruel smile twisted Lascilion's leonine face. 'We will tear down those walls. We will fall upon the city that stands beyond them. The last city of Shyish will be our playground. Your kinsmen will be free to loot and pillage, to defile and desecrate. You will abandon yourselves in murder and delight, and every indulgence will be an offering to Great Slaanesh.'

Greed and lust shone in the eyes of Tokresh. He had heard the stories from his tribe's elders about the old days, when the hordes of Chaos had descended upon the mighty kingdoms and cities of Shyish. Long had he dreamed of such wantonness and savagery. 'I will tell my people,' he said. 'We will see this city.'

'You will do more than see it,' Lascilion promised. 'You will tear it apart. After we have finished, nothing of flesh or stone will have been spared our attentions. Nulahmia exists only to sate our desires.'

The warlord watched Tokresh as he marched back to his tribe. Lascilion had rekindled the chieftain's lust, but not his loyalty. When the battle began, he would give the Sorroweaters the honour of acting as the vanguard. Whatever defenders Nulahmia possessed, they could inflict the worst of their efforts against the marauders. They would expend resources and spare Lascilion the effort of dealing with Tokresh later.

Lascilion's tongue slithered out and licked the air once more. The exquisite taste of depravity burned his senses like an exotic spice. When the walls came down, he would lead his Amethyst Guard through the rubble. Let the others indulge their petty appetites. For Lascilion, there could be no treasure more precious than the creature that could preside over such a legacy of atrocity.

Neferata would be his.

CHAPTER TWO

From behind the battlements atop the Jackal Gate, Lord
Harkdron glared down at the wormfields. A vast stretch of
loamy ground spotted with ghoulish stands of morgueweed
and the cadaverous blooms of cryptfronds, the fields were
a carefully prepared killing ground for any foe so reckless
as to threaten Nulahmia. Every foot of ground bore its hidden, eldritch mark, visible only to those versed in the dark
art of necromancy. Each sigil denoted the distance from the
walls, allowing the necromancers and vampires gathered on
the ramparts to direct the arrows of the skeletal regiments
under their command with fiendish precision.

There were more malefic magics bound into the morbid
soil of the wormfields. Pockets of lethal corpse-gas erupted
at a gesture from the necromancers, bursting beneath the
marching feet of the Chaos horde and searing the life from
their veins. Nests of marrow-maggots bubbled up from the
earth to fasten their leech-like mouths about the toes and

ankles of the invaders, digging fresh burrows in living flesh. The broken, mangled dead that over the centuries had been dumped into the wormfields like so much rubbish were reanimated with a spark of dark magic, clawing up to the surface. The maimed, battered things were too miserable to visit any true hurt upon the foe, but their noxious presence brought fear and confusion to the barbarians and beastmen, slowing their advance as they probed the ground ahead of them with spear and axe.

Crackling bolts of death magic hurtled down from the gnarled hands and skull-tipped staves of necromancers, withering clutches of brutish invaders at every turn. Gravestones launched from catapults smashed down upon the savage herds of horned gors. Spears of bone loosed from ballistas impaled hulking Chaos warriors, tearing through their heavy armour in sprays of gore. Showers of arrows rained down from the walls, lancing through the flesh of mutants and marauders. Havoc and carnage riddled the Chaos horde, yet still they came onward, trampling their wounded and dead underfoot as they continued their march.

Harkdron scowled at the enemy's tenacity. He had expected them to relent under such punishment, to slink away in fright at the losses they were suffering. Perhaps he had grown too accustomed to the craven, servile mortals who dwelt in Nulahmia. Maybe it was his contempt for these crude, decadent creatures that made him underestimate them. Whatever the cause, Harkdron had to admit that the victory he had promised Neferata wouldn't be as simple as he had thought it would be. The vampire could feel his queen's eyes on him, watching him from her palace on the Throne Mount. He could feel her evaluating him, judging his every decision, noting his every mistake.

The Slaaneshi dead that littered the wormfields would be small consolation to his queen if Harkdron failed to keep them off the walls. Already there had been a few determined warbands that had managed to bring ladders to within a hundred yards of Nulahmia before the undead shot them down. A section of the Vulture Reach had been reduced to a steaming quagmire by the spells of a Chaos sorcerer. Other witches and warlocks cast withering lights and bolts of fiery magic up at the defenders, decimating scores of skeletal warriors beyond the potential of reanimation. One goat-headed shaman held his scalp-laden staff towards the Jackal Gate and evoked a soporific cloud that reduced a pair of deathmages to babbling wretches. Harkdron ordered his grave guard to dispatch the maddened spellcasters, then set his own magic against the bestial shaman. A bolt of dark energy speared down from his hand and burst the beastman's heart. The shaman's herd bleated in fright and fell back from the Jackal Gate.

The vampire lord looked away from the routed gors. He scowled at the sight of a large company of men and beasts advancing towards the Jackal Gate. At a glance Harkdron could tell these were more formidable foes than the marauders and brayherds they had faced thus far. This would be the main effort; he could feel it in his bones. Not only were these Chaos warriors better armed and equipped than the rest of the horde, but they also drew a hulking siege tower after them.

Harkdron stared at the tower behind the advancing horde, a mammoth cylinder of iron and wood, its top bound by a crown-like cap. He saw men behind the exposed framework of the tower, clinging to chains and ropes as the siege engine rolled forwards. He snarled a command to the ballistas mounted atop the Jackal Gate, directing them to engage the tower. As they hurled their missiles at the siege engine, a purplish light shimmered around the structure, shattering the bolts before they could strike it. Harkdron cursed at the stifled attack. He snapped a command to one of the necromancers who had survived the shaman's spell, but even bolts of dark magic couldn't pierce the arcane wards that shielded the structure. The enemy had their own fell magic to draw upon, and it seemed the most potent of their sorcery had been directed to keeping the tower from harm.

The vampire observed the tower's advance with suspicion. Why was there only one tower? Were the invaders so arrogant that they thought they could seize the city from a single foothold? To defend the walls Harkdron had roused battalions of grave guard from their deathless sleep, and summoned dread wight kings from the oldest tombs to command them. Wherever the enemy brought their tower, they would find a remorseless foe waiting to receive them.

If such was truly their plan. Harkdron wondered if the tower was simply a ruse, a trick to capture his attention. All the elaborate precautions to protect it were perhaps nothing more than flavouring to make the deception more convincing. Down there, among the teeming mass of brayherds and warbands, the invaders might be hiding grapnels and ladders, or even more esoteric means of scaling the walls. The malignant spirits entombed beneath the gatehouses might claim some of the attackers, the skeleton warriors atop the walls still more, but if the assault was spread broadly enough, the foe might yet succeed in their purpose.

Harkdron gripped the edge of the crenulations before him, his fingers digging into the limestone as he gnashed his fangs in frustration. He wouldn't abide the shame of failing his queen. Neferata was just cruel enough to let him linger in disgrace rather than destroying him outright. She had charged him with keeping the enemy outside the walls. If even a single barbarian made it into Nulahmia, he would know the queen's wrath.

The tower. Deception or arrogance? Harkdron had to know. Pulling off his left gauntlet, he raised his bared hand to his mouth and brought his fangs stabbing into his pallid flesh. The stagnant blood of his undead veins bubbled up from the wound. Stretching out his hand, holding his bloodied palm towards the crawling tower, the vampire hissed an incantation. He was calling upon the vicious hunters that nested deep within the Black Grotto, calling to them in their hungry slumbers. He felt the creatures stirring, answering his call. Soon they would take wing and come to claim the prey he had chosen for them.

Harkdron smiled as he anticipated the onslaught to come. The invaders had preserved their tower against a few spells and spears, but how would they fare against a few hundred ravenous fell bats?

The shrieking, chirping cacophony that wailed across the wormfields drew every eye skyward. Lascilion was no exception. He cursed when he saw the swarm of gigantic bats that flittered above his army. Each of the monsters was as large as a horse, leathery wings torn and tattered, mangy fur peeling away from rotten flesh and yellowed bones. Sorcerous fires gleamed in the hollows of their broad faces, blazing with the most bitter malignancy.

Lascilion shouted commands to the warriors around him, calling them to guard against attack from above. The warning, he soon discovered, was unnecessary. The huge bats took no notice of the men and beastmen below but instead sped onwards. He cursed when he understood the objective towards which the fiends were flying. The aerial horrors were making for the great column of iron and wood his warriors were rolling towards the walls of Nulahmia.

'With me,' Lascilion snapped at his bodyguard. Arrayed in heavy coats of mail that glistened with stolen jewels and plundered gemstones, the Amethyst Guard looked too ostentatious to be dangerous. Many foes had spilled their lives on the axes of Lascilion's warriors after dismissing them as pampered fops. The Amethyst Guard were connoisseurs of the blade, relishing the excitement of combat with the same ardour as a drunkard with his wine. In the whole of his horde, there were no fiercer fighters than these refined killers, at least not among his mortal followers.

Even with the Amethyst Guard ready to follow him, Lascilion hesitated as he drew the reins of his snake-like steed and turned its head towards the threatened siege engine. The swarm of bats was nearly on its objective now, rancid bits and pieces falling from their decayed bodies as they swooped in for the attack. He couldn't reach the hulking spire of iron and wood in time to intercept the enemy. The wards and charms the horde's sorcerers and shaman had woven to protect the construction from hostile magic would be of little effect against the undead bats. It was doubtful any of the warriors near the siege engine would climb up to confront the attackers; they were too aware of what it would mean if they were to fall inside the framework.

Lascilion looked away as the first of the bats struck at the framework, scrabbling at the iron fastenings, gnashing its fangs against the wooden supports. Instead, he studied the distance between the siege engine and the walls of Nulahmia.

A bark of grim laughter rumbled from the warlord. Neferata had waited too long to unleash her flock. She had let Lascilion get too close, let his horde draw too near the atmosphere of wickedness and depravity that saturated her city. He could feel the defiled energy reaching out to him. Soon it would reach out to others, invigorating and intoxicating his warriors, feeding their lust for conquest. There was naught that her bats could do now to change the situation.

Or was there? Lascilion turned back to the great spire. The upper reaches were now coated in the leathery wings and decaying bodies of the giant bats. He could imagine the raw terror pounding through the hearts of those within the spire as the ravenous monsters tried to tear their way inside to reach them. It always struck Lascilion as ironic how even a man who knows he is going to die can still feel fear in such magnitude. Of course so few appreciated the strange relish of fear, or the thrill of anticipating one's own mortality. Rare were those who could truly appreciate the art of a novel death.

'Hold,' Lascilion told his bodyguard as he stood up in his saddle. In a single motion, he drew Pain and Torment from their scabbards and held both swords above his head. As the two blades touched, a nimbus of purple light flashed from the contact, a signal to the siege masters following behind the lumbering spire.

Another flash of purple fire answered Lascilion, a flicker that started just behind the spire and then quickly grew into a conflagration that swept up the skeletal framework. Like a colossal torch, the whole of the spire was quickly engulfed in the sorcerous flame, from the base of the wheeled carriage to the spiked crown at its summit. The undead bats were consumed in the arcane pyre, some of the vermin trying to fly away, spinning through the air like blazing torches before plummeting earthward. Others were immolated as they clung to the framework of iron, their wings curling into charred strips, their bodies bursting as the deathly gases within them exploded.

Shrieks of nigh-unbelievable torment sounded from the spire. From top to bottom, the occupants were caught in the same flame that had devoured the bats. It was a fire that seared not only the flesh but the soul as well. Lacking the vitality to feed the abominable sorcery, the undead bats had been destroyed outright, but for the living victims within, a far more lingering and excruciating doom was their lot. What the vampires had mistaken as the crew of a siege tower were in fact offerings, sacrifices chained inside the framework, mortal fuel to feed an infernal flame.

The flames wouldn't burn long. Had the bats set upon the spire a moment sooner, Lascilion would have faced a potential catastrophe. The undead had waited too long, however. The flames would last until the weapon was pulled to the walls. Indeed, the extra measure of fear the fell bats had extracted from the sacrifices was lending the fire an even greater potency.

Lascilion watched in fascination as the spire swung downwards. The Chaos horde scattered as the blazing framework slammed down upon the bed of the wheeled carriage. Ahead of the gigantic conveyance, immense mammoths were being harnessed to drag the construction forwards, their angry trumpets echoing across the wormfields. Small streamers of purple fire flickered along their harnesses, scorching the immense war mammoths and goading them to pull faster towards the city.

Howling his delight, the giant daemon Mendeziron marched

to the rear of the carriage and gripped the base of the prone spire with his four arms, clinging to it as though to a lost lover. The agonies of the burning sacrifices rushed through him, blazing through his monstrous frame. The enormous daemon reared back, shrieking in obscene ecstasy. Scores of nearby marauders collapsed as the sound smashed down upon them, overwhelming their minds in a riot of sensation.

Mendeziron's cry echoed back into the Realm of Chaos, reaching into the senses of his kindred daemons. The burning spire acted as a beacon to the ravening hosts that scratched at the barriers of reality. Shimmering rents opened across the wormfields, disgorging packs of depraved creatures. Lithe daemonettes with sinuous bodies and monstrous claws sprang from the fissures opened by Mendeziron's shriek. Crab-like fiends scuttled out of glowing cracks, squealing with infernal delight as they drew in the debauched scent of Nulahmia.

The Keeper of Secrets cried out again, and in reply more daemons came creeping out from the gashes inflicted by his malign power. The defenders now realised the true nature of the siege weapon Lascilion's horde had built. Not a tower to climb the walls, but an arcane altar to summon a daemon army to tear them down. A storm of arrows pelted the carriage, bolts of necromancy crackled from the claws of vampires and the staves of deathmages, stones flew from the arms of catapults. None of the attacks were sufficient to overcome the malignant magics that rippled across the fallen spire. Arrows were reduced to ash as they hit the purple flames, skull projectiles shattered into bony fragments and wisps of impotent enchantment, spells fizzled out into clouds of harmless smoke.

The agonies of the mammoths pulling the carriage drove them to ever-greater effort. By the time the purple fires overcame them and left them sprawled along the ground, the carriage had come less than a hundred yards from the Jackal Gate. Still shrieking his ghastly cry, drawing more daemons onto the wormfields, Mendeziron stepped down from the now-unmoving altar. His body steaming with purple flames, the daemon took hold of the burning spire. Wrenching it from the carriage, the Keeper of Secrets dragged it towards the gate. As a last effort by the defenders to halt the daemon, a torrent of boiling blood spilled from the jaws of the stone jackal that looked out over the gate, but it was to no avail. The blood sizzled as it struck the flames, sending an eerie crimson mist steaming into the air above the ram.

With a monstrous roar, Mendeziron struck the Jackal Gate – not at the gate itself, however, but at the walls of the gatehouse to the side of the archway. One arm still clenched about the burning spire, the daemon was bristling with the eldritch energies and supernatural sufferings of the sacrificial victims. Enticed to the edge of mania by the depraved atmosphere that saturated the whole of Nulahmia, the daemon's blow connected with the force of a hundred battering rams. The tremendous magic that fed the purple flames was unleashed in a heartbeat. With a deafening clamour, the entire left side of the Jackal Gate exploded, flung back into the city by the perverse sorcery brought against it. Slabs of stone weighing several tons came slamming down into the streets, pulverising undead defenders, pelting the outer wards of the city with a crushing shower of debris.

Thousands of barbarous war cries boomed across the wormfields as the horde cheered the incredible destruction. A great surge of beasts and men rushed for the immense gap in the wall where the Jackal Gate had been. The Sorroweaters were in the vanguard, their chief Tokresh-khan leading his warriors into the breach. Lascilion saw some of the undead work their way free from the rubble and try to block the marauders, but they were too few to oppose the oncoming tide. An armoured vampire, his cape torn and tattered, appreciated the fact more keenly than the fleshless skeletons and wights he commanded. After cutting down a dozen of Tokresh's men, the blood-drinker turned and retreated into the city.

Lascilion laughed at the vampire's flight. The creature was only delaying the inevitable. The rest of Shyish was given to Chaos. Now Nulahmia would be added to those conquests.

Slithering across the rubble, flanked by the Amethyst Guard, the warlord's steed carried Lascilion into the broad plaza just behind the ruined gate. All around him, swarms of marauders and daemons were streaming into Nulahmia. He saw a brayherd of goat-like gors battering their way into a squat building, and an instant later he heard the screams of the structure's inhabitants. Neferata had peopled her city with the living as well as the dead, but they were a wretched and broken breed. Men who had spent generations brutalised and oppressed by the vampires would not suddenly discover the courage to fight now.

It was a far different story with the undead who served the Mortarch. The Queensroad, the main avenue through the city, was thronged with legions of armoured skeletons, shambling zombies and even worse horrors. While part of his horde dispersed to sate the obscene appetites that called to them, Lascilion mustered his own reserves of discipline. Twelve warlords had been dispatched by Archaon Everchosen to find Nulahmia and conquer it. Even the Bloodking had failed to conquer the city. Lascilion alone had succeeded. He wouldn't allow his own desires to turn victory to defeat now, in the final hour.

Lascilion raised Pain and Torment once again, letting the purple light flash a second time. It was a signal, a summons to his horde, a command only the most debauched and depraved would defy. In an army such as his, Lascilion knew there were many who lacked the restraint to deny themselves. He scowled when he saw the hulking figure of Mendeziron lumbering off towards the inner wards, seeking the largest concentrations of mortal victims to glut his daemonic hunger. A great flock of lesser daemons followed the Keeper of Secrets, like scavengers loping after a hunting lion, eager to feed off the predator's leavings.

The warlord cursed Mendeziron's disobedience. It was true enough that the daemon had broken the walls and drawn multitudes of his own kind to augment Lascilion's forces, but clearing the Queensroad would be far more difficult without his might. The lesser daemons and marauders engaging the undead legion were unable to break through the skeletal ranks. Their ferocity and savagery could not break the determination of beings devoid of thought or fear. The undead had to be annihilated, destroyed outright. There would be no rout, no easy victory.

'With me,' Lascilion ordered the Amethyst Guard. Digging his spurs into the flanks of his snake-like steed, Lascilion slithered across the skull-paved roadway and between the rows of impaled corpses that lined the street. He tried to deafen himself to the cries of outrage and brutality that rose from the dying city, smothering the urge to feed his own appetites. Later. Later there would be time for any abomination he could imagine. Once the city was conquered.

The warlord turned his face towards the summit of the Throne Mount deep within Nulahmia's temple district. His forked tongue licked out. He could smell his prey. Neferata was up there, entombed in her palace. Her tyrannical scent was unmistakable. She'd had a long time to perfect her cruelties against her subjects, but Lascilion would show her what it was to truly be devoted to depravity. From her palace, she would listen and watch as Nulahmia perished.

The spectral blaze of the spirit-beacons stabbed into the smoky sky, staining the plumes with a ghostly green luminescence. Phantoms could be dimly glimpsed flickering in and out of the glowing beams, struggling to draw shape and form from the necromantic energies. Far below, spaced about the flattened plateau of the Throne Mount, the immense bone-clad braziers continued to consume the lost souls that fed the beacon lights. The shambling, grotesque creatures that bore the canopic jars to feed the fires were sometimes themselves consumed, their own miserable energies sucked out from their decayed bodies, their crumbling corpses shattering as they struck the bloodstone platforms upon which the braziers stood.

Neferata watched the eerie spectacle from the balcony high up in her palace. How many times had she stood here, gazing down upon her city, revelling in the golden lustre of nostalgia? She was more than queen and Mortarch for Nulahmia; she was the city's mother. Every structure had been raised to her exacting specifications, demolished and rebuilt until they shone with the glory of perfection. The inhabitants, the mortal subjects who bestowed upon the city its vivacity, had been pampered and nurtured to excess. They wanted for nothing; even the least among them was spoiled beyond the imaginings of most men. They wore robes of velvet and gowns of silk, supped from golden plates and drank from cups of sapphire. Even their deaths were things of splendour, spectacles to be remembered and recorded.

All that Nulahmia had been was vanishing before her eyes. Neferata's arcane vision allowed her to see through the smoke and darkness that enveloped the city. She could see the Chaos warriors pouring through the shattered Jackal Gate, ransacking and despoiling at will. The beasts and barbarians slaked their crude thirsts upon the flesh of her subjects, glutted their appetite for plunder with the treasures of her people. Among the throng she could see the lithe shapes of creatures devoid of mortal blood, daemonettes that danced through the streets butchering whomever aroused their fiendish interest. The vampire queen felt a shiver course through her. She had faced the handmaidens of Slaanesh before when they had sought her out. It was an experience even she found abhorrent.

Her legions still held the northern limits of the Queensroad, though they were sorely pressed by the forces of Chaos. That they had held this long was a testament to how much of the horde had quit the battle to ravage the city. Had the full might of the horde been loosed against the Queensroad, the enemy would already have prevailed. As it was, they were obliterating the skeletal warriors and zombies faster than her vampires and necromancers could reanimate them. Once the horde was finished there, only the temple district would be left. Then, the enemy would move against the Throne Mount itself.

Neferata raised her gaze to the spirit-beacon. She had resisted lighting the fires for as long as she dared. Perhaps some of her court would be motivated to fight harder if they thought help was coming. The delusion of hope could instil a terrible tenacity in the weak-minded. For her part, she doubted any of her fellow Mortarchs would answer the summons. If they hadn't been overwhelmed by Archaon's hordes, then they would be like herself – a hunted thing trying to survive in the shadows. To expose themselves to the enemy simply to relieve Nulahmia was something she doubted the likes of Arkhan or Mannfred would risk. Certainly, if the roles were reversed, she would not go to their aid. Not with the odds so heavily weighed against them.

That fool Harkdron! Neferata had expected him to fail, but she had anticipated an interval during which she could consider her options and plan her next move. The speed with which her consort had been defeated, the rapidity with which the hordes of Chaos had poured into Nulahmia, had caught her off guard.

The vampire queen turned her back on the view of her dying city and watched as one of her handmaidens stepped out onto the balcony. Though she appeared as the merest wisp of a youth, Kemsit had existed for millennia as a creature of the night. In better days, she had attended Neferata on royal hunts into the Cobweb Forest to kill werebloods and flayworms. During the great battles against Archaon's armies, she had served as both spy and shieldbearer for her queen. Now, as she walked between the skeletal morghasts who flanked the balcony, the expression on her face was vulnerable and uncertain.

'My queen, Lord Harkdron has returned,' Kemsit announced, bowing before Neferata.

Neferata's eyes blazed. For just an instant, her rage focussed upon Kemsit. If any other of her handmaidens had brought such tidings to her, they would have been pitched over the balustrade and down to the streets below. Her attachment to Kemsit made her hesitate for the split second she needed to compose herself. Callous bloodshed had its place, but right now it was cunning and strategy that would serve her best.

'Send the fool to me,' Neferata snarled, dismissing Kemsit

with an imperious flick of her hand. All effort at remaining composed drained from her as her morghast guards stepped aside and allowed Harkdron onto the balcony. The regal glamour of the queen vanished from her pale face, driven out by the viciousness of a cornered predator. Fury smouldered in her eyes as she watched her lover advance towards her. His armour was battered and dented, soiled with the stinking gore of things human and inhuman alike. As he bowed before her, the vampire's mail creaked and groaned.

Lord Harkdron kept his face lowered as he bowed to his queen, unable to meet her wrathful gaze. 'My queen,' he said, his voice subdued. 'They were too many. I have failed you.' He dared to look up at Neferata and immediately fell silent. There was death in his lover's eyes.

Once more, Neferata hesitated as she forced some of the fury pulsing through her heart to dissipate. Harkdron had failed her, but the wretch still had his uses. 'Of all my vassals, you have been the most precious to me,' she told him. 'I entrusted my city into your care and you vowed you would protect it from harm.' She thrust a finger at the smoke rising from the burning city. 'Your failure I could excuse, but you have done worse to me. You have broken your promise.' Harkdron tried to answer his queen's anger, but she gestured for him to keep silent.

'I will give you a chance to prove yourself to me,' Neferata decreed. 'The enemy will soon move against the temple district and Throne Mount. A zombie dragon has been summoned as your new steed. It awaits in the crypts. You must keep them off Throne Mount. Help is on the way, but you must hold them.'

Neferata turned and pointed to the gibbous light of the spirit-beacon. Harkdron watched the spectral energies blazing up into the sky. The vampire nodded, a new determination settling across his visage. 'When next we meet, you will think better of me,' he swore.

'See that I do,' Neferata declared, turning her back on her lover and gazing out across her city. She could hear Harkdron rise and march away, hastening down to the crypts to claim his steed and hurry back into battle. His eagerness to redeem himself in her eyes would have been pathetic if it wasn't so useful.

From her vantage, Neferata could see that the fighting on the Queensroad was all but over. A few wights and morghasts remained, but the creatures were surrounded by Chaos warriors and beastmen. Even the warlord who led the horde paid the lingering resistance no notice. She saw him slide off the back of his snake-like mount and remove his plumed helm. For an instant, she could feel his eyes staring up at the palace, almost as though the man were seeking her out. The sensation quickly passed. The warlord turned away from Throne Mount and the Queensroad, sprinting towards the nearest building. She soon lost sight of him as he vanished inside what had once been a bathhouse.

Let the scum gratify himself, Neferata thought. Distracting the slaves of Chaos was the last service Nulahmia could render its queen. When the horde turned to the temple district, Harkdron would have his defence organised. He might even hold them at bay for a time.

Neferata smiled, pleased at the act she had put on for Harkdron. The fool would do his best for her because she had led him to believe there was something to hope for. She didn't ask him to annihilate the horde by himself, only keep them back until help arrived. That was all he needed to do to win his redemption.

Only there would be no redemption. While Harkdron fought, his queen would be making good her escape. Nulahmia was lost, but she needn't burn with her city. Dozens of catacombs burrowed through Throne Mount, and one of them eventually opened to a realmgate. Neferata had already told Kemsit to prepare her most precious things. With her handmaidens, she would steal into the catacombs and withdraw before the enemy could complete their conquest.

A boom of thunder caused Neferata to look skyward. Somewhere above the smoke and the ghostly glow of the spirit-beacons, she could see vast stormclouds stretching out across the heavens. There was something uncanny in the manner with which the clouds spilled across the sky, as though they were being poured into the air from some phantasmal chalice. She could see flashes of lightning crackling within the angry clouds.

Then, with a near-deafening crack, great sheets of lightning crackled from the sky, forking downwards into the ravaged streets of Nulahmia.

CHAPTER THREE

Knifing down from the clouds, a blinding tempest of lightning slammed into Nulahmia. Across the despoiled sprawl of the noble quarter, where the manors of the city's deathless elite sprawled across walled estates and morbid gardens, pillars of elemental fury plummeted earthward. Each thunderbolt sent a tremor rolling over the ground and a booming roar surging through the air. Smoke and steam rose from toppled walls and cracked streets, spiralling upwards to merge with the flashing flames of burning ruins. The marauding hordes of Chaos, those nearest to the storm's violence, turned away from their depredations, staring in confusion at the sudden havoc.

Figures stalked out from the violence of the stormstrike. Huge shapes clad in ebon armour emerged from the smouldering craters inflicted by the lightning, mighty warriors encased in plate, their faces locked behind the glowering masks of their helms. Upon their breastplates they bore the symbol of the comet; on their shields was an anvil wreathed in lightning.

Shouts of obscene glee rose from the rampaging warriors of Chaos when they saw the black-clad knights. Their lust for atrocity whetted by the carnage they had inflicted upon the people of Nulahmia, the devotees of Slaanesh rejoiced at the prospect of further depravity. Howling their debased ululations, they rushed through the backstreets of the noble quarter, leaping over garden walls to converge upon the enemies who had so suddenly manifested among them. Even the most savage of the Slaaneshi creatures could sense the vitality that burned within the knights, for these were no undead horrors conjured by the Mortarch of Blood, but beings of flesh and substance, victims to torment and defile.

The knights met the first foes with swords and axes that crackled with lightning. A score of marauders were struck down in the blink of an eye, dozens of beastkin killed as they charged out from the wreckage of a mortuary garden, and baying hounds slaughtered as they came loping down alleyways. Unlike the snarling and shrieking of their foes, the knights preserved a grim silence as they brought death to the creatures of Chaos, plying their weapons with a stoic purposefulness that had more in common with the unfeeling undead than the wanton savagery of the barbarians.

Leading the remnants of his tribe, the immense Tokreshkhan rushed at the ebon warriors. The chieftain's bare flesh was stained with the lives of his victims, strings of gruesome trophies dangling from his neck and arms. The barbarian pounded his chest in savage delight when he saw the ranks of enemies ahead of him. The soft, pampered subjects of Nulahmia had perished much too quickly to make a fitting offering for Slaanesh. These bold enemies would provide much more satisfying fare for the jaded god's appetites.

Before the Sorroweaters and their hulking chief could assault the line of ebon knights, the sinister warriors opened their ranks. From their midst, a great dragon-like reptile lumbered forwards, steam hissing from its nostrils and sparks snapping about its horns. A knight in armour more resplendent than that of his comrades sat upon the beast's back, a golden halo of metal radiating from the back of his helm and a long cloak hanging from his shoulders. In his hands, the rider gripped an enormous sword that sizzled with divine power. He raised the runesword and pointed it at Tokresh and his tribe.

'Slaves of Chaos,' the rider's mighty voice rumbled, 'the Anvils of the Heldenhammer bring you judgement. We give you the same mercy you've shown your victims.'

The jaws of the giant lizard-steed gaped wide, and from its maw, a blast of blue lightning immolated a swathe of charging marauders. Cries of agony rose from barbarian throats as their bodies were reduced to charred, blackened husks. A litter of smoking corpses lay strewn across the street, fouling the path of the men following after them. The armoured rider didn't give the barbarians a chance to recover. He urged the scaly dragon-beast onwards, ploughing into the reeling tribe. Reptilian claws and fangs ripped into the barbarians, slashing armour and rending flesh. The dracoth's lashing tail shattered bone and sent mangled men hurtling through the air. Upon its back, the rider brought his sword flashing down, cleaving through collarbones and splitting skulls with each blow.

Tokresh shuddered at the ferocity of the assault, but his fear only urged him onwards. The novelty of crossing blades with the ebon rider, the prospect of feeling the crackling bite of his reptilian mount – these would present new sensations, fresh delights to be experienced. For the first time in many years, the almost-forgotten delight of anticipation flowed through the chieftain's veins.

He waited until the dracoth had set its jaws about the torso of a shrieking tribesman and the rider was plunging his sword into the breast of a fur-clad reaver before he lunged at his foe. Tokresh was stunned by the speed with which the rider reacted and the incredible strength he displayed. When the knight brought his sword whipping around to block Tokresh's attack, he fairly flung the body of his dying enemy at the chieftain. Tokresh felt the impact throbbing through his bones, could almost hear the ensorcelled steel of his axe split as it met the intercepting blade.

'Tokresh-khan will feed your soul to Slaanesh,' he growled at the ebon knight. He brought his axe swinging around for another blow, putting all the strength in his brutish frame into the attack.

The rider met the assault with withering scorn. His crackling sword cleaved through the head of the axe, slashing Tokresh's face with shards of metal. 'Your god goes hungry tonight,' he told the chieftain as he brought the sword's edge raking across his throat.

Tokresh saw the sky flash above him then watched as the world rose up around him. His last sight was of the ebon rider and his mount. A hulking figure with tattooed and scarred flesh swayed unsteadily beside the reptilian creature. It was only when the headless bulk crashed to the street that he understood the body was his own. The realisation was a last novelty to speed him into the darkness.

The smell of burning flesh and spilled blood filled Lascilion's senses like the aroma of sweet perfume. Cries of agony fell upon him like music. He could taste the smoke of blazing homes, could feel the warm lick of destruction tingling across his skin. Too long. It had been too long since he had felt these things, since he had surrendered himself to the abandonment of sensuality.

The Lord of Slaanesh finished buckling his breastplate, tightening the straps until he felt the delicious bite of leather digging into his flesh. He took up his plumed helm from where he had tossed it aside on the gore-stained floor, a goat-headed beastman sprawled where it had fallen after refusing to surrender to Lascilion's urges. He stared for a moment at the tangle of purple entrails that spilled from the dead gor, caught up in the play of hue and shade as firelight flickered across the slimy organs. A moan from the thing that was splayed upon the wall behind him broke the fascination. The warlord glanced back at the creature he had pinned across the tile mosaic with the same knives he had played across its flesh. With all the skin removed, it was difficult to determine sex or age, not that such matters were of consequence to him. Since leaving the Queensroad to satisfy his appetites, Lascilion had claimed many victims. It was tiresome to remember them all.

As he stepped out into the street, Lascilion saw the amusing sight of his steed crushing some shapeless mass of meat and bone in its coils. He wondered if it was one of his own warriors or some luckless Nulahmian who had caught the daemon's notice. Either way, he was certain their final moments had been deliciously excruciating.

He was less pleased to find Amala crouched upon an overhanging archway. The mutant stretched out one of her talons, displaying for him another one of her flesh-scrolls. Lascilion's displeasure mounted as he read the winged monstrosity's report. The black lightning he'd seen earlier had indeed struck the outskirts of the city. Amala had flown to investigate and come back describing an army of plate-clad knights unlike any she had seen before. Whoever the warriors were, they were cutting down the scattered elements of Lascilion's horde that tried to oppose them.

The warlord cast the scroll into the gutter and glowered at the mutant. If he turned his army around, brought them against these strange foes, then the offensive against the temple district would suffer. It mattered little to him how much of his army these knights killed; what he wouldn't risk was letting Neferata slip through his grasp. The conquest of Nulahmia would be a pyrrhic victory if the vampire queen escaped.

'Bring me the Siren!' Lascilion growled at Amala. The winged mutant had expected the command. Unfolding one of her beetle-like wings, she gestured at his steed and the object wrapped in its coils. On his order, the daemonic mount withdrew from its captive. What had been caught in its sinuous body was no being of flesh and blood, but the lithe body of another daemon, one of Slaanesh's daemonettes.

Nothing remained of the warrior whose flesh served as the Siren's vessel. The possession had erased his being entirely. Now there was only the Siren. Cast in the voluptuous semblance of a sensuous maiden, the daemonette's beauty was marred by the barbed claw that engulfed one of her arms and the nodules of horns that sprouted from her scalp. The fibrous mane of hair that flowed down her bare shoulders was more like the fur of some anemone than anything that should grow from a woman's head. The face was a maddening admixture of desire and horror, lustrous lips parting to reveal needle-like fangs and dagger-like tongue. In her eyes burned a rapacious hunger even more fierce than that of Lascilion himself. Only the coils of his steed had prevented the Siren from slipping away to glut herself on obscenities.

'I am the chosen of Slaanesh,' Lascilion reminded the snarling Siren. He raised his hand to his head, pushing back his hair to display the mark that grew just behind his ear. 'My will is your command, my word is your law.' He saw resentment smother hunger in her glare. He had been the one who summoned her and gave her a mantle of flesh to possess in the Mortal Realms. That power over her was a festering bitterness in the Siren's mind. He was indifferent to the daemon's anger. Let her hate, so long as she obeyed. He gestured to the gnarled horn hanging from the straps of the leather bodice she wore. 'Sound your horn,' he demanded. 'I have need of my army.'

The Siren raised the grisly instrument to her lips, biting down upon it with her sharp fangs. The note that resounded from the infernal horn was less a sound than a vibration, a call that was heard not with the ear but with the soul. Anything that bore the mark of Slaanesh, anything that had sworn itself to the Prince of Chaos, would feel the call reverberating through them. Some, too debased and primitive to understand, would refuse the summons, content to indulge themselves on petty pleasures.

Most would come. Tribes and herds and covens, they would flock to the summons. Lascilion knew this. The greater their orgy of depravity, the more irresistible the call would become. The havoc they had inflicted on the city was but an appetiser, something to whet their hunger. Greater delights awaited them in the ornate halls of Neferata's palace, pleasures undreamed and unspoken. Across the burning city, he could hear other horns being blown as more daemonettes hearkened to the call and rallied the ravagers to them. Throughout the city, his forces were converging, becoming once more an army of conquest.

Lascilion snapped his fingers and his serpentine steed lowered itself so that he could step into its saddle. Spurring the daemonic beast onward, the Lord of Slaanesh hastened to rejoin his Amethyst Guard. His course took him across crumbling avenues and corpse-strewn boulevards, the wreckage of a city on the edge of collapse. He fought the temptation to linger over the scenes of atrocity he passed, to study them with artistic appreciation. He had to remember his discipline, had to maintain his focus.

The intoxicating soul-scent of Neferata was more than a trail to follow now. It was his guide, his purpose. To Lascilion, it had the savour of ambrosia, a gift from Slaanesh himself if the warlord could but find the perseverance to claim it.

Lord-Celestant Makvar scowled at the few Sorroweaters who tried to flee back the way they had come. Arrows from the Judicators behind him brought the barbarians down, bolts of lightning stabbing into their backs. There was no pity to be spared for such degenerates. The creatures of Chaos warranted no respect in battle. They were a pestilence, vermin to be crushed underfoot and exterminated with utter dispatch.

Firelight flickered from the dark armour of Makvar's Stormcasts, the glow of a dying city. The Chaos horde had been thorough in their campaign of havoc and destruction. Somewhere deep within him, he could feel revulsion for the depravity that was on display here. That many of the perpetrators of such outrages wore at least the semblance of humanity only made their crimes more abominable. The Ruinous Powers were aptly named and the greatest ruin they left behind was the blackened souls of those who worshipped them.

Makvar looked across the wanton devastation all around him. Nowhere had been spared the spectacle of violence and horror. Smoke and flame gushed from the windows of slender towers, blackening their marble facades. Mangled bodies bobbed in the alabaster basins of elegant fountains, darkening their waters with the corruption of death. Plunder lay heaped in courtyards, precious jewels glittering among stacks of stolen cutlery and crystal goblets, elegant tapestries sprawled beside bloodied piles of silk robes. The primitive despoilers had even pried wood wainscotting from walls and carved shutters from windows. Two ornate doors, ripped from their fastenings, leaned against a wall as though standing guard over the sandstone statuary collected beside them.

Nulahmia had been a rich city. It pained Makvar to see its splendour blotted out. Across the realms, the hordes of Chaos had already taken so much, destroyed so many things. Now here was yet another outrage to be added to the tally.

The Lord-Celestant let the sense of righteous fury smoulder in his heart. The God-King, Sigmar, had not sent him to the Realm of Death simply to avenge the destruction of Nulahmia. There was a greater purpose to the deployment of the Anvils of the Heldenhammer. Makvar had been sent into Shyish to broker a treaty with the Mortarch of Blood, to renew the old alliances that had once seen the armies of death fight alongside Sigmar's pantheon against their common foe. Saving the city had no place in the God-King's plan, not when there were far more things of incomparably vast import at stake. Knowing this, accepting it, didn't lessen Makvar's disgust at the ravages of the Slaaneshi hordes.

He would use that fury, harness it, draw strength from it.

Makvar and his Anvils of the Heldenhammer had descended upon Nulahmia to the rear of the Chaos hordes, where the enemy was dispersed and distracted by their pillaging. The Slaaneshi forces would have no time to converge upon them before the Stormcasts brought the fight to the barbarians.

'Form ranks!' Makvar called out, his voice echoing from behind the mask of his helm. 'Liberators to the fore! Judicators at the centre! Paladins to the rear!' He tugged the reins of Gojin's harness, urging the dracoth to one side as the Stormcasts spread out across the road, stretching across it in a solid wall of ebon sigmarite plate. At his signal, the knights began to march deeper into the city. Woe betide whatever stood in their path, be it depraved barbarian, prowling beast or capering daemon.

From the midst of the marching Stormcasts, an officer with a golden halo about his stern helm and a shuttered lantern chained to his belt moved towards where Makvar sat astride his reptilian steed. Lord-Castellant Vogun dipped his halberd in salute to his commander before addressing him. 'We have suffered no casualties from this skirmish,' he reported, 'but I fear we cannot depend on the enemy to throw themselves at us in so piecemeal and reckless a manner. Lord-Relictor Kreimnar is concerned that the stormstrike has put us too far from our objective.'

Makvar shook his head. 'Sigmar has placed us where we need to be,' he stated. 'From this position, we can strike at the enemy where he is weakest and slaughter him before he can bring his greater numbers to bear.' He pointed between the burning towers and smoking rooftops, indicating the flat-topped Throne Mount and the immense palace spread across it. The ghostly spirit-beacons stabbed their light skyward from behind those walls. 'Chaos has yet to complete its conquest. The one we seek will be behind those walls. Queen Neferata is too vain to suffer the despoiling of her palace while her forces have strength to defy the enemy. The grace and might of Sigmar has given us passage through the veils of illusion by which Nulahmia was hidden. Now it is left to us to carve a path through the disorder of the enemy and reach the Mortarch's stronghold.'

Vogun shifted uneasily as he heard Makvar's speech. 'Sigmar grant that we do not trade one evil for another,' he said. He brought the butt of his halberd cracking down against the ground. Embedded in the roadway, frozen in a soundless scream, was a fleshless skull. One of many dispersed between the flagstones. 'This city was beset by depravity long before Chaos breached the walls.'

'These lands have been without the light of Sigmar for a long time,' Makvar said. 'They have been forced to find other sources of strength.' He looked skyward once more, at the ghoulish spirit-beacons. 'Sometimes to fight a monster, you must become a monster.'

The hordes of Chaos were advancing upon the temple district once more. From scattered bands of ravaging sadists, they were regrouping into an army again, an enemy united in malignant purpose. Neferata watched them for a while, saw the fur-clad marauders and armoured Chaos warriors crashing against the legions of skeletal warriors Harkdron now led. The vampire's defence was tenacious, but he couldn't do more than hold back the tide. The forces of Chaos knew that victory was within their grasp. All they had to do was smash through the undead to claim it.

The vampire queen watched as a file of grave guard was overwhelmed and the first invaders reached the Pathway of

Punishment, the great road that climbed Throne Mount to end at the very gates of her palace. Neferata turned her back on the scene, withdrawing from the balcony into the shadows of her antechamber. Kismet and her other handmaidens were waiting for her, ready to attend their queen. Neferata unclasped the bloodstone broach that held her gown in place. The sable folds collapsed about her feet. A single step and she was free of them and gliding towards her attendants.

'Quickly,' Neferata snapped at her handmaidens. It was not modesty that provoked the demand that they redress her at once, but rather a sense of urgency. Neferata stamped her foot with impatience as the vampires slid a silken underdress up her naked body and drew a padded surcoat down her shoulders. Bit by bit, Kismet and the others strapped pieces of ornate armour to her, encasing her lithe frame in ancient plates of wightbone and steel. She could feel the protective enchantments woven into each piece growing, surrounding her in a shell of defensive magic. The golden war-crown of Lahmia dropped about her head, framing her face in the royal splendour of antiquity.

Kismet bowed before the queen, offering with outstretched hands the infamous Dagger of Jet. Countless innocents had perished upon that blade, the purity of their souls swelling the deadly magics bound into the dark dagger. Neferata nodded, raising her arms so that her servant might buckle the weapon belt about her waist. From another handmaiden, she received the potent Staff of Pain, each hieroglyph etched into its ancient haft laced with agonising sorceries and diabolical curses.

Arrayed in the accoutrements of war, Neferata looked down at Kismet. 'You will remain here and keep things in order,' she said. Was it disappointment or relief she saw flicker through her handmaiden's eyes? She couldn't be certain and it would make no difference. There was no other she could trust to keep the escape route ready for her in the event this gambit failed.

Neferata listened to the screams rising from Nulahmia. There was nothing that could be done to save her city now. It was lost, defiled and despoiled. Whatever the hordes of Chaos didn't destroy would be too unclean to salvage. The very air would bear the taint of their triumph. No, her city was finished, but that didn't mean there was nothing to be gained here.

The strange lightning that had slammed down into the outskirts, the weird warriors she had discovered in her scrying stone – these were things that presented opportunity for Neferata. For some time now, her agents in other kingdoms in the realm had brought her stories of storm-knights who opposed the hordes of Chaos wherever they were to be found. From captives and converts of a hundred lands, she had heard tales that these knights had been seen in Shyish, seeking the Mortarchs, trying to reforge the ancient pacts that had once united the Realm of Death and the Realm of Heavens against the corruption of Chaos.

Much might be gained by the one who received these emissaries of Azyr. They would be powerful allies if even part of the stories told about them were true. Neferata smiled to herself as she imagined the advantages she would enjoy. There was no man alive who could resist her charms and no mind clever enough to see through her intrigues. To wrap an alliance with Sigmar around her own ambitions was a prospect too enticing to jeopardise. She always considered the crudity of battle a last resort, but she couldn't allow this opportunity to slip away.

The storm-knights had found Nulahmia despite all her spells and illusions. Neferata wondered if they might do the same with the other Mortarchs. Though she didn't know where they had hidden themselves, or even if they yet lived, the knights might. She couldn't risk another Mortarch spoiling the chance to establish an alliance with these warriors. Worse, she couldn't allow the likes of Mannfred to exploit the storm-knights before she could.

Neferata stretched forth the Staff of Pain, letting the ancient relic add its own magic to her spell. Thrusting the gilded head of the staff towards the balcony, she drew upon the morbid essence of her palace, channelling it into the conjuration. Necromantic energies crackled and flashed through the archway, condensing into an expanding sphere of darkness.

Gradually, something took shape within that sphere, a fleshless apparition that swelled in size with each crackle of arcane power. Huge blackened ribs, claws as long as swords, massive plates of bronze and gold, an immense eyeless mask – all of these flowed into existence around a clattering core of skulls. Gigantic jaws stretched out from beneath the mask, fangs snapping at the spectral shapes that rippled around the huge, leonine creature. A tail of fused bone stretched out from the beast's hindquarters until it was a dozen feet and more in length, a wicked barb thrusting out from its tip.

Neferata walked back out onto the balcony as the energies of the summoning dissipated and left a huge, skeletal abomination standing beside the balustrade. The grisly horror was Nagadron the Adevore, a dread abyssal bound into the Mortarch's service. The Mortarch of Blood mounted the undead beast. At her gesture, Nagadron rose into the air, carried upon the spirits of those who had died to give it shape and substance. Neferata could hear them wailing to her, despairing of their plight. A simple spell deafened her to the ghostly protests. She was in no mood for such distractions now. She had to see these storm-knights for herself, determine to her own satisfaction their strength and capabilities. Only then would she know if she should linger over the bones of Nulahmia or make good her escape through the realmgate.

Behind the vampire queen, the skeletal morghasts flew after her, their phantom wings carrying them through the sky. Loyal beyond the limitations of mere flesh, her bodyguard would follow Neferata into the very Realm of Chaos should she demand it of them. For now, it was enough that they kept close to her. She had no intention of leading the defenders on the Pathway of Punishment or the other undead legions that yet struggled to protect the temple district. That task was Harkdron's, and the fool was welcome to it.

No, Neferata was after much bigger things.

Mouldering armour and bleached bone crashed to the ground as Lascilion brought his glaive shearing through the advancing rank of skeletons. Around him, the warriors of his Amethyst Guard shattered limbs and smashed skulls with each swing of their axes and thrust of their swords. The fighters who followed behind those in front were careful to visit further destruction upon the bones of the fallen, smashing and scattering the vanquished foes. Too often during their slow slog up the Pathway of Punishment, some deathmage or vampire had infused the vanquished skeletons with a new store of unnatural vitality. Many marauders, and even a few of his Amethyst Guard, had been killed by such treacherous sorcery. It was the delay such tactics caused rather than the casualties inflicted that wore on the warlord's temper.

Since spurring his steed onto the Pathway of Punishment,

Lascilion's obsession with conquering Neferata had swollen beyond measure. Everywhere he turned, he was confronted by the gruesome evidence of the Mortarch's depravity. He felt humbled to behold such a blend of savagery and artistry. It was an effort to compose himself as he gazed upon the sadistic displays. Rows of iron spikes lined the road, a severed head gracing each stake. Gibbets cast their morbid shadows across the way, withered bodies contorted inside each cage, mummified faces stretched in expressions of incredible misery. At each turn of the switchback avenue, torture wheels waited to greet the invaders, the corpses strapped to each instrument betraying almost unimaginable brutality in their broken bones. Pillories with shards of glass lining each opening were interspersed along each approach, rusty stains flowing down their sides in mute testament to the fate of their prisoners when endurance at last deserted them.

Had the cavalcade of horrors been merely an ornament of past tyranny, Lascilion would have been impressed. Instead he was fascinated, captivated by the outrages of the vampire queen. Neferata had employed her dark arts to instil in the exposed corpses of her victims a heinous echo of life, compelling them to languish in their death agonies. Bodiless heads moaned from atop their spikes, withered skeletons begged for food from behind the bars of gibbets, bloodless corpses struggled in the grip of glass-edged stocks, vainly trying to keep their slashed veins away from the wicked shards.

Yes, Neferata was indeed a fellow artist, a connoisseur of agony. It was small wonder that her soul-scent had called to Lascilion, had allowed him to pierce the arcane veils that hid her city. Never had he experienced a mind so in harmony with his own. Once she was subjugated, once she was exposed to the glories of Slaanesh, she would be a fitting consort for him. Together they would rebuild the wonders and obscenities of the lost god.

Lascilion stabbed his spurs into the sides of his daemonic steed, forcing the creature to raise its sinuous body upwards. His forked tongue flickered in irritation at the seemingly endless ranks of fleshless warriors who filled the road before him. Beyond them, he could see the vampire general from the Jackal Gate using his magic to invigorate the undead legion. The vampire had secured the decayed carcass of a dragon to act as his mount, scaly strips of rotten meat dripping from its yellowed bones. Knowing that such a monster was ahead of them might have blunted the zeal of his warriors as they fought their way up the path, so Lascilion was careful to keep the presence of the dragon to himself. When the time came, he would employ his sorcerers and daemons to overcome the beast.

The roar of conflict from far below drew Lascilion's attention away from the skeletal defenders ahead of him. Peering down the slopes of the Throne Mount, he could see the despoiled streets of the city below. Clutches of beasts and barbarians yet ravaged the outlying districts, and at first he thought it was infighting among these warbands that he had heard. He was swiftly disabused of such misconceptions.

Marching out from the burning city was a phalanx of armoured warriors unlike anything Lascilion had seen before. From head to toe, they were arrayed in ebon plates and the mighty hammers they bore crackled with dark flashes of lightning. These were the foes Amala had spotted, the enemies she had warned the warlord about. Now, as he watched them stalk towards the temple district, Lascilion appreciated the reason the mutant had been so alarmed. The rearguard he had left at the base of the mountain wasn't half as strong as it needed to be. These lightning-men would plough through the tribes and herds at the rear in short order unless he reinforced them swiftly.

Lascilion glanced up in the direction of the Mortarch's palace. He resented anything that would delay his conquest, felt the tugging of depression at his heart as he contemplated the frustration of his desires. There was no other choice to be made. He had to deal with the threat posed by these lightning-men, had to annihilate their menace before his army was trapped between two enemy forces.

'Mendeziron!' the warlord shouted, thrusting his glaive at the ranks of lightning-men advancing towards the mountain. He wasn't certain where the great daemon was, what diversion he had found to amuse himself in the defiled city. Wherever he was, the Keeper of Secrets would hear his command. He would hear, and obey.

Lascilion hoped Neferata was watching. When Mendeziron was roused, there was no limit to his cruelty. The daemon might even teach her a thing or two about torment.

CHAPTER FOUR

Howling reavers crumpled before the onslaught of the advancing Stormcasts. Marching in formation, shields foremost, the Anvils of the Heldenhammer were like a moving wall of sigmarite as they marched through the temple district and towards the slopes of the Throne Mount. Such enemies as refused to give ground before the black-armoured knights were smashed by the crackling heads of mighty warhammers or chopped down by flashing swords. The Judicators following behind the protection of the shield-bearing Liberators raised their bows and sent volleys of lightning searing down into their brutish foemen.

Yard by yard, Lord-Celestant Makvar could see their objective drawing nearer. At the same time, he watched the Chaos forces upon the Pathway of Punishment with dismay. As rapidly as the Stormcasts were gaining ground, the vanguard of the Slaaneshi horde was cutting their own route through the undead.

'We must draw their attention from the summit,' Makvar declared, addressing his words to Lord-Relictor Kreimnar. Among the grim Anvils of the Heldenhammer, Kreimnar presented a sinister figure. His skull-shaped helm and the macabre ornamentation of his ancient hammer were trappings that wouldn't have looked out of place adorning a wight king or Soulblight vampire. Kreimnar had a greater affinity for spirits and sorcery than any of his comrades, often experiencing eerie premonitions and uncanny twists of fortune.

The Lord-Relictor looked up towards the pinnacle of Throne Mount and the ghostly spirit-beacons blazing into the sky. 'Neferata calls for help. Even if no other purpose drives them onward, the enemy will want to smother those fires before anyone hearkens to that call.'

'Then we will offer them a menace greater than the one they fear lies ahead of them,' Makvar said. He urged Gojin forwards, the files of Stormcasts parting as the dracoth lumbered out from behind their ranks. Kreimnar fell into position beside him, guarding his flank. Makvar only advanced a few yards before he directed his steed to attack. A stream of blue lightning erupted from Gojin's maw, blasting into the Slaaneshi forces clustered at the base of the hill. A dozen of the enemy were reduced to smouldering husks in a heartbeat; others ran screaming through their own forces, their hair and rags set alight by the dracoth's attack.

Kreimnar raised his relic-weapon to the sky, invoking the divine fury of the God-King. From the angry heavens, a shower of lightning bolts came crashing earthward, slamming into the barbarians with devastating force. Charred bodies were sent flying through the air, crashing through the roofs of abandoned temples and shrines. Smoking craters pitted the street, shreds of armour and bone the only reminder of those caught in the elemental barrage.

Makvar urged his steed onwards, sending another blast of lightning streaking above the rearguard to crackle into the armoured file of Chaos warriors climbing the path behind them. Only a handful of the Slaaneshi warriors were killed by Gojin's assault, but it was enough to surprise them and make them forget their ascent while they sought cover among the nearby buildings. To ensure the Chaos warriors would stay where they were, the Judicators sent a volley of arrows crackling down into the rooftops.

'Advance!' Makvar called out to his knights. The clatter of sigmarite armour became a dull rumble as the Stormcasts moved on the hill, surging towards it like a black tide of retribution. Those marauders and beastmen that had escaped the assault of Makvar's dracoth and Kreimnar's spells were now confronted by unyielding ranks of ebon knights. Retinues of Paladins emerged from gaps in the Liberators' shield wall, charging into the confused mobs of barbarians with gigantic mauls and enormous axes. What followed was more massacre than melee, but after the carnage they had seen in the streets of Nulahmia, there were none among the Anvils inclined to offer the Slaaneshi honourable combat.

Inhuman shrieks and roars rattled down from the winding path above the Stormcasts. Makvar looked up to see a clutch of goat-headed monsters struggling to send a stone sepulchre from some hillside tomb crashing down upon the heads of the knights below. Judicators sent a flight of searing arrows up into the monsters, the lightning lancing through the fur and flesh of the beastmen. For each brutish corpse that went sliding down the slope, another half-human savage rushed out to take the place of the fallen. Just as it looked like the gors would send the sepulchre crashing downwards, a strike of celestial fire pelted them from above. The heavy slab of marble exploded as the elemental force slammed into it, slivers of stone ripping through those beastmen not slain outright by the blast.

By calling down the power of Sigmar's wrath, Kreimnar destroyed one threat to the Stormcasts, but in doing so, he left opportunity for another. The barrage of lightning he'd invoked against the path ahead had been diverted against the beastmen, and mounted warriors were swift to exploit the respite. Huge knights on hideously mutated steeds came galloping out from the first bend of the switchback, levelling barbed lances and hooked spears as they charged downwards. Behind them, leaping and lunging with alluring abandon, was a pack of claw-armed daemonettes.

The sight of such merciless foes charging towards them would have strained the resolve of even the bravest mortal warrior. The Anvils of the Heldenhammer were more than mortal, however. They had transcended many of the limitations of mere flesh, their valour magnified to superhuman degree by their Reforging within the armouries of Sigmaron. Instead of dread, the Stormcasts felt a rush of expectancy, even eagerness to come to grips with their obscene enemies.

Makvar smiled behind the stern visage that fronted his helm. His ploy had worked. The Chaos commander had taken notice of the Stormcasts' advance. The enemy was now sending some of his stronger warriors to assault the Anvils. When they vanquished the Chaos knights and daemonettes, the warlord would have to send more of his forces back down the hill – perhaps even some of those he was using to push his way to the summit. Every fighter the Stormcasts could lure down was one less blade trying to pierce Neferata's defences.

Foot by foot, foe by foe, Makvar would cut his way up the Throne Mount.

Lascilion lifted the skeleton impaled upon his glaive high into the air. The undead myrmidon continued to slash at him, refusing to return to the grave its masters had called it from. The warlord leaned away from the struggling skeleton, keeping out of the reach of its sword. With a savage shake of his glaive, he dislodged the bony body and sent it hurtling down the hillside. He watched it for a moment, seeing different bones fracture and shatter as the creature tumbled down the slope. By the time it reached the Slaaneshi warriors on the path below, the skeleton had lost both its arms and one of its legs. The boot of a barbarian jarl crushed the snapping skull and extinguished the stubborn spark of animation that lingered in the dismembered husk.

The warlord's steed slithered back, allowing some of the Amethyst Guard to move forwards and engage the fleshless defenders. Ancient spears scraped against their baroque armour in a futile effort to bring down the elite warriors. The blows from the jewelled axes and gilded swords of Lascilion's bodyguard were far more telling, shearing through both iron mail and the bony limbs within.

Lascilion drew his mount upwards, unfolding its coils so that he might observe the battle raging both ahead and below. Before him, the undead maintained their stubborn defence, their numbers seemingly as vast as they had been at the start of the fighting. A few arrows flew at the warlord from archers deep behind the front ranks, taking advantage of his momentary exposure. The missiles glanced from his enchanted armour, and those that stabbed into his daemonic steed merely caused the beast annoyance, its unnatural flesh excreting them in a slime of ichor.

It wasn't the archers that concerned Lascilion, nor the deathly magic of the necromancers who guided the skeletons. His worry was the vampire commander and the zombie dragon. So far, the pair had taken no direct role in the fighting. That worried Lascilion. He had fought vampires before, and though they could be as duplicitous and cunning as a Tzeentchian sorcerer, they weren't known for timidity. The undead general was waiting for something. Try as he might, Lascilion couldn't figure out what strategy his enemy had in mind.

Looking below, towards the foot of the hill, Lascilion could see the sable ranks of the lightning-men steadily gaining ground. He had sent a good portion of his reserves down the pathway to hold the knights back, yet the infusion of fresh troops hadn't stopped their advance, merely slowed it. He felt a sense of both fascination and disgust at the formidable magic the dark warriors deployed against his horde – sheets of eldritch lightning drawn down from the heavens that blasted smouldering craters into the hillside and left even the stoutest formations shaken and mauled in their wake. The leader of these knights, himself mounted upon some manner of dragon-beast, wasn't as shy of battle as the vampire general. He pressed the attack at every turn, bolts of lightning blasting out from his steed's maw to cut through the Slaaneshi ranks, his own gleaming sword flaring out to claim any opponent bold enough to stand against him.

The Lord of Slaanesh grimaced, his forked tongue flickering in irritation. There was only one thing that could stop the advance of the lightning-men – an attack at their rear, something to put them on the defensive. Where was Mendeziron?

Had the Keeper of Secrets become so lost in his perversity that he was defying even the Crying Tower's profane Cup of Sorrows? Had the dominion of the lost god become so fractured that even his daemons no longer trembled before his authority?

A shrill horn blast sounded from among the lightning-men. The note was of such strange and pristine nature that Lascilion could feel it sting his ears. His daemon steed hissed its own irritation, offended by the noise. He clapped his hand against its wormy neck, trying to soothe its displeasure. The warlord had already forgotten his own discomfort. From his vantage, he could see why the lightning-men had sounded their horn. It was a call of alarm.

Lumbering out from among the burning buildings and ransacked palaces was the enormous figure of Mendeziron. The streets around the greater daemon teemed with his smaller kin, the infernal scavengers that had followed him through the Jackal Gate. A swarm of clawed fiends scuttled towards the base of the hill, long tongues flashing from their crustacean maws. Packs of daemonettes pranced through the rubble of fallen temples, their squeals of delight and depravity rising even to the Pathway of Punishment. Behind them all, the gigantic Keeper of Secrets himself marched forwards. Lascilion could feel the daemon's eyes staring up at him, peering into his very soul.

Mendeziron is no mortal's lapdog. Lascilion could feel the daemon's words shiver through his mind. *By pact and by promise do I suffer the summons of flesh. But though you live a hundred lifetimes, know the humility of flesh. Know that when death takes Lascilion, his spirit belongs to Mendeziron.*

The daemon's threat reverberated through Lascilion. For just an instant, he felt a tremor of doubt. Angrily he crushed the fear. He was a Lord of Slaanesh, marked and favoured by his god. He had been granted dominion over Mendeziron and his ilk. Even if such power one day was withdrawn, for now it was his. And he would use it.

'Obey,' Lascilion snarled. The sound of his command wouldn't reach Mendeziron, but the daemon heard it just the same. Throwing back his horned head, the daemon vented a shivering roar and charged towards the hill, heedless of the lesser daemons he crushed beneath his hooves. The lightning-men had fared well enough against Chaos warriors and marauders, but an enraged Keeper of Secrets would be a far different foe. Doom was upon the ebon knights.

The sound of great pinions fanning the air drew Lascilion's eyes back towards the slope above. A foul, rancid stink washed over him as he saw the zombie dragon take wing. The rotten corpse sprang from the roof of the mausoleum upon which it had been perched and circled above the massed legion of skeletons packed onto the pathway. The warlord called out to his sorcerers and warlocks. It was against this menace that he had held them in readiness, conserving their magic to protect his vanguard from the dragon's breath.

The threatened attack never manifested. Instead of striking at Lascilion's warriors, the dragon peeled away, diving down the far side of the hill. The warlord could see it soaring towards the ruined temple district. At first, he thought the vampire general was moving to intercept Mendeziron, for it was clear that the greater daemon's arrival upon the battlefield was what he had been waiting for. But the dragon made no move towards the daemon or to prevent the assault against the lightning-men. Instead, it wheeled around the base of the hill and towards one of the defiled temples. Lascilion saw the rotting beast land amid the rubble. The vampire on its back stood in the saddle, gesturing at the Throne Mount.

Lascilion could almost see the necrotic magic suffusing the vampire lord as he invoked the dark powers. The hordes of Chaos had imagined their foe to be trapped on the Throne Mount. Now the Lord of Slaanesh wondered who had trapped whom.

Rusted gates and hidden doors creaked open in answer to the vampire's call. Timeless catacombs and secret crypts gaped wide as necromantic spells called out to the entombed. From yawning tunnels all across the hill, mouldy legions of the undead emerged. A host of bone warriors and dead-walkers, the carcasses from untold generations, shambled out into the streets. By the hundreds, by the thousands, the armies of the dead surrounded the hill, moving with the uncanny precision of the unliving.

Once the undead encirclement was complete, the vampire lord drew his sword, crimson fire glowing deep within its blackened steel. His voice snarled across the smoking rubble as he ordered the ghastly host to the attack.

'Kill!' the vampire commanded. 'Kill! Kill! Kill them all!'

The purifying light of Lord-Castellant Vogun's warding lantern brought blessed oblivion to the grisly trophies that lined the Pathway of Punishment. Bodiless heads shrivelled under the purging glow of the lantern, caged skeletons crumbled into ash. From each corpse, a mote of luminance rose, flickering away almost in a heartbeat. None of the Stormcasts could say to what fate the released spirits were bound, but it could be no worse than their tortuous imprisonment upon the hillside.

Lord-Celestant Makvar detached a retinue of Decimators

to guard Vogun as he brought mercy to the long-suffering spirits. As the Anvils moved up the Pathway, the opposition was growing steadily more fierce – too fierce for Vogun's gryph-hound to protect its master. The warding lantern's light was anathema to all creatures of darkness, repulsing daemons and rousing the ire of corrupted mortals. Packs of mutant hounds and clutches of beastmen tried to quench the offending light, rushing at Vogun from the shadows of blasted shrines and shattered ossuaries. Once, a troop of Chaos knights drove past the Liberators in an effort to reach the Lord-Castellant, heedless of the peril they invited by turning their backs on the Stormcasts. The silver-armoured leader of the knights had actually managed to strike Vogun with his lance, but had been cut from the saddle by a sweep of the officer's sigmarite halberd in return. The Lord-Castellant's personal crusade faltered for a few moments as he turned the healing magics of his lantern upon himself to mend the wound he had been dealt.

It was more than mercy that made Makvar agree to Vogun's entreaty to bring peace to the cursed dead. The Stormcasts were filled with an even firmer resolve when they saw the relief Vogun bestowed. The palace atop Throne Mount was still far above them, but these damned souls were all along the road. Every yard, every step they gained brought with it an immediate and visible victory. It now became something of a personal affront to the Anvils, the persistent defiance of their Chaos foes. They had become more than just a hated enemy. They had become an obstacle between the Stormcasts and those they would help. Never did the Anvils of the Heldenhammer fight with more ferocity than when they felt the helpless crying out to them.

Makvar brought his sword shearing through the shoulder

of an armoured beastman, its perfumed blood splattering across Gojin's scales. A kick of his boot knocked the dying foe free and the carcass tumbled down the slope until it became caught in one of the gibbets.

It was a hard thing, to reconcile himself to the cruelty Neferata displayed across the Pathway of Punishment. Still, Makvar could only imagine the necessities that had demanded such extremes. With the whole of Shyish consumed by Chaos, the call of the Dark Gods would have reached even to the sanctuary of Nulahmia. To keep her own people from surrendering to Chaos, to drive the corruption from her city, the Mortarch had to present them with a threat even greater than the horrors of the Ruinous Powers. Only terror of their queen had kept Nulahmia from rotting from the inside. Without the light of Sigmar to guide them, any land could be driven to tyranny in its desperation to survive.

The strident blare of Knight-Heraldor Brannok's battle-horn drew Makvar's attention away from Vogun and his cleansing of the Pathway. The call Brannok sounded was one of not only divine wrath but of alert and alarm. Positioned with the Stormcasts' rearguard, the clarion report could indicate only one thing. Enemies were moving upon the Anvils' backs. Not the deranged stragglers that had harassed them throughout their march across Nulahmia, but a force large and powerful enough to pose a real threat to them.

'Vogun, hold the advance here!' Makvar called out to the Lord-Castellant. Until he knew what manner of threat had come stealing out of the conquered city, it would be imprudent to ascend further up the hill. By the same token, Makvar refused to surrender an inch of ground his warriors had fought to wrest from the foe. It was his conviction that no patch of earth was worth bleeding on twice.

Vogun saluted the Lord-Celestant as Makvar rode his dracoth back through the ranks of Liberators and Judicators. 'Kreimnar, with me,' he called out to the Lord-Relictor as he began a hurried descent. As a precaution, he also drew two retinues of Paladins from the flanks. On the Pathway, their thunderaxes and lightning hammers were seeing only sporadic use, striking down the odd Chaos warrior hiding among the funerary shrines. Below, there might be more immediate need for their weapons.

The rush back along the Pathway soon revealed to Makvar what had alarmed Brannok enough to sound his destructive battle-horn. Packs of daemons were slinking out of the ruins. Not by the ones and twos, but by the score. Obscene fiends of Slaanesh scuttled across the skull-strewn roads on chitinous legs, clouds of musk oozing from their slimy bodies. Demure daemonettes danced through the rubble, their laughter at once enticing and murderous.

Brannok winded his battle-horn once more, unleashing a violent thunderblast that roared through the daemons. An ancient temple toppled into the street, its foundations shattered by the pulverising clamour. Tons of rubble smashed down upon the daemons, bursting them in foul sprays of ichor. Yet still more of the abominations rushed towards the Anvils.

Makvar felt the presence of the Keeper of Secrets long before he saw the daemon's bulk striding through the streets. It was an oily, repulsive sensation that seemed to seep through his armour, a sickly sweet stench that reached inside him and tried to defile his soul. Images of corruption and abandon struggled to plant themselves in his mind, fumbling to pierce the bulwarks of faith and devotion that fortified every Stormcast against the lures and lies of Chaos.

A snarl of frustration rattled above the ruins of Nulahmia. Stalking out of the smoke of a blazing temple, the Keeper of Secrets glowered up at Throne Mount with eyes of ice and fire. The daemon was colossal, four times the height of a Stormcast. Its body was cast in a rude semblance of human shape, with two sets of arms erupting from the shoulders. One pair rippled with muscle and ended in hands that sported vicious claws; the others were gigantic chitinous claws that glistened like pitch. The daemon's pillar-like legs ended in a pair of stomping hooves, while its head was crowned with vast horns that curled away from a broad skull, both features suggestive of some bovine nature. Across its forehead were a series of welts not unlike those left by the kiss of a whip. The marks formed a symbol perverse and obscene, a rune that violated the eye of any that gazed upon it – the mark of Slaanesh himself.

Mendeziron. Makvar felt the name thrust itself upon him. A sneer stretched across the enormous daemon's monstrous face, exposing the gigantic fangs lining his leech-like maw.

Kreimnar raised his relic-weapon, drawing down once more the celestial fury of the God-King. Lightning crackled all around Mendeziron, searing into the horror's loathsome body. Flesh bubbled and bone melted in the divine wrath pronounced by the Lord-Relictor, but it wasn't enough to overwhelm the daemon. Saturated in the essences of the victims he had claimed in the sack of Nulahmia, the Keeper of Secrets channelled his own magic, drawing on the perverse energies of his god. Destroyed bones re-formed and scorched flesh regrew. In just the time it took the Stormcasts to cover a few dozen yards, the huge daemon was whole and restored.

Brannok and the rearguard were under attack when Makvar reached them, beset on all sides by the smaller daemons of Mendeziron's circle. The thick, reeking musk of the scuttling fiends saturated the air, a fug that crawled down inside the Stormcasts' armour. Few were the mortal men who could withstand the allure of that reek, but those reforged upon the Anvil of Apotheosis carried within them the celestial fires of Azyr. The soporific musk that could drown a man's mind found small purchase in the fastness of a Stormcast's resolve. The daemonic foulness could discomfit the ebon knights, but it couldn't debilitate them.

Not so the pincers and fangs of the hideous fiends. Two Liberators at the furthest end of the line were pulled down by the strange daemons. The arm of one was snipped from his shoulder by a crab-like claw, sigmarite plate and reforged flesh sheared clean through by the daemonic grip. The other was knocked off his feet by the whipping tail of his attacker. Before he could recover, or one of his comrades could render aid, the fiend was atop him. From the thing's fluted proboscis, a razor-tipped tongue shot out and pierced the Liberator's throat. Glowing streams of light erupted from each of the fallen Stormcasts, their vibrancy and purity at odds with the spectral flares that haunted Nulahmia. Swiftly, the soul-energies streaked into the stormy sky, drawn back into the God-King's keeping.

The daemonettes followed close upon the scurrying fiends. Some of the feminine abominations wielded barbed swords and cruel whips; others were content to use the monstrous claws that grew from their pallid arms. Moving with a supple grace and lethal agility, they darted between the hammers and swords of the Liberators, lashing out with diabolic viciousness to break through the formation.

The agility and ferocity of the daemons was unlike anything Makvar had seen before. A daemon was no easy foe to overcome, even for a Stormcast Eternal, but these seemed endowed with a malignancy beyond what was to be expected of their kind. Whether it was the innocent souls upon which the horrors had so recently glutted themselves or if it was the malign influence of Mendeziron himself, he didn't know. All he could be certain of was that the situation was dire. Even with himself and the Paladins to reinforce them, Brannok's line might not hold.

A blast of lightning from Gojin's maw immolated a clutch of daemonettes, bursting their voluptuous bodies in a spray of purple ichor and sweet-smelling smoke. Makvar rode to the line's left flank, where the enemy was making the greatest effort to force a way through. His sword decapitated a slavering fiend, pitching its twitching body into the monstrosities behind it. Pressing his attack, he brought his dracoth's clawed forelegs slamming down on the reeling daemons, stomping them beneath the reptile's immense weight and sigmarite barding.

Mendeziron's roar boomed across the rubble. Perhaps tiring of watching his lesser kindred battle, perhaps despairing of their ability to breach the line now that Makvar had reinforced it, the Keeper of Secrets prowled towards the Stormcasts.

As the greater daemon advanced, Makvar saw something soar through the sky above. The rotten husk of a dragon flew towards the base of the hill. Upon its back, an armoured vampire howled his defiance of Chaos and called on the ghostly might of Shyish.

At once, Makvar could feel the change that surged through the air, a numbing chill like the cold finger of death itself. All around the base of the Throne Mount, rusted portcullises were raised, revealing black passageways into the necropolis beneath Nulahmia. From that underworld, decayed legions marched. Skeletal warriors in corroded mail, desiccated corpses with withered flesh stretched taut over ancient bones. Armed with bronze falchions and iron spears, bearing adzes and khopeshes, the undead legion crept out from their timeless crypts. Dead eyes and empty sockets gaped at the daemonic onslaught. Then, without uttering either cry or challenge, the deadwalkers and bone warriors fell upon the Slaaneshi abominations.

Daemonettes were dragged down by gangs of skeletons, hacked to ribbons by the merciless action of rusted swords and axes. Fiends were pierced through by spears, impaled by cadaverous enemies immune to the numbing musk oozing from their pores. A veritable flood of deadwalkers besieged Mendeziron, cutting into the daemon's hide with tomb-blades, clawing at him with rotten talons, worrying at his skin with decayed fangs. Like angry ants, the undead engulfed Mendeziron, defiant of his efforts to annihilate them. By the dozens, the undead lay smashed at the daemon's hooves, yet still they came, relentless as an ocean tide.

A pulse of purplish light rippled through Mendeziron, a discharge of eldritch energies that burst apart the deadwalkers scrabbling at his body. Rotten flesh and mouldering bone exploded into greasy tatters and splashed across the streets. The daemon's claws lashed out, skewering dozens of the undead. Arcane fire leapt from his eyes to sear the decayed warriors climbing up from the catacombs.

Makvar gripped Brannok's shoulder, directing the Knight-Heraldor's attention to the soaring temple across from the rampaging daemon. 'Do you think you can bury that monster?'

Brannok nodded and raised his battle-horn to his mouth.

The thunderous blare that issued forth from the instrument smashed into the old temple, blasting apart its tiled facade and spiral pillars. Mendeziron reeled, shaking his head as the sacred note assaulted his hyper-acute senses. His disorientation was already passing when he turned his glowering gaze upon Brannok. Mendeziron's fang-filled grin promised that he would give the Stormcast no chance to sound another note.

The Knight-Heraldor had no need to. Weakened by the magical blast of the battle-horn, the temple spilled down into the street. Bat-winged gargoyles and skull-capped minarets hurtled down upon Mendeziron. The Keeper of Secrets raised his arms in an attempt to catch the descending avalanche of stone, but he had exerted too much of his energies against the deadwalkers and the openings of the catacombs. The cascade of rubble smashed into the daemon, entombing him beneath a mound of broken stone and a cloud of grey dust.

Whatever sense of relief Makvar felt at seeing the Keeper of Secrets buried was soon vanquished. A pack of bone warriors, after slaughtering a daemonic fiend, set upon a Retributor who had been fighting it. The Stormcast was savaged by the undead assault, pulled down to the ground to suffer the same fate as the vanquished daemon. A Liberator had his shield ripped away by the hooked axe of a deadwalker, before being impaled upon the spear of a skeletal champion. Pulled from the line of defenders, he was soon overwhelmed by the host of undead trudging up from the underworld.

'Can they not see we are allies?' Brannok cursed.

'They make no distinction between Stormcast and Slaaneshi,' Kreimnar agreed, bringing his relic-hammer smashing down upon the head of a decayed adversary, crushing its rotten skull.

'Form a shield wall!' Makvar called out. 'Close formation! Don't let them bring their numbers to bear!' Warrior for warrior, the Stormcasts were far superior to the undead soldiers. But for every knight under his command, Makvar could see ten, maybe twenty of the undead, with more crawling from their tombs every instant.

'It would appear that Neferata isn't interested in parleying with us,' Kreimnar said.

Gojin whipped his powerful tail around, swatting a daemonette into the air and pulverising half a dozen zombies. Almost at once, a new rank of undead lurched forwards to take their place. 'We don't know that our offer has been rejected,' Makvar said. His sword lifted a bone warrior from the ground and sent its wreckage crashing down on the heads of those behind it. 'It may be she is unaware of who we are and why we've come here. There is no mind within these creatures. They do not differentiate between us and the invaders because no one has told them to.'

The rearguard began to fall back onto the Pathway, wary of being completely surrounded by the undead and the remaining daemons. The narrower constraints of the hillside would make it easier to guard against such strategy. Brannok kicked the severed torso of a deadwalker down the path, almost instantly finding another foe lurching towards him. 'They had best decide we aren't enemies soon,' the Knight-Heraldor said. 'This fighting will only benefit the Chaos vermin.'

Makvar looked up at the heights above. The delay here would impede the Anvils and prevent them from pressing the attack, perhaps giving the forces of Chaos the time they needed to gain the palace-temple and seize Neferata.

'We need to make them aware of our mission,' Kreimnar declared.

Brannok pointed at the zombie dragon and the vampire on its back. 'He would be the one to talk to, only it doesn't seem he's interested.'

Makvar disagreed. Every moment more of the undead were converging upon the shield wall. A dominating will was directing the mindless corpses, an intelligence malignant and powerful. The vampire was deliberately setting his legions against the Stormcasts, aware that the Anvils were enemies of the Slaaneshi hordes. The question was, did he act on his own, or was he following orders from his queen?

If it was the latter, Makvar's mission had already failed.

CHAPTER FIVE

As Nagadron flew through the smoky skies above the Throne Mount, Neferata was struck by the vicious tenacity of her foe. The reserves Harkdron had summoned from the necropolis beneath the temple district had surrounded the hordes of Chaos. Skeletons encrusted with centuries of calcification, deadwalkers with their rotten flesh lost beneath layers of mould and muck; these climbed up from the depths, bursting from concealed flues and chutes to spring upon the enemy from every quarter. Daemonettes darted among the animated corpses, snipping off limbs and heads with each sweep of their terrible claws. Silent files of grave guard stabbed at gaudily adorned barbarians with spears of bronze. Barbarian chariots thundered down the path to crush the ungainly bone warriors, smashing them to splinters beneath iron wheels and the pulverising hooves of foul daemonic steeds. Lurching mobs of zombies hacked branded beastmen into gory litter. Sorcerers in pastel robes and crystalline cloaks shattered scores of the undead with their obscene spells. Wight kings butchered armoured Chaos knights with their ensorcelled tomb blades.

Neferata could see that her forces atop the hill were without a commander. The vampires and deathmages had been exterminated by the enemy, leaving the lesser undead to maintain a stubborn but uninspired defence. Like a clockwork machine winding down, the skeletons guarding her palace were losing their momentum.

Angrily, the vampire queen peered through the smoke, searching for Lord Harkdron. At first, she thought her consort had been destroyed, though what she found instead was even more infuriating. Her general had flown down to the base of the hill to summon the catacomb-legions, but instead of focusing them upon the hordes of Chaos, he had set them against the storm-knights as well! She could see her consort on his dragon in the wreckage of the temple district, exerting his magic to push his attack upon the ebon-armoured warriors.

Neferata's first impulse was to speed her abyssal steed down to Harkdron, to issue the vampire new commands. Even he had to see the absurdity of attacking the storm-knights when they shared a mutual foe. A cold fury running through her, she glared down at the general. He would pay for his poor judgement.

Focussed upon Harkdron, Neferata let her concentration falter for just an instant. The warding spells that shielded her from the Slaaneshi sorcerers below suffered from the momentary loss of focus. Beams of corrosive energy shot up towards her, searing into the flanks of her abyssal steed and causing several of the skulls trapped within its skeletal frame to crumble into powder. Her morghast bodyguards flew forwards, flinging themselves between their queen and the magic being turned against her. A pair of the winged skel-etons burst apart into shimmering fragments as the arcane rays slammed into them. Neferata commanded the others to loose arrows from their bows into the enemy warlocks, and then quickly urged her injured mount earthward.

Driven from the skies, the vampire queen landed amidst her fleshless legions. She fumed at the indignity, frustrated that she would be incapable of reaching Harkdron to call off his attack upon the storm-knights. Every spirit and minion bound to her service was already committed to the fight-ing, leaving none to carry a message to either Harkdron or the storm-knights. All she could do was command those undead within her reach to refrain from combat with them and fix their efforts strictly against the hordes of Chaos. She could only hope the storm-knights would notice her efforts and understand that not all within Nulahmia were hostile towards them.

Drawing upon her magic, Neferata sent a surge of nec-romantic force rushing from the Staff of Pain. The pulse of dark energy saturated the broken bones and mangled husks of those that had fallen in battle upon the upper reaches of the Pathway. Only the most grievously damaged among the invaders' dead didn't respond to her conjuration. Hundreds of the slain enemy lurched back onto their feet and hooves to assault those who had once been their comrades, while the carcasses of the vanquished undead drew themselves back into a ghastly animation, all but the most brutally damaged rallying to the call of their queen.

Neferata scowled at the results of her magic. It wasn't enough. The forces she had at her command wouldn't be able to hold the hill. Not on their own. She glanced up at the palace-temple behind her, picturing the maze of tunnels that would bring her to the realmgate. Yes, there was escape for her there, but nothing more.

Looking below, she could see the storm-knights relentlessly forcing their way through Harkdron's legions and the Chaos host alike. Never had Neferata seen such warriors! They were engines of destruction, elemental wrath unleashed. Nothing stood against them, not wight nor daemon. To reach an accord with these warriors, to harness their power to her own ends – that was a purpose worth tempting the caprices of battle. But as she watched the enemies closing around the ebon knights, she wondered if even they could prevail against so many.

If they fell, Neferata would hurry back to her palace. But if they could succeed... what power might then be at her service!

'Close ranks!' Lord-Celestant Makvar called out to his warriors. The Anvils had suffered only a few casualties in the fighting against both the daemons and the undead. Makvar wanted to ensure that they could keep it that way. The Liberators brought their shields in close, forming an unbroken wall of sigmarite at every side of the wedge-like formation they had adopted. In the middle of the wedge, Judicators raised their bows and sent lightning snaking down into the masses of enemies all around them. The Paladins held their thunderaxes and lightning hammers at the ready, waiting for any foe persistent enough to breach the defences.

'We can hold, but for how long?' Knight-Heraldor Brannok wondered.

Makvar shook his head. 'We gain nothing holding this ground,' he declared. He pointed his sword up at the Pathway of Punishment. The road was swarming with skeletons and deadwalkers, a sea of decayed corpses reanimated by dark sorceries. 'That is where we're going. We march to rejoin Lord-Castellant Vogun. And then we force our way to Neferata's palace.'

Kreimnar raised his relic-weapon, drawing down an electrical blast that annihilated a dozen bone warriors. The Lord-Relictor grumbled in frustration when he saw several of those felled by his arcane assault begin to stir once more. 'As many of these things as we destroy, the vampire's magic simply brings them back to life.'

Kicking his heels into Gojin's sides, Makvar caused the huge dracoth to rear up onto his hind legs. A bolt of lightning shot out from his gaping maw to splinter the restored skeletons once more. 'We are the Anvils of the Heldenhammer, chosen by Sigmar!' Makvar shouted, his words carrying to every Stormcast in the formation. 'If these lifeless husks rise a thousand times to stand against us, we will smash them down. They will not keep us from standing beside our comrades. They will not cause us to falter in our sacred mission. Woe betide any who try!'

Slowly, the wedge began to climb up the Pathway. The crackling swords and hammers of Liberators battered down the files of skeletons that rushed at them, solid shields of sigmarite thrust back the decayed troops that tried to block the way. Flights of crackling arrows rose from the Judicators, cooking rotten deadwalkers and blackening ancient bone warriors. Foot by foot, then yard by yard, the Anvils pressed their advance.

Resistance intensified. Malignant spirits rose up from the very flagstones to drag at marching feet and claw at armoured legs. The wails of banshees and wraiths shuddered through the mind of each knight, a litany of pitiless malice and cruel sorrow to freeze the soul.

The Anvils pressed on, forcing their way through the deathly gauntlet. Shrieking banshees were knocked down by lightning-spitting bows, while other spectral horrors were seared by the blazing discharge of colossal maces wielded by Retributors and Decimators. Kreimnar drew the destructive powers of the storm down upon the undead formations waiting ahead of them, breaking their ranks and leaving their mangled remains strewn across the pathway. As their advance gained momentum, the Stormcasts smashed the undead underfoot even as the vampire sought to reanimate them yet again.

Through it all, Makvar's voice rang out, reciting the holy catechisms and orisons sacred to their warhost. 'Sigmar is my light in the shadow. With him there is no darkness. From the tomb are we redeemed and no death can lift from us the burden of duty. Fear has been burned from our blood, doubt has been scorched from our minds, and damnation has no claim upon our souls.' With each recitation, Makvar could feel the cries of the ghosts weaken, the reach of their phantom claws lessen. Soon, their hold was as inconsequential as morning fog, and their howls little more than whispers.

Makvar could see the welcoming blaze of Vogun's warding lantern ahead. He could feel the celestial light reaching out to him, pulling at him like a beckoning finger. The rest of the Stormcasts felt it to, their pace quickening, the ferocity of their attack upon the undead and Slaaneshi forces redoubling. Remorselessly, they smashed their way through their foes, eager to rejoin their comrades.

Vogun redeployed his warriors, spreading them out into a solid line. Judicators armed with boltstorm crossbows sent a withering barrage into the faces of the Chaos marauders who packed the road between the two contingents. A retinue of Protectors issued forth from Vogun's ranks, plying their stormstrike glaives with murderous ferocity as they carved a path through the Slaaneshi invaders.

As Makvar urged the wedge onwards, he noted for the first time that, unlike the legions of undead that the rearguard had been forced to fight their way through, those around Vogun's warriors exhibited no interest in the Stormcasts. They were fixed entirely on attacking the Chaos horde. It was tempting to put the change down to the light of the warding lantern, its energies repulsing the undead, but Makvar thought it must be more than that. The skeletons and zombies appeared to finally be drawing a distinction between ally and enemy.

'Brannok!' Makvar called out to the Knight-Heraldor. 'Have the warriors bringing up the rear stay their attack. Keep the undead from breaking the wall, but otherwise visit no harm against them.'

The Knight-Heraldor was puzzled by the command but didn't hesitate to execute it. Sounding a call upon his battle-horn, he relayed the order to the Liberators holding the base of the wedge.

For a time, the seemingly endless tide of undead that had pursued the Stormcasts up the hill continued to hurl themselves upon the shield wall. The Liberators drove them back, using sword pommels and hammer hafts to repel the decayed soldiers, but they quickly returned, stabbing and slashing at the Anvils with mindless tenacity. However often the undead were repulsed, they came again.

Then a change came upon the skeletons following behind the wedge. As they advanced towards the Stormcasts, they suddenly lowered their weapons. Without a sound, they marched onwards a few paces, but made no effort to assault the shield wall. When the wedge gained ground and moved forwards, the skeletons did likewise, but they didn't make any further attempts to engage the Liberators. From Gojin's saddle, Makvar could see the rear ranks of the undead continuing their menacing advance. Once they climbed to a certain point on the path, however, all the hostility seemed to drain out of them, as though they had crossed some invisible barrier.

'Keep a careful watch on them,' Makvar told Brannok. 'Sound the alarm if they try to attack again, but I don't think they will.' He looked at the slope above, at the fearsome Chaos chariots ploughing through the undead warriors. 'At least not while we share a common enemy.'

What happened after that, Makvar knew, would be the difference between success and failure.

From the back of his decayed dragon, Lord Harkdron watched as the storm-knights smashed their way through his warriors. Again and again, he used his magic to reanimate the fallen, to pour into their mangled flesh and shattered bones the eldritch power that would restore them to a semblance of life. However quickly he tried to reform and reassemble the broken skeletons and mangled zombies, though, he couldn't match the rapidity with which the strange knights were destroying his troops.

The hordes of Chaos were likewise redoubling their efforts. Harkdron's undead threatened to engulf the flank of the Slaaneshi army. To counter that threat, bands of daemonettes flitted through the skeletal regiments, hewing and hacking with their ghastly claws. Two terrifying chariots drawn by daemonic steeds sped through the streets of the temple district, their spiked wheels pulverising the undead warriors who fell beneath their charge. After them, an even larger chariot thundered across the broken corpses, reducing them to such shattered debris that even Harkdron's magic could find nothing to infuse with animation.

Packs of daemons raged and howled, trooping through the wreckage of Nulahmia on slobbering mounts that were neither reptile, horse nor insect, but an impossible amalgam of all three. Crab-like fiends of Slaanesh scuttled along rooftops and clambered down walls, their slimy hides exuding clouds of musk. Hulking spawn, maddened wrecks of Chaotic energies and tortured flesh, dragged themselves through the ruins, striking all that dared to stand in their way with gigantic claws and whipping tentacles.

As his dragon flew above the battlefield Harkdron tried to direct his forces, to draw new legions from the most ancient of Nulahmia's crypts. It was then that he saw a stirring of the rubble below. The Temple of the Bloodbat had been demolished by the storm-knights, cast down by the thunderous magic they bore with them. Beneath the mound of debris, the great daemon Mendeziron had been entombed. Much like the catacombs the vampire was emptying, the mound of rubble made for an unquiet grave. Lesser daemons flocked towards the shifting mound, gathering about it with a terrible air of expectancy.

Harkdron sent his will rushing through the companies of bone warriors and deadwalkers he had summoned, commanding them back towards the fallen temple. If he hurried, if he brought enough force to bear, perhaps his warriors could vanquish Mendeziron while the daemon was still weakened by the storm-knights' attack.

Hope withered in the vampire's heart when the rubble

suddenly exploded outwards, chunks of stone spinning through the air as the thing buried under them erupted to the surface. Mendeziron had been bloodied by the storm-knights, his flesh ripped to tatters by the crushing enormity of the temple. Smoke rose from skin scorched by the electric fury of the battle-horn; steam vented from rivulets of boiling ichor that dripped from his wounds. Charred clumps fell from the daemon's body as he stalked out from the rubble. The pain of a Keeper of Secrets, the unique agony of one of Slaanesh's most terrible manifestations, was like a lodestone to the daemons that were marked by the Prince of Chaos. From across Nulahmia they came, intoxicated by the sensations flowing from Mendeziron. And as they drew near to him, their identities were subsumed under his hideous malignance. Ensnared by the power of Mendeziron, the daemon host could do naught but obey his commands. The command was to kill and conquer.

Pride kept Harkdron from repenting his decision to focus on the storm-knights, allowing Mendeziron to slip through his fingers. The daemon was a mighty tool of the enemy, but the storm-knights were something worse. They were interlopers. Chaos could defeat him, but the storm-knights could steal his victory from him. How would he redeem himself in the eyes of his queen if her salvation were bought only with the aid of these storm-knights? Harkdron would be her rescuer; he would allow none to take that from him! He would share the esteem of Neferata with no one!

Harkdron's dragon soared above a pack of daemonettes, the rotting beast's stench washing across them as it raked its claws through their ranks and used its bony tail to swat a handful of them into the rubble of a mausoleum. The bone warriors opposing the daemonettes rallied for a moment, revivified by the vampire's necromancy. But it was only a momentary resilience. Harkdron had been pushing his arcane talents to their limit and beyond. Each spell he cast felt like drawing blood from a dry vein. He could feel his mind growing fuzzy as the residual harmonies of the spells he evoked broke through his overtaxed defences.

Seeing the resurgent Mendeziron and his daemons, Harkdron knew that only an even greater magic could stand against them. Something beyond his own fading energies. The vampire snarled defiantly at the Keeper of Secrets, letting his mockery stab at the abomination's ego. There was a way to summon the power he needed to destroy the daemons, though only a warrior of Harkdron's calibre was brave enough to draw upon it.

Even as Mendeziron sent a ray of searing magic rippling towards him, Harkdron turned his dragon's climb into a sweeping dive. Over the heads of snarling daemons, he flew his steed onto the ruined Queensroad. There, rising amidst the wreckage of war, stood an object of such menace that even the rampaging hordes of Chaos had given it a wide berth – the Obelisk of Black, a forty-foot spire darker than night itself, a frozen fang of death. The hieroglyphs that shone across its obsidian surface hadn't been cut into the Obelisk, nor had they been painted or seared into the glass-like stone. It was as if they had been pressed into the skin of the structure, pushed just under the surface so that they seemed to be scratching at it from within, as though trying to force their way free.

Harkdron didn't know what the hieroglyphs said. They were of a time from beyond time, a relic of the world-that-was and hoary with age even in that mythical era. Once, in an unguarded moment, Neferata had told him even she could read little of their meaning, and even that much was enough to haunt a Mortarch.

The vampire lord didn't need to understand the hieroglyphs to recognise the power bound within the Obelisk. It filled him with a sort of frightened awe, like staring into the fires of a volcano. The magnitude of the arcane force entombed within the obsidian monolith was such that even now he hesitated to draw upon it. *Summon not that which cannot be dismissed* was the first law of necromancy, a warning to all who would violate the rules of death.

Out from the smoke, the enormity of Mendeziron stalked towards Harkdron. The daemon's hooves shattered the skulls embedded in the street, his claws smashed the statues lining the road, and his seductive malevolence dragged the ghosts of Nulahmia into the furnace of his infernal heart. The vampire could feel the Keeper of Secrets pawing at his mind, promising him the most excruciating torments before his spirit was consumed. Such was the fiendish lure of the daemon's voice that it made Harkdron anticipate the promised torture with almost overwhelming desire.

It was the thought of Neferata, of failing his queen, that moved Harkdron to indulge his instinct for survival. Mendeziron was nearly upon him, reaching towards him to pluck him from the saddle of his zombie dragon, when he broke free of the daemon's spell. Crying out in rage, he spurred his dragon to attack. The rotted beast reared back, its bony jaws gaping wide as it spewed a blast of decayed flesh and corpse gas into the face of the daemon.

Mendeziron stumbled back, skin bubbling and sloughing from his bovine skull as the dragon's pestilence washed over his flesh. The daemon's eyes flashed with pitiless enmity. A great sliver of scintillating flame erupted from one of his hands, swiftly cooling and solidifying into a gigantic blade. A second blast of draconic breath scorched Mendeziron, burning a great hole through the monster's chest – but even such grievous injury wasn't enough to blunt his assault. His mighty claws snapped closed about the dragon's body, sinking deep into its rotting carcass. Held fast in Mendeziron's grip, the dragon couldn't avoid the giant sword as the daemon rammed it into the creature's gut. Withered organs and nests of carrion worms spilled from the beast's carcass as the daemon wrenched the blade crosswise. Heedless of the raking claws and smashing wings of his foe, Mendeziron twisted the sword deeper and drew the beast closer.

Harkdron jumped from the saddle of his mangled steed, leaving the zombie dragon trapped in Mendeziron's clutches. Impaled upon the daemon's blade, the beast could only writhe helplessly as its adversary ripped it apart. The vampire could feel Mendeziron's rage clawing at him with obscene persistence, assuring him that he would suffer far greater atrocities of flesh and spirit before his own existence was extinguished.

The vampire looked to the Obelisk of Black. Rushing to the monument, he ripped the gauntlet from his hand and buried his fangs in his own flesh, tearing open his palm. Glancing back at Mendeziron as the daemon continued to butcher the dragon, Harkdron pressed his bloodied hand to the Obelisk and called out to the power buried within it. At once, the infernal whispers of Mendeziron were burned from his mind, exorcised by a deafening tide of spectral wails and ghostly moans. Through that tempest of phantoms, a commanding presence enveloped him. Without conscious thought, without even the concept of resistance stirring inside him, Harkdron found strange words of an unknown language slithering across his lips. Fresh legions of the undead stirred at his call, but so too did something else.

Mendeziron cast aside the mutilated ruin of the zombie dragon and turned towards Harkdron. The Keeper of Secrets grinned with what was left of his face, deciding to savour the vampire's torment. All around him, flocks of lesser daemons came stealing up the Queensroad, eager to draw their own vicarious amusement from Mendeziron's depravity.

The great daemon took one lumbering step towards Harkdron, then froze in place. His eyes fixed upon the Obelisk, growing wide with alarm as he saw the power slumbering within the monument respond to the vampire's call. Before Mendeziron could retreat, that power erupted into a spectral wave of death. A black storm of ethereal energies spilled across him and his followers, ripping and tearing at them with ghostly claws. The chill of ancient graves stifled the burning ferocity of Slaanesh's daemons, shredding their unnatural essence into tatters of desire and sensuality. The forms the daemons had taken on were cast down, burned away by the shrieking maelstrom.

The Keeper of Secrets crossed his arms, evoking the infernal magic of Slaanesh. A shimmering trapezohedron flared around his body, a cage of light to hold back the darkness. For an instant the barrier crackled with purple sparks and jade flickers, then the ghostly forces seeped through the breaches they had torn in the arcane ward. The daemon banished the first surge of phantoms with a nimbus of arcane flame, but more spirits swiftly rushed in to take the place of those he vanquished. As the howling phantoms swirled around him, the daemon found himself being consumed, his physical presence devoured by the maelstrom of spectres. Mendeziron's claws crumbled as they were reduced to dust, his horns wilted like melting wax, his howls of defiance collapsed into a death rattle. Mighty as the daemon's magic was, it was unequal to the power that now raged across Nulahmia and the dread being that was its master.

Spirits from the world-that-was, ghosts of the legendary past, the slumbering dead of numberless millennia – the spectral storm overwhelmed the Slaaneshi along the Queensroad, annihilating them utterly. Then, the ghoulish tide poured out across the burning streets, striking down the scavengers and despoilers prowling among the debris, slaughtering the few inhabitants yet hiding in secret refuges. The storm rolled onwards, sweeping into the temple district. The hungry spirits smashed down the hordes of Chaos trying to fight their way up the Pathway of Punishment. They crushed the regiments of bone warriors and deadwalkers trying to hold the approaches to the Throne Mount. The Anvils' rearguard was beset by the spirit storm, even their mighty valour incapable of denying the spectral fury of Shyish's dead. One after another, black-armoured Stormcasts were dragged from the shield walls to be consumed by the swirling fog of undeath.

The daemonette fell, the severed halves of her body streaming ichor. Neferata swung away from her fallen adversary to face a second snarling enemy, sending a bolt of withering sorcery searing into the clawed daemon's limbs to leave the creature twitching upon the ground. Around her, the queen's morghast bodyguard struggled to hold back the mob of Slaaneshi attackers, their halberds glistening with the filth of daemonic veins.

Though the undead continued to hold most of the Slaaneshi horde as they battled to reach the summit, the daemonettes had been able to slip through the lines. Stalking the vampire queen, they had proven persistent and malicious foes. Neferata's steed had been so savaged by the claws and whips of her enemies that she could feel its energies draining out of it with each step it took. To restore Nagadron's vitality, she let the dread abyssal feast on the lifeless husks of her fallen morghasts.

Distracted by raising new regiments of bone warriors to oppose the Slaaneshi forces, Neferata had lost track of the storm-knights and their progress punching through the Chaos horde. When she was at last able to spare a glance down the hillside, she was surprised to see how far they had come. Despite the fact that a veritable horde of enemies still stood between them, the ebon knights were proving unstoppable. Though the undead had ceased attacking them, the storm-knights remained wary of their decayed allies – a wariness that did as much to impede their advance as the blades of Chaos. Once again, Neferata cursed Harkdron's foolish decision to attack the newcomers.

Casting her gaze further afield, Neferata looked across the burning ruin of Nulahmia for some sight of her lover. Instead of Harkdron, however, she saw a black cyclone of spirits raging through the desolation, a tempest of destruction that was obliterating all in its path. She could see the glowing apparitions that swirled out from the midst of the eldritch gale, spectral warriors that slew whatever stood before them. Phantom swords cut down skeletal soldiers while storm-knights expired on ethereal spears, their spirits streaking into the sky in bursts of blue light. The cyclone's greatest havoc was turned upon the legions of Chaos, however. Droves of barbarians and beasts perished as the spirit hosts spilled across their ranks.

For an instant, Neferata wondered if, despite her doubts, one of the other Mortarchs had seen the spirit-beacons and come to her aid. The manifestation was certainly a feat of necromancy on a scale far beyond that of a deathmage or vampire lord. At the same time, it didn't have the eldritch imprint of her fellow Mortarchs. There was nevertheless something familiar about the phantom storm, something that sent an icy chill rushing through her blackened heart.

Another swarm of daemonettes came dancing up from the Pathway, overwhelming her remaining morghast guards. Neferata set her magic against the assault, driving the creatures back. She could see the ghastly hunger in their eyes, the lascivious sneer on their faces. For the moment, she stood alone against them, a fact that emboldened these creatures of Chaos. Slithering up the jagged slope, bypassing the regiments of undead filling the Pathway, a serpent-like daemon-beast carried the Slaaneshi warlord himself into the Mortarch's presence. The lion-faced mortal brought his glaive shearing through the skull of the last of her morghast defenders, the weapon's enchantments shattering the ancient bone like an eggshell.

Before the warlord and his daemons could charge Neferata, however, they were beset by a barrage of crackling lightning. Winged storm-knights flew overhead, hurling javelins down upon the Slaaneshi horde. Each projectile became a lance of celestial fire before it smashed into the daemonettes. The infernal creatures shrivelled under the fulminating assault, their essence steaming away.

The fury of the lightning failed to stop the Chaos lord. Spurring his snake-like steed onwards, the warlord made one final push to reach Neferata. She could read the grisly determination in his eyes, the obsession that drove him to claim her even in the face of certain defeat. He cast the scorched ruin of his glaive aside, reaching for the swords hanging from his belt.

A thunderbolt struck just then, a blast more brilliant and furious than any that had come before. Neferata recoiled before it, driven back by its violence. When the blinding flash dissipated, she saw a black-armoured warrior standing in the smoking crater left by the lightning, a storm-knight with wings like those of the warriors flying overhead. Unlike his comrades, the lone knight bore a golden halo around his helm and a great lantern was clenched in his upraised hand. The vampire queen screamed at the searing sting of the light that blazed from within the lamp.

The winged knight noticed her aversion, angling the lantern away from her so that she was shielded from its rays. Even so, she could feel the azure glow piercing her with a sensation that was at once both cool and warm. She felt revulsion at the purity of the energy, yet also a desperate craving for it.

The Chaos lord's steed hissed in terror as the azure light spilled across it, its charge arrested as it drew back in fright. Sparks glanced from the daemon's steaming hide as the purifying rays washed over it. Only the vicious urging of the warlord goaded the monster onward. Swift as a striking tomb-cobra, the daemon's head shot towards the winged knight. Swifter still was the flash of that warrior's sword, shearing through the serpentine head in a gout of purplish ichor. The decapitated daemon crumpled back upon itself, writhing in agonised spasms. The lion-faced warlord was smashed against the ground, crushed beneath the undulating coils of his steed. The maddened thrashing of the monster at last brought the chaotic tangle of rider and mount to the edge of the cliff. With a final twitch, the daemon-snake rolled over the side, hurtling down the face of Throne Mount. As the creature's vitality dissipated, its body faded away, leaving its master to plummet alone to the burning streets below.

The blinding light was extinguished as the winged knight snapped closed the latch of his lantern. He turned towards Neferata, bowing to the vampire queen. 'Greetings, Lady Neferata,' the warrior said. 'I am Huld, Knight-Azyros of the Anvils of the Heldenhammer. I hail from the Realm Celestial, and come seeking alliances as were of old.'

Before Neferata could answer Huld, the spectral tide that had been raging across the ruin of Nulahmia rose up from the city, sweeping across the summit of the Throne Mount. A black veil of death, glowing phantoms swirling within its current, howled all around them. The bones of her morghast guard were drawn up into the tempest, vanishing into its titanic whirlwind. Only the Mortarch and the Knight-Azyros remained, standing in the very eye of the morbid cyclone.

A hellshriek rose from the black storm, a sound of such enmity that it rattled across the whole of Nulahmia. Out from the swirling eddies of phantasmal forces and spectral warriors, a maleficent figure strode. Prodigious in stature, the fleshless revenant marched across the summit. Black robes were draped about his bony body, and chitinous plates of deathly armour shrouded his skeletal frame. In his withered hand, he bore a tall staff of bone surmounted by a funerary icon. Atop his skinless skull, he wore a tall crown of obsidian and gold that pulsated with arcane energies and glowed with an amethyst light.

Shakily, Neferata dropped from Nagadron's back, prostrating herself before the advancing apparition. No mere Mortarch had descended upon Nulahmia, but rather the one being in all existence before whom even she knew terror. The Great Necromancer himself, Master of the Deathly Realm. The Death God, Nagash.

She could feel the gaze of Nagash upon her, studying her

from the depths of empty sockets. Though he had long ago withdrawn to his underworld, she knew he was aware of her secret kingdom, her manifold manipulations and schemes by which she had thought to expand her own power. Nothing could be hidden from him. Nagash saw all, and what he saw did not please him.

Even as she trembled before her master, Neferata was stunned by the courage of Huld. Could it be that the Knight-Azyros was ignorant of whom he stood before? How else to explain that he didn't fall to his knees in terrified worship? When Nagash turned his gaze upon Huld, a gaze that had reduced warlords to simpering wrecks and demigods to grovelling vassals, the storm-knight stood proud. He defied the tremendous will that emanated from the core of Nagash's being. Instead of abasing himself, he rendered only the same slight bow he had offered Neferata. His salutations to the Great Necromancer were no different; no tremor of fear polluted his voice or dulled his words.

Neferata waited in dread for Nagash to respond to such arrogance. As impressive as Huld's assault upon the Chaos lord had been, she knew Nagash could exterminate the knight almost without a thought. As the silence stretched on, her fear continued to mount. All of the ambitions she had entertained about harnessing the might of the storm-knights would be extinguished the instant Nagash loosed his wrath upon Huld.

'Spoken like a true son of Sigmar,' the sepulchral voice of Nagash hissed. The Great Necromancer swept his staff through the air, dispelling the swirling maelstrom of spirits, sending them streaming back into the underworld from which they had been called. He advanced towards Huld, staring down at the winged knight. 'Unbowed. Unbroken. How like your god you are. An echo of his dream.'

A malignant glow rose within the pits of Nagash's skull. 'How many dreams may fade into nightmares.'

CHAPTER SIX

Stretching across the wilted fields, a vast double-column of bleached bone and withered flesh marched. What remained of the armies of Neferata, Mortarch of Blood, advanced with grim silence, only the rattle of rusted armour or the creak of ancient bones giving note of their passage. At the centre of the column, carried within funerary carriages, were the vampire queen and her handmaidens. The revivified morghasts surrounded the carriages, their bestial skulls leering with menace at the lands through which they passed. Ahead of the queen's attendants rode Lord Harkdron and the few remaining blood knights of Nulahmia.

Behind Neferata's entourage, a massive throne of bone hovered across the earth, supported upon phantasmal energies that moaned with spectral malice. Even the regiments of skeletons and zombies that marched silently to either side of the throne were loath to draw near to it, the embers of awareness within their rotted heads drawing back in fear from the entity that reposed upon the throne. Living or undead, all trembled in the presence of Nagash.

Trailing behind the column of undead strode the ebon ranks of the Anvils of the Heldenhammer. Hundreds strong, the Stormcasts kept pace with the advancing skeletons and zombies but made no move to close the gap between them, observing the separation with an almost religious fervour.

The smoke rising from the ruins of Nulahmia was fading away in the distance, absorbed into the miasma of icy fog that inundated the dominion that had once been Neferata's kingdom. The city they left behind was now as desolate as the terrain that had once hidden it, another lifeless necropolis littering the lands of Shyish. The ghosts and spectres that haunted Nulahmia's cursed ground now did so without the interruption of mortal life and immortal sorcery.

A part of Lord-Celestant Makvar felt regret that the Anvils of the Heldenhammer had come too late to save the city and preserve its inhabitants from the depredations of Chaos or the spectral carnage that followed. He had not been deaf to the misgivings of Knight-Heraldor Brannok when the Stormcasts marched from Nulahmia. Brannok had wanted to detach a few retinues of Liberators and Prosecutors to search the ruins and ensure they were not abandoning any pockets of survivors. He felt that to do so would be a blemish on the honour of their Warrior Chamber, but even Lord-Castellant Vogun, who was sympathetic to Brannok's concerns, felt such a dalliance would be a waste of time. Nothing alive had been spared by the black storm that descended upon Nulahmia – only those upon the slopes of the Throne Mount had escaped its consuming malevolence. To tarry in the haunted streets would simply tempt the anger of the unquiet dead or draw the attention of such daemons as had managed to slip away during the battle for the Pathway of Punishment.

Makvar's concerns were more pragmatic. They had to be. The benefits of lingering to rescue a few dozen – even a few hundred – survivors hidden amidst the havoc had to be balanced against the scope of their mission to the Realm of Death. He simply couldn't justify the risk. Not when so much depended upon their success. Not when the Anvils had been presented with an opportunity far greater than that which had been entrusted to them when they left the Realm Celestial.

They had come to Shyish to broker an alliance with a Mortarch, to secure the aid of one of the realm's deathless lords. Instead they found themselves confronted by a god, a being that had walked among the divinities of Sigmar's pantheon. Nagash, the Master of Death, one of the mightiest entities in all the Eight Realms. The daunting prospect of parley with a god was eclipsed only by the enormity of what stood to be gained by such discussion. If Makvar could sway the mind of the Great Necromancer, then it wouldn't simply be the might of a single Mortarch but that of the Realm of Death itself which he would bring into the arsenal of Azyr.

'To what purpose do we march?' Lord-Castellant Vogun wondered. He held his warding lantern out, its rays dispelling the grave-gas that swirled all around the Stormcasts, pawing at them with phantom tendrils that left lines of frost on their armour. As far as the rays could pierce the fog, there was only the barren wastes of a withered land, lifeless fields spilling into stands of dead trees and jumbles of craggy grey stone. 'These lands are spent, bled dry by the hunger of their masters as much as the rampaging armies of Chaos. What refuge do they think to lead us to?' The question brought a worried growl from the gryph-hound that loped along beside him.

'A crypt would be sanctuary enough to the undead,' Lord-Relictor Kreimnar reminded Vogun. 'The hordes of Chaos may have overlooked much in their rush for conquest and glory. A living city might draw the invaders like moths to a flame, but would a cairn offer the same lure to their ilk? It is the living they seek to dominate and corrupt, not the bones of the dead.'

'It is a cheerless thought,' Vogun said, 'to leave one grave-yard behind only to seek another.' He turned and looked back at the winged Knight-Azyros Huld. Of them all, only Huld had stood in the presence of Nagash and traded words with the Death God. 'Again, I question the reason for our sojourn and the reason we couldn't be given an audience in Neferata's palace.'

'I can only repeat what was said to me,' Huld replied. 'There was concern that the taint of Chaos hung heavy about Nulah-mia, that the presence of the Ruinous Powers lingered upon the Throne Mount. It is enough that the enemy is aware that we have descended upon Shyish, should we also reveal our mission where daemonic ears might be listening? No, I find this display of caution to be well reasoned.'

Brannok shook his head. 'It is vexing,' he said. 'If we march, then we should be told where we march. Not simply commanded to follow where *he* would lead us.' The Knight-Heraldor pointed to the retinues of Liberators march-ing behind the officers. The Stormcasts strained under the colossal weight of the obsidian obelisk that had been uprooted from the Queensroad. More than the physical mass of the monolith, it was the ethereal taint that exuded from its glassy surface that tested the endurance of the knights. The warriors carrying it had to be rotated every few hours lest its uncanny emanations become onerous to them.

Brannok's words fed Makvar's own concerns. Nagash had commanded haste in debarking from Nulahmia. A prudent decision, for if one army of Chaos could find the hidden city, there was no reason to believe another wouldn't be quick to follow. Indeed, Neferata had been given little time to summon her attendants from her palace-temple and gather a few of her most treasured belongings. But the Obelisk of Black, for the plinth to be excavated and removed – for that the retreat from Nulahmia had delayed. Under the exacting supervision of Lord Harkdron, the vampire general who had fought against the Anvils during the battle for the Throne Mount, the Stormcasts had cut away the ensorcelled paving that grounded the obelisk. The lanterns of both Vogun and Huld had been necessary to hold back the gales of phantoms that swirled around the site, angry that the relic was being disturbed.

The potency of the arcane power infused into the Obelisk of Black was something it didn't take someone of Kreimnar's or Vogun's nature to sense. It was a thing saturated in the dark energies of Shyish, a shard of death itself. Makvar didn't need to understand its workings to know that the relic was a weapon, hideous in its potential. That Nagash would entrust the relic into the Stormcasts' care was something that gave him hope for the success of his mission. However much of a burden the Obelisk might be, by carrying it they would be returning the faith the Great Necromancer had extended to them.

'If you leave a battlefield, do you leave your sword behind?' Makvar turned in his saddle and looked down at Brannok. 'Our weapons are sigmarite and steel. The weapons of Shyish are those of magic. The more disquieting the instruments of that magic, the more potent its power.' He swept his gaze across the rest of his officers. 'We came here to gather warriors for the God-King. It is towards that goal we must all persevere.' He nodded at the Obelisk. 'However arduous our trials, we will persevere.'

Rising above the stagnant depths of a festering tarn, the castle snarled at the moonless sky with fang-like battlements and the jagged parapets of broken towers. The great rock upon which the fortress perched was pitted and scoured, immense fissures snaking down the crumbling cliffs and deep caves yawning blackly from ledges and overhangs. Swarms of bats flitted from the caves, swooping across the scummy water below to snatch insects from the rank air. Packs of wolves howled from the darkness of desiccated forests, their lonely cries echoing across the windswept moors.

The towns and villages that they had passed since leaving Nulahmia had been desolate and abandoned, not so much as a rat prowling among their ruins. Here, however, in this blighted place, signs of habitation greeted the Stormcasts. Lights shone from the windows of the castle and the murmur of voices rose from behind its walls, accompanied by the discordant sound of an untuned harpsichord.

All at once, the undead column came to a halt. Makvar raised his fist into the air, arresting the advance of his Stormcasts. The knights kept a wary hand near their swords, bracing themselves for whatever would soon unfold. Their wait wasn't a long one. Riding out from among the undead ranks upon a steed as fleshless as any bone warrior, Lord Harkdron approached Makvar and his officers. Gojin snorted with agitation as the deathly stench of the skeletal steed struck the dracoth's senses.

Harkdron scowled at the reptile, and the look with which

he favoured its rider was no less hostile. 'I bring salutations from Queen Neferata,' he said. 'She requests the company of Lord-Celestant Makvar and his officers.'

'And where does her highness expect to entertain us?' Lord-Relictor Kreimnar asked.

'You are to be guests in the castle,' Harkdron stated, waving his hand in the direction of the sinister fortress. 'Your troops may bivouac on the plain below.' A malicious gleam shone in his eyes. 'If they are vigilant, they should come to no distress.'

Makvar leaned back in Gojin's saddle and studied the vampire general. He might be uncertain of Neferata's intentions, and be even less sure of what he could expect from Nagash, but there was no mistaking the hate boiling inside Harkdron. The only question was how far he would go to indulge that hostility.

'What of your queen's master?' Makvar asked. 'When may we expect an audience with Nagash?'

Harkdron bristled at the note of expectation, the almost demanding turn of Makvar's words. 'Mighty Nagash will receive you in the great hall of Schloss Wolfhof,' he said. The vampire's lips pulled back, revealing his fangs. 'It is rare quarry that is so eager to tempt the hunter's hunger.'

Makvar returned the vampire's cold stare. 'Return to your mistress,' he said. 'We were sent here to treat with the rightful lords of Shyish, not bandy words with one of their more ineffectual minions.' He drew back on Gojin's reins, causing the dracoth to raise his head, the reptile's jaws only inches from Harkdron's shoulder. 'Tell Queen Neferata I eagerly anticipate our conference, and my audience with the Great Necromancer.'

Seething at his curt dismissal, Harkdron wheeled his skeletal horse around and galloped back towards the motionless ranks of the undead column. Makvar waited until the vampire was well in the distance before addressing his comrades. 'Brothers, the castle above us appears to be the refuge to which we have been marching. It would seem this is the setting Nagash has chosen to formally receive us. My presence and that of the officers of our Warrior Chamber has been requested. If fortune favours us... If my eloquence be equal to the task, it may be that our mission will soon be accomplished here.'

The Lord-Celestant's announcement brought a subdued response from his warriors. Reserved even by the standards of the Stormcast Eternals, the spirits of the Anvils were further depressed by their sombre surroundings and the grim influence of the Obelisk they carried with them. As the Liberator-Primes and the commanders of the Paladin retinues issued orders to the knights to prepare the camp, Makvar noted the visible relief with which those carrying the plinth lowered it to the ground. Already it seemed to be drawing nebulous, ghastly wisps of energy up from the earth upon which it rested.

'Vogun, I want you to remain behind,' Makvar told the Lord-Castellant. 'Your warding lantern may be necessary to fend off whatever wayward ghosts the Obelisk attracts to it. It seems to become at least partially dormant when a celestial light falls upon it.' He shrugged as another thought occurred to him. 'Besides, I need to leave someone familiar with Gojin's habits and temper to look after him while I am being feted in Schloss Wolfhof. However dilapidated their castle has grown, I doubt they would welcome a dracoth in their great hall.'

Huld approached Makvar as he started to dismount. 'Shall I remain behind as well?' he asked. 'It may be prudent to have my celestial beacon to support Lord-Castellant Vogun's warding lantern.'

'No doubt it would,' Makvar agreed, 'but I fear I need you with me. My pride can suffer the reality when I confess that my eloquence is that of a child beside your own. In a duel of blades one chooses to have his best swordsman at hand. It is no different in a contest of words.'

The Knight-Azyros bowed his head. 'Sigmar grant that I am worthy of the trust you place in me.'

'The God-King knows the strength within every soul,' Kreimnar stated. 'He knows the hour when that strength must be called upon, when each man must show his mettle.'

Yes, Makvar thought, but how often is the test of a man's mettle to parley with the Death God?

Though it was a shameful thing to feel, Makvar was grateful that it was upon Huld's shoulders and not his own that such an enormous feat had fallen.

The great hall of Schloss Wolfhof was a squalid, rotting ruin. The tapestries that hung from its walls were faded, moth-eaten and caked in mould – incapable of stifling the cold drafts that whipped through the multitudinous cracks that rippled through the stonework. The rugs that lay strewn across the floors were stained and threadbare, doing nothing to lend a semblance of refinement, or to dull the chill of the flagstones underfoot. The timber tables were splintered, their surfaces gouged and dented, the wood discoloured by the substances that had seeped into the grain. The chairs were worn, the carvings upon armrests and backs rubbed down to shapeless bumps by centuries of misuse and neglect. The cushions upon the seats stank of mildew, their feathers squeezed and compressed until they had a stony firmness. The candelabras that were arrayed about the tables were caked in verdigris, and wobbled on feet that had long ceased to be even. Overhead, a dusty mess of cobwebs and rust struggled to present itself as a chandelier.

More unsettling than the decayed splendour of the great hall were the efforts expended by its inhabitants to cling to the grandeur of the past. The lord of the castle, a decayed and monstrous vampire calling himself Count Zernmeister, draped his twisted body in scraps of rotten velvet and wore a crown of tarnished metal too small to fit about his misshapen head. The abhorrent made a great show of playing host to his guests, exhibiting a courtly solicitude that took no notice of the dilapidated surroundings.

Zernmeister's court were no less hideous than their lord. Snarling, atavistic ghouls sat around the tables wearing ruffled rags and perfumed wigs, golden rings jammed down about their scabby claws. A naked, bat-winged monster stinking of crypts and coffins played the part of major-domo, announcing each guest by stamping its clawed foot against the floor and croaking out a stream of inarticulate garble from its fang-ridden mouth. A huge monstrosity with splinters of bone piercing its leprous flesh sat behind the ramshackle harpsichord that leaned against one wall, prodding the keys with clawed fingers and pumping its pedals with taloned toes. A bestial creature the size of an ogor sat in the chair beside Zernmeister, an embroidered collar pinned about its neck, and a gilded pectoral hanging against its furry breast. When the vampire introduced the thing as the Prince of Wolfhof and his heir, the monster stood up and spread its leathery wings wide.

The madness of the ghoulish entourage was heightened by the abominable repast they presented their guests. Platters of raw flesh were set before each table, sometimes exhibiting the curve of a rib or the tapering point of a finger. Soup was a broth of blood and worms. The wine was nothing but sludge drawn up from the tarn below. Yet to Zernmeister, the fare was extravagance itself and the vampire took pride as he described the wondrous boar hunt by which the main course had been brought to the table, utterly oblivious that what stared back at him from the tarnished trencher were the butchered remains of some luckless marauder.

Makvar shook his head as the horrible fodder was set before him. Turning to where Zernmeister sat, he apologised to their crazed host. 'Forgive me, your grace, but I and my brothers have taken strict vows. We may neither sup nor drink until our sacred duty has been accomplished.'

The vampire crooked his deformed head to one side, as though suffering some internal turmoil at this disruption of his fantasy. After a moment, Zernmeister decided to fit the rejection into his delusion. 'It is a pity, Lord-Celestant, for you will find no better fare in the kingdom. You do respect to your order by exhibiting such fidelity to your vows. There are few templars, I fear, who would adhere to such strictures.' The abhorrant turned his attentions away from Makvar to nibble at the rotten meat on his own plate, sucking such blood as remained in the collapsed veins.

The Lord-Celestant looked away, turning his attention towards the head of the table. There, reclining in a seat fashioned of bleached bones, Nagash rested his cadaverous body. The inhabitants of Schloss Wolfhof had accepted the Great Necromancer as their liege lord, making a great show of presenting to him a coffer filled with finger bones – the tax they had collected from their serfs. The vampire had further sought to placate his visiting sovereign with a series of gifts, the least disgusting being a mouldy funeral shroud. Nagash had indulged the insane dementia of the ghoul-court, treating them as faithful vassals and accepting their deranged tribute. Watching Makvar follow his example appeared to amuse the Lord of Death.

'You pay them a grand kindness, leaving them with their illusions,' Nagash declared. 'When a wretched reality persists beyond its time, there are many who would find succour in madness.'

The sepulchral hiss of Nagash's voice reverberated through Makvar's very spirit. He suspected that the Great Necromancer's words only reached those whom he wanted them to reach. Many times when he spoke, the court of Wolfhof failed to respond. At others, his slightest murmur had the debased ghouls fawning over him to attend his needs.

Makvar had to be more cautious with his words. From everything he had seen, from all that Nagash had intimated, the only thing that kept the ghouls from falling upon the Stormcasts was the delusion that the knights were their guests. Anything that broke that fragile fantasy would turn the great hall into an abattoir. Even if the Anvils prevailed, Makvar sensed that they would have failed a test, a trail that the Death God had set before them.

'Your realm has suffered greatly,' Makvar said. 'The taint of Chaos has taken much from your subjects.' He frowned as he stumbled over the words, glancing down the table to where Huld sat beside Zernmeister's monstrous 'heir'. The Knight-Azyros was the one who should be here fencing words with Nagash and trying to keep from saying anything that would unsettle the ghouls. By design or perverse whim, the Great Necromancer had singled out Makvar for his attentions, sitting the Lord-Celestant on his right at the head of the table, well away from his fellow Stormcasts. The only ally near at hand was Neferata, seated to Nagash's left, who gave a warning flutter of her lashes whenever he felt himself sliding into some verbal trap the Death God had laid for him.

Nagash took up the chalice Zernmeister had set before him, raising it to his fleshless mouth. The ghoul court was oblivious to the fact that none of the slop ever left the cup. 'Chaos is a ravenous beast,' Nagash declared. 'The more it consumes, the more it demands. Nothing can sate its hunger. Even were Chaos to devour the whole of the Eight Realms, it wouldn't be satisfied.' He lowered the chalice and leaned towards Makvar. 'There are some appetites that can never be appeased.'

'The enemy is formidable, but not unstoppable,' Makvar said. 'Sigmar has held them back, kept them from breaching the gates of Azyr. The God-King's armies range across the realms, taking the battle into the very strongholds of Chaos. Many realmgates have been wrested from the enemy, many lands and peoples have been liberated.'

'If the God-King's victories are so numerous, why does Sigmar send you to treat with me?' Nagash asked. He gestured at the decayed hall around them with a bony talon. 'Is his reality as much an illusion as that of these wretches?'

The Death God's blasphemous mockery stirred a sense of pious outrage within Makvar's heart. He held back the retort that would have so easily rolled from his tongue. It didn't need a warning look from Neferata to tell him Nagash was trying to bait him into some injudicious remark. Still, he refused to let the slight against Sigmar go unanswered. 'Chaos is a foe to test even the mightiest of gods,' he stated.

'True,' Nagash conceded. 'The War of Bones has taken its toll even upon me.' He pointed a bony finger at Makvar. 'Still, it must be remembered that I fought on while Sigmar simply locked himself away behind the gates of Azyr. Now that he has decided to stir from his seclusion and try to turn back the tide of Chaos, in his arrogance he sends his disciples to rebuild the old alliances and renew the ancient pacts?'

'The God-King seeks to reassemble the divine pantheon,' Makvar said. 'The strength of Azyr and Shyish united once more against Chaos, committed to driving its creatures from the Mortal Realms.'

Once more, Makvar found the skeletal face of Nagash turned towards him, empty sockets studying him with the fiercest scrutiny. 'Sigmar has been busy in his absence,' the Great Necromancer conceded. 'Never have I seen such armour and weaponry as those you carry. I have never encountered warriors such as your Stormcasts, men who bear the light of Azyr burning within them.'

'We are but one Warrior Chamber,' Makvar said. 'There are multitudes of us among the armies of Azyr. This is the strength Sigmar is unleashing against the legions of Chaos. This is the power which–'

Nagash interrupted Makvar's speech. 'But why does such strength seek alliances? Why is it needful for Sigmar to send his underlings scurrying about the realms to draw others into his camp?'

Makvar had braced himself for such a question. The Great Necromancer was a being of darkness, existing in a world of suspicion and oppression. It would only feed his doubts if Makvar didn't disclose the necessity that had seen the Anvils descend into the Realm of Death. 'Archaon holds the All-points, seeking to corrupt it for his masters. If Chaos could be denied possession–'

'And Sigmar doesn't have sufficient faith in his Stormhosts to carry the day for him,' Nagash chuckled. 'He seeks to add my deathless legions to his forces.' The Great Necromancer nodded. 'It is a wise course to pursue. The only method by which Chaos may be beaten is to overwhelm them utterly.' He raised his hand in warning to Makvar. 'Before I can render assistance to Sigmar, I must regather my own resources. Most of the Realm of Death has fallen to Chaos since Archaon's invasion.'

'What do you require?' Makvar asked. 'If it is within the means of the Anvils of the Heldenhammer to secure, we will see it done.'

'If it is not, then you will shake my faith in this army Sigmar has made for himself,' Nagash cautioned him. 'First we must find my other Mortarchs.' He extended a skeletal claw towards Neferata. 'My lovely Mortarch of Blood once more stands at my side, dutiful and loyal as ever. To help me in my magic, I will need her companions. Arkhan, the Mortarch of Sacrament, and Mannfred, the Mortarch of Night.' The Great Necromancer rested his claws on the table before him, listening for a moment to the off-key dirge rising from the harpsichord. 'It will be a perilous ordeal, unearthing my Mortarchs and returning them to me. Neither of them are so gracious as my dear Neferata, and they are prodigious sorcerers in their own right. Should they prove reluctant, it may be no simple task to bring them to heel.'

The taunting dismissal of the Stormcasts woven within Nagash's warning offended Makvar's sense of honour and pride, but this alone wasn't what moved him to agree to help the Great Necromancer track down his errant acolytes. It was the knowledge that his mission depended upon securing an alliance with Nagash, and that it was the Death God's province to dictate the conditions to secure his aid.

* * *

Part of the pageantry demanded to support the delusions of Zernmeister's court was that his guests should retire to chambers within Schloss Wolfhof's crumbling towers for the night. Nagash, as the count's visiting liege lord, was given accommodation in the abhorrant's own chambers, with Zernmeister displacing his son and initiating a ripple effect that would see the winged major-domo sleeping beneath one of the tables in the great hall alongside the ghoulish kitchen staff.

For Makvar and his comrades, as well as the vampiric entourage of Neferata, the 'guest rooms' within the towers were rendered for their use. Zernmeister had been most effusive in his assurances that the rooms had been exactingly prepared for them by his servants. In reality, this simply equated to the ghouls ensuring that there was still a room waiting behind the water-warped doors. The chamber Kreimnar had been given lacked an outer wall, its floor dropping away to offer an unobstructed view of the stagnant tarn. The room shared by Huld and Brannok had been a little better, though the lack of a roof overhead was worrisome considering the size of the bats flying about the castle.

Makvar almost felt spoiled when he discovered his room had both a ceiling and four walls, though the condition overall made him hesitant to touch anything. Mould and tradition seemed to be the only things keeping the place from falling apart. Even under better conditions, he wouldn't have rested comfortably in a castle infested with insane vampires and ghouls. Instead, he kept his sword close at hand when he sat down upon the floor, his eyes fixed on the swollen door, his ears trained upon the corridor outside.

It was some hours into his vigil when Makvar heard a furtive sound in the hallway. Closing his hand around the grip of his sword, he waited as the sound slowly crept nearer. When the deformed horror that served as Zernmeister's steward withdrew from his room, it had taken the creature much effort to close the warped door behind it. Now the portal slowly inched inwards, no sound betraying the creaking of its hinges or the scrape of its bottom against the floor.

The starlight shining through the narrow window of Makvar's chamber illuminated the figure that quickly shifted around the open door. The Lord-Celestant recognised the enticing presence, the sensuous curves of slender limbs and the alluring swell of a generous bosom. Framed by her raven tresses, the pale face of Neferata was a vision of beauty to melt even the stoniest heart. The soft smile that flickered across her red lips was at once both innocent and suggestive. With a kick of her bare foot, she closed the door behind her.

Even a heart of stone would have been roused by the voluptuous vampire as she entered the room, but Makvar's spirit had been forged from unyielding sigmarite, not simple stone. Yes, he could recognise the charms of his visitor, appreciate the enticing lure, but they presented no temptation to him. Neferata realised that fact when she saw the sword still clenched in his hand.

'I mean you no ill, Lord-Celestant,' Neferata said. 'I come to you as one who would consider you a friend.'

Makvar nodded at the thin gown that was doing a feeble attempt at covering the vampire. 'I dare say you've won many friends with visits like this.'

'How else to convince you I mean no harm?' Neferata asked. She turned around, holding her arms at her sides. 'You can see I bear no weapon.'

'There's no weapon half so fearsome as what you choose not to hide,' Makvar observed. 'But understand – I am not one of your thralls like Harkdron.'

Neferata smiled again, this time without any imposture of innocence or seduction. 'I was wrong to underestimate you, but do understand that my intentions are sincere. There is much to be gained through this alliance you seek.'

'Surely that is Nagash's decision to reach,' Makvar said. 'He is your master, is he not?'

A haunted look filled Neferata's eyes. 'You must be careful of him,' she warned. 'Do not trust him too far. Already he has dealt treacherously with your knights.'

Makvar sprang to his feet and seized the vampire's arm. 'What do you mean? What has he done?'

Neferata drew away from him, staring at the imprint of his hand on her milky skin. 'The Obelisk of Black,' she said. 'He asked your storm-knights to bear it away from my city. He was testing your men, seeing how mighty they truly were. He knew that nothing mortal can long endure contact with the Obelisk.'

'You knew this as well,' Makvar accused, 'yet you said nothing!'

'It isn't an easy thing to defy Nagash,' Neferata said. 'The only reason I have the liberty to do so now is because he has turned his attentions elsewhere.' A look of fear twisted her face. 'Don't trust anything he tells you. Always be on your guard.' She hesitated, as though drawing up some hidden reserve of courage. 'If I ask it, swear to me you will protect me from him.'

Makvar shook his head. 'Such a promise is one I cannot give. There are things greater than either of us at stake. They cannot be jeopardised. I cannot set aside my duty.'

'Your duty may doom us all,' Neferata told him. As quickly as she had slipped into his room, the vampire queen withdrew, retreating back into the hallway. Makvar watched as the door slowly closed behind her, cutting off his view of the corridor.

Alone again inside his room, the Lord-Celestant didn't see the shadow that emerged from the end of the hall. He didn't hear its silent approach or sense its lingering presence outside his door. Nor was he aware of it when it withdrew, following the same path Neferata chose when making her retreat.

CHAPTER SEVEN

Foul, reeking of decay and dissolution, the vast swamps seemed without end, a great sea of mud and morass that stretched away into eternity. Great stands of marrow-weed stabbed up from dank ponds and sinkholes like the bones of drowned men, their morbid flowers oozing poisonous nectar. Expanses of corpse-willows cast their shadows across boggy creeks and scummy streams, their trunks contorted into the semblance of rotten bodies, their finger-shaped leaves waving with sinister artifice in the marshland breeze. The croaking of toads bubbled up from every puddle, a groaning chorus redolent of sorrow and mourning. Crocodiles slithered down slimy embankments, their dark hides melting into the brackish gloom of sluggish channels. Crimson grave asps crawled through the shadowy branches of festering fenpines, their scales marked with death's heads.

The armies of Chaos had rampaged through the Mirefells many times, scourging the swamps of those who hid in its wastes. Though the invaders had razed every shelter, massacred each camp, the swamp itself had resisted their conquest. It had sucked them down into bottomless quagmires and drowned them under stagnant streams. Venomous bats and pestiferous spiders had taken their toll upon the intruders. Choking miasma and glowing soulblight had consumed the essence of beasts and men, leaving their ravaged bones as grim warnings to those who followed. From the hundreds of cemeteries and tombs half obliterated by the mud and muck, vengeful spirits rose to slaughter all who defiled their forsaken domain.

It had been many lifetimes, as mortals reckoned such things, since the Great Necromancer had felt the dread vibrations of the Mirefells seeping into his bones. In centuries past, entire kingdoms had vanished within the expanding mire. The spires of sunken palaces and temples protruding from muddy islands were the only testament to their passing. Yet even in nameless oblivion, the forgotten dead stirred at Nagash's approach. He could hear them crying out to him, wailing in the throes of their unquiet sleep, begging for a mercy unknown to the Lord of Death.

Nagash wondered how much of the swamp's essence Sigmar's warriors could sense. There were those among them with some affinity for the eldritch and the arcane. The morbid Kreimnar, certainly, would be aware of at least the most strident of the necrotic harmonies. Perhaps Vogun would feel some of the malignant energies, Vogun with his purifying lantern and his righteous zeal. The Stormcasts were an enigmatic admixture of honour and duty, faith and obedience. Concepts that were sometimes put at odds with one another, standards that were subsumed to the demands of their mission.

Among them all, Nagash most pondered the mystery of the knight who led them. He had lied to Lord-Celestant Makvar when he told the knight that the Anvils of the Heldenhammer were the first of Sigmar's Stormcasts that he had encountered. But then, there were many things he had kept from Makvar. There were questions that Nagash would see answered, riddles that needed solving. Makvar and his Anvils were different from the other Stormcasts in a manner that nagged at the Lord of Death. Their resistance to the Obelisk of Black's emanations was still a puzzle to him.

That experiment, at least, had run its course. After leaving Schloss Wolfhof, Nagash had commanded the better part of Neferata's undead army to bear the relic down into one of the underworlds where it would be safe from harm. There was no need leaving it exposed to the Anvils any longer, and taking the risk that they might learn its true nature. From subtle alterations in Makvar's demeanour, it seemed that he, at least, had begun to harbour suspicions about the Obelisk.

It would be a mistake to dismiss any of the Stormcasts as simple or foolish. Nagash could detect the great age of the souls bound within their physical incarnations, taste it like a vintage wine. These were spirits that had worn the mantle of flesh many times, purged in the flames of death and rebirth in a fashion far different to the black art of necromancy. Instead of being diminished, instead of carrying the taint of the grave in their bones, they had been reshaped and remoulded, transmuted into something greater than they had been. Only by the most exacting artifice could Nagash create warriors of such potentialities, and those entities often demanded the life-force of lesser creatures to sustain their might.

In the millennia since his withdrawal into the Realm Celestial, had Sigmar discovered some new path of resurrection?

Or had he merely found a different means to the same processes Nagash had mastered long ago? What was this force that sustained the Stormcasts beyond their mortal span? What were the limitations of such power? That was the great question that dominated the Death God's mind.

When he unlocked the secrets of the Anvils, then Nagash would know what course to follow.

'The stink of this place will never leave my armour,' Knight-Heraldor Brannok growled as he slogged through the filthy mire. 'I'll have to boil each rivet and plate to divest myself of this stench.'

'That should avail you little,' Lord-Relictor Kreimnar commented. He removed his skull-shaped helm, letting the foul air of the swamp strike his senses unimpeded by the layers of sigmarite armour and leather padding. After a moment, his stern features curled into a grimace of contempt. 'The smell of this swamp is going to seep into our very flesh.'

Brannok shook his head at Kreimnar's rejoinder. Reaching up to seize hold of a corpse-willow branch, the Stormcast pulled himself up onto a patch of weed-choked ground that at least feigned a semblance of solidity. Stagnant water drained out from his leg armour, streaming back into the mire in little rivulets. White leeches clung to the sigmarite plates, vainly trying to suck their way through the metal to reach the warm body within. With a grunt of annoyance, Brannok brushed the vile parasites from his legs.

'You'll only make room for new ones,' Kreimnar told him. Grabbing hold of the same branch Brannok had used, he joined him on the tiny rise. From the slight vantage, he could see the file of black-armoured Anvils trudging along the boggy creek, their boots stirring up the layers of wilted leaves and dead amphibians embedded in the sediment, further contributing to the murkiness of the water. It said much of the treacherous state of the muddy earth confining the creeks and streams that Makvar had decided their passage would be easier if they plunged directly into the shallows. Many times, the column had been forced to slow its pace while a Decimator was extracted from some hungry quagmire or a Liberator was withdrawn from the watery depths of a gator-pit that had been hidden from view by a layer of weeping grass.

The Lord-Celestant reacted to each delay as though it were a personal affront. Kreimnar found it easy to sympathise with Makvar's attitude. Nagash's entourage didn't allow the hazards of the swamp to inconvenience them. Their steady, tireless march never wavered, their course never faltered. When one of their number fell into quicksand or was caught in the jaws of a crocodile, the undead didn't bother rescuing their hapless comrade. Sentiment had no claim upon them, only the surety of purpose and objective.

The Stormcasts had too much humanity within them to slide so easily into such callousness.

'Have Huld and the Prosecutors returned yet?' Brannok asked as he plucked an especially large leech from his pauldron and scrutinised it for a moment before flinging it into the creek.

Kreimnar shook his head. Makvar had dispatched the winged Stormcasts hours ago, charging them with scouting ahead and finding an easier path through the Mirefells – a course unknown to or forgotten by their undead companions, or perhaps one that they chose to keep to themselves.

'I don't envy them the task they've been given,' Kreimnar said. He kicked the toe of his boot against the muddy soil.

'From the air, all of this muck must look the same. It can be no easy matter to decide what is solid earth and what is simply grass hiding a bog beneath its roots from that vantage point.' A cheerless laugh rose from his throat. 'At least they won't get lost. Vogun's light is the only bright spot in this festering mire.' He nodded in the direction of the Lord-Castellant. The officer was hidden around a bend of the creek, but the vitalising glow of his warding lantern could be seen through the trees and weeds.

Brannok suddenly turned from Kreimnar, his attention seized by something much closer at hand than Vogun's light. The knight crouched down beside the corpse-willow's trunk, clearing away the tangle of weeds and vines clumped around it. His efforts quickly disclosed a chunk of discoloured stone embedded in the base of the tree. The outlines of the stone were too even, too regular to be any natural formation. Uprooting more of the weeds and tearing away some of the dangling vines, he exposed more of what proved to be an oval. Leaning back, studying the sprawl of the trunk, he could detect a certain roundness about its outline, as though the tree itself had grown to conform to a definite pattern.

'What have you found?' Kreimnar asked, taking note of the Knight-Heraldor's distraction. Brannok looked upward, ripping away still more of the vines. Faintly visible, just protruding from the bark, was the stump of a stone wrist and, further down, the outline of a knee.

'A fountain stood here once,' Brannok declared, gesturing at the traces of the statue buried within the tree and the evidence of the basin hidden beneath its roots. The Stormcast looked across the dismal mire surrounding them, gazing at the swamp as though seeing it for the first time. 'There was a village here, perhaps an entire town.'

Kreimnar drew his morbid helm back down over his face. 'Almost anything might be buried under this slime,' he said. 'The hordes of Chaos have long dominated the Realm of Death and destroyed much in their rampages. There is no comfort in pondering the things already lost to the enemy.'

Brannok shook his head. 'But which enemy was this place lost to?' he wondered, pressing his hand against the corpse-willow. 'How long has this tree grown over the graves of a vanished people? Was it the depredations of Chaos that brought them doom or was it the creatures who claim mastery over the Realm of Death?'

'Would knowing the answer make any difference?' Kreimnar asked. 'War demands sacrifice, and there is no sacrifice harder to bear than the sullying of virtue. The lofty ideals of nobility and righteousness are things to keep locked away within the heart, preserved in the one place where they cannot be soiled by the demands of necessity. Chaos has many enemies, but unless they stand together, they cannot stand at all. Sigmar has seen this. It is why we have descended into this blighted realm. It would be an easier thing if those we came to befriend shared our ideas of justice and order, but we must take our allies where we find them and as we find them. We must compromise if we would see the long night of Chaos brought to an end.'

'Yes,' Brannok agreed, 'there is no need to remind me of our duty, or my role in it. Yet it is difficult to divest myself of foreboding. We have appealed to a malignant power in hopes of setting it against a greater evil.'

'Place your trust in Sigmar,' Kreimnar advised. 'Do not forget that Nagash was once a part of the God-King's pantheon and walked at his side.'

'I haven't forgotten,' Brannok said. 'My fear is that Nagash has.'

The dracoth's head plunged beneath the muddy waters of the creek, emerging an instant later with a crocodile impaled upon his fangs. Gojin shook his head from side to side in a violent burst of ferocity, cracking his prey's spine and reducing it to an inanimate mass hanging from his jaws.

'Drop it,' Makvar told his steed. The Lord-Celestant walked beside the enormous reptile, slogging through the muck. It had always been his maxim that a true leader didn't spare himself the travails of his warriors but instead shared in them. While his Stormcasts were forced to trudge through the slime, Makvar didn't have the heart to keep warm and dry in the dracoth's saddle. That his knights wouldn't begrudge their commander such comfort only hardened his resolve to shun it.

Gojin glanced back at Makvar, a snort of irritation spraying from his nostrils. The dracoth was too obedient to protest his master's command, even if he didn't understand the reason for it. With another shake of his head, Gojin sent the broken carcass crashing onto the embankment.

Makvar watched the carcass, observing the eerie animation that crept back into its sinews and set its long tail thrashing against the weeds. After a moment, it raised its head, oblivious to the broken vertebrae protruding from its scaly hide. Soundlessly, the crocodile slid back into the creek and sank beneath its scummy surface.

'See – you don't want something like that in your belly,' Makvar cautioned his steed. The dracoth shook his horned head, long tongue rolling across his fangs as though to rid himself of the aftertaste of the would-be meal. Makvar patted his steed's neck, reassuring him that he would find cleaner prey soon.

Makvar was certain the dracoth would find no such fare within the Mirefells. The further the Anvils pressed into the wasteland, the more nebulous the distinction between life and death became. On the fringes of the swamp, the demarcation between living flesh and necrotic corruption was readily apparent. Now it was all blurred together, flowing into a confusion of fecund growth and morbid decay. Swarms of hideous blue flies pestered shrivelled toads that snapped them up in turn. Bloated rats gnawed at the stems of yellowed weeds, only to have vampiric stalks wind around their throats and draw the blood from their furry bodies. Bedraggled crows pecked away at the rotted organs of cadaverous bats only to have the creatures suddenly erupt into violence and sink their fangs into the birds.

Somewhere in this ghoulish desolation, Nagash declared they would find the Mortarch of Sacrament, Arkhan the Black. Makvar knew little about the ancient liche-king beyond his name and title. There were legends, nay myths, about the skeletal warlock and his mighty sorceries, but he preferred information of a less lurid and imaginative nature. To question Nagash directly would have been to undermine the impression of staunch confidence and unwavering commitment Makvar hoped to convey. If his mission was to succeed, it was vital to make the Great Necromancer appreciate the formidable nature of the Anvils of the Heldenhammer. He had to see for himself the benefit of numbering the Stormcasts among his allies and the danger of making the stormhosts of Sigmar his enemies. Anything that might suggest weakness was something Makvar couldn't afford to risk.

The Lord-Celestant turned his head, following the progress

of Lord-Castellan Vogun as he sloshed through the sluggish water. The azure light glowing from behind the shutters of his warding lantern was a stark reminder to Makvar that Nagash needn't look too hard for evidence of the Stormcasts' strength. Neferata and her vampires could scarcely abide the revivifying glow, much less the purity of Huld's celestial beacon. As he had witnessed for himself during the fighting in Nulahmia, the arcane spark that animated lesser undead could be extinguished simply by prolonged exposure to the holy luminescence.

'I think Gojin might swallow first and ask later the next time,' Vogun said as he drew near Makvar. The Lord-Castellan had his gryph-hound, Torn, slung across his shoulders, carrying the beast well above the boggy mush of the creek. Torn seemed to appreciate the indulgence extended to him by his master, tail wriggling contentedly against the Stormcast's back.

'Then we will learn how well your healing light serves a dracoth's indigestion,' Makvar retorted. He scowled at the swamp around them. 'Though I confess, I doubt anything could conspire to make this place smell worse.'

'Never tempt the gods,' Vogun warned with severity. After a moment's thought, his voice grew still more sombre. 'Especially when you march in company with one.'

Ahead of them, the Stormcasts could just see the ancient skeletons of Neferata's army marching around the next bend of the creek. The bone warriors lacked grace in their movement, but at the same time, they showed no sign of being slowed by the mire. The Anvils prided themselves upon their stamina and endurance, but the undead legions were truly indefatigable. Neither hunger nor weariness caused them to waver in their march. So long as a greater will exerted its influence upon them, they would never stop. And there was no will more formidable than that of the Great Necromancer himself.

If there was an antithesis to the comforting glow of Vogun's lantern, then it was the aura of dread that rose from the ancient bones of Nagash. Makvar didn't need to see the Lord of Death to be aware of his presence. It was a phantasmal taint that sent a shiver through the soul, a spectral hiss just at the edge of his hearing. To a Stormcast Eternal, the sensation provoked a heightened wariness, but in mortal hearts, Makvar expected the feeling would provoke nothing short of terror.

'It is a great and terrible force that we court,' Makvar told Vogun. 'It is precisely because Nagash is great and terrible that Sigmar seeks to draw him into alliance. If the legions of Shyish stand with us when we assault the Allpoints, it will be the turning of the tide. Archaon will suffer a defeat from which he will never recover.'

Vogun shook his head. 'Can we trade the corruption of Chaos for the depravity of the undead? You saw the outrage and cruelty in Neferata's city. From your own lips, I have heard of the madness within Schloss Wolfhof. My faith in Sigmar is as unshakable as your own, Lord-Celestant, but I confess, I lack the wisdom to reconcile myself to these injustices.'

'To save the many, sometimes it is needful to sacrifice the few,' Makvar said. 'That is the hardest lesson to learn, but it is the first any leader must accept. Truth isn't always pleasant, and necessity is sometimes as ugly as what it seeks to overcome. Should the hordes of Archaon prevail, should the dominion of Chaos extend yet further into the Mortal Realms, it will mean the extermination of all. Existence itself would be devoured, sucked down into the infernal madness of the Realm of Chaos. All light, all order would be extinguished, and only the dominion of the Ruinous Powers would remain. Beside such horror, even the evil of the undead would be a thing to be welcomed.'

A motion among the bushes along the embankment drew Makvar's attention away from Vogun. His fingers tightened around the grip of his sword, ready to draw should some denizen of the swamps more formidable than a crocodile choose to show itself.

Instead, what emerged from the undergrowth was a lissom maiden arrayed in a simple gown of web-like silk. Her pale skin was nearly as colourless as her white raiment, and she shielded her eyes from the rays of Vogun's lantern. Makvar recognised her from the grisly dinner in the ghoul-court. She was one of Neferata's handmaidens, a vampire thrall named Kismet.

'Please, cover the light,' she asked, keeping her eyes averted from the Stormcasts. 'My mistress sends me with tidings for the Lord-Celestant.'

Makvar nodded to Vogun, motioning for him to swing the lantern around so that it was behind him. At the same time, he gestured to the Judicator retinues to keep a closer watch on the embankments. It was discomforting to know that they had allowed Kismet to reach them without discovery.

'The light has been withdrawn,' Makvar told Kismet, walking towards the embankment. When the vampire lowered her hands from her face he could see the furtive, almost hunted look in her eyes. 'You are safe with us,' he said, trying to ease her fear. His assurance brought no change to her attitude.

'Queen Neferata bids me pass warning to you,' Kismet said, each word becoming lower and softer until her voice was reduced to a mere whisper. 'At great risk to herself, she has used her magic to spy upon Nagash, to delve into his plans. She wishes you to know that we do not march to find Arkhan, but rather that Nagash has known where his disciple has been from the very start. Through his spells, Nagash has been in communion with the Mortarch of Sacrament. She desires that you should know of this subterfuge… and be ready for it.'

Makvar listened to Kismet's warning, turning over each word, trying to decide what to believe and what to discard. That Neferata had her own ambitions was apparent, though he doubted she would entertain any 'great risk to herself' to achieve them. Even so, she was cunning enough to exploit the intrigue of others to perpetuate her own scheming. With a being as steeped in magic as the Great Necromancer, there was little that could safely be put outside of possibility.

'Thank your mistress for her concern,' Makvar said. 'You may tell her that I will bear her message in mind and that the Anvils of the Heldenhammer will act accordingly.' Kismet bowed to him before vanishing back into the undergrowth. When he saw how stealthily the vampire withdrew, Makvar repented some of his displeasure at the vigilance of the Judicators.

'Someone is anxious to make friends,' Vogun said when Kismet had gone.

Makvar frowned behind the mask of his helm. 'Too anxious,' he said. When he had described the strange reception at Schloss Wolfhof to Vogun, he had left out the details of Neferata's nocturnal visit to his room. 'The question we must ask ourselves is if we can afford her kind of friendship.'

'You believe she is inventing this plot between Nagash and Arkhan?' Vogun asked.

'No,' Makvar conceded. 'I think she is too clever to lie to me.'

He turned and stared through the stands of corpse-willows, gazing in the direction from which Nagash's deathly aura emanated. 'What troubles me is how much of the truth she has decided I should hear.'

Harkdron watched as Kismet slipped away from the Stormcasts, dropping behind a clump of bat-thorn as she turned in his direction. At this late stage, it would be absurd for her to discover him now. Not after all the care he had taken in following her through the swamp.

The vampire glared in the direction of the storm-knights. He hadn't drawn near enough to hear what Kismet told them, but he could guess. She had brought them some offer from Neferata. The queen's pretence of fawning obedience to Nagash didn't fool Harkdron. He knew she had aspirations of power, that she would rebuild her kingdom, if not in Nulahmia, then in some other land.

Neferata had some idea that the storm-knights could win that kingdom for her. Harkdron could just imagine her offering to share her throne with that interloper Makvar. She would make that usurper her king, bestow upon him all the honours she had withheld from Harkdron!

Directing a last glare towards the storm-knights, Harkdron hastened after Kismet. He had small worry that the handmaiden would notice him following her. If anything, she would be more concerned about drawing the attention of Nagash's morghast guards. When Neferata sent her off on her clandestine liaison, it had been the Great Necromancer and his creatures they had been careful to avoid. Neither of them had given a thought to hiding their intentions from Harkdron.

The vampire gnashed his fangs as he considered that his

queen had given him very little thought since the fall of Nulah-mia. Neferata had turned a cold shoulder to her former lover and consort, treating him no better than any of her blood knights. He knew she blamed him for the ruin of her city, the breaching of the Jackal Gate and the defiling of the Throne Mount. He had done his best to redeem himself, but before he could annihilate the hordes of Chaos, Makvar and his damned storm-knights had appeared!

It was enough that Makvar had stolen from him his chance to prove himself to his queen. Harkdron wasn't about to allow him to take his place in the queen's favour.

There was no way to strike directly against Makvar. Hark-dron knew this. Even if he discounted the displeasure of his queen, there was the danger of angering Nagash. The Lord of Death was interested in the storm-knights, at least for the moment. Perhaps he was even entertaining Makvar's over-tures of an alliance with Sigmar.

No, Harkdon decided, the only route open to him was to drive a wedge between Neferata and Makvar. He had to turn her against the storm-knights and make it seem her own decision when she did so. Then she would understand that Harkdron was the only consort worthy of her.

With a powerful lunge, Harkdron threw himself across a stagnant brook. As soon as his feet struck the ground, he was dashing through a stand of gallow-oaks. Kismet would take a more cautious course as she made her way back to her queen. Haste, not caution, was Harkdron's goal. Darting around the boughs of the squat oak trees, the vampire felt the thrill of the hunt pulsing through him. He had let himself grow soft amidst the luxuries of Nulahmia. He had forgotten the excite-ment of being a predator about to fall upon his prey.

Kismet's pale shape came gliding out from the undergrowth,

hesitating as she peered in the direction of the undead column. Her fixation with the column and any threat rising from it made her oblivious to the menace stealing towards her from the gallow-oaks. Harkdron was nearly upon her before she sensed him and noted her peril.

Like a cornered tigress, Kismet spun about to meet her attacker. Raking fingers slashed at Harkdron's face, missing the vampire only by a hair's breadth. The foot she brought slamming into his midriff brought better results, connecting with such violence that he was knocked off his feet.

Harkdron was back on the attack almost at once. Snarling, he pounced at his fleeing quarry. One of his clutching hands seized a clump of Kismet's hair, wrenching it out by the roots and spilling the handmaiden into the mud. The vampire loomed over her, staring down with blazing eyes.

Kismet saw death in those eyes. 'Spare me, Lord Harkdron,' she begged. 'I will tell you whatever you want to know.'

The vampire sprang at her, driving his fist into her chest with superhuman, bone-splintering force. 'Keep your secrets,' he hissed into her ear. 'You are more use to me this way.' With a vicious pull, Harkdron's hand came tearing out of Kismet's mangled chest. Clenched between his bloodied fingers was the handmaiden's dripping heart. He glared at it a moment, then tossed it into the weeds. Crouching over Kismet's body he removed the silver talisman he kept hidden in his boot. He averted his eyes from the tiny hammer, an ancient relic from the ages when Sigmar had walked the kingdoms of Shyish. The God-King was long gone from the Realm of Death, but his power lingered on in the few symbols left behind. Symbols that were potent against the undead.

Harkdron stuffed the talisman into the gaping wound. There were times when he had disposed of vampiric rivals for Neferata's attentions, using the little hammer to ensure they stayed dead when he destroyed them. While the hammer rested in the place where Kismet's heart should be, she would remain with the truly dead. If some friend found her resting place, they might dispose of the talisman and allow her to revive, but Harkdron would ensure that didn't happen. He picked her up and stalked off into the swamp. He had seen an especially deep bog when he had followed her away from the column. Just the place for someone to disappear.

Harkdron wondered what Neferata would think when Kismet failed to return from her meeting with Makvar. With some care on his part, he was certain he could help her come to the right conclusions.

Blackened hills and barren fields rushed past Lascilion's foggy vision. Dimly, he perceived the dried beds of dead lakes and the gnarled boughs of charred forests, the broken walls of ruined castles and the shattered foundations of fallen temples. The rubble of despoiled tomb cities lay strewn across meadows of bleached bone. The husks of vanquished armies withered upon groves of stakes, fleshless skulls grinning up at the sky.

Everywhere, the taint of Chaos was in bloom. The megalithic flagstones of ancient roads were split and broken by the fibrous stalks of colossal flowers with petals of ice and fiery nectar. Streams of corrosive ooze eroded primordial barrow mounds, sending pillars of greasy vapour screaming into the air. Vast, amorphous things rippling with unclean vitality washed across the ghostly streets of desolate villages, caking all they touched in crystalline growths.

Awareness came roaring back into Lascilion's brain, threatening to devour his senses in a paroxysm of pain. Reluctantly, the Lord of Slaanesh fought back the agonies that threatened to consume his reason and render him a dumb, mad thing. With his resistance came memories, the crushing torment as his daemon steed rolled across him and crushed the strength from his bones, the searing light of the storm-angel's lamp as it pierced his eyes and stabbed his spirit. Most of all, he remembered the sight of Neferata, the delicious vampire queen, so close to him that his tongue swelled with the scent of her cruelty.

He had fallen then, hurtling down the side of the Throne Mount, the burning city rushing towards him as though eager to draw him into its dying embrace. Then, everything was lost in the darkness. The warlord knew no more.

Lascilion tried to move, to discover for himself the extent of his injuries. The effort sent a new spasm of pain rushing through him and a trickle of blood down his back. He could feel the sharp claws that were dug into his flesh, the bite of his splintered armour as it cut his skin. Managing to tilt his head, he could see the hideous face of Amala staring down at him. He knew then that he was held fast in the mutant's claws as she soared across the sky. There was no hint of intention to be found in her inhuman eyes and no clue of her purpose to be had from the inarticulate slobbering that dripped from her jaws. Amala had been a dutiful enough servant when he had been the Lord of Slaanesh with an army of men and daemons under his command. Now, broken and disgraced, he wondered if any sense of loyalty lingered in her.

Amala's purpose soon became clear to Lascilion, and when it was, he considered that it might have been better for him if she had simply carried him off to some craggy mountainside to devour his flesh. A vast encampment lay sprawled across the terrain below, a veritable city of hide tents and wooden shelters that stretched away into the mist-shrouded horizon. Lascilion could see huge stone idols with their blood-drenched altars. He could see massive slave pens with their spiked fences. There were great fighting arenas gouged where the followers of Khorne offered up the skulls of their victims, and the diseased cesspits where the disciples of the Plague God sought Nurgle's putrid blessings. Eldritch towers bound in chains of copper and adorned with arcane sigils of gold flickered with weird energies and eerie lights as the students of Tzeentch practised their sorceries. Lascilion looked for the perfumed pavilions of Slaanesh's initiates, but soon despaired of the search. Most of those who honoured the Prince of Pleasure in this realm had flocked to his banner and followed him to their doom in Nulahmia. Those who remained would view him with loathing, an affront to their absent god.

The winged mutant tightened her grip upon Lascilion's shoulders. Wheeling through the air, Amala headed towards the gigantic tent at the centre of the encampment. Stitched from the hides of mammoths and dragons, it was supported by enormous pillars of skulls, each head branded with the grisly rune of the Blood God. Pennants of flayed flesh fluttered above each pillar, flags cut from the still-living bodies of kings and hierophants and stained with the murderous symbols of Khorne. Encircling the tent, their skinned bodies nailed to posts, were the eighty-eight warriors chosen as offerings to the Lord of Skulls. As each tortured warrior expired, he was replaced by another, an endless cycle of blood to ensure the Blood God's favour.

This, then, was the stronghold of Bloodking Thagmok, mightiest of the generals left by Archaon to secure the Realm of Death in the name of the Dark Gods. Lascilion had been filled with pride when he had last stood in Thagmok's presence, arrogantly boasting that he would succeed where so many others had failed. He had promised to find Nulahmia and capture its queen. The Bloodking wasn't known for his mercy, nor his indulgence of broken promises. As Amala descended towards the tent, Lascilion found his gaze roving across the exposed muscles and organs of the warriors on the posts. He trembled as he imagined joining the gory offerings.

If Thagmok even considered him worthy of such a fate.

CHAPTER EIGHT

Huld soared across the blighted wasteland of the Mire-fells, keeping close to the oozing earth, vigilant for any path that might provide his comrades a speedier journey than the creek they followed. Except for a few rocky islands and the occasional stand of twisted forest that seemed rooted in something with more solidity than a bog, his efforts had come to naught, as had those of the Prosecutors who shared in his labour. The nearest any of them had come was the discovery of a stone causeway sprawled across some fens, its supports dragged down into the muck so that the road was tilted on its side. The dilapidated construction looked as treacherous as the boggy ground that was slowly consuming it. Even had it been in a more amiable state, it was useless to the needs of the Stormcasts, winding its broken course away from the backwaters into which the Lord of Death was guiding them, as though the land itself were telling them to turn back.

Yet the Anvils couldn't turn back. Too much depended

upon their mission. Makvar cajoled every effort from the Stormcasts to keep from falling too far behind the undead. The winged scouts did their best to guide their comrades to paths less onerous than that taken by Nagash and his creatures, but never could they seem to find a route which would allow them to gain upon the undead. Makvar was compelled to keep pushing the Anvils and prevent them from losing all contact with the undead column.

The Knight-Azyros didn't envy Lord-Celestant Makvar his burden. Every decision he made had to be weighed against the success of their mission. Whatever lengths it took to convince Nagash to lend his support to Sigmar and unite his deathless legions with those of the Realm Celestial, Makvar had no choice but to pursue them. Even when it meant putting his comrades at risk and marching them into a trackless mire. Huld's comrades sometimes said he had been reforged with a silver tongue, but he wondered if his gift of eloquence would have counted for much when it came to negotiating with the Great Necromancer. He felt that it was deeds, not words, that were needed to sway Nagash.

Huld's wings snapped tight against his armoured body as he sent himself into a dive, skimming just above the moss-ridden treetops with deceptive grace. His aerobatics were more than simple exuberance. He was keeping close to the trees to avoid being spotted from afar. Only the most debased and forsaken of the enemy's minions would linger in a place like the Mirefells, but if there was one thing Huld had learned about the hordes of Chaos, it was to never underestimate the depths to which they could lower themselves. Some of the things he had seen perpetrated by the bloodreavers of Khorne would have made a ghoul's gorge rise.

There were also the noxious creatures of the swamp itself

to avoid. Several times, immense bats had taken wing at the approach of the Stormcasts, whether from hunger or to defend their territory. Most of the flying vermin had been routed easily, a single stormcall javelin enough to scatter their flocks and send them hastening back to the shadows. A few of the larger beasts had been more persistent, their eyes aglow with an appetite that uncomfortably recalled to Huld the hideous feast at Count Zernmeister's castle. Only by sending their steaming carcasses plummeting down into the bog were the Stormcasts able to fend off the attentions of these unliving horrors.

The faint sounds of battle drifted back to him on the rank wind and made Huld forget about giant bats. The distinct clash of metal against metal rang through the air, but with the sound came even more savage noises. Ferocious howls and fearsome screams, bestial and exultant, the cries of wanton carnage and brutal conquest. Somewhere ahead of him, a vicious battle was being fought.

Signalling the Prosecutors, Huld sped onwards, towards the roar of combat. The stands of trees below became more sparse, their trunks wizened and even more twisted than the others he had seen in the Mirefells. Ugly patches of mist and vapour billowed up from the marshy ground, pulsating with a phosphorescent glow. Here and there, he could see clumps of broken masonry poking out of the mud and the severed stumps of stone columns half-engulfed by weeds and moss.

Evidence of ancient habitation increased the closer Huld drew to the clamour of battle. The few trees that thrust their trunks from the muck became still more sickly and dwarfish, their branches reaching out like decayed claws. The heaps of rock and stone protruding from the mire were now recognisable as structures, empty windows gaping from their abandoned walls, morbid carvings nearly obscured by sediment and slime. Certainly, Huld thought, what lay below him had once been a great city, perhaps a seat of empire in some long-lost epoch.

The sound of battle drew him still farther. He began to wonder if what he was hearing was some ghostly echo of this city's death, some grim haunt conjured to lead him astray. The Knight-Azyros shook his head. The only way to be certain what was real and what was phantom was to press on and discover for himself where the phenomenon would lead him. Only then could he tell Makvar what lay ahead of the Anvils.

The obscuring mist suddenly evaporated, and Huld had an unobstructed view of what lay beneath him. Many strange sights had filled his eyes – the frozen fires of Chamon and the living forests of Ghyran – but never had he seen such an uncanny vista as what now lay below. He hesitated to call the surface either ground or sea, for it seemed to be a translucent substance which refused to be either. He could see through its wraith-like essence, peering straight down into the drowned streets and smothered buildings of the vanished city. At the same time, the ectoplasmic sludge was viscous enough to provide support for the few trees and weeds stubborn enough to persist this far into the forgotten ruins. He saw something resembling an enormous rat go skittering across the surface, plunging through the phantom muck like an ice-fox hopping through the snows of Yvir in the far-reaches of the Celestial Realm.

Now, the clash of steel and the cries of combat were close at hand. Warning the Prosecutors with him to be still more cautious than before, Huld soared close to the half-smothered roofs and crumbling minarets of the drowned city. Ahead, beyond the narrow streets, some tremendous conflict was raging.

When he was clear of the sunken streets, Huld could only gaze in amazement at what he had discovered. Before him, stretching away for thousands of yards, was a great clearing, a plaza covered with the translucent phantom sludge. Here and there, the top of some monolith protruded from the ecto-plasm, the angular tips of colossal pyramids and the eroded faces of stone kings. The summit of a smothered mountain reared at one end of the clearing, its barren slopes littered with a carpet of bones.

Here was the site of the battle Huld had heard. Across the transparent slime, legions of fleshless warriors marched. Even from a distance, the Knight-Azyros was struck by the impres-sion of antiquity conjured by their corroded armour and archaic weapons. The armies of Nulahmia had arrayed them-selves in the relics of a living people, but the skeletal warriors he now beheld seemed devoid of even so fragile a connection to the mortal coil. The bronze breastplates strapped about their ribs had been pounded into the shape of leering skulls, and their tall helms were the shape of bony hands. The ser-rated edges of the falchions and adzes they carried had been cast into the semblance of rending talons.

Beyond the fleshless legions of infantry, Huld could see troops of cavalry mounted upon skeletal steeds, their capar-isons as rotten and tattered as the shroud-like cloaks that clung about their undead riders. Ghoulish flames rose from each skeletal rider, flickering from beneath their tattered robes and rusted helms, rippling across the glistening edges of the wicked scythes they bore. With eerie precision, the malignant riders wove between the advancing formations of infantry, the ethereal slime doing nothing to arrest their speed.

Other, even less corporeal things wound their way through

the undead legions. Masses of spectral energy eddied about the periphery of the battlefield, sometimes coalescing into great pillars of ghostly malevolence that rolled forwards before forsaking whatever cohesion held them and dispersing into wisps of glowing fog. When he tried to follow the flittering lights, Huld would see them draw near one another once more, again merging into clouds of deathly faces and spectral talons.

To the rear of the graveyard army, Huld could see baroque chariots and strange carriages; catapults fashioned from bone alongside hulking giants with fleshless faces; a strange altar lit by corpse-fires and borne aloft by a vortex of howling spirits and vengeful apparitions. Above them all, however, was the solitary presence that stood upon the summit of the drowned mountain. At such distance, Huld could only discern a skeletal shape mounted upon an abyssal steed similar to that favoured by Neferata. The aura of power and malevolence spilling from the figure was undeniable. He could almost sense the belligerent motivation exuding from the undead lord to fill the decayed ranks of his army with murderous purpose and animation.

It was an effort for Huld to look away from the sinister presence on the mountain, to turn his gaze from the undead legions to the foes they battled. Only the pronounced horror of the undead could have eclipsed the noxious foulness he now beheld. As vile as the decay and filth of the swamps themselves, a vast host of disease and corruption seeped across the clearing. As though responding to his regard, Huld's senses were now struck by the fecund reek of that horde, the dirty taint of the pestiferous Nurgle.

Knights in corroded armour charged across the spectral slime, the hooves of their diseased beasts throwing up great swathes of translucent sludge as they galloped into the massed ranks of skeletons, smashing them to bony splinters with their lances. Hulking Chaos warriors, the fly-rune daubed upon their shields and helms, trudged through the ghostly mire to slam into the lines of their deathless opponents, shrieking their outrage as they brought destruction to the fleshless corpses. Grotesque brayherds plunged across the morass, shattering skulls and crumpling armour with clubs of stone and axes of bone. Prowling amidst the havoc, daemonic plaguebearers and swarms of giggling nurglings brought corrupt dissolution to even these lifeless enemies.

Gigantic and heinous, the bloated bulk of a greater daemon squatted behind the hordes of Nurgle. A veil of flies and gas rose from the monster's leprous flesh and exposed organs, a discharge of abominable black liquid trickling from its limbs to sizzle on the ghostly surface that supported it. The daemon's squat, toad-like head seemed to sink beneath the weight of its own horns, its single eye struggling to shrug off the fatty folds of its own lids. The monster's cavernous mouth spread in a hungry grin, thousands of sharp, diminutive fangs jutting from its bleeding gums. Gesturing with one of its gigantic hands, the Great Unclean One encouraged its infectious followers to press their attack.

Huld lingered only a moment, then peeled away from the surging battle. Mighty as the undead legions might be, he knew they were no match for the enormity of the Chaos horde that opposed them. How long the undead could hold against their enemy was something he couldn't say, but unless they could be reinforced, the outcome of the fight was certain.

There was little the Knight-Azyros and the Prosecutors could do to tip the balance, but the rest of the Anvils of the Heldenhammer could. They had fought greater odds before and emerged victorious. From what he had seen and felt, he was certain the undead general was the creature Nagash had brought them into the swamps to find – the Mortarch of Sacrament, Arkhan the Black. His duty now was to bring such news back to Makvar. The decision to intervene belonged to the Lord-Celestant.

The Lord-Celestant and the Great Necromancer.

Lord-Celestant Makvar was silent as he pondered Huld's report. He balanced the Knight-Azyros' observations against the warning that had been passed to him by Kismet. It would seem that even if Nagash knew where Arkhan was, if this foray into the swamp was a pretext of some kind, then his plot had developed a severe complication. The hordes of Chaos had discovered the missing Mortarch first.

'Our course is clear, commander,' Lord-Relictor Kreimnar said. 'Arkhan fights the slaves of Chaos. We must come to his aid.'

'It is certain that he will need it ere long,' Huld agreed. 'These bone warriors are enormously resistant to the pestilence carried by the disciples of the Plague God, but contagion isn't the only weapon they carry. The horde I saw descending upon Arkhan's army numbered in its thousands, with more emerging from the swamps to join it.' There was a dour look in his eyes as he turned back towards Makvar. 'There is a realmgate not far from the city, a pillar of mud and slime from which the creatures of Nurgle are vomited into the Mirefells. If we aren't swift, Arkhan may be overwhelmed.'

Knight-Heraldor Brannok shook his head. 'You forget, brother, that the armies of death are unlike those of mortal kings. What means their losses if with a few conjured blasphemies they can reinvigorate them and put their fallen back into the fight? Many and abominable are the powers of Chaos, but they do not infuse corpses with fresh vitality.' He removed his helm, wiping away the sweat beading his brow. His face bore a hardened expression, implacable and resolute. 'I advise caution,' he said.

'Caution is a luxury for the army in the field,' Lord-Castellan Vogun declared, recalling a quote from the Fifteenth Canticle.

Makvar knew the parable well. Many times had he thought about its meaning and the wisdom locked within it. *Quick to hesitance, slow to action.* Recklessness could drive an army to destruction, but too much reserve could lead them to an even worse fate. Disgrace.

'You surprise me, my lord,' Brannok told Vogun. 'I saw your indignation upon the Pathway of Punishment. You understand the limits to which these creatures may be trusted.'

Vogun patted the feathered neck of his gryph-hound, feeling the old scars where Torn had been struck by a Khornate daemon on campaign in the Realm of Fire. 'There is no truce with Chaos,' he stated, remembering the scene of unspeakable carnage they had found in the duardin tunnels. 'Shyish has languished a long time under the invading hordes. They will have learned the lesson a thousand times over since the War of Bones. Whatever else they may be, they are no friends of the Ruinous Powers.'

'If all had the nobility and valour of Sigmar,' Kreimnar said, 'then the Mortal Realms could never have been assailed by the hosts of Chaos. Archaon would have been hurled back into the shadows long ago. Such is not the way of things. Even among gods, such fortitude is rare.' He laid his hand upon Brannok's shoulder. 'It is fruitless to despise the desert because there is no water within it. You must accept it for what it is, not what it isn't.'

Brannok was unswayed. 'This realm is a reflection of its god. Harsh and unyielding, devoid of pity or compassion. I don't–'

Whatever more the Knight-Heraldor might have said never fell from his tongue. The Anvils of the Heldenhammer went on the alert as the chill of sorcery rushed along the creek, speckling the mud with beads of frost and turning the breath of each Stormcast into icy mist. A sandbar in the middle of the channel began to darken, becoming shadowy and indistinct. Liberators marched forwards, forming shields around the conclave of officers while Judicators raised bows and crossbows.

The shadow lengthened, thickening until it stood like a pillar of night. From its depths, the Great Necromancer stepped. The armour that enclosed his skeletal frame pulsed with dark energies, seeming to feed the nebulous doorway Nagash had conjured. The Lord of Death stared across the massed Anvils, contemplating their defensive formation and their readiness for action. His focus soon settled upon Brannok.

'You are in error,' Nagash declared. He wagged a bony talon at the dismal marshland that bordered the creek. 'Much of this realm has slipped away since Sigmar's leaving.' Stretching his clawed hand, he caused one of the corpse-willows to wither, blackening to a crumbling husk in the blink of an eye. As it collapsed in upon itself, grotesque green moths dug themselves out from the ruin. Spreading their blotched wings, the insects quickly took flight. Brannok didn't fail to note the unsettling pattern the markings of their wings assumed – three swirls that intersected in emulation of Nurgle's fly-rune.

'The force of death shaped the Mirefells,' Nagash explained, 'but no longer does it rule alone. Chaos has found its own strength here, drawing its own sustenance from the swamps. Even in this place, the enemy seeks to pervert my domain into its own semblance.'

Makvar stepped out from behind the line of Liberators. 'Did you know the enemy was here?' he asked. He pointed at Huld. 'My scouts have found the second of your Mortarchs. He is beset by a horde of invaders commanded by one of the Plague God's vile daemons.' He tried to find any hint of surprise or emotion in the Death God's reaction to his words, but the fleshless visage was as inscrutable as ever. 'I have been conferring with my officers. If we don't hasten to his aid, your vassal is certain to be overwhelmed.'

'Is that your counsel, then?' Nagash asked. He loomed over Makvar, his death's head staring down at the ebon knight. 'Would you advise a swift foray against the foe to rescue my layman?'

Makvar looked across the black masks of his knights. He knew each of them would follow his command without hesitation. Even if they had their reservations, like Brannok, they wouldn't allow their concerns to influence their duty. It was upon him that the decision to act or hesitate would depend. What was it that Sigmar would expect of him?

'We will march to relieve Arkhan,' Makvar said, feeling no doubt that the decision was what would please the God-King. The Stormcast Eternals had been forged as warriors, an army to bring battle to the foe. It was their purpose and their strength. He trusted that, in his wisdom, Sigmar knew that these were the things which would bring them honour in the Realm of Death.

The shadowy gate behind Nagash expanded, seeming to reach out and enfold the Great Necromancer in its essence. 'My layman makes his stand in the ruins of Mephitt, upon the slopes of Mount Khaerops,' he said. He waved his claw at Huld. 'It is a simple thing to find what is lost when you know where to look. I will bring my subjects against the enemy's left flank. If your storm-knights can strike from their right, we will have only the foe between us.' The darkness wrapped itself around Nagash, his final words echoing on as the shadows consumed him. Almost before Makvar was aware of it, the sorcerous cold was banished and the column of darkness evaporated. The Lord of Death had returned to his cadaverous subjects.

'Which of us do you think he intends to bear the brunt of the fighting?' Kreimnar asked as he drew near Makvar.

The Lord-Celestant shook his head. 'I think the question counts for little with him,' he said. 'As Brannok observes, whatever losses his armies incur can be redeemed.' He stared back at the spot where the Great Necromancer had faded from view. 'The greater question is whether this battle is by chance or by design?'

'You think Nagash means to see for himself our quality?' Kreimnar asked.

'We ask him to leave his realm and take the field against Archaon himself,' Makvar said. 'Before giving my answer, I think I'd want to know who I would be fighting alongside.' He clapped the Lord-Relictor's shoulder and led his friend back towards their knights. As Huld had said, they would have to be swift if they were to be any good to Arkhan. The Primes would have to get their retinues moving quickly.

Even as he relayed his commands to his men, Makvar couldn't shake the warning Kismet had given him. How much of this conflict had been engineered? He felt certain he knew what Sigmar expected of him, but what was it that Nagash expected?

* * *

Mist boiled up from the spectral slime that had consumed the ancient ruins of Mephitt, rolling across the city in a ghoulish fog. The warriors of Neferata's army became little more than hazy shadows in the grey veil, even the creak of their dry bones and the rattle of their rusty mail smothered by the glowing vapours. The vampire queen could barely detect the stolen life-energies that pulsated within the bodies of her blood knights, much less see them as they slowly trotted through the eerie expanse.

'Shall my knights lead the charge, my queen?' Lord Harkdron asked, his voice reduced to the merest whisper.

Neferata shifted around in Nagadron's saddle, glowering at her vampiric consort. 'You will hold *my* knights until I tell you to attack,' she snapped. Since abandoning Nulahmia, Harkdron had become by turns insufferably presumptuous and annoyingly attentive. She knew he was fearful of his position, trying to impress upon her the invaluableness of his services. Ever since the Stormcasts descended from Azyr, he had gone to great pains to exhibit his ardent devotion to her. Neferata wasn't certain if the display was pathetic or simply irritating.

'Of course, my queen. Forgive me.' Harkdron clapped his hand to his breast in salute.

'Obedience pleases me more than initiative,' Neferata told him. She smiled at the flicker of pain her reproof provoked on the vampire's face. It was comforting to know that there were some things still firmly under her control.

Obedience and initiative. She turned the words over in her mind, sickened by the sound of them. Since the resurgence of Nagash from his underworlds, she had felt his abominable spirit towering over her like some smothering force. The least exertion of his awful malice and she would be crushed beneath him, her independence smothered by his all-consuming power. The Mortarchs drew their power from Nagash, a legacy bestowed upon them by the Lord of Death. Neferata feared for the moment when her dark master might repossess that power and leave her little more than a withered shell. She tried to convince herself that some things were beyond even the Death God, but there were times when such arguments sounded hollow even to her.

Now, riding through a sorcerous veil conjured by the Great Necromancer, feeling his dark spirit all around her, knowing that somewhere close by his corporeal form glided through the ruins, it was hard for Neferata to quiet the shivers that rippled through her dead flesh. Nothing seemed beyond him, not when his presence surrounded her. She wondered if everything might not be a facet of one of his eternal schemes – the War of Bones, the hordes of Chaos, even Archaon and Sigmar – all of them pieces he was moving in his endless game of domination.

The sounds of battle reached Neferata through the fog. She could smell the blood of Arkhan's foes, the rancid, sickly stink of polluted gore and daemonic ichor. Idly, she wondered if the Chaos horde had simply stumbled upon her fellow Mortarch or if he had baited them to him. Of one thing she was certain – whatever Arkhan's purpose in the wastes of Mephitt, it was by Nagash's design. Of all the Mortarchs, Arkhan was most in the Great Necromancer's shadow, sometimes seeming to be naught but an extension of his master. He could no more be separated from Nagash than one of the Death God's hands. What, then, were they trying to accomplish?

The answer certainly revolved around Makvar and his storm-knights, but Neferata couldn't be certain how. For her,

Makvar and his warriors represented power and independence, a way to be free from Nagash's dominion. They were a force strong enough to oppose the hordes of Chaos and perhaps even defy the malice of Nagash himself – if only she could harness them properly. Her overtures towards Makvar hadn't been successful and she was troubled by the vanishing of Kismet. Was her handmaiden's disappearance a reproof of her efforts to insinuate herself into the confidence of the Stormcasts? She had seen for herself how devoted Makvar was to cementing this alliance between Azyr and Shyish. At the same time, she prided herself on ferreting out the measure of the men she sought to catch in her web. Makvar's sense of honour made it doubtful he had any penchant for intrigue of his own.

That left Neferata with the frightening possibility that Nagash himself had intercepted her messenger. Perhaps Makvar had never even received the warning about Arkhan. Certainly, if he had, it hadn't been enough to keep him from marching to Mephitt.

The crash of battle rumbling from behind the fog intensified. Neferata could see flashes of blue light crackling behind the grey veil. War cries, too proud and righteous to bubble up from the diseased throats of Nurgle's slaves, rang out. Makvar had sent his knights into battle. The Anvils of the Heldenhammer were on the attack, charging to rescue Arkhan's beleaguered forces.

Neferata turned towards Harkdron. She tried to tell her consort to spur his knights into the battle, to fall upon the flank of the Chaos horde. The command faltered on her tongue, crushed into silence by a will far greater than her own.

Nagash would tell her when it was time to help the

Stormcasts. Until then, she would keep her forces back and stay hidden within the fog.

Until Nagash decided otherwise, Makvar was on his own.

'For Sigmar!' The battle cry rose from the throats of every Stormcast as they rushed out from the veil of mist, rolling like thunder across the brooding desolation of Mephitt.

Once again mounted on the back of his dracoth, Makvar led the charge of his warriors through the sunken avenues and out into the vast clearing Huld had described. The translucent ectoplasm had a viscous quality about it, sloshing around the feet of the Stormcasts like mud but at the same time proving far firmer than the bog they had crossed to reach the ghost city. He noted at once that it was more than physical laws that governed the substance. Despite Gojin's immense weight, the reptile sank no deeper into the translucent sludge than the Liberators around him. It was as though the spectral muck refused to draw an animate body more than a few inches into itself.

The fog soon thinned and Makvar had an unobstructed view of the clearing. It was like a great plaza, bordered at one end by the sunken mountain and on the other sides by the ruinous sprawl of the city. A thick veil clung to the far side of the clearing, concealing the forces Makvar expected Nagash to bring against the Chaos horde. The end opposite the mountain had no such misty shroud clinging to it, but instead was a maze of walls and rooftops. Ahead of these ruins, squat and colossal, was the horned daemon Huld had seen. Around the diseased abomination, a scummy host of mortals and daemons gathered, abasing themselves before its frog-like feet before rushing away to give combat to their foe.

True to Huld's dire prediction, that foe was swiftly fading.

The great legions of bone warriors, the troops of malignant cavalry, the swarms of vengeful spirits – these had been battered and shattered by an adversary as persistent as they were obscene. The broken shells of skeletons lay strewn about the plaza, slowly being sucked into the ectoplasmic mire as the sludge drew the inert material down into its depths. The fleshless giants were gone, as were the catapults and chariots. Everywhere, the hordes of Chaos surged and swelled, engorged in their victories and inflamed by the noxious presence of the Great Unclean One. They poured into the undead ranks with an almost fearless ferocity. Beyond the dwindling line of skeletons, Makvar could see the figure of Arkhan on his gruesome steed. It wouldn't be so very long before the enemy was climbing up the bone-littered slopes to reach the Mortarch.

'For Sigmar!' Makvar cried out. The foremost of his knights had already reached the flank of the Chaos horde. They struck down dozens of skin-clad marauders and goat-headed beastmen, slaughtering them with hammer and sword. The sparking flashes from their attack shone with magnified brilliance, an aspect of the arcane battlefield that caught Makvar by surprise and which drew the attention of the Nurglesque warriors. Those not embattled by the undead turned to address the assault on their flank. Howling their diseased fury, the brutish throng came rushing at the black-armoured Stormcasts.

Makvar drew back on Gojin's reins. The dracoth spat a gout of lightning skyward. It was the signal to the Judicators massed behind the advancing Liberators and Paladins. From the archer formations, a withering volley of lightning came hurtling down into the charging brayherds and marauder tribes. Chaos warriors crumpled as smoke steamed from their scorched mail, and lesser daemons burst in greasy gouts of ichor. From above, the winged Prosecutors swooped down, hurling their stormcall javelins into knots of cavalry and the slithering foulness of Chaos spawn. A sheet of searing lightning hurtled into a swarm of nurglings, exploding the diseased mass before it could come flooding into the ranks of Liberators.

A note from Brannok's battle-horn saw the Liberators fall back and close their line as the pulverising wrath of his clarion cracked one of the monoliths and sent its debris slamming down upon the Nurglesque warriors. Each Liberator braced his shield and secured his place in the new formation. The disorganised mobs of gors and barbarians crashed ineffectually against the shield wall, swiftly repulsed by blazing swords and crackling hammers. The Stormcasts pushed them back, taking no pride in repelling these simple foes. The real test of their stamina would come when the heavier troops came against them, when daemons and sorcerers turned their eldritch attentions upon the Anvils.

Makvar looked beyond the oncoming enemy, watching the far side of the plaza. Before the hordes of Chaos could turn the full strength of their diseased malice against them, he hoped that Nagash would give them something else to worry about.

A tremor rippled through the translucent ground, but this time it wasn't provoked by Brannok's battle-horn. Makvar felt his gaze drawn towards the end of the clearing. The horned daemon was moving, waddling across the carcasses of its own minions as it moved towards the fray. Content to sit back and watch before, now the Great Unclean One had taken it into mind to play a more direct role in the fighting.

With an obscene grin on its monstrous face and a malicious

gleam in its cyclopean eye, the daemon was moving towards the Stormcasts.

CHAPTER NINE

From the shadows, the Great Necromancer watched as Makvar's warriors met the rancid forces of Chaos. He observed the Stormcasts with cold deliberation, scrutinising their actions as he would any novel specimen he found worthy of study. The conditions were at variance with what he had intended to arrange, but there were things to be learned from this unexpected conflict.

Nagash was already aware of the steely resolve and nigh-unshakable courage that burned within the spirit of each Stormcast. It was a phenomenon that was, in many ways, an antithetical process to the black art of necromancy. Even amongst the highest forms of the undead, their revivification involved a diminishment of the soul, the peeling away of layers of identity until the spirit was reduced to a blackened core. Such reduction was needful, stripping away the residue of mortal attraction and confusion that would pollute the resurrection process. Only by breaking that connection to

161

the mortal plane, breaking the link between life and undeath, could a new sense of purpose be instilled into the undead. Without that diminishment, there were few souls with the will to endure, capable of embracing eternity without a destructive yearning for the things lost with their mortal existence. Those undead with the strongest attachments to their prior existence would become crazed, hateful things, either denying the reality of their altered state or mindlessly lashing out at whatever recalled that condition to them.

Sigmar had found some different path to redeeming the spirits of his warriors. The process employed by the God-King was such that his Stormcasts weren't reduced by their resurrection, but instead were magnified by it. Nagash appreciated the amount of effort and power it took to craft undead of strength and versatility near to what he had seen the Stormcasts exhibit. The thought that Sigmar could draw upon such a magnitude of arcane energy was something the Lord of Death found both disturbing and enticing. It made the armies of Azyr more formidable than he had imagined, but it also meant there now existed a power strong enough to drive back the spread of Chaos.

A power that could serve Nagash as well as Sigmar.

The burn of celestial light lanced down into the Chaos horde. Nagash's might was such that he drew no discomfort from the purity of the blaze, but he could sense the painful reaction it provoked from Neferata's vampires. Nearer to that discharge of celestial energy, the lesser undead that formed the basis of his legions would find the arcane bonds that invigorated them coming apart, breaking the cohesion of the spells that endowed them with animation. It gave the Lord of Death pause to consider how his creations could be dismantled by this oppositional force. It made him wonder if there might be a similar force that could break the magic which had reforged each Stormcast from a fragile mortal spirit into a mighty warrior of the God-King.

The Chaos horde, so near to overwhelming Arkhan's battered regiments, was now turning the brunt of its fury against Makvar's knights. Bleating brayherds trampled their own dead as they charged through the volley loosed upon them by Stormcast bows, rabid froth bubbling from their jaws as they snapped and slavered against sigmarite shields. Howling barbarians flung aside the smouldering bodies of their own tribesmen as they endured the divine storm set upon them by Kreimnar's relic-weapon, brutal axes and flails crashing against the unyielding formations of Makvar's knights. Despite the distance that separated them, Nagash could hear the Lord-Celestant calling out to his warriors, rallying them against the teeming masses of their foes. Lightning crackled from the scaly jaws of his steed, burning marauder horsemen from their saddles and reducing their grisly standards to smoke and ash.

Nagash watched as the first packs of daemons came boiling out from the Chaos tide to assault the shield wall of Makvar's knights. How often he had watched mortal formations crumple before such an attack, their very flesh recoiling from the presence of creatures shaped from the raw stuff of Chaos. The malign aura of a daemon could even disrupt the crudest forms of undead, reducing their motivation to such a degree that they became easy prey for raking claws and slavering fangs. Yet the Stormcasts exhibited no change in their determination. They endured the rush of daemons with the same resolve with which they had opposed the advance of their mortal foes. Just as they had withstood the lascivious malignance of Slaanesh's minions in the rubble of Nulahmia, so they found no terror in the diseased claws of Nurgle's obscene progeny.

Courage and determination could accomplish only so much. Here and there, one of the Anvils fell before the enemy, slain by the blade of a daemon or incinerated by the bilious magic of a Nurglesque sorcerer. From each vanquished knight there blazed forth a flare of celestial light that streaked up into the darkened sky before vanishing into the aether. Nagash could feel the spirit nestled within each flare, could sense its trajectory as it pierced the veils of Shyish to return to Azyr.

The Great Necromancer reached out with his mind to those of his Mortarchs. His acolyte Arkhan responded immediately to the call of his master. Without hesitation, he acted. The undead legions around Mount Khaerops rallied for a renewed offensive. Necromantic energies crackled about their fleshless limbs, pouring redoubled ferocity into their desiccated frames. The deathly host surged forwards, smashing and battering their way through the brutish tribes that had only the instant before threatened to overwhelm their position. Arkhan remained upon the slopes of the mountain, dropping from the back of his steed and crouching upon the corpse-strewn ground.

Nagash's commands extended to Neferata and her warriors. On his order, she spurred her vampiric knights into an assault against the enemy horde. The blood knights would act as the tip of the spear, plunging deep into the corrupt mass of Chaos. After them trooped regiments of grave guard and deadwalkers, flights of morghasts and covens of deathmages. The ghostly fog would magnify the scope of Neferata's attack, inflicting upon the invaders the illusion of a far greater threat. Already he could see the waddling bulk of the Great Unclean

One turning away from the Stormcasts, shifting his attention from Makvar's knights to this new undead attack.

The pressure against the Anvils lessened as the minions of Chaos found their focus shifting. Nagash was pleased by the rapidity with which his design unfolded. He had seen how the Stormcasts acquitted themselves against the creatures of Nurgle, there was no reason to bleed their strength further by prolonging such an engagement. Not when there were far more important observations to be made.

Exerting his will once more, Nagash seized control over a swathe of Arkhan's legion. At his command, the bone warriors flung themselves forwards in a reckless advance against a warband of hulking Chaos champions. The undead assault was swiftly broken, their shattered bones sinking into the spectral sludge. A bubbling cry rose from the savage victors, a shout of diseased jubilation. Vanquishing these last skeletal foes brought the Chaos warriors an unexpected boon. They had created a break in Arkhan's lines, exposing a gap that left them with a clear path right to the slopes of Mount Khaerops. It was an opportunity the murderous invaders were quick to seize.

From above the clearing, Huld's shout of alarm rang down to the other Stormcasts below, alerting Makvar to the peril that threatened Arkhan.

Now the real test Nagash had planned for the Anvils would begin.

Makvar brought his sword crunching down into the shoulder of a festering plaguebearer, a stream of putrid liquid and maggots bubbling up from the wound. Before he could strike again, Gojin's claw came raking across the creature's torso, ripping its organs and snapping its bones. The mangled daemon was smashed beneath the dracoth's feet, its remains swiftly evaporating into a greasy smoke. The reptile threw his head back in a bellow of anger, offended by the unnatural dissolution of his prey.

Around the Lord-Celestant, the Anvils of the Heldenhammer slowly pushed their way through the morass of Chaos creatures. Blocks of Liberators sought to channel the monsters and marauders into the waiting axes, hammers and glaives of the Paladin retinues. Judicators armed with vicious boltstorm crossbows prowled behind the shield wall, ready to loose a deadly barrage the instant any hole appeared in the defences. More Judicators sent a steady wave of crackling arrows arcing down into the attacking barbarians, leaving their scorched bodies strewn along the course of the Stormcasts' advance.

Overhead, Huld and the Prosecutors kept a wary vigilance, monitoring the ebb and flow of battle and warning Makvar the instant they spotted any shift among the Chaos forces. He knew the winged knights well enough to appreciate the frustration such restraint provoked, but the Lord-Celestant needed to conserve them until the last moment. Until it was too late for the foe to react and redeploy their warriors.

Grateful as he was that Nagash's army had emerged from the fog to fall upon the Chaos horde, Makvar felt a sense of frustration as well. The undead who attended Neferata and the Great Necromancer had inflicted many casualties and an enormous amount of confusion with their sudden charge. Many of the enemy tribes and herds moving to engage the Anvils had withdrawn to confront this new threat to their rear – including the gigantic daemon that appeared to be commanding the diseased throng. It was only the lessening of pressure against his own lines that allowed Makvar any freedom of movement.

He had need of such liberty, and it was this that discomfited Makvar. The diminished regiments defending Arkhan had rallied and attempted to mount an assault upon the Chaos horde they simply lacked the strength to achieve. Whether they sallied forth to support Nagash or to aid the Anvils was of small consequence now. The damage had been done – the minions of Nurgle had ripped a hole in the undead ranks, enabling them to penetrate the perimeter the skeletons had been maintaining. A rancid mob of Chaos warriors now rushed unimpeded towards the rise where the Mortarch of Sacrament stood.

Even if they annihilated the whole of the Chaos horde it would bring no victory to the Stormcasts if they lost Arkhan. Nagash insisted his Mortarchs were essential to rebuilding the strength of his armies. How much truth there was in his claim made no difference. Finding Arkhan was one of the conditions Nagash had set before Makvar. If the Anvils failed now it would threaten the alliance they had been sent to broker.

'Onwards!' Makvar cried out to his knights. 'For Sigmar and for glory!' He spurred Gojin forwards, crushing another plaguebringer beneath the reptile's immense bulk. His sword flashed out in a vicious arc, raking the face of a snarling daemon and sending the furry arm of a beastman flying into the air. More foes swarmed towards him to replace the slain and wounded, the stink of their oozing sores and corrupt breath blotting out even the musky smell of the dracoth he rode.

Press ahead. That was the tactic the situation demanded of Makvar and his command. If they couldn't fight their way through the Chaos host, if they failed to reach Arkhan before the enemy, then nothing else would matter. A flash of light rose off to his right, a sombre reminder to him of the price such haste demanded. When the fighting was finished, he would learn the names of those Stormcasts who had fallen. For now, it was enough to know they were sustaining losses and that with each knight overwhelmed by the foe, the task ahead of them became that much harder.

The invigorating glow of Lord-Castellant Vogun's lantern shone upon Makvar. He could feel the healing energies rushing through him, fending off the contaminated filth that dripped from his blade and spattered his armour. Gojin uttered an exultant hiss as the gashes in his scaly hide began to close and heal. Wails of pain rippled from the fanged maws of the plaguebringers, and they threw up their scrawny arms to cover their monstrous eyes from the celestial light. The resemblance to the aversion exhibited by their undead allies wasn't lost on Makvar, and did little to comfort the dark turn his thoughts had taken.

'Break upon the Anvil!' Vogun shouted, holding his lantern high in one hand as he brought his halberd smashing down into the bearded face of a marauder with his other. The barbarian staggered back, clutching at his bloodied visage with something that more resembled a tentacle than a hand. Before he could recover his thoughts enough to resume his attack, the marauder was borne down by the raking claws and slashing beak of Torn. The gryph-hound made short work of his adversary and hastened back to Vogun's side, ready to kill all who threatened his master.

By degrees, the Stormcasts were gaining ground, forcing the Chaos warriors back onto the rusted spears and primitive swords of the undead. Pressed between two foes, the marauders and beastmen broke ranks, descending into utter disorder. In their panic to escape destruction, they stampeded over their own comrades, turning their axes and clubs upon the daemons and chieftains who tried to force them back into the fight. The routed barbarians and gors were ripe for the slaughter. Makvar felt no compunction ordering his knights to obliterate their reeling enemy. The Stormcasts had seen for themselves the mercy Chaos extended to those who felt helpless before them.

The dark shapes of Huld and the Prosecutors soared close to the Anvils before climbing once more and speeding away to the right. Makvar responded to the arranged signal and urged his knights to leave their broken enemies to the pitiless attentions of the undead. Their own objective was elsewhere. Smashing through the few packs of beastmen and warbands of marauders who stood in their way, Makvar led the Anvils in pursuit of the armoured Chaos warriors trying to converge upon the summit of Mount Khaerops.

The Prosecutors cast their javelins down into the charging Chaos warriors as they flew past them. The missiles cracked against the spectral sludge with elemental fury. Great craters opened up in the ectoplasm, gouged from the ghostly material by the explosive bursts of electricity. The scorched bodies of mangled warriors were sent spinning through the air. Others fell into the ghoulish pits, screaming with the horrors of the damned as the translucent muck came flooding back in to fill the depression. Trapped within the spectral mud, they struggled to claw their way back to the surface before the ectoplasm smothered them. Few proved equal to the effort.

Huld landed on the bone-littered slopes of the mountain, wings unfurled, the light of his celestial beacon blazing around him. The Knight-Azyros put himself between Arkhan and the Chaos warriors who still sought to overcome the Mortarch. The first armoured brute who rushed towards him was sent flopping down the slope, cut in two by a sweep of Huld's sword. A second warrior crashed to his knees and pitched forward among the bones after the winged knight sent his horned head bouncing from his shoulders.

The Prosecutors made a second pass over the Chaos warriors, scattering their enemy and breaking the momentum of their charge. A stream of sizzling foulness shot up from the mouth of a diseased warlock, the boiling spew engulfing one of the flying Anvils and knocking him from the sky. As the stricken Prosecutor slammed into the ectoplasm, a blue flare streaked skyward. Before the sorcerer could try to repeat his murderous feat, Kreimnar brought a cascade of retribution roaring down from the sky, engulfing the enemy warlock in a shower of thunderbolts.

Then, Makvar was leading the vanguard of his force into the scattered Chaos warriors. Steel plate pitted with corrosion and rust flattened beneath his dracoth's claws, pox-ridden flesh branded with the viral sigils of Nurgle split before the cleaving edge of his sword. A bolt of lightning from Gojin's jaws reduced a charging foeman into a steaming husk, the spiked mace in his hands splashing across the ground in a molten puddle.

Liberators rushed to support the Lord-Celestant, forming up to either side of Gojin to guard the dracoth's flanks and keep Makvar from being surrounded by the enemies who remained. Though they had the numbers, Makvar doubted the Chaos warriors still had enough unity of purpose to coordinate such an attack. Those who came rushing at the Stormcasts did so as individuals, sparing no thought for any strategy greater than coming to grips with the ebon knights. The Anvils, by contrast, fought as though they were bound into a single sigmarite body. The Liberator who struck down a flail-wielding invader was guarded by the broad shield of the knight beside him when a slobbering axeman sprang at him.

The Decimator who failed to finish a fly-headed Chaos champion with a blow of his thunderaxe was spared the bite of his enemy's rusty claymore when a Judicator sent several bolts from his crossbow punching through the warrior's chest.

Some few of the Chaos warriors still tried to climb the slopes of Mount Khaerops. Thinking to overwhelm Huld with ferocity and numbers, they failed to account for the speed and finesse of the Stormcast. Weaving between a half-dozen foes, Huld visited upon them a flurry of glancing cuts and shallow slashes. Death wasn't the dominating concern of his swift blows, but simply a measure to dull the haste of the rancid invaders. Diseased blood spilled from each of the Chaos warriors as they tried to recover their momentum and make another rush up the slope.

Flapping his great wings, Huld hopped higher up the bone-strewn rise, keeping himself between the enemy and Arkhan. He risked a look back at the kneeling liche. He could make no sense of the incantation that tumbled from the Mortarch's bony jaws or the symbols he scratched into the earth with his skeletal claws. But he could feel the power Arkhan was evoking, the magical chill that crept into the air and turned his sweat into beads of frost.

The enemy could sense it too. Huld could see the lethal resolve that wriggled in their eyes. Whatever spell Arkhan was working, these minions of Chaos were determined to disrupt his conjurations.

Huld pointed his sword at the biggest of the brutes, a barbarian with such a swollen gut that his iron armour had split open to expose the bulge of his belly. The Stormcast could see the blistering fury in the diseased man's eyes. 'You'll have to get past me if you want him,' he warned the invader. The bloated warrior scowled at him with what little of his face

wasn't hidden behind the rusted mesh of his helm. His pudgy
fingers clenched tighter about the haft of the twisted axe he
bore. Huld nodded as he prepared to receive the Chaos warrior's attack.

Then the Knight-Azyros found himself thrown into the
air. Before he could catch himself, he slammed into the litter of bones and started rolling down the slope. As his vision
swirled, shifting between the slope and the sky, he had the
impression of something rising up above him.

Something unbelievably gargantuan.

Something unspeakably monstrous.

Makvar gazed in disbelief as the entire top of Mount Khaerops
reared up. An avalanche of bone was sent crashing down the
slopes, spilling across the clearing in a clattering cascade of
grinning skulls and broken skeletons. Up from beneath the
mound of bones, an enormous talon erupted into the air,
slamming down with pulverising force against the exposed
rock of the mountain. Two smaller claws flanked the huge
talon, all of them attached to a great skeletal framework that
somehow recalled to Makvar the outline of a colossal hand.

The immense fingers stretched, revealing a skein of tattered
flesh between them. Leathery, hideous, the decayed skin gave
off a charnel reek. A dozen yards from where the first talon
gripped the rock, a second enormous set of claws burst from
beneath the mound of bones. These talons smashed through
the layers of bleached bone to seize the rock buried beneath.
Again there was the vast finger-like framework with its can-
vas of rotten skin stretched between each digit.

With both talons anchored in the rock of the mountain,
a fresh avalanche of bones came crashing down the slopes.
Rearing up from beneath the skeletal heap was a titanic

shape. As big as a dragon, more hideous than anything that had haunted the cursed streets of Nulahmia, the beast lurched up from its hidden tomb.

Makvar saw now that the limbs it had first thrust forth were the behemoth's forelegs, attached to its shoulders by thick knots of wiry sinew and exposed muscle. Its body, broad at the chest, tapered off to a long tail of naked bone. Masses of mouldy grey fur clung to the beast's torso, rents in its skin displaying the raw meat and organs within. A great gash along its left side exposed the skeletal frame of its spine and ribs, and the withered husk that should have been its heart.

The colossal beast's head jutted forwards on the merest stump of a neck. It was a hideous countenance, at once possessed of a long jaw and a squashed forehead. Grisly eyes gleamed from the pits that opened to either side of the yawning nasal cavity. Long fangs jutted from the bone stretch of its jaws, curving downward like scimitars, stabbing upward like a phalanx of pikes. The tatters of leathery ears dangled from the sides of the monster's bestial skull, strips of skin and fur dripping from their rotted lobes.

The terrorgheist will destroy us all. The words echoed through Makvar's brain, stabbing into his awareness like a knife. His gaze turned from the gigantic creature, drawn to the one who called out to him. He saw a skeletal figure retreating from Mount Khaerops on the back of an abyssal steed. Whatever relief he felt at seeing Arkhan intact was quashed by the realisation that the thing looming above the mountain was mighty enough to make even the Mortarch withdraw from it.

My magic has roused it, but I underestimated its strength. I can exert no control over it. Each thought Arkhan thrust upon Makvar carried an icy lack of emotion. There was no

apology or shame that the creature his necromancy had conjured wouldn't obey him. It was a statement of fact, nothing
more. Arkhan had certainly adopted his master's air of pas-
sionless detachment.

Makvar swung around in Gojin's saddle, looking across the
battlefield. The Chaos warriors who had been engaged with
the Anvils were all but exterminated, and he could see that
the remnants of Arkhan's army had fared much the same. It
was the army of Neferata that now bore the brunt of the enemy's effort. He could see the grotesque Great Unclean One
waddling about, snatching vampire knights from their saddles with his flabby claws or incinerating grave guard with
bile from his gaping maw. Though he could feel the sinister
presence of Nagash, he saw no trace of the Lord of Death
within the raging melee.

The Lord-Celestant looked back to Mount Khaerops and
the gigantic terrorgheist that now squatted upon its slopes.
Gazing upon it, experiencing the air of hostility and evil that
rolled off it, he didn't doubt for a moment that the behemoth
had the potential to turn the tide of battle all on its own.
Under Arkhan's control it would have ensured the annihila-
tion of the Chaos horde. Free to vent its malignance at liberty,
it represented a threat that couldn't be ignored.

'Makvar!' Vogun cried out, gesturing with his halberd. 'The
beast has spotted Huld!'

It was true, the terrorgheist's head had turned downward,
contemplating the cadaverous mound beneath it. Among the
litter of bones, the dark armour of Huld fairly shouted his
presence to the gigantic undead bat. The Knight-Azyros was
keeping still, refraining from any sudden motion that might
provoke the beast.

'The terrorgheist has slipped free of the Mortarch's control,'

Makvar declared, his voice loud enough to reach every Stormcast gathered near to him. 'How is a question for later. What
concerns us now is what to do about it.' He looked at Vogun's
lantern, thinking about the adverse way the undead reacted
to the light of Azyr. Leave this task to us, he thought, hoping
his intentions would reach Arkhan's mind as the Mortarch's
had his own.

'The undead are leaving us!' Brannok called out. The Knight-
Heraldor indicated the battered legions of Arkhan. The bone
warriors were leaving the positions they had held, advancing across the clearing to support Neferata's embattled forces.

'Leave them,' Makvar declared. 'Against this enemy, the
Anvils of the Heldenhammer will fight the better for being
alone.' He turned towards Kreimnar. 'Call down Sigmar's
wrath against the beast.'

The Lord-Relictor nodded his skull-like helm. 'One strike
may not be enough to consume that monster,' he warned.

'So long as it gives Huld a chance to slip away, and the rest
of us a chance to draw near,' Makvar said.

Kreimnar raised his relic-weapon. On the mountain, the
terrorgheist was slowly moving one of its clawed hands, gradually shifting the talons closer to Huld. Perhaps the undead
beast thought if it moved slow then its prey would be oblivious to the peril. Perhaps it simply thought the Knight-Azyros
was paralysed with fear. Whatever its motivation, the gigantic
brute was unprepared when a crackling deluge of lightning
seared down upon it from the dark skies above. As it reared
back in shock, strips of fur and flesh burning in the fury of
Kreimnar's magic, Huld sprang to his feet and stretched his
wings. The Stormcast became a dark blur as he threw himself
from the slopes of Mount Khaerops and soared away from
the bat-like behemoth that had been ready to devour him.

Enraged both by the blast of lightning that had scorched its bones and by the escape of its prey, the terrorgheist threw back its head and uttered a deafening shriek. Spreading its tattered wings, the beast rose into the air, diving down from the summit straight towards the Anvils' black ranks.

The beast's flight was too swift for Kreimnar to draw down another thunderbolt to intercept it. Instead, Makvar called upon the Judicators to loose against the oncoming behemoth. At the Lord-Celestant's signal, the massed archers sent a volley of crackling energy searing up into the terrorgheist. Most of the lightning simply steamed against the beast's hardened bones or tore ribbons of decayed flesh from its desiccated body, but a few provoked angry snarls and flicks of its bony tail.

Diving down upon the behemoth from above, the Prosecutors were the next to assault the flying horror. Throwing their stormcall javelins into the gigantic brute, the explosive spears detonated in the beast's decaying bulk. Shreds of meat and bone were ripped from the behemoth, and its tattered wings were further mangled as skeletal shrapnel tore through them. A living beast, even one of the mighty dragons, would have been felled by such havoc, but if any spark of true life had ever burned within the terrorgheist, it had long ago been extinguished by the fell magics of Shyish. Abruptly turning its dive into a vicious climb, the gargantuan horror snapped at the Prosecutors flying above it, catching one of its tormentors in its enormous jaws. The sound of splintering mail echoed down to Makvar and his knights as their winged comrade perished under the bat's piercing fangs.

Once more, Makvar called for the Judicators to loose against the titanic beast. This time, Gojin's electric breath was added to the barrage that rose up to strike the terrorgheist. Again, the havoc visited upon the beast was hideous, but largely cosmetic to a creature that could endure with a shrivelled heart and bloodless veins. The gigantic bat wheeled about in the sky, chasing after the Prosecutors as though they were mosquitoes flying above the stagnant waters of Wolfhof's tarn. A flash of celestial light marked the end of another Anvil in the monster's jaws.

'Keep after it!' Makvar commanded. The Stormcasts spread out along the drowned plaza, trying to keep the terrorgheist overhead. Retinues of Judicators kept their skybows trained upon the beast, loosing whenever it drew within range. Among the Paladins, those armed with the brutal starmaces gripped their weapons with frustrated anticipation. Let the monster descend for but a moment, and they would let it taste the might of the Anvils.

The terrorgheist swung around once more, hurtling after a Prosecutor it had missed in its previous rush. Now the bat intended to finish its foe, its jaws stretched wide as it flew towards him. Before it could close with its prey, another winged Stormcast dived towards it. Makvar thought he caught the gleam of the golden halo fastened to Huld's helm. An instant later, he knew for certain the interceptor was the Knight-Azyros. Interposing himself between the terrorgheist and the Prosecutor, Huld held his celestial beacon before the undead monster, letting the purifying rays sear into its grisly essence.

Stunned, shrieking, the huge monster plummeted earthward, slamming into the translucent syrup that covered the plaza with the force of an earthquake. Monoliths and statues that had stood so long above the spectral sludge now toppled under the force of the beast's impact, sinking with eerie lethargy into the mire. The terrorgheist itself floundered in the

ghostly slime, the crater inflicted by its impact swiftly filling again and threatening to suck the beast into the depths.

'Before it can free itself!' Makvar called out to his knights.
Dozens of Stormcasts charged toward the trapped terrorgheist,
striking it with swords and hammers. Makvar noted the blazing discharge of a starmace and watched as several feet of the
monster's thrashing tail went sailing through the air.

The beast's claws lashed out at its attackers, crushing one
Liberator and ripping a Retributor open from collar to groin.
Then the terrorgheist drew back, seeming to fold in upon
itself like a coiling serpent. For a moment, it held itself still,
then it lurched forwards, its jaws stretching wide to let loose
a murderous shriek. The terrorgheist's cry proved as deadly as
the blast from any dragon's maw. Blue light erupted from several Stormcasts unfortunate enough to be too near the bat's
head when it gave voice to its rattling scream. The howl had
extinguished their vitality in less than a heartbeat, hurling
their spirits back to the Realm Celestial and the armouries
of the God-King.

Makvar urged Gojin towards the hulking beast, hoping
to save more of his knights from the terrorgheist's malevolence. The brute turned its head towards him, coiling back to
unleash another deadly shriek. Two things happened before
the gigantic bat could sound its cry. The first was the bolt
of crackling lightning that flew from Gojin's jaws to blast
one of its ears to ruin. The second was the blinding blaze
of Vogun's warding lantern as the Lord-Castellant shone it
into the terrorgheist's eyes. The beast's agony was such that
it forgot about Makvar and his dracoth, instead snapping its
huge jaws at Vogun.

Vogun darted away from the terrorgheist's bite and retaliated with a slash of his halberd that sent fangs rolling across

the clearing. Growling at the undead monster, ignoring the colossal difference in their sizes, Torn sprang at the beast that had tried to eat its master. The gryph-hound's beak ripped into the terrorgheist's rotting face, slashing such meat as yet clung to its skull.

A snarling sheet of lightning crashed down into the terrorgheist as Kreimnar brought the fury of the God-King descending upon the undead horror. Flesh steamed in the elemental blast, bones blackened and fractured. One of the monster's wings withered into a charred stump. The shriek that hissed from the monster's jaws now was one of agony as the dark magic which fuelled its abominable animation was burned away.

Makvar brought his sword chopping down into the stumpy neck that supported the terrorgheist's bat-like head. The blade sheared through the rancid flesh, gouging the thick vertebrae beneath. The decaying beast swung around, trying to snap at him with its blackened jaws. A crack of Gojin's tail broke the momentum of its assault and sent more of its fangs tumbling onto the ground.

Gripping his sword in both hands, Makvar brought the blade slashing down in a vicious stroke. The sharp edge sheared through the already weakened bone. The terrorgheist's head crashed to the ground, dislodging Torn from his worrying grip on the beast's ear. The massive body twitched and writhed, tail whipping out in blind malignance, the remaining wing closing and opening in mindless spasms. A ragged shout of victory rose from the Stormcasts around the vanquished monster, their triumph tainted by the loss of their comrades to the beast's rampage.

'Now we must return to the real fight,' Makvar declared, rousing his knights and recalling to them the greater battle raging above the drowned streets of Mephitt. Even as he did so, Vogun drew the Lord-Celestant's attention to the turn that battle had taken.

The corrupt Chaos horde had come the worse for their struggle against the undead. Between Neferata's vampires and Arkhan's bone warriors, the slaughter had been monumental. Dire spells leapt from the eldritch staves the two Mortarchs carried as they rode about the periphery of the conflict, decimating entire warbands with each of their conjurations.

The bloated, toad-like daemon which led the forces of Nurgle, the hulking Great Unclean One that had seemed so formidable to Makvar when he led his knights to Arkhan's rescue, was now beset by a power even more destructive. Nagash had sallied forth from the darkness to confront the daemon. The skeletal Lord of Death sent masses of clawing wraiths screaming across the huge daemon's cancerous body, tearing great rents in his hide. He hurled shrivelling magics into the thing's exposed organs, reducing them to empty husks. Chilling energies streamed from Nagash's staff, cracking and splitting the Great Unclean One's oozing skin, freezing its horns and nose, making them so brittle that they shattered when his foe tried to strike at him with a giant diseased sword.

Nagash's other hand gripped a sword of his own, a blade of such immense darkness and malice that it seemed to drain the vitality from the very air around it. When the Lord of Death brought his blade against that of the daemon, the bilious sword was shorn in half, split asunder as though it were naught but a twig. The deathly weapon continued its murderous sweep, slashing into the daemon's body, hewing through its vast maw and cyclopean eye. Relentless to the last, Nagash gave the blade a twisting flourish before tearing it from the daemon's body.

Almost before Makvar understood what he was watching, the immense daemon of Nurgle lay corroding at Nagash's fleshless feet in four gory segments.

The Stormcasts had exhibited their might for the undead. Now Nagash had shown the warriors of Sigmar why the God-King was so keen to restore the Lord of Death to his pantheon.

CHAPTER TEN

The translucent morass that had consumed Mephitt surrounded the Anvils of the Heldenhammer as they descended
into the depths of the ruined city. Wispy orbs and weird lights
flittered through the sunken streets, darting down empty
avenues and through abandoned archways. Colossal statues
sitting atop huge pedestals of marble and malachite flashed
into view as the ghost-brands rushed past them. Pyramidal
obelisks and ovoid menhirs were revealed as glowing motes
swirled around their bases.

More macabre than the drowned echoes of the forgotten
city were the gruesome objects that hung suspended within
the ectoplasmic lake. Bones of every description, human and
inhuman, hovered within the opaque mire, slowly drawn
down into the depths of Mephitt. The corpses of beasts and
men killed in the recent fighting, the splintered remains of
Arkhan's vanquished warriors, could be seen oozing their way
down from the surface, sinking with almost glacial lethargy

into the shadowy underworld. The broken husk of the terror-gheist was there, gargantuan and hideous, its monstrous bulk drawn down towards the long-hidden flagstones of Mephitt's great plaza.

'I can feel the chill of this place chewing into my bones.' The words were spoken by Knight-Heraldor Brannok, but they could have come from any of the Stormcasts. The clammy, dank atmosphere was inescapable, too persistent for even Lord-Castellan Vogun's lantern to hold at bay. It was a cold not of temperature but of spirit, the frigid clutch of an open grave, the slumbering malice of the dead towards the living.

'This necropolis is offended that we are here,' Lord-Relictor Kreimnar stated. Boldly, he reached out his hand, feeling the translucent wall beside him recede ever so slightly at his touch. 'It has been a long time since anything that drew breath walked these streets.'

It didn't take Kreimnar's arcane sensitivity to feel the sullen hostility that oozed up from the ruins. Lord-Celestant Makvar felt it all around him, a creeping sensation that crawled through his skin. It was like having a thousand eyes watching him, glaring at him with pitiless hate. Every instinct in his body and all the fighting reflexes he had honed and developed were shouting to him, crying out to him to beware. It wasn't fear – that emotion was all but unknown to the Stormcast Eternals. It was something more subtle, welling up from some primal aspect of his being. It was the same anxiety he could feel pulsing through Gojin's reptilian bulk, could see hovering about the feathered head of Vogun's gryph-hound. As Kreimnar said, life wasn't welcome in Mephitt, and even the basest creature could feel itself trespassing upon a world in which it had no place.

Yet for all the malice, the atmosphere of bitter threat Makvar felt pressing in around them, he knew that the Stormcasts were in no danger. The spirits that haunted the desolation, the spectral malignity of Mephitt's ruins, the deathly essence of the translucent mire, all of these were manifestations of the Realm of Death. Nothing of this sinister land would do them harm. Not while they were in the company of the god who claimed dominion over Shyish.

Makvar gazed at the eerie tunnel through which the Storm-casts marched, boring its way through the submerged streets, lit by a ghostly glow that followed the knights as they pressed deeper into the city. Ahead of him he could see the fleshless ranks of Arkhan's skeletons, the crimson armour of Nefera-ta's vampires. Beyond them, towering over the undead legion, was the morbid throne upon which Nagash reposed, carried upon a phantom tide of writhing spirits, surrounded by the black essence of the Great Necromancer's power.

When he had descended from Azyr, Makvar had imagined Nagash to be a dwindling force, a fading deity whose powers were waning. They had come to broker alliance with Neferata because they had believed the Mortarch to be a more active opponent of Chaos, a leader of such defiance as yet lingered within Shyish. Nagash, he had thought, was in retreat, sealed off within his underworlds, unable or unwilling to oppose the hordes of Archaon. Seeing his swift dispatch of the Great Unclean One proved to Makvar that whatever else, Nagash's powers were still far from extinguished. Watching him stretch forth one of his bony hands and bore a passage through the ghostly sludge which buried Mephitt impressed upon him that this was still the realm of the Death God.

No, there wasn't any question that Nagash was still a for-midable power. He could stand against the tide of Chaos. What Makvar wondered was if the Great Necromancer was willing to do so. Perhaps he had been too long in his hidden vaults and underworld catacombs to believe victory was still possible.

'Lord-Celestant, a rider comes,' Huld called to Makvar. The Knight-Azyros waved one of his wings as something emerged from the undead ranks and crossed the gap that separated the Stormcasts from their allies. Makvar almost expected to see Neferata's handmaiden drawing towards them, to relay tidings from her mistress or to pass along some veiled warning. Instead, what he saw was a withered husk perched atop a skeletal steed. The mounted corpse bore a bony standard in one of its fleshless claws, a golden icon mounted to the top of the morbid pole. The thing regarded the Anvils with its empty sockets, then dipped its head in a creaking extension of honour.

'Mighty Nagash wishes you to attend him,' the rider said, its jaws moving too slowly to match the words that rattled from them. 'If Lord-Celestant Makvar would follow, he will be shown where he will be received.'

Brannok drew close to Makvar's side. 'Don't go alone, commander,' he cautioned.

Makvar cast his gaze up at the mass of ectoplasm above them, pondering how far below the surface they were now. 'If Nagash willed, it he could bring this tunnel crashing down upon our heads,' he said. 'No, he has no need for subterfuge. Not while we are so completely in his power.' It was hardly a comforting sentiment, but then they hadn't been sent to the Realm of Death to play things safe. They had been sent to accomplish their mission and accept whatever risks were demanded to execute that purpose.

'You should take someone with you,' Kreimnar said, studying the undead horseman. 'Someone to offer advice and council should it be needed.'

Like Brannok, Kreimnar was more worried about Makvar's safety than any strategic concerns, but unlike the Knight-Heraldor, he was more cunning about expressing himself. The suggestion even had merit in its own right. Makvar was wise enough to appreciate that his focus on the success of their mission might blind him to other matters. Nuances of possibility that might have an oblique effect upon the alliance he strove to build.

'I will take Brannok, Huld and Vogun,' Makvar told Kreimnar. 'I trust that will allay some of your worry, old friend?' Of all of his officers, Brannok and Vogun were the ones most critical of the powers they had been sent to court. As a result, they would be the ones paying the most attention when he conferred with the Lord of Death. Huld, with his keen tongue, was someone he was certain would prove essential in any event.

'Bring such servants as you deem needful,' the skeleton declared. 'Great Nagash will be waiting.' Its message delivered, the undead herald collapsed in upon itself, its bones losing their cohesion. The horse disintegrated in similar fashion, crashing to the ground in a mess of decay.

By its disintegration, the undead rider impressed another message upon Makvar. It was that whatever served Nagash existed only because it had a purpose useful to him. Once it became superfluous, its existence could be snuffed out in a matter of a few heartbeats.

The weight of ages lay wrapped about the royal palace of Mephitt. The tomb-mire that had smothered the city made it impossible for dust to gather or spiders to spin their webs between the columns. No vermin scurried in the shadows, no decay pitted the gruesome frescos painted on the walls.

Yet time had left its stain just the same, the years seeping down into the marble floors and limestone walls, tainting the bronze sconces and brazen braziers. A miasma of antiquity clung to it all in defiance of the arcane preservation of the spectral lake that had drowned the once-mighty city.

It needed only a wave of his hand for Nagash to send the tomb-mire rolling back, to drive the opaque sludge from the great hall where the necro-kings of Mephitt had once lorded over their people. As he marched to the barren throne where the ashes of the last necro-king lay heaped, he let the ancient vibrations of the dim past inundate him, welcoming him with ghostly harmonies and the silent howls of the grave.

The Great Necromancer seated himself on the jewelled throne. Dimly, he could feel the lingering essence of the last necro-king, its final agonies and entreaties bound into the place of its dissolution. Nagash banished the irritation with a thought, hurling the royal spirit into the formless shadows of the realm it had once ruled. The Mortarchs who followed him into the hall sensed his casual obliteration of the spirit. He felt the tremor of fear that pulsed through Neferata and the shiver of adoration that coursed through Arkhan's ancient bones.

So vastly different in character, these two scions of death, yet each had an important part in Nagash's vision. Makvar and his Stormcasts had their own role to play, even if they were as yet unaware of it. Their performance in the plaza had revealed much to him, allowing him to better place them within his design. Their potential was enormous. As hard as it came to him to accept Sigmar's withdraw from the Realm of Death, he had to concede that the God-King had accomplished much behind the gates of Azyr.

Nagash looked up as he felt the presence of the Stormcasts

enter the hall. The celestial energy that burned within them, the mark of Sigmar's Reforging – he knew the alarm it evoked from Neferata's vampires. The Mortarch of Blood's reaction was more layered, less clearly defined. It was like her to view anything new in the context of both threat and advantage. If she felt the reward was grand enough, there was little she wouldn't risk to further her pursuit of power. Sometimes she was overbold in her recklessness. Sometimes her lack of restraint left her exposed to hazards even she couldn't see.

Arkhan's contemplation of the Anvils was more like that of his master. The Mortarch of Sacrament pondered the methodology behind their creation, the limitations invested within them. He would be thinking of their armaments both as menace and as asset. Not with an eye towards his own advantage, but with the cold detachment of expanding his knowledge so that he might be of even greater use to the Great Necromancer. If Neferata's failing was her selfish ambition, then Arkhan's was his lack of the same. He suffered from a deficiency of imagination, an inability to ferret out the possibilities, to follow hope and fear to their furthest limitations.

Of course, when it came to dreams of avarice and schemes to power, there was one who made even Neferata's intrigues appear childishly simple. Nagash intended to call upon that twisted mind quite soon. With the help of Makvar and his knights.

'Lord Nagash,' Makvar greeted him. The Great Necromancer noted that the black-armoured knight made no obeisance before him. It was more than pride – the Mortarchs had that in abundance yet they didn't hesitate to prostrate themselves in his presence. No, it was that rarest of all things – an absence of fear. For why should a warrior feel fear if death would simply speed his soul back to the halls of Sigmar to be cast anew in the forges of the God-King?

'I have summoned you, knight of Sigmar, to make my intentions known,' Nagash told Makvar. He looked across the warriors who accompanied the Lord-Celestant. The flare of purity shining behind the shutters of the lantern fixed to the belt of one companion evoked a twinge of amusement. Such a weapon would discomfit Neferata or Arkhan, possibly even destroy some of the vampire queen's entourage, but it was nothing to a being who had once walked beside Sigmar and withstood the aura of the God-King himself.

Makvar stepped forwards and pointed towards Arkhan. 'We have helped to restore your disciple to you,' he said. 'It is my hope that we have displayed to your satisfaction the quality to be found in Sigmar's servants and the advantage of fighting beside us against the common foe.'

'Your command sustained casualties in the fight,' Nagash stated.

Makvar's voice had just the faintest edge to it when he answered. 'Most of our losses were suffered putting down the monster Arkhan summoned with his magic.'

Nagash nodded, shifting around so that his deathly countenance glowered down at the liche-king. 'Explain yourself,' he hissed at Arkhan.

The Mortarch of Sacrament fell to one knee, bowing his head before his master's ire. 'The fault is mine, my liege. The invaders had forced their way past my guardians. In my rush to work my spells and conjure a servant mighty enough to defy them, I made an error in my incantation. My haste is to blame for rendering the terrorgheist beyond my control–'

A wave of Nagash's skeletal claw silenced Arkhan's apologies. 'Your carelessness has brought harm to those that would befriend us,' he said. 'Be grateful that they were able to put down that which you so recklessly summoned.' He turned back towards Makvar. 'It is my hope that your casualties were not too severe.'

'We still have strength enough to accomplish our mission,' the winged Stormcast Huld answered. It was the sort of ambiguous response a skilled diplomat would give, acknowledging the situation while assuring it made no impact upon the relative positions of all involved.

'That remains to be seen,' Nagash cautioned. 'Confidence is but the prelude to achievement.' He waved one hand towards the undead who stood beside his throne. 'I must rebuild the might of my legions if I would help Sigmar wage his battles. To do so, it is needful that my Mortarchs assist me in my labours. Two of them now stand at my side, but there is a third whose help is essential to me.'

'You ask that the Anvils of the Heldenhammer find this missing vassal for you?' Huld looked aside to Makvar before continuing. 'Are you making that a condition...'

'There can be no alliance based upon disparity,' Nagash declared. 'I will not treat with Sigmar unless it is as his equal.' The Great Necromancer extended one of his fleshless hands. From his bony claws, a ripple of dark magic poured away, striking the cold floor of the forgotten palace. In response, streamers of spectral essence billowed upwards, growing like phantasmal vines. As the deathly energies wound about each other, they merged, fusing into a single pillar of writhing green light. When the pillar stood higher than any of the assembled Stormcasts, its summit began to fold in upon itself, transforming into a nebulous sphere-like shape. With each gyrating shudder that passed through it, the form grew more defined and distinct until finally the Anvils found themselves staring up at a grisly visage. It was almost bestial in its degree of cruelty, menace dripping from the vicious set of the jaws and the sharp beak-like nose. The eyes were sunk deep within shadowed sockets, the bald pate distorted by nodules of bone.

'This simulacrum is the face of Count Mannfred, the Mortarch of Night,' Nagash said. 'I will need his powers to restore my legions.' At a flick of his talon, he caused the phantom image to alter, now showing the vampire riding an abyssal steed into battle, wielding a ghoulish blade against unseen foes. 'Of all my vassals, Mannfred has fared the best in his efforts to defy the spread of Chaos.'

Makvar pointed at the apparition Nagash had conjured. 'There is no need to remind us of Mannfred's visage. Well do we know that countenance. It is the face of an adversary the warriors of Sigmar have found themselves in conflict with before.'

The simulacrum disintegrated in a burst of wailing light as Nagash extinguished his spell. 'He rests once more within the expanse of my realm, like a prodigal son slinking back to his home. Perhaps your comrades have taught him humility, or maybe the lesson he has learned is merely to be less audacious in what he would claim for himself. Repentant or unbowed, he is necessary just the same.' Nagash let his gaze bore into the stern mask that covered Makvar's face. 'There are many past slights which must be set aside if there is to be an understanding between us. Do not think the Stormcasts are alone in the matter of old enmities they must forgive… if not forget.'

Silence hung over the hall as Nagash let his words echo in the air. Even if he had heard only Sigmar's side of the tale, Makvar couldn't be unaware of the manner in which the old alliance was broken, or of the fate which came upon the

Realm of Death as a result. The Lord-Celestant was far from a stupid man – he had imagination enough to conceive how those events were regarded by the Great Necromancer and his followers. Beside the abandonment of an entire realm to Archaon's hordes, of what consequence were the reckless aspirations of a power-hungry Mortarch?

'As you say, Lord Nagash,' Makvar stated, 'there is much that must be set aside so that we may all focus upon the task before us. The fact that Sigmar has sent us to you is proof enough that the God-King understands this and is ready to forgive old conflicts.'

A rattling chuckle hissed across Nagash's fangs. He turned aside, looking across his Mortarchs and their followers. 'Eloquently spoken,' he decided. 'The very nature of an embassy is compromise. But do all your warriors share your sense of vision, Lord-Celestant?' Nagash leaned forwards, fastening Brannok in his spectral sight.

The Knight-Heraldor met the Lord of Death's cadaverous stare. 'It isn't necessary to share my commander's clarity of vision,' he said. 'It is only necessary that I obey. That I remain faithful to my vows, my duty and my faith.'

Brannok's answer both amused and provoked Nagash. 'Faith?' he repeated the word, turning it over as though dissecting it with his voice. 'What is faith but a mask to hide doubt? What is it but a deceit evoked to goad the feeble-minded beyond the limits of reason? I had imagined it was something noble and rational that endowed the Stormcasts with such remarkable potential, yet within I discover only the atavism of faith.'

'Faith is the source of my strength,' Brannok retorted. 'Faith in Sigmar God-King, trust in his divine power and wisdom.'

'Be wary where you place your trust, knight, lest you find yourself abandoned.'

'That is a warning which should be turned towards the creatures which haunt your court,' Brannok said, pointing at Neferata and her vampires. 'They are the ones that have been abandoned and left to slink through the shadows.'

'You understand little,' Nagash said, 'and least of all what it means to serve me. Those who do are never far from my reach.' He dismissed Brannok from his notice, instead focusing once more on Makvar. 'There is nothing that transpires within the Realm of Death that can long escape my attentions. When Mannfred returned to this realm, he sought to hide himself within the vastness of his old castle of Nachtsreik. Within that labyrinth of crypts and vaults, he defies the hosts of Chaos that hunt for him.'

'If he is so well hidden, how will we find him?' Makvar asked.

'By uniting our powers,' Nagash answered. He gestured at Huld's celestial beacon. 'With the light of Azyr we can penetrate Mannfred's illusions.' His skeletal hand closed into a bony fist. 'And with my might, the prodigal son can be brought to heel.'

The rich silks of the divan upon which he rested caressed Lascilion's abused flesh the same way the sensuous perfume anointing their folds teased his nose. There was something almost tortuous about such indulgent luxury after the carnage of battle and the agonies of defeat. He wondered if Bloodking Thagmok had the acumen to appreciate the subtlety of such torment. If he did, then he had forgotten the desires of those who devoted themselves to the Prince of Chaos, those who plunged into that excess of experience and sensuality where the borderland between pleasure and pain wasn't simply breached, but ceased to exist entirely. If Thagmok wanted to punish him, the worst he could have done to Lascilion was to shut him up in an empty box and leave him to rot.

'You aren't being punished. You are being offered the chance for redemption.'

The words drifted to Lascilion in a husky whisper, redolent of lewd suggestion and hedonistic promise. The Lord of Slaanesh felt his body longing to submit to those seductive tones, but the fierce will that burned within him resisted the temptation. It was all too easy to allow sensation to eclipse desire, to plunge into vacuous indulgence and lose all appreciation of the very lusts that enslaved the flesh.

'I have told you before to stay out of my mind,' Lascilion snapped, rising up from beneath the silk coverlet that sheathed his body. The companions disturbed by his sudden motion went scampering off into the scented darkness of his pavilion.

Strolling out of that darkness was a slim figure arrayed in a long cloak of feathers. A tall helm of reflective gemstones and mirrored glass cradled the proud head that rose above the onyx clasps that held the cloak across narrow shoulders. A pectoral of beads and bones spilled over the swell of more-feminine charms. Small, delicate fingers curled around the haft of a slender staff that seemed at once to be shaped from both crystal and clay. Nodules of metal embedded in its length blazed with some inner light.

Even if her features hadn't been reshaped by the mutating gifts of the Lord of Change, Lascilion would have been hard-pressed to judge either age or origin when it came to the sorceress Molchinte. That she had strayed far from whatever tribe had produced her was obvious. Such was the way of Chaos. The gods favoured the wanderer, the one who always strove to go beyond the next horizon, endlessly seeking some new novelty of sensation with which to honour their god. Or, in Molchinte's case, some new ember of knowledge to trap in the web of her scheming mind.

'If you would put barriers between us, then you shouldn't have allowed my magic to heal your wounds,' Molchinte said. Though no sound issued from it, the vestigial mouth that opened across her cheek parroted the motion. 'Of course, Thagmok would have small use for a crippled hedonist unable to leave his bed. A tidbit for the flesh hounds to toy with, certainly nothing more.'

'Your ministrations have healed my injuries,' Lascilion conceded, turning his head and looking at his recent playthings cowering in the dark. 'I have regained much of my old stamina.'

Molchinte ignored the boast. 'Thagmok feels you are whole enough to perform the task for which you were spared death upon the skull-wheel.' A flick of her hand and the sorceress caused Lascilion's forked tongue to rasp across his lips. 'You found Neferata once, when all others failed in the task. The Bloodking demands you do so again.'

Lascilion scowled at the sorceress, baring his leonine fangs. 'I have told him my condition. I have told him that I will hunt the vampire queen only with the understanding that she is *mine*.'

A contemptuous laugh rose from both of Molchinte's mouths. 'How childish are your ambitions, Lord of Slaanesh! Can you not rise beyond your brute instincts! Are you so dull that you don't understand how things have changed! Did you truly think Thagmok spared you simply so you could glut your depravity!'

The warlord's temper rose as the scorn of the sorceress whipped out at him. 'I am the favoured of Slaanesh!'

'The broken servant of a broken god with a broken army strewn about the ruins of Nulahmia,' Molchinte returned. 'Think, Lascilion! Why were you driven to defeat? The lightning-men, the warriors who came down from the sky. Yours isn't the first horde to be decimated by them. Across the Mortal Realms, strange armies have appeared to oppose the hordes, seeking to stem the ascendancy of Chaos.' Her voice dropped to a subdued whisper. 'The Everchosen himself has communed with Thagmok and given the Bloodking his commands. Neferata has become a triviality, an inconsequence in the greater skein. Archaon is concerned that lightning-men have appeared in the Realm of Death, that they have struck where not even his daemon prophets predicted them to appear. He has seen possibilities behind their presence here. Possibilities that will not be allowed to come into being.'

Lascilion fell silent under the weight of Molchinte's words. Even daemons trembled at the name of Archaon, the Everchosen who bore the favour of the Dark Gods and had been granted honours and powers beyond the scope of any mortal. There were some who venerated him as a god, and Lascilion wasn't certain they weren't right to do so. To know that the Everchosen had heard of his defeat made the warlord's stomach sicken. But the idea that it was within his power to render a service to Archaon sent his pulse quickening.

'Thagmok would have me sniff out Neferata as I did before,' Lascilion said. 'What then?'

'Slaughter,' Molchinte said.

At a gesture, Molchinte drove the shadows from where they clung about the pavilion. Lascilion was startled to find that others had entered the tent with the sorceress. In one corner, he saw the diseased bulk of Alghor Wormsword, his corroded armour straining to restrain the cancerous organs slowly oozing up from beneath his flesh. The semi-daemon Vaangoth, his limbs clothed in shaggy strips of crimson fur, his body encased in arcane armour that dripped with the blood of his countless victims. Orbleth the Despised, arrayed in a patchwork cloak woven from the scalps of wizards and priests, his pallid flesh scarred with the marks of all the Dark Gods and the brand of Chaos eternal.

Amala was among them, the winged mutant's eyes somehow conveying a sense of uneasiness. Lascilion could imagine her disappointment, expecting reward for carrying the disgraced warlord to the Bloodking's doubtful mercy. Instead, the Lord of Slaanesh once more held dominion over her. It was a temptation to reach to the table beside his divan and take up Pain and Torment. Striking down the treacherous mutant would be a delightful diversion. But Lascilion denied himself the pleasure. Amala had been useful to him before and could be so again. Later, once she wasn't so useful, would be the time to dispose of her.

'These are the most vicious killers among the Bloodking's warbands,' Molchinte said. 'Between us, we carry the marks of the Ruinous Powers, the favour of the Dark Gods. We can slip unnoticed to the places where Neferata seeks to hide. Our command is to kill her, and those who would befriend her.'

Lascilion shook his head. 'Thagmok expects a handful of warriors to succeed where my entire army found destruction? I have seen these lightning-men. Each of them is worth a score of warriors.'

'We don't need to kill them all,' Molchinte said. 'Only their leaders. Only those who would draw the armies of death out from their lurking seclusion in this realm...'

* * *

Knight-Heraldor Brannok paced across the dead court-
yard, staring up at the terraces which climbed the side of
the ancient palace. He tried to imagine what this place had
been like when Mephitt was a living city and not a vast tomb
buried beneath the Mirefells. The empty basins of fountains
evoked the gurgle of bubbling water, the barren confines of
planters conjured the smell of flowers, the skeletal frames of
trellises summoned the comforting shade of vines. A little
platform projecting from the flagstones suggested the sound
of musicians drawing harmonies from flute and horn.

He closed his hand about the gilded horn that hung from
his belt. Those who had dwelt here had been men, people
with lives and dreams. At least of such sort as the Lord of
Death permitted them to have. Brannok wondered if the city
had perished before the conquering hordes of Chaos or if its
end had been brought about by some caprice of Nagash, some
offence that had provoked the Great Necromancer.

No good could come from such contemplation, Brannok
realised. When the rest of the Stormcasts set up camp in
the empty halls of the palace, he had drawn away to medi-
tate upon the turmoil he felt within himself. Why was it so
difficult for him to accept the situation? Why couldn't he
resign himself to his duty the way Makvar and the others
did? Even Vogun, who shared Brannok's misgivings, seemed
more accepting of what was demanded of them.

Brannok didn't for a moment doubt the wisdom of Sigmar
in seeking this alliance with Nagash. The might of the undead
was undeniable, the menace of Chaos unquestionable. For
the greater good, Brannok knew this merging of forces must
come to pass. Yet knowing it and feeling it were two different things. His conscience kept crying out to him, reminding
him of those who had suffered under the dominion of Nagash

and his disciples. Try as he might, he couldn't still the loathing he felt for the monsters they had been sent to befriend.

A rustle of cloth and the sound of a footfall stirred Brannok from his meditations. Spinning around, his sword half-drawn from its sheath, he was surprised to see Neferata watching him from the shadows. The vampire queen's expression was almost contrite, almost embarrassed. Almost. As she smoothed the dark gown that hugged her body, Brannok reminded himself that this was no woman walking out from the shadows, only a monster pretending to be one.

'Forgive my trespass,' Neferata said. 'I didn't mean to intrude on you.'

'If there was any truth in that claim, you would have passed me by without making a sound,' Brannok told her. 'I am certain a predator like yourself has become quite skilled at moving unseen and unheard.'

Instead of responding to him with the regal disdain and arrogance Brannok expected of her, Neferata lowered her gaze, staring down at the flagstones. 'You have seen through my pretence,' she said. 'I wished to speak with you.'

Brannok started to turn away. 'If you want to talk, seek out Lord-Celestant Makvar or Huld. They have the authority and the skill to negotiate with a personage of your status. I am naught but a soldier doing as his duty compels him.'

Neferata walked towards him. 'You hate me,' she stated.

'What I saw in your city makes it easy to hate,' Brannok said. 'The suffering and terror you inflicted upon your subjects–'

'They should have fared far worse, storm-knight, had they been given into the grip of Chaos,' Neferata answered. She shook her head, a tinge of disgust on her face. 'Who are you to judge, who has only known the righteous protection of Sigmar? Do you know what it is to see everything around you despoiled and corrupted by Chaos? What lengths would you go to if it meant you could stave off that destruction?'

'Lord-Celestant Makvar has proffered the same explanation,' Brannok said. 'I can find no sympathy for it. If everything good and innocent is destroyed to oppose Chaos, then for what do you fight? No, my lady, you should speak with Makvar. As you say, I have no kindness towards you.'

'That is why I must speak with you,' Neferata said. 'Your antagonism towards us is known. None will expect me to seek you out.' She hesitated, watching Brannok to see what impact her words might have. 'In the swamp, I sent my hand-maiden Kismet to pass warning to Makvar. She didn't return.'

'How can you be certain the Anvils aren't responsible for her disappearance?' Brannok asked. Despite his animosity and suspicion, he saw the threat such circumstances could cause the Stormcasts and their mission.

'I am a judge of some quality when it comes to men,' Neferata said. 'If you were to reject my overtures you would do so openly, not in such sordid fashion. No, it is someone else who seeks to prevent any understanding between us.'

'Nagash?' Brannok nodded as he considered the notion. From what he had seen, what he knew, the Great Necromancer exerted complete control over his vassals. He wouldn't abide one of his Mortarchs acting on her own.

Neferata merely nodded. 'I cannot pretend to know his intentions, but understand that he does nothing without a purpose.' She paused, her voice falling to a whisper. 'When we seek Mannfred in Nachtsreik, Arkhan will not accompany us. He has been set another task by our master. While we are hunting for Mannfred's crypt, Arkhan will be here removing the obsidian domes from the Temple of the Vulture. I don't expect you to understand the import of that, but know the domes are fashioned from the same stone as the Obelisk of Black that was removed from Nulahmia. Such relics have arcane potential that can magnify the potency of any spell focussed through them.'

Brannok was silent a moment, trying to put himself in Makvar's place, trying to find the arguments his commander would make. The explanations that would make him still believe in an alliance between them. 'Maybe he needs these relics to summon the army he will send to aid us.'

'Don't be deceived,' Neferata warned. 'The terrorgheist that slew your comrades. You were told it slipped free of Arkhan's control. Arkhan assumed responsibility for its attack. Yet I tell you, next to Nagash himself, there is no more skilled practitioner of the Art than the liche-king. There was another purpose behind that attack.'

Brannok drew closer, listening intently while Neferata whispered to him her theories of intrigue and deception.

Neither the Knight-Heraldor nor the vampire queen was aware of the eyes watching them from the darkness.

Or felt the burning malignance of that gaze.

CHAPTER ELEVEN

Wan, gibbous light flickered through the blackness, revealing just enough of the subterranean vaults to make the shadows beyond its reach still darker and more menacing. Arches of bone curled overhead, mineral encrustations dripping from them in gnarled spears and jagged fangs. Underfoot was a grainy surface of ash and dust, rippling and flowing as a phantom breeze wafted across it. The walls, when they loomed out from the shadows, were shaped from countless skeletons, each body entwined with its fellows, melding into stony solidity. Bare skulls stared out from the walls, seeming to bemoan the fate that had claimed them... or inviting those who gazed upon them to share in it.

'This is an unclean place,' Lord-Castellant Vogun declared, making the sign of the hammer with his hand as he gazed upon the morbid vastness. At his side, Torn whined in sympathy with his master's uneasiness. The gryph-hound kept close to Vogun's side, lingering near the warding lantern hanging from his belt as though to draw some comfort from the holy light.

'We tread upon the dust of nations,' Lord-Relictor Kreimnar said, emphasising his words by stomping down on the sand-like surface. The added pressure caused him to sink up to his knee in the ashes. One of the Liberators marching alongside him helped Kreimnar pull free from the hole. Throughout the dark tunnel, the rest of the Stormcasts pushed through the morbid drifts of ash and dust. Sometimes eerie energies would rise up from the ground and swirl around lone knights, fumbling at their armour with wispy hands and vaporous claws. Usually, the spirits vanished as swiftly as they appeared, but several times their persistence had drawn angry sparks from the black sigmarite plate. At such times, the repulsed apparitions uttered dejected wails before flying away into the darkness.

Worse dangers prowled the underworld of Shyish. The Anvils had caught fleeting glimpses of gangrel shapes lingering at the edges of the light. Things with gleaming eyes and slavering mouths, dripping claws and decaying flesh. Some of the stalkers were diminutive, wasted creatures, while others were grotesques far larger than a mortal human. Others still bore no resemblance at all to human shape, but instead suggested slithering reptiles and venomous arachnids in their nebulous outlines. Human or inhuman, tangible or phantom, the hostility and hunger radiating from the stalkers was undeniable, impressing upon each Stormcast that he was trespassing in a forbidden land. Only the presence of Nagash kept the horrors from rushing out of the shadows and consuming the intruders. It was a lesson that wasn't lost on the Anvils.

Lord-Celestant Makvar felt the weight of responsibility pressing against him as never before. At every turn, the

Stormcasts were exposed to the enormity of Nagash's power. The grisly underworld through which the Great Necromancer led them was like nothing they had been prepared to imagine. The scope and magnitude of these endless vaults fashioned from the materials of death staggered credulity. The dust through which they trod represented an ocean of graves, each mote and speck a particle of some extinguished life. From these ashes, Nagash had shaped an entire world, an empire buried beneath the conquering hordes of Chaos.

Yes – when Kreimnar said the Anvils marched across the dust of nations, he spoke the truth. How many peoples had been vanquished? How many kingdoms drawn into the endless night? In death and destruction, they served Nagash more completely than they could ever have in life. Mortal debris became the brick and mortar of the Great Necromancer's domain, spirits became the fuel of his magics. The transition from life to death fed Nagash's power. It was this that made the Death God so mighty. It was this which also made the Lord of Death so formidable and fearsome. Each display of his power impressed upon Makvar not only his strength but the grisly source of that strength.

To cement the alliance between Azyr and Shyish, Makvar knew he had to gain the trust of Nagash. Without the undead to support the assault upon the gate of Gothizzar, the Anvils of the Heldenhammer would be unable to press their attack into the Allpoints. They needed the creatures of Shyish at their side. Facilitating that meant stifling his own qualms and suspicions. He had to believe in the purpose of his mission, had to embrace it with uncompromising conviction. He had to accept the realities of what they had seen in Nulahmia and Schloss Wolfhof and Mephitt, to appreciate that such extremes were the price of defying Chaos when the enemy had all but devoured the entire realm. Cruelty and terror were often the only things that could defy the lure of Chaos, to keep a people fighting when all seemed hopeless. Compassion was a luxury the conquered couldn't afford.

It was towards a greater good that they had to rouse Nagash from his seclusion and draw his undead legions into the larger fight. Anything else had to be ignored. Even the security of Makvar's own warriors. He knew how completely they were in Nagash's power now. The forces of death were all around them, waiting in the dark. The slightest gesture, the simple withdrawl of Nagash's protection, and those hungry wraiths would flood the Stormcasts in a sea of death. Even if they could find the path back to the desolation of Mephitt, Makvar couldn't envision many of them making it back to the surface.

'How much further do you reckon we must march?' The question came from Knight-Heraldor Brannok. He kept his sword drawn as he walked beside Gojin's flank, eyes roving across the lurking shadows. Of all the Anvils, it was Brannok who exhibited the most suspicion of their grim allies. It was telling of his sense of loyalty and duty that he expressed that suspicion by keeping close to Makvar in hopes of shielding the Lord-Celestant from harm.

'The Realm of Death is vast,' Makvar said. 'Nor can we be certain these vaults can be measured in leagues or miles as we understand them. I cannot say how far we've come. It would be even more impossible to say how far we have yet to go.'

Makvar studied Brannok for a moment. It wasn't the length of their journey that disturbed him, but the question of what they would find waiting for them at its end. He had brought Neferata's message to the Lord-Celestant, tidings that gave Makvar much to ponder. The disappearance of Kismet in the Mirefells was certainly an ill portent, if it was truly as mysterious as the vampire queen suggested. The Mortarch of Blood had her own aspirations, a facet that added a new wrinkle to the web of intrigue that characterised the shadowy world of the undead. She was most eager to prove her friendship towards the Anvils, even at the expense of her fealty to Nagash. That very fact forced Makvar to be sceptical of her warnings. She could be trying to curry favour with him by sowing suspicion of her master.

Still, Makvar had to admit, there was some truth bound into Neferata's warnings. Whether she was genuine or simply clever enough to clothe her deceptions in a mantle of reality, he couldn't say. It was certainly true that the Obelisk of Black had exerted a disturbing energy on the Stormcasts who bore it away from Nulahmia. It was also true that Arkhan had remained behind in Mephitt, ostensibly to replenish the forces lost combating the minions of Nurgle by reanimating the city's ancient dead. Might he also be gathering the relics Neferata had described?

Brannok stepped ahead of Gojin, placing himself between the dracoth and the rider who came galloping towards the Stormcasts. It was a messenger from the entourage of Nagash and Neferata. No skeletal herald this time, but a leering vampire in blood-red armour. Makvar recognised the cruel visage of Lord Harkdron as he drew his decayed horse to a halt several yards ahead of the Anvils.

'Great Nagash extends his salutations to you, Lord Makvar,' Harkdron announced, not quite able to keep the distaste he felt from tainting his words. 'He commands me to inform you that the redoubt of Lord Mannfred is near.' The vampire leaned forwards in his saddle, his face curling back into a sneer. 'The seclusion of Nachtsreik has been disturbed. The enemy lays siege to it, seeking to force their way past its defences.'

'Nagash expects us to lift the siege?' Brannok returned Harkdron's scorn.

Harkdron glared back at the Knight-Heraldor for a moment, his eyes glittering with hate. 'The Great Necromancer expects nothing,' he snarled back. 'What Nagash commands is that Lord Makvar select a small contingent of his storm-knights to accompany him into the fortress.' The vampire shifted his attention back to the Lord-Celestant. 'Much time will be lost if we try to fight our way through the enemy host,' he explained. 'Mighty Nagash is aware of the urgency of your embassy and would spare a needless effort. A handful of your warriors – no more than a score – should suffice.'

'What is Nagash's intention?' Makvar asked.

'There are ways into Nachtsreik known only to him,' Harkdron said. 'Passages too small for an army but where a smaller company can move with ease.'

'And, of course, Nagash will join this foray,' Brannok's voice came like an audible scowl. Makvar gave the warrior a reproving glance.

Harkdron nodded. 'Great Nagash and Queen Neferata will accompany you, along with such attendants as they feel needful.' The vampire smiled, displaying his sharp fangs. 'Without them, it is doubtful you could even find Mannfred's sanctuary, much less treat with him before he ripped out your throats.'

Holding his hand towards Brannok, silencing whatever rejoinder the Knight-Heraldor might be tempted to make, Makvar dismissed Harkdron. 'Tell Nagash that the Anvils of the Heldenhammer stand ready to aid him in restoring contact with his vassal. Tell him that we appreciate this concession to the urgency of our mission and the furtherance of an alliance that will benefit both our realms.'

The vampire started to ride away, then turned back, an almost frightened look on his face. He hesitated a moment before relaying one last command from the Great Necromancer. 'When you decide which storm-knights are to join you, Nagash asks that you include those who carry the Light Celestial among your entourage.'

Brannok watched as Harkdron rode off, then turned and spoke to Makvar. 'Why does Nagash want to draw Lord-Castellan Vogun and Knight-Azyros Huld from our ranks? Why them specifically?'

Makvar felt he knew the answer. From all he had witnessed, even Arkhan and Neferata were sensitive to the light Vogun and Huld carried in their lamps. 'I think Nagash is unsure that Mannfred will be as eager to submit to his master as the other Mortarchs. He may feel that Sigmar's light is necessary to subdue the Mortarch of Night.'

A shroud of mist marked the doorway between the forbidden underworld and the secret redoubt of Nachtsreik. Even to Neferata, the mist had a clammy, parasitic feel to it. She knew that for a mortal, the phantasmal barrier would be even more repulsive, sucking at their veins and drawing out their essence. Such spectral walls had the potential to ward off all but the most powerful slaves of Chaos, though the arcane demands to maintain such barriers went beyond the abilities even of the Mortarchs to sustain for long. Only Nagash had such power. Walking through the mist, Neferata was reminded of his dominance and the strength of his fell shadow.

The barrier opened into the mouldy confines of an ancient crypt. The caskets had long ago been pulled from their niches in the walls, the bones of their occupants strewn about the floor. A winding series of steps rose up from the tomb, climbing towards the smashed timbers of a narrow doorway. Neferata could see the skeletal figure of Nagash already ascending those steps, one bony hand curled around the haft of his staff, Alakanash. With his other hand, the Lord of Death evoked the ancient spirits of the crypt, surrounding himself in a circle of ghostly energy.

Only a few of Neferata's vampire knights accompanied her from the underworld, the rest remaining behind with the remainder of her army. Lord Harkdron followed the blood knights through the mist, his expression sullen. Her lover had grown increasingly attentive to her since his failure to defend Nulahmia, as though his eagerness to please could blot out his deficiencies. She had made no secret of her displeasure, fully aware how her disapproval only fed the vampire's devotion. In the presence of beings like Nagash and Arkhan, it did her pride immeasurable good to have someone at her side who still worshipped her as a goddess.

The fearful adoration she had enjoyed in Nulahmia would be hers again. Neferata was determined to regain everything that had been lost. Even if it meant defying the intentions of the Great Necromancer.

Neferata turned to face the veil of mist, watching as Makvar and his Stormcasts marched out from the underworld. Not so much as a shudder passed through their armoured frames. The only evidence of their fearful passage was found in the gryph-hound that crept alongside Vogun. The half-bird's feathers were ruffled and his lean body shivered with the trauma of his trot through the veil. Neferata considered it a testament to the might of the Stormcasts that they not only withstood the barrier, but had even been able to compel a simple beast to follow them through.

The vampire queen noted that Brannok was among the warriors Makvar had chosen to accompany him. She took that as a reassuring sign, evidence perhaps that he was taking her warnings to heart. Whether Nagash intended to support the Stormcasts or not, Neferata saw only advantage for herself by gaining their goodwill.

The rest of Makvar's followers consisted of a mixture of archers and swordsmen, as well as the winged storm-angel Huld and the formidable healer-priest Vogun. The skull-helmed Kreimnar wasn't in evidence, however. Left behind to command the rest of the Anvils while they awaited the return of Nagash and their commander.

Makvar looked around the crypt, seeming to take especial notice of the layers of cobwebs and mould that coated the walls and filled the niches. 'What is this place?' he asked Neferata.

'You might call it an antechamber,' she said. 'A threshold between the underworld and the rest of Shyish. There are many such places in the Realm of Death, though only Nagash knows them all.'

Huld came forward, gesturing at Harkdron and the other blood knights. 'Forgive me for what may seem an imprudent observation, but I expected you to bring more warriors.' The words brought a frown to Neferata's face and a glower to that of Harkdron.

'You are in the presence of the Lord of Death,' Nagash's words echoed through the crypt. 'There is no mightier power in this realm.' The Great Necromancer turned from the top of the steps, staring down at the Stormcasts below. 'If it is disparity of numbers that unsettles you, I will put your fear to rest.'

Neferata felt the power gathering into Nagash's claw as he

pointed down to the floor of the crypt. She recognised the nature of the magic he was conjuring, though it was of a magnitude that surprised her. The litter of bones tossed about the tomb began to tremble, bouncing upon the cold floor with spasms of animation. A green nimbus of energy gathered around each fragment and with a speed she found to be incredible, they leapt from the floor. A dozen whirlwinds of shattered bone gyrated about the crypt, waves of necromantic energy streaming from Nagash's hand into each eddy.

The spirals of bone began to take a distinct shape as Nagash's magic fused the fragments together. They were forms which Neferata realised could never have been natural to the occupants of the crypt. Skeletal apparitions, each as big as a Stormcast, that had tattered wings sprouting from their backs and canine jaws distorting their bestial skulls. The Great Necromancer wasn't reanimating the dead, he was using the mortal debris as a shell to house the primordial spirits of his own guard. In appearance, they were not unlike the morghasts who served Neferata, but she knew the spirits that lurked within these skeletal monsters were far more powerful. These belonged to divine avengers dispatched aeons ago to destroy Nagash, only to fail in their purpose and be enslaved by the Lord of Death. These were the morghast archai.

The Stormcasts weren't cowed by the frightful feat of necromancy that unfolded before them. Still, Neferata noticed that Vogun drew slightly ahead of his comrades and had one hand poised above the lantern he carried. Brannok, too, exhibited an increased wariness, drawing closer to Makvar. The Lord-Celestant himself, however, gave no sign of trepidation. Boldly, he walked towards the steps.

'Lord Nagash,' Makvar called up to the Great Necromancer.

'We have no doubt as to your power. Accept my apology if any offence has been paid to you.' He pointed to the shattered door at the top of the steps. 'Mannfred's refuge lies beyond that portal?'

Nagash turned, waving his staff towards the door. At his mere gesture, the remaining timbers decayed, collapsing into a heap of black dust. Through the doorway, a sinister red light spilled into the crypt. 'Nachtsreik,' he declared. 'The Stronghold of Night.'

Neferata felt the mockery in Nagash's voice, the sardonic amusement woven into his words. She glanced aside at the Anvils, but it appeared none of them had noticed the sinister tone. Yet when Makvar climbed the steps, the Lord-Celestant drew back. He had stood without flinching within a few feet of the morghasts as they clothed themselves in shards of bone, yet now he retreated from the doorway. The vampire queen rushed up the steps to see for herself what could alarm the stalwart Stormcast.

What she found beyond the door of the crypt was something that shocked even her jaded sensibilities. The crypt in which they stood looked out across an immense cavern, its furthest reaches lost in shadow. It wasn't the size of the cavern that stunned her, however, but the fact that everything seemed inverted. When she gazed up, she saw not the roof but the floor of the cavern, covered with pools of murky water and a twisting road of colossal flagstones. Immense statues lay shattered about the rocky terrain, sprawled between a forest of stalagmites. More, there were creatures moving along that road and within the stony forest, a teaming mass of verminous shapes cloaked in filthy robes. It was as though the mouth of the crypt in which she stood was positioned above the cavernous landscape, and those within the tomb were hanging over it like flies on a ceiling. Even the sight of the great pulsating light that smouldered at the heart of the cavern like some miniature moon couldn't match the uncanny sensation of standing on the roof of the world.

Nagash stepped between Neferata and Makvar, pointing outward with his staff. 'When the War of Bones looked uncertain, Mannfred prepared this refuge for himself by pulling the city of Dyre deep beneath the ground.' He drew their attention away from the scene below – or was it above? – them and to that which stretched away across the roof of the cavern. As far as could be seen, the streets and houses of a crumbling settlement were visible, the crypt itself standing within a great cemetery. 'The lives of Dyre fed his power even as their souls were bound into the hidden moon he wrought for himself.'

Makvar had already overcome his surprise at the strange vista. He pointed at the fortress the swarms of skaven struggled to penetrate. 'That is Nachtsreik? It seems we must hurry if we would find Mannfred before the ratkin.' As he spoke, a section of the black walls was brought down by a great ball of corrosive gas hurled against it by a monstrous catapult.

A dry chuckle rattled from Nagash. 'These walls have withstood the hordes of Chaos for many lifetimes. Every stone is steeped in blood, and the mortar made from bone. They are imbued with the same magic that feeds Mannfred's moon. If the walls are brought down they will restore themselves. Speck by speck, they will draw themselves back.' The Great Necromancer was silent for a moment, contemplating the scene below. 'If the enemy were to bring sufficient force to bear, they might break the old spells long enough to get inside. Mannfred realised this when he left his refuge. Now that he's returned, it is possible the enemy is aware of it and will stir themselves to greater effort.'

'How do we get inside?' Makvar asked.

Nagash leaned out from the doorway. As he did so, Neferata noticed that his cloak fell upwards, drawn towards the floor of the cavern. 'We cross the city,' he stated. Thrusting a bony claw, he indicated a slender tower that stabbed up from the mammoth fortress. The narrow window that opened just below its roof was only a few feet below the suspended streets of Dyre.

'With a retinue of Prosecutors, we could cross that distance without delay,' Makvar said, shaking his head. He stared at Nagash for a moment. 'You desire to see how resourceful we are.'

'Before entering any battle,' Nagash said, 'it is wise to know the capabilities of your allies.'

The moment he stepped out from the crypt, Huld found himself falling towards what had seemed the roof of the cavern. It was a simple matter to arrest his fall, unfurling his sigmarite wings to keep himself aloft. Reorienting himself to the strange geometry of Mannfred's stronghold was another matter entirely. The eerie sight of Dyre's streets inverted and hanging from the roof of the cavern was confusing enough, but when he drew close to the abandoned city, he found himself being pulled towards it rather than the true floor of the cavern. Whatever arcane spells governed the crypt exerted their influence across the rest of Dyre. Huld suspected it was some residue of the magic Mannfred had employed to drag the city below the earth, but the nature of that magic and its limitations were things beyond his knowledge and experience. The city appeared to be more than suspended in space, but in time as well, locked in that moment when it had been captured by the Mortarch.

He didn't need to understand the Mortarch's sorcery. He only had to overcome it. Makvar was depending on Huld, and that meant their entire mission was in the balance. It did no good to bemoan the conniving nature by which Nagash had arranged this test of the Stormcasts. As Makvar had pointed out before, whatever ordeals they had to endure to bring the undead into battle beside them at Gothizzar, the Anvils would overcome them.

Keeping just beyond the pull of Dyre, Huld flew towards the desolate sprawl of what had once been the city's harbour. The spells Mannfred had used even captured part of the sea adjoining the city. Huld could see the weird reflection of the red moon shining from the suspended pool. Ships dangled from the frozen water, their masts and sails jutting out at weird angles as the pull from below fought to wrest them from the opposing pull emanating from the ceiling. It was towards these ships that Huld climbed, preparing himself for the instant when he would be drawn towards the ships rather than away from them, turning his climb into a dive. When he landed on the deck of a trireme, it was a descent of such ungainly awkwardness that he prayed none of his fellow Stormcasts were able to see him. That the most likely observer was Makvar at the door of the crypt only made the sense of embarrassment more pronounced.

Hunting across the decks of the ship, Huld inspected the thick coils of rope heaped beside the gunwales. Choosing the stoutest mooring line he saw, he drew a length between his gauntlets with a savage grip. His eyes studied the rope with dour scrutiny, watching for the slightest fraying of the cord. Only when the Knight-Azyros was convinced it would hold did he draw the heavy stack of rope away with him as he spread his wings and leapt back into the air.

Navigating the sorcerous inversion was even more difficult with the heavy rope in his hands, but it was a feat Huld was able to accomplish without the cord becoming tangled in his wings. He knew he would have to repeat the performance several times in his labours and made careful calculations about the best way to manage the manoeuvre. Of particular interest to him was the border between the drag from the ground and the pull from the suspended city. He saw how the phenomenon could be harnessed to serve the Anvils.

Huld flew back to the crypt, the rope trailing after him. By pulling it along the edge of the competing gravitational influences he was able to negate much of the burden, only that portion actually in his hands weighing him down. The rest snaked out along the border, levitating in the grip of the oppositional forces. Another complex mid-air contortion of his body and the Knight-Azyros was back in the crypt, proud to make his landing with much more finesse than he had before.

'Your idea will work, Lord-Celestant,' Huld said as he saluted Makvar. He proffered his commander the end of the rope he carried.

'We will secure this length here,' Makvar said, handing it off to Brannok.

The Knight-Heraldor looked at the cord with some surprise. 'It is much hardier than I expected.'

Huld nodded. 'Dyre appears to be caught in the very moment Mannfred dragged it from the surface. There are carriages standing in the streets, stalls lining the market place, boxes and barrels stacked along the quays.' He looked towards the deathly shape of Nagash. 'Everything is just as it was, as though the population had withdrawn into their temples for some religious observation and will be back at any moment. It is disturbing to understand that they are gone.'

'It is their life-force that shapes the magic of Mannfred's redoubt,' Nagash told him. 'Without the extraction of their spirits, this place wouldn't exist. The most potent spells are those that demand the greatest sacrifice.'

'I wonder if Mannfred offered these people a choice,' Brannok said.

A cold snarl rose from Lord Harkdron. 'The cowherd doesn't ask the opinion of cattle. Mortals cannot be expected to understand the struggle against Chaos. They cannot look beyond their own brief existence, their own fears and pain to truly see the war for what it is.'

Vogun stepped between the two, silencing Brannok's retort. 'You are wrong, Harkdron,' he told the vampire. 'Perhaps you haven't seen the fire of defiance that can burn in a mortal heart because you've sought to quench it under a shroud of subservience. We have fought in lands throughout the Mortal Realms. I can attest to the valour of men, how they can be inspired to fight on even when the outcome is hopeless. How they will willingly sacrifice themselves if their belief in victory is great enough.'

Harkdron laughed. 'I will believe such courage exists when I see it for myself.' His laughter fell away when he felt Neferata's disapproving eyes on him. He sketched the merest apology to Vogun and withdrew to the recesses of the crypt.

Huld turned away from his observation of the exchange when Makvar asked a question of him. 'How far do you think the rope will reach?'

The Knight-Azyros leaned from the doorway, pointing across the graveyard to the tile roof of a stonemason's workshop. 'I will need to secure the first line to that building. From there I can draw a second over to the market square. In total it will need four separate lengths to reach the tower.' He paused, then gestured at the suspended line, explaining the phenomenon. His suggestion was that the Stormcasts could use the cord to pull themselves along, flipping themselves around once they were clear of the crypt so that they would be walking across the streets of Dyre rather than hanging above the cavern floor.

Makvar had another idea. Unbuckling his sword from his belt, he held the weapon across the cord, gripping its sheathed length by either end. He made a tentative sliding motion with it. A sigmarite blade was far stronger than mere steel. It would bear his weight without warping. Quickly, he explained his idea to Huld. 'We will make better time if we slide down the ropes. If anyone gets into trouble, he can flip around as you suggest and let himself drop to the street. A far better prospect than plummeting down into the cavern.'

Huld nodded, inspired by the wisdom of Makvar's plan. 'I will secure each end of the rope so that they describe an arch. It shouldn't be difficult to find appropriate heights to anchor them.'

'Admirable strategy,' Nagash said. He waved his skeletal claw towards Neferata. 'Assist my Mortarch and her attendants across. I shall await you in Nachtsreik.' Without another word of explanation, the Great Necromancer walked out from the crypt. Huld was stunned to see him glide across the cavern, a glowing nimbus of spectral energies billowing all around him. The skeletal morghast archai he had conjured into being leapt after their departed master, flying towards the distant tower on their tattered wings.

'His magic is such that he could have carried all of us across,' Huld heard Neferata say.

'Perhaps he needs to conserve his powers,' Makvar said. 'He has expressed concern that when we find Mannfred your fellow Mortarch may not be so agreeable as we might hope.'

Huld found that prospect far from cheering. After all that he had seen, the thought of any being which could provoke caution from the Great Necromancer was a daunting one.

The morbid energies of Nachtsreik spilled across Nagash, soaking into his skeletal frame and seeping into his malignant spirit. Truly the castle Mannfred had built for himself was a thing of impressive horror. The few details of its construction he had revealed to Makvar's knights were but a sampling of the atrocities that had given it shape. He could hear the shrieks of the souls bound into the foundations of the castle, envision the chained victims lying in their holes, watching as each stone block was lowered into the pits, listening to the screams of those who perished ahead of them.

Blood and terror, these were the true bricks and mortar of Mannfred's redoubt. The souls of all those entombed within and beneath its walls were the force that guarded his stronghold against conquest. Nagash could feel the necromantic energies dripping from the stones around him, rivulets of blood that pooled upon the floor before evaporating back into the aethyr. Apparitions winked in and out of his vision, struggling to manifest yet always sucked back into their stony prisons.

Far below, he could see the verminous skaven trying to batter their way through the walls. The bones and debris of the many armies that had besieged Nachtsreik before them lay scattered about the cavern. For an instant, Nagash was tempted to stir the rotten carcasses and set a legion of skeletons loose in the midst of the ratkin. The enmity he bore the skaven was almost primordial, cascading back into the Age of Myth and beyond. Massacring them would be a delight, but at the same time, a frivolity. The slaughter could contribute nothing to his greater design.

Nagash gazed out across the suspended streets of Dyre. The ingenuity of Makvar and his knights reminded the Great Necromancer of the great failing that settled into the bones of his creations. Even the highest of the undead lacked the inspiration and enthusiasm of mortal minds. The luxury of time dulled their sense of immediacy. They were slow to conceive new ideas, slower still to adopt them. Time after time, they would fall back upon the same strategies they had employed before, like corpse-moths locked into the same migration. Of all his disciples, only the Mortarchs had any real ability for innovation.

The Stormcasts slid down the lines, gliding across the cavern high above the swarming hordes of skaven. They displayed no hesitation, no fear of the hazards they courted as they made their way towards the tower. Whatever doubts they had were subsumed to the demands of their mission. It was a degree of obedience absent even in Neferata's vampire knights.

Truly, Sigmar had unlocked methods of resurrecting the life-force that were far different than those Nagash had crafted. The black art of necromancy devoured all it claimed. Something of the identity was lost, a spark of essence that refused to linger in the reanimated husk. Sigmar had found a way around that, a way to maintain the vibrancy of the soul while expunging all fear and doubt. Instilling an almost unshakable loyalty and obedience.

Nagash considered his past encounter with Stormcast Eternals. He had failed to learn all he needed on that occasion, but it had served to make him more aware of where his observation should be focussed. The might of the Stormcasts was something he had to quantify before he could properly fit them into his plan to purge his realm of Chaos.

The Great Necromancer turned from the window. Makvar would reach the tower soon. Then the search for Mannfred's sanctum would begin. Nagash was interested to see how quickly the Anvils could penetrate the shroud of illusion his errant Mortarch had woven around himself. Would they fall prey to the phantasms conjured by his necromancy, or would they be the first to uncover the vampire's secret refuge?

CHAPTER TWELVE

The moment Makvar climbed through the tower window, he was struck by a sense of lurking menace. Clambering down from the rope, descending the face of the tower, he had felt as though the very stones were trying to push him away, to send him hurtling to the floor of the cavern. When he looked at his gauntlets he found them slick with blood that evaporated before his eyes.

'The blood is the life, son of Sigmar,' Nagash's voice rose from the gloom within the tower. The fleshless Death God drew one of his claws across the wall, gore dripping from his bones. 'Mannfred has gone to great pains to invest his refuge with a life of its own.'

'I doubt the pain was his,' Makvar observed. He leaned back out the window, watching as Brannok began his own descent. 'Mannfred has worked great evil in other realms. It fell to our brethren, the Hallowed Knights, to bring an end to his infamies.'

'Forcing him back to this refuge,' Nagash stated. 'Your brothers are to be congratulated for sending my errant child back to me.' The Great Necromancer stepped towards Makvar, his morghast bodyguards following him across the barren room. 'A fearsome foe will be just as fearsome when set against the enemy. Bear that in mind, Lord-Celestant. Whatever discord there may be between Mannfred and the Stormcast Eternals, remember that he is no friend of Archaon.' He waved his staff at the dripping walls. 'The might of the Mortarch of Night will be a great asset in taking Gothizzar from the hosts of Chaos.'

'But will he see it that way?' Makvar wondered. 'As you've said, it was Stormcasts who drove him from the Realm of Beasts to seek refuge in Nachtsreik.'

Deep within the hollow sockets of Nagash's skull, a flash of fiery light briefly blazed. 'He will obey,' the Great Necromancer said. 'It is his choice what condition he is in when he submits, but he will submit in the end.'

Makvar turned away, helping Brannok as the Knight-Heraldor reached the window. He clapped the other Anvil on the shoulder as the warrior gained his footing. 'Help the others through,' he told Brannok. 'This fortress is immense and I suspect Mannfred will have concealed his sanctum with great care.' He looked back towards Nagash. 'Unless your powers can narrow our search.'

Nagash clapped the end of his staff against the floor. Ribbons of ghostly energy snaked away from the relic, crackling across the ground and shining up the walls. 'Mannfred has soaked this castle in so much necromatic power that its vibrations crash together in deafening discord. With time, I would of course be able to extract his presence from the clamour that surrounds him. I could follow the signature of his magic back to whatever hollow he's found for himself.' He thrust his skeletal finger towards Makvar. 'You have told me that your mission is urgent, that the God-King will need my legions soon. If that is the case then we shouldn't tarry over rituals and spells.'

'How are we to find Mannfred then?' Makvar asked.

The Great Necromancer gestured at the stone steps leading down from the tower. 'By defying the tricks and traps with which he guards himself. By using your remarkable abilities to uncover his hiding place.'

Makvar looked back to the window, watching as Brannok helped Neferata into the tower. The vampire queen looked alarmed by what she had overheard. Makvar wondered what kind of tricks and traps she anticipated her fellow Mortarch to have laid to ensnare those who trespassed within Nachtsreik.

Lord-Castellant Vogun was the first to descend the narrow steps which wound down through the tower. He held his warding lantern before him, its purifying rays burning through the cloying darkness ahead of him. The phantasmal blood dripping from the walls sizzled as the light struck it, vanishing in greasy puffs of smoke. Bodiless shapes woven from naught but shadows and malice fled from the Celestial glamour, their moans of pain and protest echoing through the dank corridors. Torn stalked just ahead of his master, snapping and snarling at the more tenacious apparitions before they could draw near to Vogun. The ghosts retreated from the gryph-hound, fading into the walls and floor before his beak and claws could strike them.

Makvar, Brannok and a retinue of Liberators followed after Vogun, each knight keeping his weapons at the ready. Despite the comforting glow of Vogun's lantern, the sense of hostility that had greeted them when they climbed into the tower had only intensified as they penetrated deeper into the fortress. The air was growing heavier and more stifling, endowed with an abominable moistness that crawled down into the lungs. The high ceiling and empty chambers of the tower conspired to create eerie echoes that refused to conform to any rhythm or rhyme but persisted in rolling back to the Stormcasts in the most distorted and disordered manner. The play of light and shadow evoked fleeting suggestions of motion at the edge of vision, the images vanishing when an Anvil turned his head to face them directly.

Neferata and her vampiric guards were behind Makvar's group, lingering just far enough back that they were spared the hurtful light of Vogun's lantern. While content to allow the Stormcasts to precede her and assume the risk of whatever traps Mannfred had set, she was less comfortable with Makvar's decision to split his knights into two groups. The second was following after the vampires, counting among them the Judicators and Knight-Azyros Huld. Makvar had claimed the deployment was to protect Neferata and Nagash should anything unexpected happen and they be forced to withdraw from the castle. Try as she might, she couldn't reconcile herself to the Lord-Celestant's claim. There was still the chance he expected treachery, and had set Huld and the others behind her so that the vampires would be caught between both groups of Stormcasts.

It was with a feeling of bitterness that Neferata reflected on Nagash's own decision to remain at the rear with his morghasts. Though she knew her own sorcery wasn't able to sift Mannfred's presence from the arcane signature he had left imprinted in the stones of Nachtsreik, she was suspicious about the Great Necromancer's claim that such a feat was beyond his abilities. The question that nagged at her was why he would make such a pretence. What did he hope to achieve by feigning weakness? Simply to conceal the extent of his power from Makvar? After his efforts at Mephitt, Neferata didn't think such humility had a part in his intentions. He had gone to great effort to impress upon the Anvils the extent of his might, vanquishing the Great Unclean One under their watchful gaze.

No, there was some deeper purpose bound into Nagash's decisions. A design that had so far eluded Neferata. It was certain that he was making use of the Stormcasts in some fashion, but towards what end? Did he truly intend to aid Sigmar's forces?

The vampire queen had given that question deep thought. The Realm of Death had suffered tremendously after Sigmar withdrew from Shyish. That Nagash had provoked the God-King's retreat was something she doubted the prideful Lord of Death would allow to mitigate his resentments. Still, even if Nagash didn't forgive an injury dealt to him, he was a cunning pragmatist. If he saw advantage to be gained by helping Sigmar, he would set upon such a course. Regardless of who he had to sacrifice to realise his ambition.

In that, Neferata reasoned, lay the chief difference between her master and Makvar. Makvar had a firm code of honour by which he abided. Duty and necessity might force him to bend that code, but he wouldn't break it. If she could set him into her debt just once, make him personally beholden to her, she felt she would have the key to the Lord-Celestant. If he felt obligation to her, she would enjoy the protection of his entire Warrior Chamber. She had once enticed the grandmaster of a warrior brotherhood into her grasp, gaining the use of his entire army as a result. The mortal had been possessed of notions of honour and loyalty, fealty and piety not so dis-similar to those the Stormcasts espoused. In the end, he had become her thrall all the same.

'Highness, do you think these storm-knights can truly find Mannfred's lair?' Harkdron's question had a hopeful note about it as he addressed Neferata.

'Beware of wishing failure upon our allies,' Neferata hissed at him. 'Now that Nagash has decided to collect his errant Mortarch, if the Stormcasts fail to find him, the duty is likely to fall to us.'

Harkdron drew himself up as he turned towards Neferata. 'I will protect you from any danger Mannfred could offer you.'

Neferata sneered at her consort. 'A fool is always certain of things he knows nothing about,' she hissed. 'If you knew Mannfred as I have known him, you would be wishing suc-cess to the storm-knights. Mannfred is a shrewd adversary, as relentless as he is cruel. Cross him, simply get in his way, Harkdron, and you'll have an enemy who will haunt you to the end of your days.'

Amala crouched within the frame of the window, her inhu-man eyes roving across the darkened chamber. She kept raising her paws to her face, sniffing at the blood oozing from the walls. Lascilion left the winged mutant to her loath-some ministrations. He had more vital things to concern him than the eldritch seepage of a deathmage's castle.

The Lord of Slaanesh pulled the plumed helm from his head, giving his leonine face its freedom. From between his fanged jaws, his forked tongue flashed forth, wriggling with ecstatic glee as it drew the scent of Neferata from the dank air. The object of his obsession had been here, and recently. There were other smells as well, but these were insignificant to him beside that of the vampire queen. Once more she was within his reach!

'Focus upon the task Thagmok has set you.' The warning rose from outside the window. Amala leapt down from her perch, stalking into the room as the feathered figure of Molchinte appeared outside. The sorceress hovered in the air, her feet sunk into the slimy back of an ovoid creature, a daemon of Tzeentch she had summoned to follow Lascilion into the tower. Beyond her, also supported upon disc-shaped daemons, were the other Chaos champions the Bloodking had sent to destroy the lightning-men.

Lascilion's face curled in an expression of distaste. Perhaps, under other circumstances, he would enjoy the novelty of Molchinte pawing through his mind. Now, however, he found it to be an abominable violation. Even if it was doomed, his dream of claiming Neferata for his own was still the force that drove him on.

'The lightning-men,' Molchinte demanded as she stepped into the tower, wrenching her feet from the limpid flesh of the daemon. The weird disc broke apart in a burst of lights as soon as she was quit of it. 'Were they here? Were their leaders here?'

'Yes,' Lascilion told her. 'Not long past either. There is no mistaking the sting of their scent.' His gaze strayed from the sorceress to the Chaos champions as they stepped through the window. Just as Molchinte's daemon steed had done, the fleshy discs broke apart the moment their riders were clear of them. Alghor Wormsword and Orbleth the Despised paid small attention to their surroundings, unaffected by the sinister atmosphere and the dripping walls. Vaangoth the semi-daemon couldn't keep his furry hands from the gory walls, dragging them across the surfaces before wiping the blood across his own dripping armour. Lascilion thought he saw a ripple pass through the bloodied plates each time he did so.

'Then let us be about our task,' Molchinte said. She stared about the room, eyes wide with alarm. More attuned to magic than her companions, she could feel the magnitude of necromantic energy flowing through the fortress. Lascilion decided it couldn't hurt him to make the sorceress still more uneasy.

'They aren't alone,' the warlord said. 'I picked out other scents as well. The smell of vampires and reanimated bones.' A cold smile played across his face. 'And something more. Something powerful. Perhaps another of the Mortarchs.'

Molchinte gave that information a good deal of thought. The prospect of confronting one Mortarch and some lightning-men had been imposing enough. The idea of facing two of the powerful undead lords was fearsome. It took her only a moment to decide it wasn't as frightful as defying the commands of Thagmok... or displeasing Archaon.

'If they are colluding with two of the Mortarchs, then our task is even more vital,' she said. 'We must strike down these lightning-men.' Her eyes glittered as she gave Lascilion a stern look. 'Could you tell how many lightning-men were with them?'

'Less than I encountered in Nulahmia,' Lascilion conceded. 'A dozen, perhaps more. Their smell is strange to me, so it is difficult to be certain.'

The sorceress was silent for a moment. Then, without warning, she spun around. A blade erupted from beneath the folds of her feathered cloak, a fat knife etched with cabalistic sigils. Before Amala could react, the knife was slashing across the mutant's throat, sending a gout of her foul blood spraying across the haunted walls. Molchinte crouched over the twitching body, sawing her knife across the back of the neck. Soon, she had Amala's head severed from the spine.

Much as it pleased him to see the treacherous mutant dispatched, the suddenness of her murder alarmed Lascilion. He and the other champions held their weapons ready to repulse the murderous witch, but Molchinte made no move towards them. Instead, she was dipping her finger in Amala's blood and drawing strange symbols across the mutant's dead eyes. A scratchy incantation rose from the sorceress, an invocation drawn from the squawks of birds and the yaps of dogs more than anything that resembled intelligent speech. As she worked her conjuration, a weird purple light shone from behind Amala's eyes.

'A shield of oblivion,' Molchinte explained as she held the head before her. 'A gift from Tzeentch. Its magic will hide us from our prey.' A vicious laugh twisted her lips. 'At least until we are ready to strike.' She motioned to her remaining companions with the hand that yet held her dripping knife. 'Draw near to me or its power cannot help you.' She laughed anew when she noted their hesitation. 'We need only one shield. Be thankful the mutant was the least valuable among you.'

Still keeping hold of Pain's hilt, Lascilion approached Molchinte. The fact he could still see the sorceress seemed to belie the efficacy of her murderous spell, but when he drew close to her, he felt a shock run through him. As Alghor and Orbleth joined them, he could see the same expression of surprise and discomfort pass through their misshapen features. Certainly Molchinte had surrounded herself with some sort of magic.

'Vaangoth!' Molchinte snapped at the bestial champion of Khorne. 'There is no time to waste.'

The semi-daemon had turned back to the dripping wall, once again raking his hand through the gore and then anointing his armour with it. He turned his brutish face towards Molchinte. 'Go,' he snarled. 'I follow.' Offering no explanation, he continued to paw at the ghostly blood oozing from the walls.

'How he find us when we invisible?' Alghor asked.

'He won't,' Molchinte snapped at the Nurglesque champion. Without further delay, she stabbed the knife into Amala's forehead. At once, the air around the sorceress and her companions took on a shimmering, hazy quality.

Lascilion smiled as he drew his helm back over his head. He had been mistaken to doubt Molchinte's magic. If the spell performed as she claimed it would, they would be able to strike at the lightning-men with complete surprise.

What Lascilion had to do now was figure a way to exploit that magic to achieve his own purpose. It had to be the favour of Slaanesh that Neferata was being offered to him once more.

'Look out!'

The cry sounded from Brannok as the Knight-Heraldor threw himself towards Makvar. The Lord-Celestant and his rescuer pitched forwards, spilling into the chamber they had been about to enter. The doorway through which they had passed was no more, sealed by the massive stone block that had come slamming down from the arch above it.

Makvar had to give a grudging degree of respect to Mann-fred's inventiveness. The trap had been deliberately calibrated to let the first few intruders pass before activating. Behind the doorway, he could hear the anxious shouts of concern from the other Stormcasts. Vogun and Torn, who had passed through moments before, turned in alarm at the sound.

Brannok rolled to face the block. He reached for his battle-horn, then hesitated. He could use the horn's magic to shatter the block, but he didn't know what else might be caught in the thunderblast.

'Back!' Makvar shouted. At the same time, he seized hold of Brannok's arm and dragged the warrior with him deeper into the room.

Lying against the floor, Makvar had heard a faint sound, like sand running from an hourglass. It was all the warning there was. Fortunately, it was all the warning he needed. Glancing back at where they had been sprawled on the ground, he now saw a yawning pit. He had been wrong about Mannfred being inventive – he was a fiend. A pit timed to open shortly after the block fell, catching whoever went hurrying back to aid those caught beneath the crushing stone.

Snarls of rage rose from the corridor outside. Makvar at once guessed its meaning. Not content to catch those inside the room, Mannfred had set a second pit to open in the hall outside as well.

'Quiet!' Makvar called out. 'We are unharmed on this side. How have you fared on that side?'

A grim voice called back to him. 'Brothers Xi and Pericles fell. The bottom of the hole was lined with stakes. Their spirits have returned to Sigmar.'

Makvar clenched his fist in silent fury. To lose his knights in battle was hard enough, but at least there was honour and dignity in such defeat. For some of his Anvils to be snatched away through such deceitful enterprise was obscene. That the trap had been laid by a monster they sought to draw into alliance with Sigmar only made it still more enraging.

'I find myself hoping Mannfred won't submit to Nagash,' Brannok said. His fingers closed around the hilt of his sword. 'It will be a pleasure breaking him.'

'Only if you find him before I do,' Vogun said. Torn loped

along at his side, feathers ruffled as he sniffed the mouldy air. Cautiously the Lord-Castellant came towards them, tapping the butt of his halberd against the floor to verify its solidity.

'I doubt any of the Mortarch's snares can be so easily uncovered,' Makvar said. He looked around the chamber. It looked to be some sort of trophy room, grisly displays standing in dusty silence upon wooden platforms. Some of the stuffed creatures in the exhibition were beasts, others, hideously, had once been men. Still a third category represented a ghoulish hybrid of human and animal anatomy, pieces of mummified flesh and bleached bone that Makvar found it impossible to accept could ever have survived in such a state. Even compared to the mutations of Chaos, these things were blasphemies.

'The exit is across from us!' Brannok shouted, then drew up short, shaking his head as he found the doorway was no longer where he thought it had been. He turned about in frustration, only to spot the doorway now on his left.

Makvar appreciated Brannok's confusion. Since descending the tower stair, the Stormcasts and their companions had been beset by a bewildering maze of halls and chambers, galleries and vaults. No sane mind could have conceived of such a castle, with stairs that climbed up to blank walls, windows that stared into chimney flues, doors that opened upon rooms sunk several feet below their threshold. More unsettling was the impression that the architecture shifted itself around when it wasn't being observed. It was an idea so absurd that Makvar tried to dismiss it as soon as it suggested itself to him. Then he remembered Nagash's warning that Nachtsreik had been fashioned from blood and bone, endowed with its own nightmarish vitality by Mannfred.

Makvar shook his head. He turned about, looking back

towards the enormous stone that had so nearly crushed them. 'Wherever it is, we'll go nowhere unless we rejoin our comrades.'

Even as he spoke the words, Makvar was interrupted by the frenzied barking of Torn. The gryph-hound was glowering at the nearest of the trophies, a hulking mass of bones that looked like a troggoth with the skull of a crocodile fitted to its vertebrae. The animal backed away from the thing slowly, feathers ruffled and hackles raised. An instant later, the undead creature turned its saurian head around, staring at the Anvils with its empty eyes.

Vogun stepped towards the thing, brandishing the warding lantern. The light, however, did nothing to repulse the animated horror. With a creaking step, it dropped down from the wooden platform. Across the room, other trophies could be seen doing the same. Even the most twisted of the creatures, those horrible amalgams of man and animal, had been infused with a new vitality.

'We are the Anvil...' Makvar told his comrades as they readied themselves for the monstrous pack. They would make a good accounting of themselves, but he had no illusions about their chances against such odds.

Suddenly, a flight of crackling arrows seared across the room. The skeletal automatons shattered as shafts of lightning seared into their decayed frames. Before the rest of the gruesome host could advance, the icy chill of sorcery engulfed them. 'Dust you are, to dust return!' Neferata's voice rang out. The Mortarch's potent magic at once wrought havoc upon the shambling monsters. Bones crumbled to powder, shrivelled flesh fell away like dead leaves. One after another, the creatures collapsed into piles of funereal decay.

Advancing into the room were Neferata and her entourage,

along with the Stormcasts Makvar had left with Huld. They emerged from a gash in the wall, an opening Makvar hadn't seen before. He shook his head. Of course it was some secret door, allowing ingress without disturbing the traps Mannfred had set. Or had it? Perhaps opening the hidden door had provoked the animation of the Mortarch's trophies.

Neferata walked towards Makvar, though her gaze kept shifting back to the demolished trophies. Even in their current state of dissolution, she appeared wary of them. Given her knowledge of necromancy, Makvar decided that if she was concerned then he should be as well.

'Huld!' he called to the Knight-Azyros. Makvar pointed to the heaps of dust. 'Bring your beacon to bear upon that carrion. If there is any arcane life lingering in them, burn it away.'

Neferata turned away as Huld unshielded his celestial beacon and set its rays across the demolished skeletons. 'I am uncertain if even that will work,' she told Makvar. 'At least in this place. Everything here has been perverted by Mannfred's machinations. It is more than natural laws he defies in this place, but the rules which govern even the darkest magic.' She pointed over her shoulder at the shattered skeletons. 'That menagerie was his creation. He considers himself an artist in his way. Always seeking some new way to display his mastery of the black arts.'

The image of the vampire count cobbling together those monstrosities was a repugnant one. Makvar only prayed Mannfred's 'materials' had been dead when he exploited them for his macabre art.

'Thank you for your timely assistance, my lady,' Makvar told Neferata. 'Was it you who found the hidden entrance?'

Neferata nodded. 'The moment the block fell and the pit opened, I knew there would be another way in.' She frowned, a vengeful gleam sneaking into her eyes. 'I underestimated Mannfred's cunning, however. I didn't expect even his private door to be trapped. I fear it was opening that door which set his menagerie in motion.'

Makvar mulled over her words. 'I was loath to suggest it before, but you have some insight into the mind of your fellow Mortarch. Such knowledge could spare us the attention of more traps. If I were to send Vogun back to the main body, would you join me in the vanguard? I will try to mitigate whatever dangers such exposure presents to you.'

A brief smile flickered on Neferata's face. 'You must keep Vogun ahead of you,' she said. 'Without his light, the spirits of this place would beset you at every turn. It is their repulsion of the light that sends them fleeing before us.' She threw back her head, tossing her dark hair in a regal flourish. 'I will endure my own repugnance of the light,' she declared. 'My discomfort cannot be measured against the dangers that threaten your knights.'

Makvar bowed and took her hand in his. 'Again, you have my gratitude. I am in your debt.'

'It is a strange thing,' Neferata said, 'to have an Anvil of the Heldenhammer indebted to me.'

The fortress of Nachtsreik was proving as sinister and forbidding as Nagash had expected it to be. The illusions Mannfred had woven into the castle, the ghostly vitality that endowed every brick and stone with a malicious presence, the murderous traps that lay in wait for the unwary – all of these things combined into a vicious gauntlet to test any warrior. It was a creation the Mortarch could be proud of. Knowing the nature of Mannfred, that pride would be dressed in a robe of arrogance and perfumed with deceit.

Nagash followed behind the Stormcasts as Neferata led them through the treacherous environs of Mannfred's refuge. It was a concession he was willing to indulge. Leaving the Anvils to their own devices had revealed much to him, but observing their interactions with the vampire queen was just as instructive. By it, he was able to gauge the earnestness of their overtures of alliance. The more he watched them, the more he came to appreciate that they had no facility for duplicity. Their faith in the God-King and their devotion to their mission were qualities each of them held to be inviolate. It was in regards to their own person and needs that they were given to compromise. Each of them was subsumed to the demands of his Warrior Chamber.

Even Knight-Heraldor Brannok, the Anvil with the most misgivings about the nature of their mission, had set himself at risk to rescue Makvar. Certainly Brannok had to know that without Makvar, their embassy was likely to fail, and he had hurled himself into danger without an instant of hesitation.

Such selflessness was to be expected from creatures like his morghast archai, beings without any true individuality or essence of their own. Nagash could command legions of such undead to march into the maw of a volcano and there would be no murmur of protest. Even the thought of disobedience was impossible for them.

Nagash was coming to believe that Sigmar's Stormcasts were instilled with an equal degree of obedience. Yet it wasn't compulsion that forced them to obey. They did so willingly, indeed, they drew a sense of honour from their unquestioning fealty. Brannok, steadfast and selfless as any of his comrades, was unsettled by the very virtue of his doubts.

The Great Necromancer listened to Neferata conferring with Makvar in Mannfred's gallery. The vampire queen's ambitions were almost as interesting as the Stormcasts themselves, and possibly of equal value to him. At least, once he set all the pieces in play.

Nagash stared into the gems set into the head of his staff. Images of the shifting vaults and halls of Nachtsreik flowed within the stones. His gaze penetrated the maze, piercing the mirages and illusions Mannfred had evoked to conceal himself. He saw the thousand snares by which the Mortarch thought to keep himself safe – the deadfalls and firetraps that lay under floors and within walls, hidden garrisons of deadwalkers and bone warriors, the cellars where still mightier guards lurked. The enormity of Mannfred's defences could stave off armies even if they pierced the morbid walls. For a handful of Stormcasts, the prospect of finding the vampire's secret tomb would border on the miraculous.

A miracle was just what Nagash would bestow upon his unsuspecting allies. As Lord of Death, there were no secrets in Shyish that could hide from him. It was a reality his Mortarchs always strove to deny, no matter how many times they were forced to re-learn the lesson.

Touching one of his claws to a huge bloodstone, Nagash conjured the image of Neferata in the crimson gem. Holding the staff close to his fleshless face, he began to whisper to the image, using great caution and subtlety as he worked his magic.

When Nagash was finished, Neferata wouldn't be aware that she wasn't guiding Makvar to Mannfred's tomb on her own. Of course, there would be a few traps in the way, a few hazards and illusions to beset the Stormcasts. If the path was too clear, someone might get suspicious.

The time for suspicions would be after Mannfred joined them.

* * *

The stench of evil rose from the floor, crawling across the Stormcasts as they marched into the crypt. The caskets which lined the walls now stood empty, their inhabitants having risen in a mass of rotting flesh and decayed organs. Hundreds strong, it had taken Makvar and his comrades some time to destroy the revenants, even with the necromancy of Neferata keeping the things from rising again. Huld and Vogun shone their lights upon the carcasses, striving to banish whatever fell influence yet lingered within them.

Makvar glowered at the charnel house that stretched away as far as he could see. The ceiling above was vaulted, rising far into the darkness, supported upon pillars of fused bones that dripped with the same spectral blood they had encountered in the tower and throughout much of the castle. There was something about the way the disembodied gore slithered along the bones that offended him, some quality about the sight that rendered it more obscene than everything else around it.

'Mannfred's lair is here,' Neferata declared. The vampire queen and her followers advanced towards a gruesome pillar. At first, Makvar thought it was simply their unholy hunger that attracted them, but then he noticed that sigils briefly flared upon the bleached surface of the bones whenever the Mortarch reached towards them. Each time the wards appeared she staggered back, a quiver of pain crossing her features.

After their arduous trek through the seemingly unending vaults and corridors of Mannfred's fortress, Makvar was almost reluctant to hope they had come to the end of their search. Four more Stormcasts had been claimed by Mannfred's traps and guards, as well as one of the blood knights who attended Neferata, yet never had there been any sign they were making progress. Now it was almost too much to believe the ordeal could be at an end.

'Anvils of the Heldenhammer!' Makvar called his warriors. 'To me!' While his knights rallied to him, Makvar approached the pillar. The reek of evil, if anything, was more pronounced around the grisly structure.

'My lady, if you would,' Makvar said, waving Neferata away from the pillar.

Harkdron rounded on the Lord-Celestant. 'Do you presume to give orders to the Queen of Nulahmia?' he demanded, oblivious to how empty the title had become.

'No,' Makvar told the vampire. He pointed his sword at the bleeding pillar. 'I intend to bring that abomination down.' He turned from Harkdron and addressed his Stormcasts. 'Set the light celestial upon this thing,' he told Huld and Vogun. 'Judicators, keep your bows ready. Brannok… bring it down.'

As it had above, so the spectral blood again reacted to the light of Azyr, steaming away in puffs of greasy vapour. While the purifying light denuded the pillar of its cascading gore, Knight-Heraldor Brannok stepped away from his comrades. Drawing the gilded battle-horn from his belt, he raised the instrument to his lips.

The note that sounded from the horn wasn't a simple battlefield signal or a rallying cry. It was a thunderous peal, a tremulous note that slammed into the pillar with pulverising violence. Such necromantic power as had saturated the pillar with its evil resilience now shattered as slivers of bone exploded across the crypt. The thunderblast cracked the base of the structure, splitting it in half and sending both monolithic sections smashing to the floor in a cloud of dust.

Gradually, as the dust dissipated, the Stormcasts could see the gaping hole exposed by Brannok's demolition of the pillar.

A flight of marble steps descended into the darkness. Instead of banishing the aura of evil that clung to the crypt, destroying the pillar had simply intensified it.

The source of the malefic energy was somewhere in the depths below.

CHAPTER THIRTEEN

The darkness closed around Lord-Celestant Makvar like the coils of some vast and monstrous serpent. Descending the steps wasn't unlike plunging into deep waters, the pressure tightening around his body, crushing the breath in his chest. Steadily mounting, growing more burdensome the further he went, it was only his faith in Sigmar and the trust placed in him by the God-King that gave Makvar the strength to persist.

He knew the weight that dragged at him wasn't a physical manifestation, but the repulsion Makvar's noble soul felt for the miasma of evil that saturated the sunken tomb. The cloying, violating taint of the place wrapped itself about him, striving to defile his purity and righteousness with its spectral blight. He felt like an open flame exposed to a torrential downpour, his ardour sputtering as the rain strove to quench his fire.

Makvar forced himself onward, reciting canticles and

orisons that described the holy might of Sigmar and the beneficence he extended to those who persevered in his name. Foot by foot, step by step, the warrior walked down into the secret refuge of Mannfred von Carstein, the infernal Mortarch of Night.

The tomb was prodigious in its dimensions, a long hall with an arching ceiling from which the wizened husks of immense bats were suspended. Gigantic statues lined the walls, sandstone idols hoary with age, jewels gleaming in the eyes of each animal-headed sculpture. Gothic columns stretched up from the tiled floor, iron sconces bolted to their sides. It was from these fixtures that a pallid blue light shone across the tomb, a sickly glow that somehow evoked images of midnight graveyards and prowling wolves.

At the very centre of the chamber, resting upon a raised dais, was a stone sepulchre, its sides richly sculpted with martial scenes. An ancient coat of arms, etched in gold, stood out amidst the carvings, its polished sheen gleaming in the eerie light. Surrounding the sepulchre, standing atop hexagonal pedestals, were an array of glassy black stones. Makvar could feel the nether-energy that throbbed within each of the stones, see the phantasmal forces trapped within their curiously angled facets. Streamers of ghostly power crawled down each pedestal before slithering up the sides of the sepulchre.

The sense of pressure and resistance against him swelled as Makvar approached the sepulchre. The effort to take each step became ever more difficult, like being back in the Mirefells and slogging through its bogs. He could understand how this forbidding atmosphere would ward off less determined intruders. Makvar, however, wouldn't retreat. The vampire Mortarch had much to learn about the resilience of the Stormcasts.

While Makvar had been the first to descend into Mann-fred's lair, he wasn't alone. The other Anvils had followed him, with the exception of a retinue of Judicators standing guard above. Neferata and her retainers had come along as well, the vampire queen's expression unsettled by the for-bidding environment in which she found herself. Makvar imagined that she knew far better than he did the amount of arcane power her fellow Mortarch had expended to pro-tect this tomb. Also, she might be discomfited by the fact that her master Nagash had once again sent her forward while he lingered behind. The Great Necromancer was nothing if not cautious. The devious traps which infested Nachtsreik more than justified such caution.

Here, in the very heart of his stronghold, Makvar was cer-tain that Mannfred would have surrounded himself with his most fiendish snares. Yet as he probed ahead, no phys-ical menace presented itself, only the unseen aura of threat that pressed in around him. All such nebulous belligerence served to accomplish was to make him still more determined to reach the sepulchre.

'Lord Makvar!' Neferata finally called out to him. 'Go no further! Stop where you are!'

It was with a strange reluctance that Makvar turned his head to stare back at the steps. He could see Neferata and her vampires standing there, but without exception, the other Stormcasts had drawn ahead of them, ranged across the floor of the tomb as they marched towards the sepulchre. Almost without volition, he found himself raising his foot to continue his advance. Firmly he stamped his boot back down upon the floor. It was an effort to fend off the urge to go onwards. He knew it was more than his own determination that was drawing him towards his objective.

'Anvils!' Makvar shouted. 'Stand fast!' He could hear the rattle of sigmarite plate as his knights strove to obey his command. Under normal conditions, such an order would have been implemented instantly, but now his warriors were uncharacteristically reluctant to arrest their advance.

A new appreciation for the subtlety of Mannfred's sorcery filled Makvar. The Mortarch had indeed anticipated the intrusion of Stormcasts into his sanctum... and he had prepared accordingly. The frightful aura, the atmosphere of brooding evil – these were manifestations to simply distract the Anvils from a more insidious influence. Some eldritch force that sought out their courage not to fend them off, but to draw them in. A fiendish beacon to lure them to the doom von Carstein had devised for all who threatened his repose.

Makvar glowered at the sepulchre and the sinister stones that surrounded it. He still couldn't see the danger that waited for them, but he was certain it was there. Fortunately, the Anvils had a beacon of their own.

Makvar turned around, gesturing to Neferata. 'My lady, your warning is timely. It is best, however, if you withdraw and await us above. I fear the means to oppose Mannfred's sorcery would be hurtful for you.' He waited while the vampires retreated back up to the crypt before gesturing to Huld. 'Ascend, brother,' he told the Knight-Azyros, then pointed at the sepulchre. 'Shine the light of your celestial beacon there. We will see if the purity of Azyr can overcome the spells which seek to entrap us.'

Spreading his wings, Huld flew up into the murky roof of the tomb, wheeling around the carcasses of the enormous bats dangling from the ceiling. Holding forth his lamp, he threw open its shutter and directed its holy light against the sepulchre. At once, a foul, penetrating odour filled the chamber, the stink of singed hair and burning flesh. Along with the reek came a cacophony of wailing moans, disembodied shrieks of agony that shivered through the room.

As the celestial beacon's light purged the tomb of its malignant aura, Makvar could see the sepulchre changing. The strands of deathly energy trailing into it from the surrounding pedestals drew back into the black stones, reminding him of a child wrenching its hand away from a fire. A strange discolouration began to creep through the sepulchre, grey vines of ghost-rot that snaked through the carvings, causing them to split and fragment. The weird corrosion grew more pronounced with every heartbeat, soon denuding the sepulchre of its ornamentation, the scenes of war and slaughter reduced to piles of dust strewn about the dais.

Finally, with a shuddering groan, the coat of arms fell, clattering across the floor. The sound reverberated through the tomb with supernatural intensity. The Stormcasts tightened their hold upon their weapons as the dolorous crash pounded against their ears.

Makvar was the first to advance, motioning for his Anvils to stand back but keep themselves at the ready. Before him, the sepulchre continued to crumble, disintegrating as though millennia of decay had suddenly been poured into it. At the back of his mind, he wondered if this was the fate that should have taken them if they hadn't broken Mannfred's spell. Perhaps Huld's beacon had turned the magic against itself.

A final shiver saw the unadorned sepulchre collapse. Its dissolution exposed its contents. An octagonal coffin fashioned from some impossibly dark wood now rested upon the dais, the same coat of arms nailed to its sides. Scarlet cloth woven from the pungent silk of the corpse-moth lined the lidless coffin's interior, exuding a sickly sweet aroma of decay. Shining with an oily glitter, a haze hung about the coffin, some last magical ward that was strong enough even to oppose the unleashed fury of the trap that had consumed the sepulchre itself.

Disgust rose up within him as Makvar gazed upon the creature lying inside the coffin. Wearing armour that seemed to consume the light that struck it, the body of Mannfred was twisted with a monstrousness more vile than that of subhuman gors and the diseased mutations of Chaos. The abominations of the enemy were savage and unrefined, caprices of the Dark Gods. The horror that was the Mortarch of Night had been deliberately fashioned into its repulsive form. The long, lean hands with their predatory claws. The pale, clammy skin so devoid of health and vitality. The grisly countenance itself with its bare pate and sharp nose, close-set eyes and narrow mouth, high cheekbones that strained against the withered flesh, and bulbous nodules of bone protruding from the forehead.

The vampire's eyes were open, gleaming like embers from within his ghoulish visage. A vicious smile drew pale lips away from long fangs. Around Mannfred's body, several glassy rocks rested on the silk lining, small chips cut from the same stones resting on the pedestals. Fingers of necrotic energy extruded themselves from the rocks to vanish into the Mortarch's body.

Just as it had sent the emanations from the larger stones retreating back into the glassy rock, so did Huld's celestial beacon drive the ribbons of spectral force back into the stones surrounding the vampire. The reaction was immediate. Mannfred's smouldering eyes blazed with a fearful intensity and the coffin around him exploded into a hail of wooden splinters. The slivers flew at the Stormcasts with murderous ferocity, uncannily darting at the gaps in their armour. Makvar felt one tear into his face, missing his eye by a hairsbreadth. The other Anvils were similarly afflicted by the coffin's explosion. Huld was thrown back, smashing against the roof of the tomb. The rays of his beacon were diverted, no longer fixed upon the dais.

'So the storm-men have hunted me to my lair?' Mannfred rose from the debris of his coffin, his body alight with necromantic power. The vampire glowered at the reeling Stormcasts. 'You will rue the misfortune that brought you to this impasse. But you will not regret for long.' Stretching forth his hand, the Mortarch expended the merest portion of the fell magic that saturated him.

All across the tomb, things long dead answered the command of Mannfred. From the bases of the inhuman idols that lined the tomb, hulking monsters emerged, smashing their way out from hidden vaults. Crafted from both stone and bone, the monsters lurched towards the Stormcasts with immense khopesh swords. Secret graves beneath the floor disgorged malodorous skeletons, their armour clinging to them in strips of blackened decay. The awakened wights stole towards the intruders in a march of menacing silence. On the ceiling, the desiccated bats shrieked into hideous life. They flew after Huld, pursuing the Knight-Azyros through the tomb, preventing him from focusing the purging rays of his beacon. Out from the walls themselves a cloud of screaming apparitions manifested. The bodiless spirits surged around Vogun, striving to drown out the glow of his own warding lantern, heedless that they were being vaporised by his light.

Makvar knew it would do no good to tell Mannfred that the Anvils had violated his sanctum not as foes but as friends.

Feeling cornered and pursued, the vampire wouldn't listen. Not while there was any fight left in him.

The Lord-Celestant blinked away the blood dripping into his eye and brought his blade scything through the leg of the hawk-headed monster stalking towards him. Electricity crackled about his sword as he hewed through the obscene amalgam of bone and stone. Makvar swung again, tearing through the creature's neck and sending its skull spinning into the darkness. Stubborn vitality lingered in the beast and it struck at him with one of its stony hands. Makvar fended off the stricken creature's attack with a parry that hewed fingers from its fist. Unbalanced, the monster crashed to the floor, yet even then, its tenacious urge to kill caused it to crawl towards him.

All across the tomb, the other Stormcasts found themselves similarly beset by undead that simply refused to be destroyed. Disembodied arms clung to ebon armour, raking at the sigmarite plates as they tried to reach the warrior within. Huge bats fell in smouldering cascades as Huld's beacon savaged their unnatural flesh, searing away their leathery wings, but the crippled beasts struggled to return to the attack by trying to drag their mangled bodies up the walls. Vogun stood in a pool of steaming ectoplasm, the residue of the waves of spirits vanquished by his warding lantern, and still more of the spectres came flying at him. Brannok stood atop the butchered debris of a dog-headed giant, driving his sword again and again into the brute in an effort to end its ability to fight.

The source of the fearsome persistence of the undead lay within the being who had conjured them from the shadows. Mannfred von Carstein exerted his infernal magic, evoking a grisly entity from the ghastly energies that saturated his sanctum. Billowing shadows spilled from the black stones that surrounded the vampire's sepulchre, converging in a mass of darkness. From the darkness a monstrous creature prostrated itself before the Mortarch. It was a beast with obsidian claws, a bat-like head and long, blade-tipped tail. Like the dread abyssals that served Neferata and Arkhan, the morbid energies of enslaved spirits coursed through the monster's skeletal body, though those bound into Mannfred's steed burned with a hellish crimson light and worked their fleshless jaws in silent screams of endless agony.

Mannfred wrapped his arm about the stony neck of his steed and swung himself up onto the creature's back. Ashigaroth, Gorger of the Meek, reared back as its master mounted it, huge claws pawing at the air. Ghostly wisps flew about the abyssal, swiftly growing from simple glowing orbs into shrieking phantoms that shot out across the sanctum to set upon the Stormcasts. The vampire howled in fury when he saw the first of the ghosts steam away as they were caught in the rays of Vogun's warding lantern. Vindictively, he exerted his powers, summoning more of the spirits from the very walls, driving them to overwhelm the Anvils and suffocate them in a veritable fog of death.

Leaping over the dismembered bulk of his stony attacker, Makvar rushed towards Ashigaroth. As he ran, the Lord-Celestant spun the weighted length of his warcloak, hurling a shower of crackling sigmarite hammers at the abyssal steed and the Mortarch riding it. The electrical assault sizzled against the shield of protective magic Mannfred had woven around himself, but he had had no time to similarly protect Ashigaroth. The monster shrieked in distress as chips of obsidian flew from its grisly frame and crimson spectres were extinguished by the flying hammers. For an instant, Mannfred's attention was diverted from the Anvils as he quieted his mount.

Makvar lunged towards the Mortarch as he tried to recover. His runeblade crackled with violence as he brought it sweeping up at the vampire. The sword glanced from Mannfred's enchanted plate, an icy shiver flowing through the sigmarite tang as the armour's foul energies pulsed into Makvar's arm. The Stormcast fought the sensation and thrust his weapon at his foe's breast. This time, the blow was fended off not by the ensorcelled armour that guarded the Mortarch but by the murderous length of the vampire's own sword, the cursed blade Gheistvor.

'You dare to touch me, storm-spawn!' Mannfred snarled. Ashigaroth spun about, striking out with a claw that flung Makvar away from its master, throwing the Lord-Celestant back as though he were a child. Gnashing his fangs, von Carstein charged his steed at his reeling foe. Narrowly, Makvar brought his runeblade up in time to catch the downward sweep of Gheistvor. The impact of the thwarted strike knocked him to his knees.

Makvar could hear some of the other Anvils cry out in alarm, redoubling their efforts to fight through Mannfred's spectral host to relieve their beleaguered leader. The vampire reacted to their alarm by conjuring still more spirits from the walls, then returned his attention to the Lord-Celestant. The Mortarch glared down at him, his face twisting into an expression of feral exuberance. The vampire took great delight in butchering the helpless.

'Tell Sigmar to send better hunters if he would contest my power,' Mannfred jeered as he slammed his foot into Makvar's chest, spilling the Lord-Celestant onto the floor. Like a huge wolf, Ashigaroth pounced towards the Stormcast, eager to feed upon helpless prey. Makvar rolled aside, the claws of Ashigaroth raking sparks from the ground as they scraped across the tiles. Before Mannfred or his steed could react, Makvar rolled back, catching Ashigaroth's claw a resounding blow with his runeblade. Lightning crackled through the undead beast, causing it to jounce back in a fit of agitation. The vampire's body likewise crackled with searing energy, his magic armour unable to fend off the reverberations flowing into him from his mount.

With a howl of outrage, Mannfred jumped from Ashigaroth's back and fell upon Makvar. The vampire's boot smashed down upon the knight's arm, pinning it and the runeblade it held against the floor. His other foot came kicking into the Stormcast's face with such force that a mortal man's neck would have snapped like a twig. As it was, the mask of Makvar's helm was dented by the impact, breaking teeth as it was driven back into his jaw.

Before Mannfred could attack again, the brilliance of Huld's beacon shone down upon him. The vampire flinched as the purifying light struck him, but it wasn't the light that hurt him. Glaring down at Makvar, his face became livid with rage as he realised what had happened. Just as the Mortarch had laid a trap that would exploit the qualities of his enemies, so Makvar had baited his own pride and arrogance. In provoking Mannfred's ire, he had distracted him from the larger fight raging around them. The enhanced ferocity and stamina he had been directing into his undead minions had relaxed, allowing the other Stormcasts respite from the vampire's spirit hosts.

Vengefully, Mannfred stretched forth his hand. Makvar could feel the necromantic power leaching into him, slithering under his armour to sap the life from him. If the vampire was to know defeat, then he would at least claim Makvar before he fell.

Before darkness could close around Makvar, a searing voice hissed through the tomb. 'The man is mine.'

The pressure upon Makvar's arm vanished as Mannfred was thrown back, cast aside by some unseen force. The draining magic that had plagued the Lord-Celestant's veins dissipated, exorcised from him with such abruptness that the rush of his restored vitality was like fire raging within his flesh. The sounds of battle within the tomb fell silent.

It wasn't hate but fear that now gripped Mannfred's features when Makvar looked at the vampire. He didn't need to guess why. He could feel the awesome presence that descended into the sanctum, the orchestrator of the words that had brought him reprieve from a sorcerous death.

Aglow with a power that made even Mannfred's exalted strength pathetic in comparison, Nagash walked towards his errant Mortarch.

The Great Necromancer could feel the terror that pounded inside Mannfred's chest. The Mortarch of Night had gambled much on his excursion into the Realm of Beasts. He had thought he could free himself of his master, thought he could rebuild his power somewhere beyond Nagash's reach. Forced back into the Realm of Death, he had thought himself safe within Nachtsreik, thought he could restore his powers by steeping himself in the energies of his sanctum.

Now, Mannfred was learning the foolishness of such thoughts. Humility wasn't something with which the Mortarch was familiar. Every so often, it became necessary to remind him that there were powers mightier than himself. Powers before which he must make obeisance.

At a gesture from his skeletal claw, Nagash dispelled the withering enchantment with which Mannfred beset Makvar.

A glance was enough to break the arcane bonds that animated the vampire's guardians, causing them to collapse in heaps of bleached bone. A gesture sent Ashigaroth back into the shadows, banishing the dread abyssal's corporeal manifestation. The Mortarch of Night was among the most powerful adepts to practise the profane art of necromancy to have ever existed, but Nagash was the father of that foul strain of magic, and there many were secrets about the art known only to himself.

It was amusing to see Mannfred retreat from his intended victim. He cringed away like some frightened animal, falling back towards the raised dais where his sepulchre had stood. The display of fright wasn't entirely genuine, but seldom was anything the Mortarch did. He retreated because he thought to draw upon the power with which he had saturated himself, to harness it for one final effort of defiance.

Nagash allowed Mannfred to pull back, letting him reach the very cusp of his objective. Then an unspoken command gripped the vampire, freezing him in place as though he had been caught in a basilisk's stare. At the last, he betrayed himself, darting a quick, longing look at the pedestals and the glassy black stones resting upon them. He even tried to cry out to them with his sorcery and draw their energy to him. It needed only the slightest exertion of his own will for Nagash to crush Mannfred's last flicker of rebellion.

'On your knees before your master, little one,' Nagash hissed at the Mortarch. A wave of his fleshless hand had Mannfred bowing before him, as abased and servile as any serf. Only the Lord of Death could sense the resentment buried deep within him, locked away in the blackest reaches of the vampire's essence.

The Great Necromancer turned towards Makvar, waiting

while the Stormcasts' commander picked himself off the floor. The other Anvils were drawing close to their leader, closing ranks around him in a remarkable display of fidelity and courage. They were battered and bloodied from their contest with Mannfred, but none had fallen in the fighting.

'You must make allowances for my vassal,' Nagash said. 'It is not long ago that he came slinking back to his old haunts to lock himself away in this sanctum. Rousing him so abruptly from his repose has brought out the worst of him. He is somewhat of a kindred spirit to the vermin that besiege his castle, and like any cornered rat, it is in his lair that his bite is at its worst.'

'These warriors are kindred to those who strove for my life in the Realm of Beasts,' Mannfred warned his master. 'The Hallowed Knights thwarted my ambition to build a refuge for you...'

Nagash glared down at the vampire. 'The Realm of Death is mine,' he hissed. 'No power will take from me what is mine.' He pointed a talon at the black stones. 'You thought you could steal from me, but all you have done is because I have allowed it.' Sweeping out from the darkness, the morghast archai answered the Great Necromancer's command. The winged skeletons descended upon the pedestals and the wreckage of Mannfred's sepulchre, poised about the glassy stones. 'If there are yet any wards guarding what is mine, you had best dismiss them,' he warned the Mortarch.

'I was keeping them safe for you, Master,' Mannfred claimed as he dispelled the magic protecting the pedestals. 'It would have been calamitous if the enemy seized them.'

Makvar rose to Mannfred's bait, suspicion in his tone as he addressed Nagash. 'What are these stones? They seem similar to the Obelisk of Black and the relics from Mephitt.'

Holding forth one of his bony talons, Nagash called one of the smaller stones to him, the object rising from the debris of Mannfred's coffin to fly into his outstretched hand. As it came into contact with him, he could feel the spectral energies coursing through his malignant spirit. 'They are vessels,' he told the Stormcasts, 'prisms through which the power of necromancy can be magnified. With these, I can raise the legions Sigmar will need for his war.'

A look of shock gripped Mannfred's face. 'You have joined forces with Sigmar? Have you forgotten the God-King's treachery so soon? Do you not understand it was his knights who fought against me!'

Nagash silenced the Mortarch with a wave of his hand. 'We share a common foe and a common purpose. Chaos must be vanquished. It must be expunged from all the Mortal Realms. Archaon will be made to account for his manifold atrocities. The gate of Gothizzar will be cleansed of its defilers. This is my command.' He turned back towards Makvar. 'There is your answer, Lord-Celestant. The Realm of Death will fight beside the Realm Celestial once more.'

Veiled in the sorcery of Molchinte, Lascilion watched from the darkness of the crypt, his pulse racing as he beheld once again the sinister beauty of the vampire queen. The frustration of his defeat in Nulahmia was smothered beneath the fiery ardour that blazed within him. She would be his.

'There are others in the chamber below,' Molchinte told the three champions who shared her arcane protection. 'Bide your time. Wait for them to return. Don't underestimate them.'

Lascilion kept his eyes on Neferata, watching her as she conferred with the vampire knights who attended her. Their crimson armour made a stark contrast to the black plate worn by the lightning-men. Three of the celestial warriors patrolled the crypt, striding across the debris of destroyed skeletons, bows clenched in their fists. The warlord knew from past experience how formidable these lightning-men were. None of them had the look of command about them, however, so he judged that the leaders must be in the vault below.

The Lord of Slaanesh plucked the enticing scent of Neferata's sadistic soul from the air, savouring it like a delicacy. The intoxicating sensation flowed through him, striking into the deepest recesses of his being. Nowhere had he ever found a spirit as cruel and inventive as his own. Never would he find such a spirit again. The vampire queen would open a new world of wonder for him, allowing him to revisit old delights and old outrages anew, to rekindle his jaded passions by dint of simply being there to share in them.

Patience! Lascilion had denied himself far too long. He recognised that Molchinte wanted the leaders of the lightning-men to offer themselves before springing their ambush. It was sound strategy, to have all of one's enemies in a single place. But he also knew the vagaries of battle. She was concerned with eliminating the leaders. His ambition was to capture Neferata. He had a good chance to achieve his purpose right now. That opportunity might not be there when the rest of the lightning-men came back.

Lascilion forced himself to draw his gaze away from Neferata long enough to look at his companions. Alghor and Orbleth were both watching the sentries, Molchinte was focussed on the steps leading below. None of them were paying any attention to him.

Silently, Lascilion drew away from the invisible watchers. He wasn't certain how far from Amala's skull the effects of the concealing magic would follow him, so he braced himself for that instant when his enemies would spot him and recognise their peril. Cautiously he advanced, gaze fixed upon Neferata and her companions. He would come upon them from the flank, angling his approach so that his presence would go unnoticed until the last possible moment even without Molchinte's spell to hide him.

When he was but a few yards away from his prey, Lascilion knew he was no longer under the veil of Molchinte's magic. The discovery announced itself in the enraged howls of Alghor and Orbleth as they rushed at the lightning-men. Aware that the ambush would be lost to them either way, the champions of the Bloodking chose to at least eliminate what enemies they could swiftly. One of the black-armoured knights was struck down by Orbleth's flail, a bright spark leaping from his body before it could crash at the champion's feet. Another writhed upon the diseased length of Alghor's vile sword, green tendrils of corruption worming through his mail.

Lascilion charged straight towards the vampires. As he reached them, he drew Pain and Torment in a flash of murderous steel. One of the vampire knights was decapitated by the vicious sweep of Pain, his body writhing on the floor like a crushed snake. The second vampire dropped as Pain slashed across his middle, all but disembowelling the undead lord. Neferata alone now stood before him.

The Mortarch of Blood raised her staff, sending a cascade of deathly magic slamming into him. Lascilion felt several of his teeth burst as the arcane energies ravaged him. The smell of his own burning hair was in his nose, tears of blood spilled from his eyes as they slowly boiled under Neferata's assault. Too late, he appreciated his mistake. When he had confronted Neferata in Nulahmia, she had been exhausted by the demands of the battle. Now she was at the height of her powers and far more than his equal.

If Lascilion had made a mistake, then so too had Neferata. She had focussed too much of herself in annihilating the war-lord and kept too little of her power back to guard against other foes. While he languished under the Mortarch's spell, Molchinte's sorcery struck out at the vampire. Bolts of cor-uscating light raced through Neferata's body, burning into her in a furious barrage. The first few bolts dissipated against the wards she had raised to defend herself, but the others drove home. Neferata was knocked back, thrown against one of the walls. Smoke rose from her branded flesh and blood streamed from the corners of her mouth. She turned to face her attacker, but even as she did, another blast of shimmer-ing light tore the staff from her hands.

Lascilion tried to rally, to subdue the weakened Neferata before Molchinte's sorcery wrought even more havoc upon her. Even as he did, however, dark shapes came rushing up from the vault below. He saw more of the lightning-men, and this time, their helms bore the crests and halos that marked them as commanders of their kind. Alongside them another vampire rushed into the vault, a being of such fearsome aspect that even the Lord of Slaanesh felt a tremor of fear.

His fear counted for nothing when a still more malevolent apparition boiled up from the sunken tomb. Spilling upwards in a cloud of blackness, a towering skeleton wearing a morbid crown commanded Lascilion's gaze. All thoughts of Neferata and his depraved desires were forgotten as the warlord stared at a being that had become legend to the hordes of Chaos infesting Shyish. He didn't need to be told who this creature was, for only the Lord of Death could evoke such terror in the heart of one who had consorted with the likes of Mendeziron and attended the court of Thagmok. Out from the domain of myth and rumour, Nagash the Accursed had returned.

The Great Necromancer pointed his staff towards Neferata and immediately a blanket of darkness swirled around her, catching and absorbing the arcane fire Molchinte hurled against her. While Nagash shielded the vampire queen, the leaders of the lightning-men charged towards Alghor and Orbleth. Formidable as the Chaos champions were, they found themselves outnumbered by the ebon knights eager to avenge the comrades the pair had cut down from ambush.

Into the tableau, a colossal shape lurched. A charnel reek preceded it, splattering through the air in a stream of foulness. The stink of blood, old and rancid washed across the crypt, causing even the faces of the vampires to twist in revulsion. A thunderous, slobbering step brought layers of mould crumbling from the ceiling. The obscene figure drew out into the light, revealing its awful aspect. Swollen, engorged with internal fluids, the thing possessed only the most mocking semblance of human form about it. The legs were short and stocky, veins bulging from the tanned skin to drip a slime of gore down knees and calves. The feet were an array of clawed pads, the hooked talons gleaming like knives as they scratched against the floor. The body itself was prodigious in its dimensions, many times larger than that of a man. Thick ropes of muscle had broken through the flesh, leaving wet strips of meat dangling from its damaged hide. One arm was little more than a withered stump flapping uselessly against the shoulder while its opposite was a tree-like bulk of sinew tipped by a bear-like paw.

The thing's head had sunk down into its torso, staring out with a nest of gigantic black eyes. Some mocking suggestion of a nose and mouth protruded just beneath the eyes. Blood bubbled up from the mouth as it cried out in a voice that filled Lascilion with horror, for it was the voice of Vaangoth, the champion of Khorne they had left behind in the tower. The bloodthirsty warrior had sampled too deeply of Nachtsreik's phantasmal gore, drawing the attentions of the Blood God to him, filling him with the raw power of Chaos. At once, Vaangoth had become both exalted and debased, one of the abominable spawn of Chaos.

'I follow,' Vaangoth howled. 'I bring doom. The Bloodking is come!'

As the spawn cried out the last words, the entire crypt was shaken by a tremor that bespoke some immense violence inflicted upon the castle itself. Lascilion chided himself for his credulity. Thagmok hadn't wanted him to merely lead Molchinte and a few assassins after the lightning-men. The Bloodking himself was following the warlord, bringing his full might against the foes he had used Lascilion to find.

Lascilion looked upon the malignant spectre of Nagash. Thagmok was coming to claim the greatest prize in the Realm of Death, the one conquest even Archaon had failed to achieve. The Bloodking was coming for the Great Necromancer.

CHAPTER FOURTEEN

The cold shell of death magic closed around Neferata, guarding her against the sorcerous barrage conjured by the copper-skinned Chaos witch. It was a small thing for Nagash to fend off the magical assault that had come close to overwhelming his Mortarch. Powerful as she was, the attacking sorceress was but an insect beside the Lord of Death. There was only so much eldritch lore Tzeentch could pour into a human mind before it collapsed into madness. Nagash had no such limitations. He could feel the sense of shock that raced through the enemy witch when he intervened, her horror that her spells could so easily be brushed away.

But it didn't suit the Great Necromancer for the Stormcasts to learn the full extent of his might. Instead, Nagash was more interested in the extent of the strength the Anvils possessed. This ambush in the depths of Nachtsreik was an opportunity to see how a small group of the storm-knights fared against foes who could pose a real challenge to them.

'Attend to the others,' Nagash told Makvar. 'I will obstruct the spells of their sorceress.' The Lord-Celestant nodded and hastened to join his warriors. The other Stormcasts were already engaged with the two Chaos champions who had vanquished the Judicators left to guard the crypt.

The bloated champion who bore the Mark of Nurgle brought his diseased blade slashing across the chest of the Liberator who rushed at him. The stricken Stormcast fell back, a black froth bubbling from the mouth of his helm as the daemonic energies within the Nurglesque sword raced through his body. The ebon knight collapsed, his hammer rolling free from his weakened grip. Nagash could feel the necrotic vibrations pulsating within the fallen warrior, ready to extinguish his life-force.

While the Liberator languished on the ground, Knight-Heraldor Brannok interposed himself between the stricken warrior and the Chaos champion. Ducking around the sweep of the Nurglesque sword, Brannok held the invader back while Lord-Castellant Vogun hurried to the dying Stormcast. He held his warding lantern over the wounded warrior, letting its rays shine down upon him. Nagash was surprised to observe the necrotic vibrations falter, gradually receding as the healing light began to burn away the daemonic infection.

Even with death so near, Vogun was driving it back. That was a power the Great Necromancer found more troubling than any he had witnessed heretofore, a power antithetical and oppositional to the very source of his own dark magics. If such power were harnessed properly, it could prove a threat to his dominion.

In the next moment, Nagash saw that he wasn't alone in appreciating the menace posed by Vogun's light. The Nurglesque champion Brannok fought lowered his guard, exposing himself to the Stormcast's blade. As the sigmarite sword slashed across his swollen belly, however, what spilled from the wound was far from what the knight expected. Instead of gore and entrails, a swarm of snake-like worms splashed onto the floor. The grotesque parasites at once slithered away, speeding towards Vogun. Brannok stamped on one of the creatures, bursting it in a spray of stinking yellow ichor. He had no opportunity to attack the rest of the swarm, for the Chaos champion was swinging at him once again with his green blade, apparently indifferent to the gaping wound in his guts.

Across the crypt, Huld and the remaining Liberator fought against the black-armoured Chaos champion with the flail. Despite their superiority of numbers, the Stormcasts were having difficulty slipping through the invader's guard. The flail swung with expert precision, the chains coiling about the blades of their swords to twist them aside each time the knights thrust at its wielder. Even the purifying rays of Huld's celestial beacon, the light that so discomfited Nagash's vampire minions, had little effect upon this barbarous fighter. Certainly not enough to dull his ferocity.

The impasse was broken when Makvar entered the fray. Coming at the champion from the flank, the Lord-Celestant swung at his adversary with his fearsome runeblade. Again, the invader turned and brought the chains of his flail whipping around to entangle and twist the descending sword. This time, however, the tactic brought electricity crackling up from the sigmarite weapon. Lightning sizzled up the flail and rushed into the champion's body. The barbarian staggered back, smoke rising from the seared flesh inside his armour. In his hands, he held a gnarled length of iron that had been the grip of his flail. The bludgeoning skulls and the chains themselves lay scattered about the floor, many of the links melted by the electric discharge of Makvar's runeblade. The stricken Chaos champion fell back, drawing an ornate dagger from his belt and reversing his hold upon the iron handle of his destroyed flail so that he might use it as a club.

Nagash noted the fearsome enchantments bound into Makvar's runeblade. He recognised the peculiar arcane crafts-manship of duardin smiths. Long ago, he had learned to his cost how potently such swordsmiths could infuse a weapon with aethyric power. He didn't envy the Chaos champion the destruction that would soon be his.

Yet before Makvar could close upon the invader, a new factor thrust itself into the battle. Lumbering through the doorway was a ghastly monster, a hideous spawn of Chaos. Nagash could see the rampant arcane energies shivering through the thing's body, changing and mutating every organ and bone with each step it took. His witchsight revealed to him the murderous Mark of Khorne branded into the one bit of chest that had resisted the riotous transformation that swept through the rest of the abomination's frame.

More than that, Nagash understood how this monstrosity had come into being. He could sense the phantasmal harmo-nies that saturated the spawn and recognised them as part of the ghostly force that Mannfred had employed to build Nachtsreik. A slave of the Blood God Khorne, this creature had glutted itself on the spectral gore seeping from the walls until it lost whatever integrity of form it had once possessed. The thing had become carnage incarnate.

A moment after it appeared, the spawn's mouth made a sav-age utterance, declaring that the Bloodking himself had come to Nachtsreik. The next instant, the fortress trembled. Nagash knew it was from the impact of some tremendous projectile, though perhaps not something more destructive than those hurled against it by the skaven. The difference wasn't in the missile, but in the castle itself. Just as the blood-soaked stones had responded to the Khorne champion, so too they were affected by the presence of the Bloodking. The necromantic resilience and regeneration with which Mannfred had infused his fortress had been disrupted. The fight in the Mortarch's sanctum had weakened the resilience of his sorcery, stifling the adaptability of his fortifications. The Khornate spawn had further upset the arcane harmonies, establishing a sympathy not with Mannfred's necromancy but with the bloodthirsty fury of Thagmok. For the first time since it was erected, Nachtsreik was vulnerable to the hordes of Chaos.

Nagash turned away from Neferata, letting his protection waver. He had no time left to play with the Chaos witch. It was time to end things. As she felt him focusing upon her, the sorceress tried to evoke the arcane concealment that had guarded her and her companions through Nachtsreik. Nagash saw the mutant skull she used to form her spell. At a wave of his bony hand, the skull exploded into morbid fragments, several slivers burying themselves in the sorceress' body. Stunned, she fell back behind one of the caskets strewn about the hall.

Nagash's skeletal fingers closed about the hilt of a sword as ancient and monstrous as himself. The wail of banshees and the shrieks of wraiths echoed in his mind as the Great Necromancer let the deathly pulse of Zefet-nebtar sizzle through his spirit. His own malignance flowed back into the Mortis Blade, establishing a fell harmony between them. As he stalked across the crypt towards his prey, the sorceress sent a coruscating bolt of Chaos magic rushing at him. Nagash whipped the necrotic head of his staff in front of him, spinning it in an arc of power that caught and dissipated the hostile vibrations. Striding through the vaporous residue of the witch's spell, he closed upon the sorceress.

The Chaos conjurer was utterly desperate now, summoning all her reserves of aethyric might, channelling reckless amounts of magical energy through her body, heedless of the strain she put upon her merely mortal flesh and spirit. She formed the rampant energies into a great shimmering ball of mutating harmonies and flung it at the Great Necromancer. As she did so, the fingers of her left hand melted away, replaced by fibrous growths more akin to fungus than flesh.

Nagash caught the malefic spell with Alakanash. It would have been an easy thing for him to hurl its energy back upon the sorceress, but he had other plans for her.

The Great Necromancer could sense Mannfred watching him as he raised his sword to strike the sorceress. The Mortarch of Night had been using his magic to drive back the Chaos spawn, but now there was a respite, a moment for him to observe his master in action. The vampire saw Nagash poised to strike. Nagash knew he also saw the black stone held tight against the hilt of Zefet-nebtar, the same glassy stone Mannfred had surrounded his sepulchre with – a fragment of which was yet hidden under the Mortarch's armour.

Feeling Mannfred's jealous gaze on him, Nagash brought the Mortis Blade slashing down. The wards the sorceress had built around herself evaporated in an instant, winking out in a flash of purple light. Then, the black sword was shearing through her body, splitting her from crown to pelvis. Nagash could feel the Mark of Tzeentch pulsate with inimical energy as the witch's spirit abandoned her dying flesh. The Great Necromancer's pull proved greater, however. He could hear her scream of disbelief as her soul was dragged away from the waiting claws of Tzeentch and down into the black stone he held in his hand.

As the hewn body of the sorceress wilted at his feet, Nagash looked towards Mannfred. He needed but a single glance to be assured that the Mortarch had seen everything. The gleam in the vampire's eyes bespoke a terrible inspiration. Nagash realised that his vassal had learned what he wanted him to learn.

Now he only needed the opportunity for Mannfred to put the lesson into practice.

All around Makvar, the crypt swayed and shuddered. It was more than the impact of the projectiles the besieging army outside the walls was hurling against Nachtsreik. The firmament itself was coming apart. Great sanguinary expulsions bubbled from wall and ceiling, spilling into the chamber in rivulets of gore. Clumps of bone rolled out from crumbling facades, clattering over the flagstones in a ghoulish tide. Clouds of wailing spectres billowed through the corridors, whipping around the Stormcasts and their Chaos foes before shrieking off into the darkness.

The fortress was tearing itself apart. The murderous necromancy with which Mannfred had built it was now sinking into a sort of suicidal madness as it responded to the influence of the arch-murderer Khorne, the Chaos God of Carnage. Makvar wondered how exalted the Bloodking Thagmok was in his god's esteem to inflict such destructive confusion on Nachtsreik.

For the moment, the question would wait. Leaving Huld and the last Liberator to finish the black-armoured Chaos champion, Makvar rushed to intercept the injured spawn as it lumbered across the crypt towards Neferata. He saw

Mannfred casting pulses of dark energy at the mutated horror, but the injuries he visited against it only seemed to make the beast even more crazed. The blood streaming from its wounds refused to splash onto the floor, but instead oozed back into the torn veins and slashed flesh.

'I am the Anvil!' Makvar cried as he rushed at the hideous monster. His runeblade lashed out in a flash of gleaming metal, hacking into the beast's nearest arm. Lightning crackled from his sword as it ripped into the crimson flesh. The blood that erupted from the wound came as a gush of scarlet steam, rushing past him in a stagnant cloud. The spawn reared back, its head snarling in pain. The brute swung around, striking at Makvar with one of its cudgel-like fists. The blow missed him as he dived away, instead gouging a pit into the floor. Flagstones crumbled, exposing the catacombs beneath the crypt.

Makvar retaliated with another slash, this time raking the runeblade down the monster's back. Again, there was the sizzle of steaming blood as the horror's corrupt metabolism reacted to the purifying surge of electricity. The spawn started to round on him once more, then was struck in the leg by a blinding flare of arcane energy. He could see the head of Nagash's staff ablaze with spectral light as the Lord of Death directed his malefic power into the monster. The beast's leg expanded like a swelling bladder and then burst apart. Wailing in rage, the thing crumpled in a puddle of its own gore as the limb dissolved under its own weight.

The Stormcast moved in to finish the beast, yet he had underestimated its ferocious vitality. The horror reared up, supporting itself on one arm and its remaining leg. The other arm came slamming down, hurling the Lord-Celestant back as its claws scraped down his black armour, leaving deep gashes in the sigmarite plate. Makvar was tossed through the air and slammed down on his back. He felt the already weakened floor crack under his impact, heard stony fragments go clattering away into the darkness below.

As he started to rise, Makvar was struck by the charging spawn, smashed back against the floor. He felt something break inside him, a flare of pain tear through his body. Keeping hold of his runeblade, he managed to slide its edge across the mutated paw that pressed down upon him. The corrupt flesh steamed as lightning coursed through it. The Chaos spawn growled and grunted, but refused to relent. The pressure mounted. Makvar could taste his own blood in his mouth and his vision began to dim.

Before the pressure against his body could crush him utterly, the blood beast recoiled, screaming in agony. Black, nebulous strands of shadow were streaming into the thing's body. It took Makvar a moment to realise that they were spirits – some of the trapped ghosts that infested Nachtsreik had been directed against the spawn. The monster stumbled back, unbalanced, and slammed down upon the floor. Cracks spread from its collapse. The fissure widened as the spawn writhed in torment. Its obscene flesh was expanding now, bubbling and undulating with grisly animation. Whatever the spirit hosts were doing to the brute, it was too much for its body to withstand. With a last howl of agony, the beast's body ruptured, splashing the crypt with the spectral blood that so engorged it. The ruined scraps of mangled meat and bone crashed down against the floor, fracturing the weakened stone. A jagged hole opened beneath it and the spawn's carcass plunged into the depths.

Makvar propped himself on one elbow as the orchestrator of the spell that had vanquished the abomination approached him. Mannfred gave the injured Stormcast an appraising look, then a smile that was reptilian in its coldness curled across the vampire's face. Silently, he drew Gheistvor and crept towards the Lord-Celestant.

Fingers of pain still crackled through Neferata's brain as she recovered from the sorcerous attack. If not for the intervention of Nagash, it was possible she would have been overwhelmed. She had invested too much of her powers in assaulting the Chaos warlord who had brought destruction upon her city. In her fury, she had allowed herself to lose focus, behaving like some newly turned thrall drunk on her own transcendence of mortality. That recklessness had left her hideously exposed, a weakness the invaders had been swift to exploit.

Neferata could see Huld and one of the other Stormcasts fighting a black-armoured Chaos champion. Across the crypt, Makvar and Mannfred struggled against the bloated Chaos spawn. Further still, Nagash pitted his powers against a barbaric sorceress, likely the same foe who had come so close to overwhelming the vampire queen. Nearer at hand, Brannok matched blades with a revolting warrior of Nurgle. She could see the swarm of hideous worms that spilled from the wounds the knight inflicted on his foe, a slithering horde that crawled away towards...

The worms were converging upon Lord-Castellant Vogun. He was kneeling beside a fallen Stormcast, using the light of his warding lantern to fend off the arcane infection that ravaged the knight's body. Directing the light upon his comrade, he struggled to protect the Liberator not only from the disease within but the worms without, for the slithering tide was crawling all over Vogun. Though the things recoiled from the direct path of the celestial light, they seemed perversely drawn to it as well. The healer's armour was slick with the wet, slimy parasites. Smoke rose from the sigmarite plate as the foul acids exuded by the vermin gradually ate away at his armour.

There was no question that Vogun was aware of his peril. Lying on the floor beside him was the corroded body of Torn. The ever-loyal gryph-hound had tried to protect his master, but without the protection of sigmarite armour, he had been overwhelmed by the slithering horde. Steam continued to rise from the animal's pitiable remains.

Weakened as she was, Neferata seized the opportunity she saw. Vogun's actions displayed for her in no uncertain terms the degree to which the storm-knights valued their comrades – and how favourably they would regard one who hurried to their aid. Mustering her concentration, she drew upon her magic, pointing the Staff of Pain towards Vogun and sending a wave of withering force into the parasitic worms.

It took all of Neferata's focus to set the spell against only the worms and not the Stormcast they engulfed. Hence, she failed to note the return of an old threat until he was nearly upon her. The Chaos warlord with the plumed helm had recovered enough to make another assault against her. With both swords drawn, it seemed he had abandoned his notion of capturing her and had determined to destroy her instead.

Before the barbarian could reach her, he was intercepted by Lord Harkdron. Neferata's lover, wounded by the warlord's blade, dived at his enemy in a feral leap. Ferocity, however, wasn't enough. The Slaaneshi warlord spun around, slashing Harkdron with the longer of his swords. The vampire's armour shredded like paper beneath the keen edge and the force of the blow knocked him back among the caskets. The barbarian sneered, lips curling away from feline fangs, and turned back towards the Mortarch of Blood.

Worms continued to shrivel under the force of Neferata's incantation. A few moments more and Vogun would be free from the parasites. Those few heartbeats would leave her exposed to the Slaaneshi warlord's blades. Reluctantly, she realised she would have to sacrifice her ambition – and with it the Lord-Castellant. Agitated by her magic, the infuriated worms would burn their way through his weakened armour in seconds.

The dilemma was resolved for Neferata when Brannok interposed himself between the vampire queen and her foe. Hurling the severed head of the Nurglesque champion at the warlord, the Knight-Heraldor glowered at the barbarian. 'She is under my protection,' he declared. The leonine face dropped into a scowl of frustration, and with a roar, he lunged at Brannok.

Stormcast and Slaaneshi traded blows. Brannok's sigmarite blade resisted the razored edge of the warlord's long sword while his agility thwarted efforts to drive the shorter knife into his gut. A return sweep of the Anvil's weapon cropped the plume from the warlord's helm, leaving its wreckage to flop against the cheek-plate. The warlord snarled in wrath, his jaws distending, revealing a long forked tongue. From this organ, a viscous slime spattered across Brannok's mask, boiling against the metal and momentarily blinding him.

Even as the warlord moved to capitalise upon the debilitation of his foe, Neferata turned towards him. Vogun was no longer threatened by the worms. Now she could direct her full attention against the fiend who had destroyed Nulahmia. A bolt of dark magic raced into his left arm, ripping through the limb in a gory discharge. Strips of armour and the deadly knife clattered away from the smoking arm.

The warlord staggered back. His gaze shifted between Neferata and Brannok, the Slaaneshi's mind turning over the odds arrayed against him. He sketched a mocking salute with his remaining sword, then turned about and threw himself into the pit that had swallowed the blood beast's carcass. Brannok rushed after him, but was too late to stop the warlord from leaping into the darkness.

A compulsion seized Neferata, diverting her attention away from the pit and to the scene unfolding on the other side of it. Makvar lay sprawled on the ground with Mannfred above him. The vampire was ready to bring Gheistvor slashing down into the Lord-Celestant. Refusing to allow her schemes to be ruined, Neferata unleashed a blast of spectral force at the Mortarch of Night. The ghostly vibration was just enough to turn aside the descending blow. Instead of striking Makvar's head, Gheistvor simply sheared through the top of his metal halo.

The respite gave Makvar the chance to retaliate. His boot kicked out, slamming into Mannfred's knee and knocking him down. Even as the Mortarch rose to make a second attack, he found a new foe leaping towards him. Hurtling across the pit was Brannok, the shout of 'Traitor!' thundering from behind his mask.

Mannfred decided not to risk himself against both Brannok and the rallying Makvar. Turning, the vampire rushed at the wall behind him. Some hidden catch responded to his retreat, opening a concealed panel and revealing a hidden passage. With Brannok close behind him, the Mortarch plunged into the secret corridor. A great block of stone came slamming down from the crumbling ceiling, sending a dolorous boom rolling through the crypt and burying the doorway beneath a mess of rubble.

'After them,' Makvar called, trying to drive his battered body towards the mound of debris. Vogun left the recovering Liberator in order to rush to his commander's side. Huld and the other Liberator, having finally overcome their opponent, started towards the buried door.

It was the voice of Nagash that held them back. 'They are beyond your reach,' he declared. 'Even should you clear away the wreckage, Nachtsreik is such a labyrinth of dungeons and tombs that it would take you years to explore them fully. And that is if Mannfred remains in the Realm of Death. The Cromlech of Avar-Sul is not so far removed from this place. It is certain the Mortarch has some way of reaching the realmgate from here.'

'We cannot abandon Brannok,' Makvar protested as Vogun shone his warding lantern on him. The Lord-Celestant's wounds, lacking the sorcerous corruption that afflicted the Liberator, responded quickly to the celestial light.

'Lord Nagash is right,' Huld said, turning away from the rubble. 'It would take too long to dig our way through.' He looked up as the castle shook once more, streams of dust rattling from the roof. 'That is if this place holds together that long.'

'Brannok will either achieve his purpose,' Vogun told Makvar, 'or he will fall and his spirit will return into Sigmar's keeping.'

Nagash raised a fleshless talon and pointed at the quaking ceiling overhead. 'There are more pressing concerns for us now. These assassins have led Thagmok's army here. They have penetrated the defences Mannfred crafted for this place. Soon they will be upon us.' The Great Necromancer raised the Mortis Blade. 'Unless we go forth to meet them. If nothing more, we can cut the head off the serpent. The Bloodking has vexed my domain far too long already.'

Neferata could sense Makvar's hesitation. It wasn't fear of the Bloodking's forces that made him reluctant to quit the crypt, but concern for his comrade. However, he was strategist enough to appreciate the uselessness of mounting a search while the enemy stormed the castle. 'What is your plan?' he asked Nagash.

The Lord of Death looked down at Makvar. 'We strike at the heart of the enemy. Kill the Bloodking, and his army will loose its cohesion.' He gestured at the pit created by the blood beast. 'As you've seen, those who follow Khorne don't react well to confusion. I will muster the spirits bound within Nachtsreik and set them against the foe. Even now, my morghasts are collecting the black stones from Mannfred's sanctum. With those to help channel my power, I will unleash a spectral flood to terrorise our enemy and grant us the opportunity to strike.'

Neferata felt more than a tinge of suspicion as Nagash turned towards her and told her to lead the Stormcasts through the vaults and to the walls of the castle. With the eerie shifting and restructuring of Nachtsreik stifled by the Bloodking's assault, the path before them would be straightforward enough. The Great Necromancer would linger behind for a while to perform the ritual that would summon the spirit hosts.

As she watched Nagash descend back down into Mannfred's sanctum, Neferata wondered if he was spending all their lives simply to give himself the chance to escape. Grimly she realised that even if such were the case, she could do nothing to disobey her master.

'Can Nagash do what he claims?' Huld asked her when the Great Necromancer had withdrawn.

'There are no limits to his power,' Neferata said, keeping her reservations to herself. She turned and glowered at the hole down which the Slaaneshi warlord had plunged. Hate blazing in her eyes, she raised the Staff of Pain and exerted her power in a spell that infused new animation into the shattered skeletons littering the crypt. The restored undead lurched to their feet and shambled silently towards the hole. One by one, without protest or hesitation, the skeletons stepped across the precipice and fell down into the darkness.

'Just in case that scum is still alive after he hits the bottom,' Neferata told the Stormcasts. She glanced at Makvar, impressed at the speed with which he had recovered. 'If you are fit enough, Lord-Celestant, I will lead you from this place.'

Walking to where the carcass of Torn lay, Vogun looked back and shook his head. 'Are you certain you can find the way?'

Neferata laughed, brushing her hand across the wall. 'Nachtsreik no longer bleeds,' she said. 'What blood is being spilled is outside where the Bloodbound and the skaven squabble over which of them will conquer the castle. If there is one thing upon which you may be confident, Lord-Castellant, it is that a vampire can always follow the scent of blood.'

Nagash descended into Mannfred's tomb. Here was one place that the Mortarch of Night had guarded with such spells and wards that even the onset of the Bloodking failed to disrupt the eerie atmosphere. Of course, von Carstein was always at his most clever when devising some safeguard to ensure his own survival. It was likely the sanctum had been created not simply to protect against Chaos and the Stormcasts alone, but to protect him from the wrath of Nagash as well. The vampire was always making that mistake, overestimating his abilities.

The morghast archai formed a circle around the pedestals.

At a signal from Nagash, they brought the black stones together, releasing a surge of arcane energy. The Great Necromancer let the magic flow into him, replenishing such power as he had expended in the battle and on the journey to Nachtsreik. It wasn't much, but the Lord of Death was always wary of even the slightest weakness.

Some of the power ebbing from the stones he channelled into a telepathic sending, linking his mind to that of Arkhan. The instructions Nagash passed to his acolyte were simple enough. The Mortarch of Sacrament already knew what to do – all he waited for was the command to proceed. Now that it had been given, he would carry out his orders.

As his body seethed with dark magics, Nagash started to exert his dominion over the spirits Mannfred had bound into the walls of his refuge. In extending his awareness outward through the halls of Nachtsreik, he detected the fading essence of Lord Harkdron. The Great Necromancer lingered over the vanquished vampire's mind.

Such a festering mire of hatred, jealousy, adoration and dependency! Neferata had done a masterful job of enslaving Harkdron, binding him to her will with such skill that the vampire wouldn't break free of her even if given the chance. Of course, such devotion brought with it a possessiveness that would brook no competition. Foremost in Harkdron's thoughts was the bitter fear that the Stormcasts intended to usurp his position, particularly Makvar and Brannok. Harkdron had even worked against his mistress in his efforts to sow discord between her and the Anvils.

Nagash decided he could use the hate he sensed in Harkdron. Expending a fragment of his energies, he sent a surge of necromantic power pulsing through the vampire. Into the reviving vampire's mind, he placed an awareness of Brannok's presence in the bleak halls of Nachtsreik and an eldritch intuition that would lead the vengeful Harkdron straight to his prey.

When he sensed Harkdron hurrying away from the crypt to find Brannok, Nagash shifted his focus back to rousing the bound spirits. It wasn't that he had any real doubt how a confrontation between the Knight-Heraldor and the Mortarch of Night would end, but with Harkdron taking a hand, he would make certain events proceeded as he intended them.

CHAPTER FIFTEEN

Lord-Celestant Makvar's heart turned cold as he gazed out across the great cavern in which Mannfred had raised the fortress of Nachtsreik. From the vantage of the curtain wall, he looked out across a veritable sea of foes, a host so vast that even with the fearsome might of Nagash on their side he didn't see any hope of victory here.

The chittering swarms of skaven that had laid siege to the fortress were thick about the walls, the rancid stink of their mangy fur and diseased flesh engulfing the castle. Clad in robes of dirty green, squeaking putrid chants and sounding rusted gongs, the congregations of plague monks worked themselves into rabid bursts of ferocity. Swinging blazing censers that seeped diseased smoke, the ratmen rushed across the cavern, hurling themselves upon the enemies that had come to contest their claim upon Nachtsreik.

The trespassers matched the skaven in both numbers and ferocity. A vast crimson horde of barbarians, howling with murderous cries, slaughtered its way across the cavern. Makvar wasn't surprised Neferata had been able to follow the scent of blood through the castle vaults, for the Chaos army was dripping in gore. Not a weapon or piece of armour had failed to be anointed with symbols of blood, or marked with the skull-rune of Khorne.

Roaring bloodstokers lashed their scourges across the scarred backs of barbarous bloodreavers, whipping the tribesmen into homicidal frenzies that found them plunging fearlessly into the choking smoke of plaguesmog congregations. Bands of blood warriors, their plate armour caked in dried gore, ripped their way through packs of rabid plague monks with axe and sword. Berserk wrathmongers, their faces locked inside horned helms, ploughed into the ratkin with crushing sweeps of the chained hammers they bore, trampling the bodies of their victims underfoot.

Where the row of plagueclaw catapults had stood, there was now only a litter of smouldering debris and mangled bodies. Amidst the wreckage, armoured barbarians mounted upon hulking daemon steeds of brass and bronze hunted the few skaven artillerists that had escaped the carnage of their charge. Makvar saw the molten metal that dripped from the jaws of the daemonic juggernauts as they worried at the ratmen, the savage glee that distorted the mutated visages of their riders as they shattered skulls and severed arms with mattock and axe.

The walls around Makvar shook once more as they were battered by a tremendous impact. He turned from the sight of the broken catapults to gaze upon the creatures that had taken their place. Three enormous gargants, their man-like bodies branded and tattooed with the Blood God's symbols, were wrenching stalagmites from the ground. Hefting their huge burdens, the towering gargants whipped them around in a swinging motion and flung them at the castle.

'The vermin are from Clan Septik,' Neferata declared, gesturing at the swarming ratmen. 'They were among the first of their breed to gnaw their way into the roots of the Bonegrooves and spread their pestilence across the Realm of Death.' She pointed her staff to where a great mass of the robed skaven were pushing an immense carriage topped by a great arch of pitted stone. From this arch a vast pendulum swung, its counterbalance drawn back by a crew of chittering ratkin, the gigantic metal cage fitted to its opposite end spewing a foul green vapour.

'Kingdoms have been exterminated by their poxes,' Neferata explained, 'the dead so defiled with disease that only a supreme effort can rouse them from their plague pits.'

'Sorcery wicked enough to overcome the black art of necromancy,' Vogun mused. The Lord-Castellant had tied Torn's carcass to his back, unwilling to leave his faithful gryph-hound where his remains might become the plaything of deathmages and corpsemasters.

'It seems their plagues aren't potent enough to avail them here,' Knight-Azyros Huld said. He pointed to where a monstrous hulk of muscle and claws ravaged a congregation of ratmen, decimating them by the droves as it splashed their black blood across its crimson flesh.

'Yet while the skaven keep the attention of the Khornate horde, we will find our own opportunity,' Makvar declared. He cast his gaze across the Chaos horde, trying to find the overlord who led them. 'If we can reach the Bloodking before they can overwhelm us...'

Neferata drew close to the Lord-Celestant, pointing across the sea of carnage. 'Thagmok will be where the scent of blood is strongest,' she said. 'The madness of Khorne burns inside him and calls out to the blood shed in murder and battle. There! We will find him there.'

The spot Neferata directed Makvar's gaze towards was a solid block of armoured blood warriors and burly skullreapers. A massive barbarian marching before them brandished an enormous icon of bronze fitted to a steel pole. Behind the mass of warriors, a red light pulsated, throbbing from a dull glow to a blazing intensity with eerily organic palpitations. Makvar couldn't gain even the slightest glimpse of what exuded this gory luminance, but he felt it had to issue from the Chaos warlord himself.

Makvar took a moment to study the battlefield, evaluating the shifting tide of carnage. There were yet enough of the plague monks to contain the Bloodbound on the right flank. Using some of the stalagmites for cover, they might be able to win their way through the conflict unnoticed for a few hundred yards. After that, it was certain to be a brutal fight to reach the overlord.

'We will make our descent as near to this position as we can,' Makvar decided. He commanded his fellow Anvils to regard the line of stalagmites he intended to use for cover. He offered no illusions about their prospects, but if most of them fell, it would be worth the sacrifice if even one of them came to grips with the Bloodking. When he had explained his intentions, he turned to Neferata. 'You should stay here, my lady. Nagash may need your abilities when he musters his legions to aid Sigmar.'

The Mortarch of Blood laughed at Makvar's concern. Reaching out her hand, she ripped a fragment from the crenulations in front of them. 'I am more than capable of acquitting myself in the fighting, and you will never reach the Bloodking without my aid.'

'I am thinking beyond this battle,' Makvar told her. 'You are more important to the battle that is coming, the fight to reclaim Gothizzar and take the Allpoints.'

Neferata turned, pointing her staff at the ground. A ghostly mist began to form, a dark shadow swelling within it. Soon, it was apparent that she was summoning her abyssal steed Nagadron to her side. 'The choice is mine to make,' she said. 'You have worked hard to broker an alliance between us. Allies do not desert one another before battle.'

Makvar could see the determination in Neferata's eyes. She wouldn't be denied. His fears that her loss here would hurt the war had to be balanced against killing such goodwill as she felt towards the Anvils and their cause. One of Nagash's Mortarchs was already their foe, could they risk making a second their enemy?

'As you wish,' Makvar conceded, 'but keep close to us.' He pointed at the skeletal Nagadron as its shape grew into a semblance of solidity. 'Don't hesitate to retreat on your steed if the fight turns from a hopeless endeavour to an impossible one. Spare no thought for us. If a Stormcast falls, his spirit returns to Sigmaron. Reforged, we will fight again.'

Mannfred von Carstein could feel the power being siphoned away from Nachtsreik. The refuge he had spent so much time and energy to construct was crumbling around him. The blood that held the stones together was being leached away by the Khornate horde outside its walls. Now the spirits themselves were being drawn out of the fortress. He didn't need to exert himself to know this was the doing of Nagash. Only the Great Necromancer had the ability to pierce the wards that imprisoned the ghostly masses.

Hate boiled inside Mannfred as he reflected upon the

prodigious abilities of his master. For truly, Nagash was the vampire's master. At the least moment, he could exert his will and reduce the Mortarch to naught but a puppet, a mere extension of the Death God.

Mannfred had had a reminder of Nagash's authority during the fighting in the crypt. The strange compulsion that had stolen upon him to attack Lord-Celestant Makvar – he knew that could only have been issued by the Great Necromancer. He suspected that Neferata's intervention, the poltergeist that foiled Gheistvor's thrust and spared the Stormcast's life, was likewise provoked by Nagash.

Left to his own devices, Mannfred would have been far more cunning about turning on the storm-knights. It stung his pride to be used in so blatant and crude a manner, moreso when his fellow Mortarch spoiled the ambush. Yet, all of it was part of a greater design, a strategy the vampire had yet to piece together. Nagash was neither impulsive or capricious. Everything the Lord of Death did was towards some ultimate purpose. He wouldn't push Mannfred into attacking Makvar just to repent the decision and move Neferata to intervene.

The scene had been staged, and Mannfred was certain that the reason for such theatre was pursuing him through the halls of Nachtsreik. His conviction was justified by the hesitance that seized hold of him when he would choose one passage over another or drop down a particular trap door, make use of some hidden portal or pass through the ghostly face of a gallowglass. He could have lost his pursuer a dozen times over, but always he had been compelled to hold himself back.

Rounding a corner, Mannfred found himself in the colossal confines of his library. Treatises and texts from across the Mortal Realms filled cavernous stacks that spiralled up to

the ceiling hundreds of feet above. Winding stairways fashioned from polished bone and yellowed ivory climbed each
of the columnar stacks, lit by the ghostly orbs bound within
the skulls that hung from their banisters. He could see the
niches cut into the base of each stack where the guardians of
his library reposed. It would be a simple thing to call out to
them, to draw to him a regiment of grave guard that would
occupy his pursuer while he slipped away.

The idea quickly faded, and Mannfred left the skeletons
to rest in their shadowy posts. Even more than the fortress
itself, he had invested too much effort creating this library.
He had razed whole towns simply to secure single volumes.
He wasn't going to throw it all away because a storm-knight
was chasing him. Instead, he drew upon the necromantic
energies residing within the guards, extracting them to fuel
a greater conjuration.

Fortunately, it seemed the influence Nagash exerted upon
him made no objection when Mannfred summoned Ashigaroth from the shadows once more. There was no protest
when he dimmed the orbs around him and used his magic
to cloak himself and his steed in a shroud of darkness. With
Gheistvor in his hand, he stared across the floor of the library,
waiting for the hunter to show himself.

The storm-knight soon appeared, his dark armour reflect-
ing the uncanny glow of the orbs. Mannfred recognised the
battle-horn that hung at the warrior's side. This was the one
his companions had called Brannok. The Mortarch always
found it amusing to know the names of his victims. It added
a certain savour to the taste of their deaths. Before he could
spur Ashigaroth to attack the storm-knight, the vampire
found his attention drawn to a figure moving through the
darkness at the base of the book-filled columns. It moved

with too much speed and agility to be a skeleton accidentally roused from its rest. Nor did it move with the bluster and arrogance he had come to associate with the storm-knights.

Mannfred smiled when he sensed the nature of the stalker and deduced his purpose. He was one of Neferata's thralls from the unmistakable vibration that coloured his aura. It appeared that the Mortarch of Night wasn't the only one with unkind feelings towards the storm-knights. Watching with keen interest, Mannfred waited while Brannok and the vampire drew closer.

Brannok was searching every shadow for sight of his quarry. As careful as he was to conceal himself, Neferata's thrall couldn't hide from the storm-knight's vigilance. Sword at the ready, the warrior rushed at the stalker. 'Traitor,' he hissed as he lunged at what he thought was Mannfred.

The storm-knight's sword clashed against the thrall's blade as he moved to parry the descending blow. Lightning flashed from Brannok's weapon, briefly revealing the face of his adversary. Surprise at finding a different enemy than he expected caused his attack to falter for an instant. It was all the time the thrall needed to twist his body around and slam an armoured elbow into the storm-knight's mask.

'Queen Neferata is mine!' the thrall roared as he strove to press his assault. Though the vampire possessed a strength many times that of a mortal man, his attack had barely phased Brannok. The storm-knight retaliated by driving the flat of his sword up into the thrall's chin, cracking teeth and all but breaking his jaw.

'I have no time to waste on you, Harkdron,' Brannok snarled at the thrall. 'Relent.'

Harkdron staggered back from the blow he had been dealt, spitting chips of tooth onto the floor. '*Lord* Harkdron,' he hissed. The vampire charged Brannok in a burst of bestial frenzy. Though the storm-knight intercepted the flurry of slashes and thrusts Harkdron directed at him, he was steadily pushed back by the intensity of the attack.

'You Stormcasts have humiliated me before my queen,' Harkdron accused. 'You think to steal her favour from me!'

Brannok continued to fall back, letting Harkdron work himself into a still greater fury. From his vantage, Mannfred could appreciate what the storm-knight was doing. He was letting the thrall slip deeper and deeper into his rage. Not with the aim of tiring Harkdron, for the undead knew no weariness, but to goad him into the unthinking savagery that would cause him to expose himself. Brannok was hoping to bring the contest to a swift conclusion.

The storm-knight would get his wish, but hardly in the fashion he had intended. By falling back, forcing Harkdron to chase him, Brannok was drawing close to the very column where Mannfred waited in the shadows. The Mortarch knew it wasn't coincidence. The will of Nagash had sent him into the library, and that same will now made use of Harkdron to move Brannok into position.

Without warning, Mannfred spurred Ashigaroth forwards and charged Brannok. The Knight-Heraldor was smashed to the floor by the impact of the dread abyssal, the sword flying from his hand. While he was stunned, Mannfred commanded his steed to rip the battle-horn from his belt with one of its black claws.

Harkdron lunged at the fallen storm-knight, sword raised for a killing blow. Mannfred glared at the thrall, a deathly blast of necrotic wind hurling him back. 'He isn't yours,' the Mortarch snarled.

From where he had been thrown by Mannfred's magic, Harkdron glared at him. 'I will have vengeance,' he declared.

Ashigaroth pressed its claw against Brannok's chest, keeping the storm-knight pinned to the floor. Mannfred dismounted and stood over the prostrate Knight-Heraldor. He held Gheistvor over the warrior's throat. His other hand closed about the shard of glassy black stone from his sanctum. 'Then let us have true vengeance,' he told Harkdron. Viciously he drove the tip of his sword into Brannok's neck.

Immediately there was a searing crackle of energy. Mannfred felt his arm go numb as power pulsed through Gheistvor. He thought of the Chaos sorcerer he had seen Nagash kill and the way her spirit had flown through the Mortis Blade and into the black stone he carried, defying the Mark of Tzeentch the witch had borne. Now, the same thing was happening, only this time it was the spirit of Brannok that was in contest and the claim of Sigmar being defied.

Pain burned through Mannfred's body as the spiritual discharge rippled through Gheistvor. He could feel Brannok's spirit trying to escape, to fly back to the God-King in Sigmaron. If the Mortarch relented for an instant, he knew the soul would escape his grasp. A will greater than his own steeled him, commanding him to endure despite the agony that ravaged him. Nagash demanded more than obedience. He demanded success.

Smoke rose from his seared skin by the time the ordeal was over and Mannfred rose from where Brannok had lain. He gazed down at his hand and the black stone he held. Faintly, he could feel the echo of the storm-knight's soul. Brannok had been killed, but the Mortarch had been unable to confound the mighty enchantments that bound the storm-knight to Sigmar. After the briefest instant, there had been a blinding flash of light and the Knight-Heraldor was gone, hurtling back to Azyr.

'What have you done?' Harkdron asked. He had seen the Stormcasts in battle enough to know that what he saw now wasn't normal.

Mannfred held up the black stone. 'Discovered something interesting,' he said. 'Something of great value.' He turned his head and studied Harkdron for a moment. 'Neferata has been friendly with these storm-knights. She won't thank you for turning against them.' He laughed, a sound as cruel as the edge of a knife. 'Fear not, she won't learn of this from me. Not while you are useful.'

Harkdron stiffened, glancing at where his sword had fallen. 'I will not betray my queen.'

'You already have by attacking the storm-knight,' Mannfred said. 'At least it will seem so to her. I know the truth, but even if I told it to her I doubt she would believe.' He shook his head. 'No, she won't have it, I think.' A sly gleam shone in his gaze as he looked again at the black stone. 'Perhaps things will be different later. Find someplace to keep yourself until then. I will send for you when the time is right.'

Mannfred exerted some of his own dominance, compelling Harkdron to return to the shadows. Neferata's consort might prove useful to him in his intrigues, allowing he could regain her good graces. It would be useful to have an agent so close to the Mortarch of Blood, one he had a hold upon that went beyond mere magic.

Plans for Harkdron were for the future, however. Looking at the stone, Mannfred appreciated that he had more pressing matters to attend to. He knew what his master had expected of him, and that he had failed to achieve that purpose. But in failure he had made a tremendous discovery, one that he knew Nagash would be most eager to learn.

For when Brannok's soul crackled through Gheistvor,

Mannfred had noticed something that he felt certain had escaped even the Great Necromancer's attention.

The screams and howls of the dying rang out across the havoc-strewn cavern. Mobs of diseased ratmen strove to pull down tribes of bloodreavers, the contagion drifting from censers scorched the lungs of blood warriors and left them choking on bits of their own burnt organs. Skullcrushers stampeded across broken swarms of skaven, the brazen hooves of the juggernauts pulverising the furry carcasses into paste. An amok slaughterpriest wallowed in the gore of butchered plague monks as he clove them with his massive axe.

Around this carnage the small group of Stormcasts made their way. Spells of concealment conjured by Neferata hid them from all but the nearest of their enemies. The Mortarch's illusions couldn't deceive those who drew too close, however. Fortunately, there were none who paid especial notice to the sounds of combat as the Anvils vanquished slinking ratmen and packs of scavenging Chaos hounds.

It was a far different matter when they drew the notice of two enormous beasts, abominable monsters that seemed the very embodiment of Khorne's primal savagery. They were bigger than ogors, immense slabs of muscle bulging from their vaguely humanoid frames. Masses of bone protruded from their crimson flesh, curving outward into enormous claws and talons. A crest of horns sprouted from each monster's back, arching over the shoulders to frame the ghastly stump of its head, almost as though in mockery of the halos worn by the Stormcasts' commanders. The heads themselves were blackened skulls leering above gigantic lower jaws rife with vicious tusks and fangs. Other skulls, wet and dripping, were embedded in the flesh of the monsters, slowly absorbed into their bodies. Branded across their chests was the murderous skull-rune itself, pulsing with a grisly hunger.

'Khorgoraths,' Neferata whispered the word. 'Wolves of the Blood God.'

Makvar tightened his grip on his runeblade. 'Whatever they are, they are in our way.' Whipping his stormcloak around, he sent a flurry of sigmarite hammers crackling into the glowing sockets that served the monsters as eyes. The assault worked no great harm upon the Khorgoraths, but the dazzle of crackling lightning was enough to blunt their charge, allowing the Anvils to take the momentum away from them.

No war cry rose from the Stormcasts as Makvar led them to the attack. Amidst the confusion of battle, the clash of blades and the screams of death might be unremarkable, but invocations of Sigmar's holy name were certain to draw attention, whatever spells Neferata used to conceal their presence. So long as there was a chance of striking at the Bloodking, the ebon knights would do nothing to worsen those chances.

Makvar's runeblade slashed across the leg of one Khorgorath, causing a slop of syrupy gore to bubble from the wound. The beast retaliated by bringing one of its huge claws snapping at him. Shaped like the disembodied skull of a dracoth, the bony claws narrowly missed him as they ripped the left pauldron from his shoulder.

One of the Liberators was rushing to support Makvar's attack when the warrior was struck by a ropey tendril that erupted from the Khorgorath's body. Shaped like a spike-tipped spinal column, the tentacle stabbed into the knight's chest, punching through his plate and bursting from his back in a welter of gore. The impaled Liberator struggled for an instant as the spinal cord wrapped about him and dragged his dying frame back to the Khorgorath.

Makvar saw the flash of light as the Liberator's spirit deserted his mangled flesh. He saw something more however. He saw a scarlet glow infuse the Khorgorath's body. The wound inflicted by his runeblade was closing, healing as the murderous aura spread across it. The monster was regenerating.

The Lord-Celestant glared at his hulking foe. He refused to accept that the thing was unkillable or that the death of the Liberator had been in vain. Strengthened by a zealous defiance, he lunged back to the attack. This time his sword met the downward sweep of the reptilian claw. Lightning seared through the Khorgorath's arm as the runeblade sheared through one of the bony claws and sent it spinning. The monster swung around, bringing its other arm pounding downwards, seeking to smash him like a bug. Makvar rolled beneath the blow, raking the edge of his weapon across the underside of the arm, splitting the crimson hide and severing the thick knots of sinew and muscle within.

Roaring more from frustration than pain, the Khorgorath reared back. Again the ropey tentacle of bone shot out, hurtling towards Makvar this time. The Lord-Celestant threw himself forwards, using the monster's own bulk to shield him from the attack. He slashed his runeblade across the beast's flank, sending a half-dissolved skaven skull spilling from the wound.

Makvar risked a glance at the other Khorgorath to see how his comrades were faring. Huld and Vogun kept the beast disoriented by alternating the rays of their lamps. The Lord-Castellant would shine his light from below and when the brute lurched away, Huld would swoop down to assault its senses with his celestial beacon. Whichever of them wasn't distracting the Khorgorath with the light would rush in to hack at it with halberd and sword. All the while, the last Liberator was circling around the monster and darting in to bludgeon it with his hammer.

The frenzied roar of his own foe set Makvar charging back around the beast. When the Khorgorath's tentacle shot at him again, he leapt past it and raked his sword across the rune etched across its chest. The monster staggered back, forgetting the Stormcast for an instant as it pawed at its newest injury. The skull-rune had been disfigured by Makvar's slash and the light that had suffused it was fading away.

Bellowing in outrage, the Khorgorath stomped towards Makvar. Even as it did so, ghastly shapes whipped around the beast's body. Spectral hands clutched at the crimson hide, withering it with their deathly touch. Phantom teeth bit into coils of muscle, worrying at the monster's strength. Charging forwards on the back of Nagadron, Neferata pointed the Staff of Pain at the brute, a spear of dark magic leaping out to strike the abomination's head. Tusks crumbled into dust as the Mortarch's hideous necromancy ravaged the Khorgorath.

As the monster languished in the grip of Neferata's sorcery, Makvar sprang at the Khorgorath. His runeblade crunched through the beast's wrist, leaving one of its claws dangling by a strip of meat and skin. He followed the attack with a lunge that brought him flying at the skull-like head. Makvar's sword flashed with holy energies as he brought its edge cleaving through the blackened pate, not relenting until the crackling sigmarite edge had ripped through not only the skull but the enlarged jaw beneath it. When he dropped back to the ground, he could see the Khorgorath stumble backwards, its head split in half by his attack. Crashing to its side, the monster made one futile effort to rise again, then was still.

Makvar turned away from his fallen foe to aid the other Anvils with their own adversary, but found that they too had prevailed, though with the loss of the last Liberator. Satisfied that Huld and Vogun at least were unharmed, he turned towards Neferata. 'My thanks for your intervention, my lady. We can only pray that there are no more like these between ourselves and our objective.'

Neferata had a distant look in her eyes as Makvar spoke to her. A cold smile finally spread across her face. 'I think the Bloodking's armies will have other concerns to occupy them now.' While she spoke, the sounds of conflict took on a new tone of agitation. The discordant strife sounded at its loudest at the back of the cavern, away from where the Bloodbound struggled against the skaven of Clan Septik.

It took Makvar only a moment to pick out the crack of thunder and the shouts of Stormcasts in these new sounds of combat. He wondered for an instant if this was some spell or illusion conjured by Neferata or Nagash, but the longer he listened, the more convinced he was that the noise was real. He could hear the war cries of the Anvils of the Heldenhammer. Somehow, his warriors had been brought to Nachstreik.

'I can sense Kreimnar and your knights,' Neferata told Makvar, verifying his thoughts. 'With them marches an undead legion commanded by Arkhan. They close against the Bloodking's horde from the rear, trapping them between the ratkin and themselves.' A frown tugged at her mouth. 'This is Nagash's doing,' she said, 'but I fear that our forces are still too few to prevail.'

Makvar looked past the dead hulk of the Khorgorath, watching as the nearby tribes of Bloodbound reacted to this new threat. Chieftains and bloodstokers strove to control their crazed warriors, alternately trying to push them ahead to continue the fight with the skaven or else trying to turn them around to engage the Stormcasts and undead. For all their numbers, it was confusion that reigned over the Chaos horde. Fratricidal attacks between bloodreavers and wrath-mongers unfolded before him as the Khornate host struggled against itself to reach its enemies. How much greater would that in-fighting and confusion become with Thagmok's death?

'They can gain us the time we need,' Makvar declared. 'We can yet reach the Bloodking.'

Lightning crashed down upon the battlefield, blasting great chunks of buildings from the ceiling as the thunder-bolts speared through the roof. The debris smashed down upon the Chaos hordes below, crushing scores of barbar-ians beneath tons of stone. The thunderstrikes themselves immolated dozens more, hurling their smouldering remains across the cavern.

The greater impact was the turmoil the elemental assault wrought upon the Bloodbound. The minions of Chaos were stunned by the devastation, their senses reeling from the thun-derous impacts. All but the most deranged among them was shaken, their rush to attack lost for several precious moments. Into that void of indecision, the legions of Arkhan charged.

Necromantic vitality pulsated from the Mortarch of Sac-rament, infusing his skeletal warriors with increased speed and agility. When they struck the mobs of barbarians that had hurried to confront the menace to their rear, the undead attacked with the supernormal vigour, stabbing and hacking their enemies with a ferocity that nearly equalled that of the Chaos warriors.

From above, the hulking shape of a terrorgheist swooped down upon the Bloodbound, its deafening shriek rupturing organs and deafening entire tribes of bloodreavers. Still bearing the scars from its battle with the Anvils, the terrorgheist now flew alongside its former foes. Black-armoured Prosecutors dived down in the wake of the mammoth bat-beast's assault, hurling their stormcall javelins into the disordered Khornate ranks. The explosive missiles sent limbs and bodies tumbling through the air.

More Anvils of the Heldenhammer came marching forth, a solid wall of shields and hammers that wheeled alongside the fleshless regiments of Arkhan's army. Volleys of lightning arced up from behind the advancing Liberators as the Judicator retinues rained death upon the enemies who thought to rush the Stormcasts. A pack of wrathmongers, swinging their brutal flails overhead, managed to withstand the punishing archery, but before they could reach the shield wall they were beset by the Paladins who emerged from behind their comrades. Thunderaxes sheared through wrath-flails, lightning hammers melted armour and flesh, stormstrike glaives impaled snarling bodies and slashed through blood-gorged bellies. The infernal aura of madness and murder that emanated from the wrathmongers enflamed the zealous disdain with which the Paladins held their foes, goading them to the most savage violence.

Lord-Relictor Kreimnar raised his relic-weapon and drew down another bolt of divine lightning from the unseen heavens. Again, the holy storm lanced through the roof, sending a cascade of broken streets and toppled buildings slamming down upon the enemies below. One of the massive slaughterpriests saw the havoc and recognised its source. The shaven-pated berserker rallied a great company of blood warriors to him, leading them straight towards the skull-helmed Stormcast. Blood dripped from the enormous axe the madman bore, steaming as the hot liquid fell upon the cold earth. His scarred body devoid of armour, trusting to the savage beneficence of Khorne to guard him, the slaughterpriest charged Kreimnar.

The berserker never reached his prey. Lumbering out from behind the Liberators, Gojin swung his reptilian head towards the fanatic. A bolt of lightning shot from the dracoth's jaws, searing through the slaughterpriest's torso, evaporating his guts in a flash of electrical violence. Blinking in disbelief, the crazed champion slumped to the ground, horrified that no blood flowed from the charred mutilation he had suffered, that in death he had nothing to offer his god. The blood warriors who followed the slaughterpriest hesitated, stunned by the abrupt dissolution of their hero. Before they could recover their momentum, a retinue of Judicators levelled their bolt-storm crossbows at the barbarians, unleashing a fusillade that annihilated them in a matter of heartbeats.

Arkhan himself led the advance on the opposite wing of his army. Troops of malignants galloped on their skeletal steeds while sinister morghasts flew overhead. A gruesome mortis engine glided forwards on a tide of phantoms, their ethereal essence supporting the exhumed reliquary of the cadaverous corpsemaster who guided the swirling ghosts with the gnarled staff he bore. Rank upon rank of skeletons marched behind the cavalry and mortis engine, the clatter of bones and corroded armour rolling from them like the rumble of an angry sea.

The Mortarch of Sacrament had called to him once more the grisly abyssal steed Razarak, the Doom of Traitors. Spurring the skeletal monster onwards, Arkhan loosed bolts of withering magic from his staff, draining the vigour from the Bloodbound before his undead warriors struck them. Weakened by the necromantic spells, the slaves of Chaos fell as easy prey to the charging malignants.

The combined forces of Arkhan's undead and Kreimnar's Anvils were cutting a path through the Bloodking's horde, but despite the impetus of their attack, they had done little more than to seize hold of the Chaos host. Their advance was certain to falter as more and more of the crazed barbarians rushed to confront them. The fatal sting would have to come from another quarter.

Even from deep within Mannfred's sanctum, Nagash watched the ebb and flow of the battle raging outside the walls of Nachtsreik. Whatever his Mortarchs saw, whatever they heard, was communicated back to the Great Necromancer.

The onset of Arkhan's attack combined with the continued resistance of the skaven had broken the cohesion of the Bloodking's horde, creating an opening through which Neferata and Makvar were pressing their advance. Nagash concentrated his focus upon the Mortarch of Blood and the Lord-Celestant, watching with grim evaluation as they stole towards the tribe of skullreapers who surrounded Thagmok.

The concealing illusion Neferata had woven around herself and the Stormcasts was shattered when they closed upon the mutated barbarians. Howling in alarm at the abrupt appearance of foes so near to them, the skullreapers hefted their massive weapons and rushed to the attack. Neferata's sorcery slaughtered the first dozen before they had taken even a few steps, the fangs and jaws of Nagadron settled for half a dozen more. Makvar's runeblade crackled as he brought his sword sweeping across the vicious steel of a spinecleaver, severing the head of the axe from its haft and rending the scarred hide of the mutant carrying it. Vogun's halberd raked through the horned helm of another snarling barbarian, a twist of his blade sending the man sprawling into the arms of the tribesmen behind him. Huld, rising above the press of bodies, shone his celestial beacon down upon the crazed horde, seeking to burn the ferocity from their brains with the divine light of Sigmar.

The swirling phantoms that billowed around Neferata swept forwards to strike at the Chaos horde, but before they drew near the Bloodbound, they were dissipated by a crimson light. The Mortarch herself tried to conjure them once more, only to lurch back in Nagadron's saddle, a stream of blood rushing from her nose. She felt the brutalising reverberation of a force inimical to magic, a blast of blood-soaked violence that streamed from the very realm of Khorne.

Through his Mortarch, Nagash could sense the source of this vibration that deadened her spells. The power pulsated from the bloodsecrator and the immense icon he bore. Hostile to all sorcery and magic, the Blood God had bestowed upon his disciples ways to oppose such powers when they were brought against them. The Great Necromancer hissed a warning to the vampire queen. Channelling energies straight from the domain of Khorne, there was no knowing the limits of the ward the bloodsecrator had created. It might even be enough to withstand the Lord of Death's own necromancy.

'Makvar!' Neferata cried out. 'The icon-bearer! He stifles my magic!'

The Lord-Celestant realised that without the arcane support of Neferata they would quickly be overcome. Calling to his fellow Stormcasts, he plunged into the mass of barbarians, leaving a litter of mangled bodies in his wake. Vogun followed at his side, guarding his commander as they ploughed a path through the skullreapers.

Before they could reach the bloodsecrator, a crimson glow appeared in their path. The skullreapers fell back, even the most crazed among them unwilling to fight Makvar and Vogun now. The two Anvils had drawn the attention of Thagmok, and now they were the Bloodking's prey.

As the barbarians parted, their gorelord was revealed. He was an enormous man, prodigious in his brawny proportions. Plates of red steel edged in bronze guarded his body, each piece of armour pulsing and flowing with a grisly light. The red patina that covered each piece of mail dripped and flowed, bubbling like molten blood. Lashed to his back was a crest, the skull-rune cast in gleaming bronze and adorned with the withered heads of fallen enemies. A cape that looked as though it might have been cut from the wing of a terrorgheist fell from his shoulders. The helm that encased his face had been crafted from a bleached skull, grisly sigils cut into its forehead. Thagmok's eyes stared out from the pits of his mask, red-rimmed pools of homicidal ferocity.

In Thagmok's hand he carried an immense double-headed axe that pulsated with the murderous power of Khorne. His other hand gripped the steel chain that restrained a gigantic creature that appeared to mix the worst qualities of lizard and hound. A frill of leathery skin unfolded around the daemonic beast's neck as it strained to reach the Stormcasts.

'A poor offering for the Skull Throne,' Thagmok growled, each word spat with a fury of contempt. In a single motion, he loosed his flesh hound, leaving the daemon to rush at Vogun while he hurled himself upon Makvar.

Makvar tried to parry Thagmok's axe, but for once, he found a weapon that was the equal of his runeblade. The lightning of his sword sparked and fizzled, unable to penetrate the blood-thirsty essence bound into the axe. The gorelord brought his fist cracking around, smashing into Makvar's mask. The Anvil staggered from the blow, narrowly blocking the savage sweep of the Bloodking's weapon.

Through Neferata, Nagash could see the deadly energies rippling across the Bloodking's axe. Like the icon carried by the bloodsecrator, the axe could cleave a rift between the Realm of Death and the brazen hell of Khorne. Only the axe wouldn't extract energy from the brass hells – it would send something through. Let so much as a drop of Makvar's blood touch the blade and he would be rent from the reality of Shyish and descend into the Blood God's domain.

The loss of Makvar would inconvenience Nagash's own plans, yet he wouldn't expose himself while the icon of Khorne yet had the power to deflect his necromancy. At his urging, Neferata cried out to Huld as the Knight-Azyros started to dive down at the Bloodking. 'The icon! You must break its power!' The vampire queen herself was beset by a vengeful crush of skullreapers. Without her magic, it was all she could do to fend off the barbarians. Huld was their only hope of striking down the bloodsecrator.

Huld angled away from Makvar and Thagmok, instead soaring towards the icon bearer. Soon he was out of Neferata's sight, and likewise beyond Nagash's vision. Through his Mortarch, the Great Necromancer again focussed upon the contest between the Lord-Celestant and the gorelord.

Makvar was a study in discipline and tactics, resisting the bloodthirsty rage the mere presence of Thagmok aroused in his mind. The Bloodking was a savage contrast, hurling himself against his foe in frenzied bursts of violence, hacking away at him in a brutal expression of insanity. The double-headed axe pounded against Makvar's armour, crumpling the sigmarite plates, smashing them out of shape. Only the swiftness of his parries denied Thagmok the force to rip through his armour, but Makvar knew the gorelord had stolen the momentum from him. He was on the defensive, simply trying to hold the enemy back.

While the skullreapers dared not intervene in the fray, the same restraint had no claim upon Vogun. The Lord-Castellant was able to blunt the ferocity of the flesh hound with his warding lantern, providing him with all the advantage he needed to vanquish his foe and send the daemonic dog howling back into the domain of Khorne. The contest hadn't left him unmarked, however, and a stream of blood flowed from the grisly bite the hound had delivered to his shoulder. The injury left his arm sagging at his side, but Vogun wouldn't desert Makvar.

The Lord-Castellant's halberd came whipping around, crunching down into Thagmok's arm. The weird crimson plates ruptured under the sigmarite blade, molten blood gushing from the gouged metal. Vogun was momentarily blinded by the escaping steam. As he shielded his eyes, the Bloodking turned on him, driving his hideous axe into the Anvil's side. There was a rending, shrieking sound like the shredding of metal, and a jagged fissure rimmed in scarlet opened around Vogun. A kick of Thagmok's boot sent the wounded Stormcast plunging through the rift.

Makvar howled in outrage and rushed at Thagmok. The gorelord turned to meet him, laughing as he gloated over the Lord-Celestant's abandonment of discipline. He caught the descending runeblade between the blades of his axe, turning the weapon around so that he could draw the Anvil closer to him. 'I have sent your friend to Hungry Khorne,' he snarled. 'Let my axe taste your blood, and I will do the same to you.'

Thagmok kicked out with his boot, smashing his foot into Makvar's knee. The Stormcast staggered but refused to fall, even when the Bloodking repeated the assault. The continued defiance of his opponent seemed to both amuse and infuriate the gorelord. He was confident of the outcome of their struggle, yet irritated that he should squander so much time on a single foe.

A dying scream rang out, crisp and sharp above the din of battle. Huld climbed into the air, the immense icon of Khorne clenched in his hands, the lifeblood of its owner splashed across his armour. With a gesture of contempt, he swung the icon downwards, sending it to crash among the skullreapers.

The warding effect was broken. The protection Khorne had bestowed upon Thagmok's entourage was gone.

From the walls of Nachtsreik, a black storm billowed outwards. A spectral tempest, a hurricane of phantoms and ghosts that roared across all in its path. Congregations of skaven vanished in the consuming darkness, their squeals of terror lost in the wailing surge. Tribes of bloodreapers were torn to ribbons as ethereal claws slashed their flesh. Spilling across the cavern, rolling in like a tide of death, the hurricane swept onwards, driving towards the heart of the Bloodbound horde.

There was no fear in Thagmok as he turned to face the oncoming storm. While his skullreapers broke and fled, he stood his ground. Raising his axe high, he shouted his resolve at the Lord of Death. 'Khorne cares not from whence the blood flows!'

Out from the raging fury of spectres, the skeletal figure of Nagash emerged. The Great Necromancer gripped the Mortis Blade in his bony claw, one of the black stones pressed close against its hilt. The fleshless face loomed over Thagmok, the pitiless depths of eye sockets piercing the skull-helm the Bloodking wore. With a howl of fury, the gorelord charged at Nagash. The Mortis Blade crashed against the Chaos lord's axe, ripping it from his fingers.

'There will be no blood,' Nagash hissed at his foe. Viciously, he drove his black sword into Thagmok's breast, tearing through ribs, heart and lungs. Into the dying gorelord's mind, he projected a final thought. *You are no longer Khorne's. Now you belong to me.* The Great Necromancer felt the tremor of Thagmok's spirit coursing through his sword, drawn down into the glassy stone.

'Such is the fate of all who oppose Nagash,' the Lord of Death declared, his words booming like thunder across the cavern.

The skaven needed no further prompting to hasten their flight, but some of the Bloodbound were too lost to their frenzied bloodlust to quit the field. Nagash sent his spirit hosts roaring about the battlefield to crush them. Dead, they would be of use to him. Alive, they were simply an obstacle.

Nagash turned away from Thagmok's corpse. There would be time enough to claim it later. For now, he was more concerned with the Stormcasts. He found both Makvar and Huld kneeling beside a ravaged carcass, the remains of Torn the gryph-hound. It seemed Vogun had cut the carcass loose before he was drawn down into Khorne's hells.

Makvar looked up at the Great Necromancer. 'It was our comrade's desire that we take Torn away with us.'

'Do as you like,' Nagash pronounced. He gestured at the carnage-strewn cavern around them. 'There is carrion enough here to build the legions we need to retake Gothizzar.' He nodded to Makvar, acknowledging the unspoken question that was on his lips. 'Yes, the Realm of Death will fight beside you for the Allpoints. The Anvils of the Heldenhammer have proven their quality. I am satisfied that together we may make Archaon Evercursed suffer for his manifold atrocities.'

The surviving Stormcasts followed their skeletal guide through the black vaults beneath Nachtsreik. Though they had lost many brothers in the struggle, Makvar felt they could all take pride that their perseverance had brought them at length to victory. They had secured the alliance with the Realm of Death. The undead legions of Nagash himself would now rally to Sigmar's cause. To the already mighty array of forces the God-King had mustered to attack the Allpoints, now could be added the terrifying creations of the Great Necromancer.

Yes, they had cause to take pride in their accomplishment, but as he led his warriors through the labyrinth, hastening towards the realmgate buried deep beneath Mannfred's fortress, Makvar couldn't quiet his own misgivings. He felt they had made a true ally of Neferata, or at least as close as the vampire queen could come to friendship. At the same time, Mannfred had proven himself a dire enemy, filled with thoughts of revenge for the Hallowed Knights expelling him from the Realm of Beasts. Though the vampire had fled from his master, Makvar worried the Mortarch would find a way to crawl back into Nagash's confidence. From all they had seen, the Lord of Death set great store in the power and council of his Mortarchs.

Then there were their missing comrades. Brannok hadn't returned from chasing Mannfred. Kreimnar echoed the sentiment that either the Knight-Heraldor would succeed in his hunt or else his spirit would return to Sigmaron, but for some reason, Makvar couldn't shake a feeling of unease regarding Brannok.

Vogun's fate was even more disturbing. Makvar patted the carcass of Torn tied to Gojin's saddle. The Lord-Castellant had been hurled into the realm of Khorne itself. The thought of him wounded and alone in such a hellish domain...

Makvar chided himself for these worries. There was enough to occupy his mind. He had to focus on the battle ahead, the titanic conflict that would be fought for control of the Allpoints. Worries about his missing companions were secondary to the greater needs of the war. Just as their reservations about the dark powers and fell deeds of Nagash and his undead had to be set aside, so too did his concerns for Brannok and Vogun.

Now, there was only the call to battle. A call every Storm-cast Eternal was bound to answer.

EPILOGUE

Thunder boomed as Lord-Celestant Makvar brought his hammer smashing down into the bird-like helm of a Chaos champion. Lightning flashed as his sword hacked through the furred shoulder of a goat-headed gor. His dracoth's jaws fell open, spewing a crackling bolt of electricity into the advancing mob of howling barbarians that turned a half dozen of them into steaming corpses. 'For Sigmar God-King! We are the Anvil upon which the foe shall break!'

All around him, the black-armoured Anvils of the Heldenhammer took up Makvar's cry. Stolid ranks of Liberators tightened their shield wall, filling in the gaps left by comrades cut down by the press of foes that surged all around them. Volleys from Judicator bows rained down on the charging masses of monsters, mutants and madmen. Fusillades from boltstorm crossbows slaughtered entire warbands, strewing the ground with misshapen bodies. Overhead, winged Prosecutors dived down into armoured Chaos knights, hurling their stormcall javelins at the cavalry with explosive effect. Knight-Azyros Huld swooped around the Prosecutors, using his celestial beacon to fend off the grotesque, manta-like daemons that slithered through the eldritch half-night that yawned above the All-gate of Gothizzar.

'The filth of Archaon will drown us in their blood,' Lord-Relictor Kreimnar called to Makvar. He thrust his relic-weapon to the sky for what seemed the thousandth time, calling down still another shower of divine retribution that came searing down into a herd of capering pink-skinned daemons. The undulating pack of horrors exploded into vivid flashes of swirling energy, some vanquished entirely by the fury of the lightning, others tearing themselves apart to reform into smaller, blue-skinned abominations. Pink and blue, the surviving horrors raised a discordant ululation of gibbering fury, rushing still faster towards the embattled Stormcasts.

'We will hold,' Makvar shouted back to Kreimnar. Gojin reared back, the dracoth's claws stamping down on the body of a mutated Chaos champion, crushing the man's armour beneath his reptilian bulk. The stink of the treacle that oozed from the smashed body was too sweet to bear any kinship to human blood.

Makvar looked across what was a vast ocean of conflict. Everywhere his gaze fell, he saw the horned helms and bestial heads of enemy warriors. The diseased hulks of gigantic maggoths, their heads reduced to masses of wormy growths, their limbs swollen with rotten gasses and putrid bile, lumbered through tribes of plague-ridden marauders as they gleefully sought to close upon the Stormcasts. Raging slaughterbrutes hurled their monstrous mass against shield walls, ripping and tearing with their savage claws and lashing tails. Armoured chosen of Chaos hacked at Paladins with their corrupt swords and arcane axes. Towering gargants cast immense boulders across the field, pulverising entire retinues of Judicators. Daemonic chariots drawn by insect-headed steeds ploughed into ranks of Liberators, the lascivious charioteers slashing at them with snapping claws and stinging whips. In the coruscating skies, daemonic flies and slavering chimeras fought against radiant-winged Prosecutors.

Makvar's runeblade hacked through the arm of a howling chosen, hurling the warrior's body back onto the weapons of his comrades. Not for the first time, the Lord-Celestant cast an anxious look at the dark portal that glowered behind the Anvils. The gateway back to Nagash's underworld. It was from here that the armies of the Great Necromancer were meant to inject themselves into the battle. With every passing moment, Makvar felt doubt swell within him that they even would.

The legions of the undead could turn the tide against Archaon's forces. The deathly magics of Nagash and his Mortarchs would overwhelm the wearied Chaos sorcerers and their daemonic masters. The horrible beasts that soared over the battlefield would be slaughtered by the terrorgheists and zombie dragons reanimated by the black arts of the Realm of Death.

The Lord-Celestant was reluctant to accept that they had been betrayed, that the Great Necromancer's armies weren't coming. As though guessing his commander's mind, Kreimnar cried back to him his own words. 'We will hold.'

Makvar turned his face from Gothizzar for the last time. He glared at the enormity of Archaon's horde. The outrage blazing inside him transformed itself into a steely defiance. 'We will do more than hold!' he shouted. 'We will win!'

Spurring Gojin forwards, Makvar led his Stormcasts into the teeming hosts of Chaos. It would take much enemy blood to blot out his failure to bring Nagash to the battlefield. He vowed he would make good the debt before he fell.

Cyclopean in its enormity, the gargantuan cavern was so immense that it could have swallowed both Nulahmia and Mephitt and still felt like an empty wasteland. In all Nagash's underworlds, there was no vault so vast as that of Nekroheim. The dead of entire civilizations had surrendered their bones to form the walls and ceiling of the sprawling expanse. Legions of ghost-wisps glowed from the sockets of the skulls that stared from the skeletal surroundings, filling the cavern with an eerie green luminescence that magnified rather than dispelled the shadows that stretched across the black, rocky floor.

Nagash enjoyed the awed silence that held Neferata as she gazed upon his endeavour for the first time. Her astonishment would swell beyond proportion when she discovered the purpose of it all. He had crafted his Mortarchs to be the mightiest of his undead, demigods to serve as extensions of his own power, yet they had their limitations. Despite the countless lifetimes of existence their deathless state had given them, they still thought with a mortal-taint dulling their minds. Even the ever-loyal Arkhan the Black suffered from this handicap, though he at least had the wisdom to recognise it and seek to overcome it through unwavering fealty.

The Lord of Death walked beside Neferata as they advanced deeper into the cavern towards the megalithic structure being raised by an army of skeletons. It was nearly complete now, its outlines unmistakable. A gigantic pyramid, half a mile wide at its base and almost a quarter mile tall once its capstone was set into place. The moment for that event had yet to arrive, however. But it would be soon. Very soon.

'A Black Pyramid,' Neferata said in a voice that was little more than a whisper. The Black Pyramids had been the centres of Nagash's power, wellsprings from which he could draw the energies of Shyish and the death-force exuding from all the Mortal Realms. By and large, they had been razed by Archaon's forces in the War of Bones, only fragments of them rescued. The Obelisk of Black had been one such sliver. So too had been the black stones with which Mannfred surrounded his sepulchre and the monoliths that had been revered by the pharaohs of Mephitt. Across the Realm of Death, deathmages and necromancers, corpsemasters and vampires, kings and priests had secreted the sorcerous rubble from the Black Pyramids, unknowingly preserving and protecting them until the Lord of Death had need of them once more.

'Not *a* Black Pyramid,' Nagash corrected the vampire queen. '*The* Black Pyramid. This is the crowning glory of my long seclusion, the result of centuries of study and experiment. It is grander in scale than any that has come before it. As its size has been magnified, so too have its arcane affinities.' He raised his claw and waved it across the expanse of the towering structure. 'This will do more than simply feed and replenish my power. It will extend it. Expand it. Allow my magic to reach into places previously denied to it.'

Nagash reached within his robe and drew forth a sliver of translucent black stone. It was one of the shards from Mannfred's tomb, but Neferata could at once see that it was changed. There was a strange energy bound within it. It took her a moment to understand. When he saw that she did, the Great Necromancer nodded. 'Yes, the spirit of the sorceress Molchinte. One who bore the brand of Tzeentch upon flesh and soul. Something that should have been beyond my power to claim.'

'But no longer, my Master?' Neferata asked.

'Anything that holds or held the essence of death within it is again mine to claim,' Nagash declared. A ghoulish laugh rattled through the fleshless god. 'Yes, even Sigmar's storm-knights,' he answered the question Neferata dared not ask. He turned from her, pointing his staff at a trio of figures walking towards them from the shadows. The presence of Arkhan came as no surprise to Neferata, but the liche-king's companion did. Mannfred von Carstein.

As he approached, Mannfred bowed in contrition to the Lord of Death. Like Nagash, he produced a sliver of black, glassy stone. 'The storm-knight's spirit couldn't be held,' he said.

Neferata turned back towards Nagash. 'You set him against the Stormcasts? You permitted it? What if his comrades should learn what has befallen their companion? What will become of our alliance with Sigmar?'

'There will be no alliance,' Arkhan stated. 'The legions promised to Makvar are needed here to speed the construction of the pyramid.'

'But if Archaon retains his hold upon the Allpoints–' Neferata started to object. Nagash silenced her with a wave of his hand.

'A victory for the hordes of Chaos would serve against me,' Nagash said. 'But I would gain nothing if Sigmar were to be triumphant. A stalemate serves me best. To prolong the war. To draw out the struggle.'

Neferata shook her head. 'I don't understand. The Realm of Death would be liberated. The hordes of Chaos would be expelled from your domain.'

A fell light blazed in the pits of Nagash's skull. 'Your ambitions are still those of flesh, my lovely Neferata.' He turned and stared at Mannfred. 'Even your scheming and plotting is limited. You do not aspire to the desires of a god!'

Nagash raised the sliver of stone in his hand, pointing it at the growing pyramid. 'The whole structure will be given a facing of these stones. The debris of its predecessors will become its skin, feeding into a grand reservoir of dark magic. I will use that power to claim the spirits of all who perish in the Realm of Death – whatever god thinks to keep them from me.'

'You will provoke the wrath of Sigmar,' Neferata said, fear in her eyes. Mannfred's sneering expression turned sour at her words, for he was only too aware what daunting foes the Stormcasts could be.

The Great Necromancer shook his crowned head. 'Sigmar busies himself with the war against Chaos. Even should he turn his attentions towards me, I have sown the seeds of uncertainty in his mind.' He extended his arms towards his Mortarchs. 'The Stormcasts know Mannfred as an enemy, rife with treachery. If I have turned against Sigmar, perhaps it is Mannfred's poisoned council that has made it so. Through Neferata's attempts to forge her own alliance with them, the Stormcasts see her as their friend. Perhaps she will be able to sway me and make me favour the God-King's war.' Nagash clenched his hand into a skeletal fist. 'Hope is a delusion that may cloud even the judgement of a god. So long as he is uncertain, Sigmar will entertain his hopes. It may yet come to pass that an alliance with Azyr will serve my purposes. But that day is not today.'

Mannfred's visage took on an aspect of haughtiness, a sly gleam in his eyes. 'Are you certain it is you who intends to betray the God-King?' the vampire asked. He held out the black shard which Brannok's soul had touched. 'There was something familiar about the storm-knight's spirit when I drew it from his body. Something so tantalisingly familiar. Perhaps you might tell me what it is, Master?'

Nagash glowered at the arrogant Mortarch. He would have punished Mannfred for his mockery, but he too had felt that unaccountable sensation about Makvar and his Anvils of the Heldenhammer. They had been different from the Stormcasts he had encountered before. Until now, he had been unable to discover why. As he wrenched the vampire's discovery from his mind, the Lord of Death suddenly understood what it was that rendered the Anvils so familiar, so dissimilar from their comrades.

The soul that had touched Mannfred's shard was from Shyish. It was the spirit of a mortal that should have passed into Nagash's keeping. Instead, it had been poached by Sigmar, reforged into one of his Stormcast Eternals. While the Great Necromancer fought alone against the hordes of Archaon, Sigmar had been stealing the spirits of his realm's mortal warriors.

The Great Necromancer looked up at his Black Pyramid. 'Do not concern yourself with matters beyond your position,' he warned Mannfred. 'I will decide when it is time to reclaim what belongs to me. What are a few dead souls when balanced against the fate of all the Mortal Realms?'

ABOUT THE AUTHOR

C L Werner's Black Library credits include the
Space Marine Battles novel *The Siege of Castellax*,
the Age of Sigmar novella 'Scion of the Storm'
in *Hammers of Sigmar*, the End Times novel
*Deathblade, Mathias Thulmann: Witch Hunter,
Runefang*, the Brunner the Bounty Hunter trilogy,
the Thanquol and Boneripper series and Time of
Legends: The Black Plague series. Currently living
in the American south-west, he continues to write
stories of mayhem and madness set in the worlds of
Warhammer 40,000 and the Age of Sigmar.

WARHAMMER
AGE OF SIGMAR

BLACK RIFT

JOSH REYNOLDS

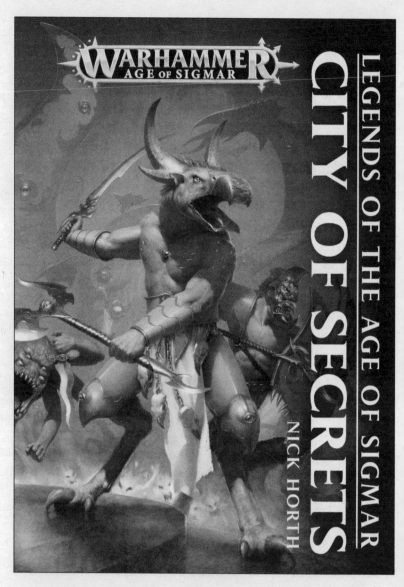

WARHAMMER
AGE OF SIGMAR

CITY OF SECRETS

LEGENDS OF THE AGE OF SIGMAR

NICK HORTH